THE SECRET LOVE
OF
HADES AND PERSEPHONE

L. E. STARDUST

Cover Design by Lauren Eilenberg - L.E. STARDUST

Edited by Amy Bigelow

Photograph of L.E. STARDUST by Kevin Eilenberg – KGE
Photography

This story is based on Greek Mythology and the author's perspective of
the gods Hades and Persephone. Names, characters, actual events,
persons living or dead that isn't part of the Greek pantheon is entirely
coincidental.

ISBN:
978-1-7329724-1-4

DEDICATION

To Hades and Persephone and to the Greek/Roman
Pantheon. To anyone who believes in them or
anything beyond the mortal realm.

CONTENTS

ACKNOWLEDGMENTS

A large expression of gratitude will never be enough for those who have supported me and my work. Of course I thank my mom, my dad, and my brother Kevin for their *encouragement*. To all of my friends and colleagues that have been *eager* for this work to manifest.

Thank you to Amy for editing in the time of need.

Thank you to the celestial beings and my spirit guides who have helped me write this book.
You know who you are.

CHAPTER 1

DEATH

Death. It is one of the most potent fears that exists among mortals. The word itself can instantly evoke feelings of anxiety, horror, sadness, and even anger. Death is an inevitable part of life and, for many people, it's still a great mystery. Everyone faces it sooner or later. This fear of death usually comes in two parts—the first is being scared of how death might actually play out. Will it be painful? Will you die in your sleep peacefully? Or will it sneak up and attack unsuspectingly? The second is the fear of the unknown—life after death.

Most mortals would do anything to avoid death. In an effort to prolong the human lifespan, many people turn toward science and medicine for answers. But others who believe in a higher power will pray to the Gods, hoping to live longer or gain immortality. For the Greeks and their spiritual beliefs, they pray to the Olympians. The mighty gods and goddesses of Mount Olympus have been there since the beginning of humankind. However, there is one particular god that everyone fears. Petrified mortals on earth are reluctant to speak his name, fearing that, in doing so, sudden death may strike upon them. Unlike other respected Greek gods and goddesses, he lacks a temple for others to worship. Hades, King of the Underworld and the Lord of Death.

Hades is always at work, for death happens every day somewhere in the world. He sends another god, Thanatos, to end the life of a mortal. Thanatos presents death to the dying mortal simply by placing his hand on their head. The dying mortal then becomes a shade or a soul, free from body imprisonment. The call for Thanatos usually happens when a mortal's body is ready to die. Mortals can encounter death in a multitude of ways, whether from a critical injury sustained during a war, a horrible accident, murder, sickness, or when old age has finally reached its peak.

A tear shed from a man's eye, as he watched his own body being prepared for burial. Today, an elderly man named Elasus, who has dreaded this moment since his days of fighting in the war were over, has died. "I can't be dead! I can't be!" Anxiety and disbelief washed over Elasus as he processed the situation. If he still had his beating heart, it would have been pounding in his ears. He tried to remember the exact moment when death had claimed his body. However, with his spirit still stunned by the fact that he was no longer living, Elasus couldn't think of anything but the present moment. He had feared this day for many years. Now, in desperation of what might lay ahead of him, Elasus feared for the fate of his soul. "Merciful Zeus, I plead with you . . . . . " he sobbed, ". . . please, I'm not ready."

Several women were now washing and anointing his dead body with blessed oil. Elasus watched his family and friends pay their respects and show their sorrows for him. His family, dressed in robes, chanted and let out their grief by striking their torsos with their fists. This was the way Greeks went about a funeral procession. The more that Elasus saw, the more evident his new fate became. Deep down he began to accept that he's now just a shade, a spirit. In his mind, Elasus couldn't help but feel that he wanted to stay. Not out of terror for the unknown afterlife, but out of worry for his family. *What will happen to them?* he asked himself. "Almighty Zeus, please bring me back to life again. I promise I'll do better," he prayed, hoping that the god would hear his bargaining.

But he doubted that the King of the Gods and Life would hear him. For the responsibility of death and the placement of souls can now only be answered by one god. The meeting of Zeus' elder brother, Hades, is the one meeting everyone must face after death. When one dies, they instantly belong to Hades. It doesn't matter whether a mortal is good or evil. After death, every soul is under his supervision.

From the corner of Elasus' eye, a shadowy silhouette crept up slowly over his shoulder. To his knowledge, Elasus already knew who this dark figure was. Thanatos approached him. His face looked human, but the rest of his body resembled an apparition. Like the Grim Reaper, Thanatos presents death to dying individuals. He makes sure that shades go to their ultimate destination. If they are ready to be given to Hades, the dead mortal will have their burial prepared and their danake coin ready to pay the ferryman before entering the Underworld. "You can't stay here," Thanatos said in a gently stern manner to the new shade.

Elasus looked at him with sorrow on his face. "I know I have to go. I just want to make sure that everyone is okay. Besides, they haven't given me my coin yet."

Thanatos nodded, "They will." Elasus watched as his family finished the burial rituals. At last, he saw his wife place a danake coin in his mouth. Now that he can pay the ferryman on his way toward a new destination, Elasus was relieved. He felt the golden coin materialize in his mouth and took it out. Elasus looked down at his hand to the danake coin that his family had given him.

Thanatos touched Elasus' shoulder, "It's time to go." Elasus nodded. He had one last look at his family, especially his wife. He sent her all of his love and prayed to the gods that they will be together again someday. Elasus shed his last teardrop before fading, as his soul beckoned to be somewhere else. Knowing that the shade had made it to his new destination, Thanatos felt satisfied and left for his next assignment.

As if in a trance, Elasus' soul was being called to another place. There he stood at the opening of a cave, which gave way to the Acheron River. He knew where he was—outside the entrance to the Underworld. Elasus and his people had feared this unknown place for as long as he could remember. Elasus stared at its opening in wonder and fear.

Apparently, he wasn't alone. Other souls who had also died that day, or even last night, were waiting for the entrance to open. Despite the cave's openness, going into the Underworld is like entering another dimension. Souls have to go through a barrier, but they can't do so without help from a guide. Which is why they wait for Hermes, the messenger of the gods, to escort the dead into the Underworld. He is needed not only to direct the path and light the way, but also to open the portal. While they wait for Hermes, the shades wander around aimlessly with fear and concern about what lies ahead for their fate.

All of them are about to face Hades. There are many stories about him and the horrors of what the Underworld provides. Some say he's cold and ruthless, just like the kingdom he rules over. Others believe that any tiny mistake they've made during their human life can instantly place them in Tartarus, the most painful prison for rotten souls. The more the souls wandered, the more their anxiety and suspicions grew.

The sound of a loud whistle suddenly caused the souls to look up and see Hermes. He hovered over them with winged sandals that help him fly from one place to another. Hermes' golden hair almost matched his gleaming sandals and his glowing tan. His short and flowing tunic allowed him to move fast. Hermes spoke loud enough for all the shades to hear. "Before we go in, please cleanse yourself in the river Acheron. Let your past and pain leave your spirit."

The souls were surprised that the messenger of gods would ask to cleanse themselves in this river since, as part of mortal belief, the river Acheron is also known as the river of pain. Hermes is aware that mortals are uneasy about the unknown. When they fear something they don't know enough about, mortals visualize the unknown to be ten times worse. Still, every shade cautiously bathed in the river. As they did, they felt the weight of the world leave their spirit. Each of them felt like a newborn baby, innocent and curious. With their worries gone, including their fear of the Underworld, the souls were ready to meet Hades.

Now it was time to enter. Hermes took a deep breath and blew into the Underworld entrance. The barrier was now temporarily gone. "Okay everyone," Hermes announced, "It's time to go, just follow my lead and you'll meet Hades shortly." He charged his voice to get the souls moving. Every soul entered the cave without hesitation, thanks to the cleansing of the river. They walked in a single file line, as Hermes slowly hovered above them with a lit torch in his hand.

The shades followed him inside the cave. Although the river had cleansed their anxiety, it started to return little by little as they continued to walk on. The souls braced themselves for the inevitable. Even with Hermes being the only source of light for them all, there was a long passageway down into the darkness. The cave was dark in its depth, and sounds of water droplets from the stones overhead echoed as they hit the floor. While the shades walked on, their fears came back in full force as they neared the entrance to their fated destination.

"We're close to the end of the road. Take out your danakes for Charon." Hermes ordered. Everyone retrieved the danake coins that their relatives had given them before their burials or burnings.

Now the group was at the gate and all they could see was the clouded Acheron river, which they still believed to be the river of pain. They were unaware of the river's ability to absorb the grief that each shade still carried. They began to wonder – was there anything else about the Underworld that appeared misguided by mortal belief?

According to their ancestors, this was the river Charon the ferryman rows the boat of souls across to reach the main River Styx. From there, they'll have to stand at Hades' judgment panel. While Hermes and the group of shades waited for Charon to arrive, Elasus looked around at his surroundings. Under Hermes' light, the man could see in the distance glimpses of amethyst and quartz dangling from the roof of the cave. The light from Hermes' torch and the dampness from inside the cave made the crystals sparkle. In that moment, Elasus felt a sense of wonder for its dark beauty.

Several moments passed, and then the group heard water splash near the gate dock. Hermes lifted the fiery torch higher. Within minutes, everyone saw a boat which looked like it could carry up to fifty souls at a time. Ancient symbols were engraved on the boat-like raft. By observing its walls, the boat looked as though it had magically survived a shipwreck. The chances that it had were likely. Charon himself was a very skinny man, looking almost like a skeleton whose bones were disguised in flesh. The smoky gray robe he wore hid his body and most of his scarred face, which was burned on the right side, near his eye. Despite his ghastly appearance, Charon always whistled while he rowed to help lighten the mood and put the anxious shades at ease.

Charon caught a glimpse of Hermes and the next group of souls who were set to meet Hades. Charon docked the boat and motioned for the souls to come aboard. As they inched toward the boat, he looked at the anxious shades and put on his best Grim Reaper voice. "Pay the fine and come aboard to your eternal doom! Abandon all hope ye who enter here!" The souls were now terrified to step onto the boat. Hermes rolled his eyes and shook his head in response to Charon's dark humor. Charon began laughing hysterically because the souls were noticeably afraid.

"Charon!" Hermes chastised, "Was that necessary? The shades are scared enough as it is, even after being cleansed. Now you've made it worse."

"Oh come on! It's just a little bit of fun!" Charon looked at the souls again, this time with a little sympathy. "So Hermes, how many this time?"

"About . . . three dozen," Hermes estimated, as he gave a quick glance at the group.

"Hmmm. . . too little for a war or some natural disaster to have ensued." Charon loved to guess how people died. It was how he kept himself entertained throughout the centuries, while passing the time. "Multiple murders? Or did they drown from a sunken boat?"

Hermes shook his head, "You need to get a little more creative my friend. I'm sure there are more than a thousand ways to die, and that is the best that you can come up with?" he asked, trying to throw Charon off track with his guesses.

"But the same incident keeps repeating itself lately. So, am I right? Multiple murders or a sunken boat?!" Charon looked at Hermes gleefully.

Hermes rolled his eyes, "Half right. Some died from a sunken boat tragedy, some from old age, and some from a small battle," he said in a bored tone.

"Ha! I won! Five gold coins Hermes!" Charon held out his bony hand, ready to take his prize.

Hermes smirked, "You haven't won anything! You only got it half right!" Charon groaned in disappointment. Most of the time, he couldn't beat Hermes at this game. For not only was Hermes the messenger of the gods, he was also the master of trickery.

"Then half a prize. Two and a half coins!" Charon tried to persuade Hermes.

"There's no such thing as a half coin, Charon." Hermes looked at him with ridicule. The shades watched in disbelief, as Charon and Hermes continued to disagree over the deaths of the mortals. How can they have fun betting on death, when the souls now fear for their fate?

Charon grumbled under his breath, "Okay fine. Two coins then!"

Again, Hermes smirked, "The answer has to be a hundred percent correct–that's the rule."

By now, Charon should've known better when placing bets with Hermes, but he was the only playing participant. As Hermes received his five coins for outsmarting Charon, the ferryman looked at the new group of souls who were waiting anxiously. Knowing it was time to get back to work, he looked at Hermes once more. "Ha—by the way, what did you mean by small battle?"

Hermes grumbled the answer, "Ares is stirring up trouble with the mortals again. He's trying to have them start a great war. Right now, it's just small fights between two lands."

Charon laughed uneasily, "Hades is not going to like that."

"Other than that, things have been pretty uneventful," Hermes shook his head, "Not much is happening on Earth or Olympus for the moment. Even Hera has been calm."

"Give it time. I'm sure one of you gods will start something . . . eventually," Charon reassured and his face brightened a little. "Want to make a bet on who starts trouble this time around?"

Hermes had to stop a laugh from trying to escape his lips. "No, it is more likely it'll be Ares. It doesn't take much for him to create chaos. "

The souls still hesitated to come on Charon's boat because of his earlier snide comments. "Oh come on! It's just a little bit of fun. I'm just playing around. Get on the boat!" The souls doubted Charon's words, and it showed on their skeptical faces. Since there was nowhere else to go, the shades reluctantly came to the boat and instantly gave Charon their danakes as payment.

Charon looked at Hermes, who was watching the shades board the boat, wondering what he was still doing here. Hermes had done his job. "You can go, you know."

"Not yet. I have to talk to your king for a minute or two."

"Well go now before I arrive. Before Hades and his judges assess the souls," Charon suggested. "Do you still not want to place that bet?"

Hermes shook his head with a smile and looked at Charon. "My friend, you have a problem."

"I don't have a problem, I'm just trying to entertain myself. You try being here, day after day, delivering souls from one place to another. This little death gamble is for my amusement, to keep me from going insane. Even though I think . . .," he paused, "I'm already insane, and I just don't know it!" Charon laughed at his own humor. Hermes smiled and laughed as he flew across the River Styx, leaving the shades with Charon. They continued to look all around the Underworld. As they went deeper, the souls were in awe by the mysteries that were revealed.

So far, the Underworld wasn't what the shades had expected. Deep into the cave, more crystals and stones were spotted once light from Charon's lantern reflected off their shiny surfaces. Drops of water dripped from the cave walls–its sound was striking and yet, almost calming.

Despite the darkness and the judgment that awaited the souls, the Underworld felt mysteriously inviting.

"Beautiful isn't it?" Charon asked all of the shades. They were all amazed by the beauty of this place, but felt slightly confused, since it did not coincide with their perceived mortal beliefs. Charon could tell what they were thinking. "What were you expecting? A running river of fire? Nothing but skulls and statues as decorations?" The shades almost nodded in response to his questions. "There might be a little bit of that, but it's very minor and it's located in a different part of the realm." Charon continued to row the boat as the shades kept observing the Underworld. To the souls and living mortals, they had no idea of the magic and mystery that the Underworld contained.

Cerberus, a large three-headed dog, suddenly passed by, barking with madness. He is the guard dog of the Underworld, and ensures that no soul leaves without Hades' permission. From a distance, Hermes saw a beautifully enormous red lava castle made out of Ammonite and Marble. As if engulfed in a shield of protection, the palace was surrounded by fine amethysts and various crystals. Perhaps their energy source was protecting the castle. Various paths wove all around the palace in different directions, leading to other dimensions. Some paths were meant only for the souls to follow, while others were designated solely for Hades.

Having lived here since that fateful day when he had inherited the Underworld, Hades has come to call this place his home. If his father Zeus ever found out how enormous and amazing the Underworld was, Hermes knew that Zeus would take it away from his elder brother. 'He really has no idea,' Hermes thought. 'It's funny how mortals keep telling stories about Hades and his desire to take over Olympus, the home of the gods. Every soul on earth thinks that the Underworld is the last place they would want to be. Mortals couldn't be more wrong.'

Hades waited patiently on his throne for Charon to arrive with his newest collection of souls. His three other judges–Rhadamanthus, Minos, and Aeacus–also waited with him. Hades' judges were more like a council, helping Hades make proper judgments more clearly. In the end, regardless of their opinions, Hades had the final say. In the meantime, Hades was busy writing paperwork and organizing the placement of souls. Along with who is reincarnated, this arrangement also included who is sent to the Isles of the Blessed. Hades was so engrossed in his work, that he didn't hear Hermes fly down. Hermes now stood right next to the throne.

"My lord?" Hermes asked gently to get Hades attention, without startling him.

"Hmm?" Hades responded, letting Hermes know that he was listening, but wouldn't stop what he had set out to finish.

"My lord, I need your attention for the moment," Hermes pleaded lightly.

"Hermes, you have my attention," Hades said in a deeply concentrated voice, but didn't look up from his work.

"I need your eyes to pay attention too, my lord."

Hades looked up, slightly annoyed, but kept his temper in check. He knew Hermes had something important to say, because he never wasted his time otherwise. Hermes wanted his undivided attention.

An annoyed Hades looked Hermes in the eyes, "Alright, I'm all ears and eyes. What is so important?"

"An invitation to Olympus," Hermes said. Ignoring his uncle's annoyance, Hermes handed Hades a scroll with a ribbon on top.

"That's it?" Hades arched an eyebrow as he took the scroll.

"Not quite. This occasion is not your typical meeting or party. Well, it is a party, but it's not just a gathering, Hermes explained. As Hermes tried to clarify, Hades was already reading the scroll.

"It's the initiation of a goddess?" Hades questioned.

"Yes."

In the daily lives of the Olympians, an initiation was a rare event. To have this initiation, one must either have a significant soul or is born to be a god. More importantly, the three kings of the earth are needed for this special initiation to occur. The three kings, of course, are Hades himself and his two brothers—Poseidon, King of the Seas and Zeus, King of the Gods—along with Olympus and the earth present. Hades continued to read the scroll.

Brother Hades,
This scroll is an invitation to Mount Olympus for an Initiation and Ceremony of the new goddess.
Your presence is required.
This blessed event will happen tomorrow night at sundown.

Your brother,
Zeus

Hades hesitantly looked up from the scroll, holding back an emotion that Hermes couldn't quite place. "Must I go?"

Confused, Hermes said, "Of course you must go, the initiation won't work without you!" Hades looked at Hermes in disbelief. Hades was sure Zeus could make anyone a god or a goddess without extra assistance. After all, the initiation was a simple procedure. Except only Hades can provide one little needed detail which, in this case, Hermes is correct. Despite how small his contribution would be, the initiation would not work without Hades. "Besides, it'll be nice to see the three king brothers together this time. . . without war being the reason for meeting," Hermes said.

"Is it one of Zeus's children?" Hades asked, even though he already knew the answer.

"Of course," Hermes confirmed.

"Of course," Hades whispered to himself as he shook his head in agitation. "I'm not going."

"What! Why?" Hermes couldn't believe what he was hearing. He was anxious to tell Zeus of Hades' answer.

"I have more important priorities that need to get done," Hades said, half truthfully. "I'm also not interested in initiating a goddess for the same reasons why Zeus made most of the gods and goddesses—protection from Hera and her jealous rage." Everyone, from gods to mortals, knows about the Queen of the Gods and her jealous rampage. Whenever Zeus has an affair with someone, Hera not only takes revenge on the lovers and wives he's involved with, but she also punishes the children too. Honestly, Hades can't blame Hera for Zeus's infidelities. She is the goddess of marriage and family, after all. But how can she be the goddess of marriage, when her own marriage is not so perfect?

"Forgive me, my lord, but Persephone is a goddess in her own right. She's not only the daughter of Zeus, but she's also the daughter of Demeter," Hermes said.

Hades paused for a moment, as he heard the name of the soon-to-be goddess. "Persephone?" His heart gave a tug of excitement, but Hades didn't show it.

"Yes, my lord, that's the new goddess we are celebrating. She'll be the goddess of spring and new life."

"How. . . appropriate," Hades whispered to himself. As her name kept ringing in his ears, a memory came flooding back from long ago. His response was serious, "I know who she is Hermes. Just because I've never met the girl, doesn't mean I don't know anything about her. Besides, the parties involved are better off without me there."

Hermes decided to persuade Hades a little, whispering in his ear, "I'm sure Persephone would love to meet the god who made her that beautiful rose choker, which she received on the evening of her birth." Hades thought about the necklace that he had made especially for her. Hephaestus may be the god of craftsman and blacksmith work, but jewelry was Hades forte. The necklace Hades had given to Persephone was an emerald rose choker. The rose was made out of actual emeralds, with a round diamond in the center. The necklace band had real gold thorn branches, which held the rose together. When he gave the necklace to Hermes who delivered it to her, Hermes was amazed by such craftsmanship. The necklace, which sparkled with beauty, was the first piece of jewelry Hermes had ever seen from Hades. He believed

Hades had conceived it with perfection from the heart. It was one of the best pieces of jewelry Hermes had ever seen.

"I had forgotten all about that," Hades lied under his breath, as he tried to focus back on the life scrolls.

"You know that means you've been here for too long," Hermes said and looked at Hades with sad eyes. "You should come to this initiation. Not only because it's Zeus's orders, but you could use a break from the Underworld. You have a wonderful place, Hades, but you need to come and see your family. It's time to meet your niece. Besides, you're not going to find a wife staying here."

Hades tried to hold back the hurt and sadness that he felt. "Hermes, I've come to accept the fact that there's no one out there for me."

"You don't honestly believe that, do you?" Hermes asked skeptically.

"I do," Hades replied, looking at Hermes with loneliness in his eyes. "Who would want to spend eternity with me in the Underworld, accompanied by death and darkness?"

"The universe has its own way of working everything out as intended," Hermes responded with care.

Suddenly, the hidden anger that Hades had been suppressing came lashing out. "Maybe the universe and destiny choose to play a cruel trick instead! They make you believe that there *is* someone out there, but leave your heart empty when you find out that there's no one actually there. You've waited for nothing!" In a defeated voice, Hades admitted, "I've waited for nothing."

Hermes looked at his uncle with sadness and then replied defiantly, "As I said, you're not going to find a wife staying here. Maybe Hades, as I said, your time just hasn't arrived yet."

Hades growled, wishing Hermes would just abandon the subject, "Is there anything else you want my dear nephew?" Hermes paused for a moment then; he could see Charon coming with the newest group of souls.

"So, are you coming?" Hermes asked once more.

Hades paused, showing no emotion, "I'll think about it. I just think it's a waste of time. I have important work to do, unlike some of my family members . . . I have priorities."

"I understand that but— "

"I said I'd think about it!" Hades responded again more forcefully.

Hermes nodded. He dreaded telling Zeus that his eldest brother would not have an answer until the last minute, most likely. "Please do, my Lord. It would be nice to have everyone together again." Hades looked at him doubtfully. "Anyway, it's time for me to take off. I've got more messages to deliver, and your new group of souls has arrived," Hermes said.

"Yes, I can see that," Hades said with a cold demeanor.

"One more thing."

"What?" Hades asked impatiently.

"Ares, he's trying to start a war. . . again. He is tired of the peace, so he now wants to play. . . or so he claims." Hades closed his eyes and groaned. "Does he not understand that the more he plays, the more work I have? The more battles he creates, the more people die, and the more I have to judge! I thought he was going to rest for some time!"

"Well, even his rest became restless."

"It was Aphrodite, wasn't it? She drove him crazy again."

Hermes shrugged his shoulders, he had no real answer. "Love makes you do the unthinkable."

"I wouldn't know," Hades said blatantly. "I'm going to have a talk with him."

"HA! So you *are* going to the initiation!" Hermes jumped as he started to fly away.

Hades rolled his eyes. At least in his mind, he had a real reason to go. "Again, Hermes, I'll think about it. Tell your King that!"

Hermes knew the conversation was over. At least he planted several seeds in Hades' head about why he should attend the initiation. This was all Hermes could do. As he flew out of the Underworld, he saw Charon park his boat at the judging panel.

Hades now had duties to carry out, and he needed to put up his guard. Not only to preserve his reputation, but also to help him focus on his job. At times, he loves what he does, and those joyous moments usually happen when souls are sent to the Elysian Fields. To see faces filled with relief and love, after facing death and judgment, is such a pleasurable experience. Putting a soul in Tartarus is not as much fun as mortals think, but still, it's not an easy job to do. After seeing what some of the subjects had done in the mortal world, Hades enjoyed watching them suffer. At other times, he felt like humankind wasn't getting any better. Despite the fact that most punishments are temporary, Tartarus is getting more occupied these days.

Charon took his boat to Hades' judgment panel. "Alright everybody out! Go to the judging panel in a single file line!"

The shades got off the boat and went toward the entrance where stairs led to the judging panel. Slowly, they walked up the staircase to Hades and his throne. Besides Hades stood two shades for security, but they weren't for him. After all, he's a god. The security was there for the souls who needed assistance or those who needed to be dragged to their destination. The souls quickly huddled together, not sure of what they were supposed to do.

Hades glared at them in all seriousness. As he sat on his throne, his vibration chilled the air. "All of you, stay where you are," Hades ordered. His voice was calmly soothing, but also stern and powerful. It was capable of shaking the souls to their core. "I will judge you all, one at a time. When it's your turn, step up into the panel circle." Every soul suddenly became nervous. The three judges were ready to begin the proceedings. Sitting in their chairs, with their faces hidden underneath the hoods of dark cloaks, it could be nerve-wracking for any being to stand at the panel.

However, despite the souls' nervousness, they were surprised by what they saw. They were expecting to see a monster or some old man with a grudge at the throne. Instead, they saw a very handsome man who appeared to be in his late-thirties. His raven-colored brownish hair flowed down to his shoulders. His piercing ice-blue eyes could make anyone shiver with fear or pleasure. He had a royal vampiric look about him, which made Hades seem like a deliberate, but fair god. Both the robes and the black armor underneath had silver trim around the edges, making him fit to look like the Lord of Death.

A soul stepped up into the circle, facing Hades. Nervous couldn't even begin to describe what the soul was feeling. He was a young man who died from illness and didn't do much with his life. If he were alive, he'd be sweating like a pig, fearing the worst. From the corner of his eye, he saw two hallways—one on each side of Hades. The young man could tell that the one on Hades' left led to the Elysian Fields. He saw a red glow in the distance coming from the hallway on Hades' right and he heard faint screaming. He knew this one was Tartarus.

Hades looked at the young man and then peered at his life scroll. "You lived a decent life, but it seems that it was cut short." There was no such thing as an untimely death. It's only in the eyes of mortals who see the end of one's life as the wrong time. Death is fated, but for some reason, it's comforting for some mortals to believe they can control their own fate.

"Y-Y-Yes sir," the young man stuttered, "My name is . . ."

"I know your name, Arion," Hades stated. "Now, you're not a hero or anything significant. In fact, your life was. . . ordinary. You just lived decently day after day, but did nothing extraordinary. You didn't help humankind in any way or form, yet you didn't harm it either. Now, you have two choices—you can either go to the Asphodel Meadows, or you can get reincarnated."

"Reincarnated?" Arion questioned.

"To be reborn, to try living on earth again. That way, you have a chance to prove yourself and to the gods that you've become a better person than you were last. The next time you die, you could get into the Elysian Fields. What do you choose?"

Arion had to think about this. First, he couldn't believe that the King of the Underworld was giving him a choice. Neither did the souls behind him, for they whispered in disbelief about what had just transpired. Arion knew that the Asphodel Meadows was designated for ordinary people, where all they did was rest and live a numbing existence. He couldn't help but yearn to live in the Elysian Fields for eternity. Since his life was short-lived, he hadn't yet gotten the chance to experience what life had to offer.

"My lord," Arion began, "If you please, so kindly allow me to be reincarnated. I didn't live very long, and I'm more than willing to do something more meaningful with my life the next time around. So that I can earn the right to live in the Elysian Fields."

"Very well," Hades signed the scroll. "This will be sent to The Fates, and within a week you'll choose what life you're going to have. You'll also choose your parents."

"Choose?"

"Yes. Everyone chooses certain things before they're reborn on earth. Which lessons needed to be learned are decided by The Fates and the gods, and will then be given to you." Arion was astounded. So many questions were going through his head. He wondered how the life and death system worked between the gods. "One of the guards will show you where you'll be staying in the meantime," Hades said as he motioned to a guard for attention. The guard immediately showed Arion where the souls hang around before they return to earth again.

While Hades judged a few more souls, the shades that were still waiting together realized that none of them had been sent to Tartarus. Each time a soul was decided, most ended up being reincarnated or sent to the Elysian Fields. The shades started to relax as they realized that they were dealing with a fair and wise god. They still were anxious about their fate, but they figured that their chances of being sent to Tartarus were slim.

It was now Elasus' turn. As he stepped into the judgment panel, he saw not only Hades himself, but also the three other judges who had remained quiet throughout the entire judging process, until now. Minos spoke up, "This shade is a war criminal! He committed crimes against humanity!"

Then Aeacus interrupted, "Except from this shades' point of view. . . he had no choice. His family would have been in danger, if he hadn't done what he was told." The third judge Rhadamanthus nodded in agreement to both accounts. There was not much else to say.

Despite that he's dead and that his body was being cleansed, Elasus could still feel the pain of arthritis attacking his knees. His fear of the unknown, of course, was what brought this sudden pain again. His strength was dissipating. Elasus was a good man, but there were some things about his life that he wasn't too proud of. Hades sensed his fear, just like he had with the others, and continued to show no emotion. He unwrapped the scroll that showed this man's life. Before Hades could talk about his final judgment of Elasus' soul, Elasus felt obligated to explain his life's actions. No matter how deadly the consequences were.

"My Lord?" Elasus spoke fearfully, but with determination in his voice. "Before you make judgment, may I please set a reason for my human behavior?" Hades gazed at the man, knowing that Elasus was about to make an excuse for his actions. However, from what he heard Minos and Aeacus say, Hades needed to consider Elasus' point of view. Hades' face remained neutral, but he nodded. "Please sir, I repent all of my wrongdoings upon humankind. I only did those horrible deeds because of the war, sir. What was I supposed to do? I had a family to take care of ...," Elasus started to ramble.

Hades lifted up his hand to stop Elasus from talking further. The man refrained immediately, now aware of a horrible feeling in his gut. Usually, Hades read the life scrolls and knew precisely what to do with a soul. Sometimes on occasion, when a soul has a complicated life or situation, he has to look within the soul. It contains an extraordinary power that hardly anyone knows about.

Hades then stood up from his throne and went to Elasus. As he held the man's face in both hands, Elasus was starting to panic. "Calm down Elasus!" Hades said impassively. "I'm just going to take a look." Hades stared into the mind's eye of Elasus' soul and saw all of the man's memories flash quickly before him. Hades saw every war duty this man had been assigned. From fighting warriors to the cruel conduct of separating and killing families under orders from his general. Elasus had even slaughtered innocents with a sword. Then he saw Elasus' family being threatened by armed soldiers. His family would have been slaughtered if he hadn't followed commands. Hades felt the guilt and burden of everything this man had done and saw the love he bestowed for his family. He would do anything to protect them.

Hades dropped his hands, stared at the man, and with a deep sigh, he slowly turned back to his throne. With the sting of tears threatening to roll down his face, Elasus was shaking in fear. He felt exposed and ashamed of every horrible thing he had done, especially now that the King of Death had seen them all. Hades sat down on his throne and stared at Elasus' eyes once again with no emotion. The silence between them intensified.

"Do you regret the things you've done as a soldier?" Hades asked Elasus.

"Yes, my lord."

"With all the war crimes you've done, you really should be sent to Tartarus."

Tears welled up in Elasus' eyes as his fear became real.

"What would you do differently with your life if you had to do it again?"

"My Lord, if I had the power to deny my general's orders, my king, I would . . . but how can I when my family's life is at stake?" Elasus pleaded.

Hades thought for a moment. He had done battle to protect his brothers and sisters before. Unfortunately, he never had a family of his own to defend, so it was difficult for him to relate. However, Hades understood the pressure that comes with making a difficult choice and fearing the consequences, especially if the decision goes against one's personal beliefs. In Elasus' case, some situations could have been executed differently. "Have you thought of going against your general by creating a small army of your own to take him down? Or trying to convince him of creating only half the damage that was previously made during the war? Like not separating the families or harming the civilians?"

"Do you think he would have listened? I was just a common soldier," Elasus said in a defeated voice. He rehashed these memories over and over again, trying to think of what choice he should have made when he was alive. How can the God of the Underworld possibly understand human situations like war?

Hades suddenly interrupted Elasus' thoughts, "Most people who become legendary start out as 'common.' Obviously Elasus, the past is something we can't change. What's done is done. I understand your situation and the decisions you made. You could have stood up to the higher ranks and voiced your opinion."

"But sir, I would have been killed for doing that."

"Not when you have people behind you. More soldiers were in the same situation as you. Gathering them together could have made a huge difference. If you had done this, more lives could have been spared from emotional and physical pain. That same pain sometimes creates more criminals on earth. Unfortunately, it's possible that maybe this was meant to be, despite the fact that there are more negative mortals now because of the war." Hades sadly concluded that perhaps this was The Fates or Zeus's doing.

Once more, Hades looked at Elasus' scroll. As part of his destiny and life lesson, he was supposed to learn self-defense. Not only for his physical well-being, but also for his mental state. Elasus had gotten the physical part down, but not the mentality.

"My judgment is clear," Hades stated. "Elasus, you've conquered self-defense as your life lesson in the physical sense. Unfortunately, you haven't mastered the right mentality just yet. You've made it here, and you are not an evil man. I order you to be reincarnated so that you can master self-defense and the right mindset. However, you will return this time as a diplomat and not as a soldier, since you've done well fighting the war. Still, heed this warning—you will receive some harsh lessons during your upbringing as a result of the war crimes you committed in your previous life. The harsh lessons that you must endure will also inspire you to become a better man. You will also learn to make wiser decisions as the diplomat that you shall become."

Elasus sighed in relief, "Thank you, sir! I'll do better next time, I swear."

"Go. The guard will show you the way." Hades said with a stony facial expression, while an inner smile reached his blue eyes.

Then Elasus had one more question, "Will I remember this? Anything?"

Hades stared at him with almost a blank expression. "I want to tell you no. I want to say that you will have a perfectly clean slate. However, I've had some mortals regain memories of this meeting through dreams and flashbacks. Sometimes your soul remembers more than the mind."

"If I'm not supposed to remember anything, how am I supposed to accomplish what you have sent me to?"

"That is what your intuition is for, and if you get confused, then call upon the gods for help."

The guard escorted Elasus to the reincarnation section of the realm. Meanwhile, Hades judged the other souls and granted most of them the chance for reincarnation. Though, some decided to stay in the Asphodel Meadows, fearing that they would do worse in their next life and end up in Tartarus. Or they just didn't want to deal with earth's problems right away. Instead, they wanted to rest for a while before returning to earth.

After finishing his duties as a judge, Hades went to his chambers and began to relax. Sitting on his luxurious bed, he looked at the invitation scroll Hermes had given him earlier that evening. He debated whether or not he should go. It's been awhile since he last visited Olympus to see his brothers and sisters. In his head, Hades kept hearing the name *Persephone* over and over. Her name was going to haunt him if he didn't go to Olympus.

He would need to reschedule things so that he could attend. *Tomorrow night is going to be interesting,* he thought. Of course, he would not tell Hermes that he's actually coming. He wanted it to be a surprise visit. Of course, tomorrow night was going to be a life-changing event. Not only for the soon-to-be goddess Persephone, but also for himself.

CHAPTER 2

THE INITIATION

"Persephone." She always heard a voice whisper her name, constantly being called, in the dark. *"Persephone."* It was always whispered in darkness, but she was barely afraid. She kept walking toward the sound of her name.

"Hello?" She called out, only hearing her own voice echo in response. "Hello?" she called out again.

Then she heard her name once more, "Persephone."

She could see a silhouette of a man in the darkness. *Who was he?* She thought. *Why does he always call out to me, but never reveal himself?* Persephone got closer and reached out with one of her hands to touch his cloak, just as she saw the detail of his face . . . .

. . . .Persephone woke up startled and frustrated. She had dreamt of a man, but she couldn't recall his name. She had dreamt of him many times, for as long as she could remember. Every once in a while, this dream would haunt her sleep–he always called out to her and she'd see him, but his figure was consistently blurred. She wanted to figure out who this man was. Though she couldn't see him in detail, Persephone felt whole and also total devotion whenever she was around him. She hoped that the dream would one day reveal itself. Until that moment came, Persephone realized what day it was–her initiation!

Persephone opened her bedroom window. It was the crack of dawn as she quietly climbed out of her window, hoping that she was quiet enough not to disturb anyone. Especially one person in particular. Wanting to pick wildflowers for the flower crown that she would wear during tonight's initiation, Persephone wanted to do this without her mother or the nymphs around. Persephone felt a small sense of freedom as she lowered herself to the ground.

The sun rose brightly overhead; it was going to be a beautiful day. The gentle breeze rolled through the grass and flowers like waves. Persephone walked through the blades of grass as she inhaled fresh air. There was no one in sight, except for a few farmers just growing their crops. It was nice being alone, without anyone hovering over her. Her mother and the nymphs watched her like hawks all the time. Persephone loved her mother, but she was overprotective.

What was so dangerous about being alone in the fields or the woods? Persephone thought. She and her mother Demeter lived in a humble house, nestled between the woods and the open fields. Although Demeter, Goddess of Harvest and Caregiver of the Earth, barely visited Olympus herself, she stayed close to earth so that she could be near her only daughter. Persephone couldn't remember going to Olympus before. She had been a newborn the last time she was there. She wished she could remember what it felt like to be at Olympus. Every time her mother had special meetings there, Persephone begged Demeter to take her along, wanting to go too. Demeter had always refused, never giving her a reason why other than, "Olympus is no place for you."

Persephone sat down and began weaving her flower band. She was already enjoying the day. No Mother, no nymphs, no responsibilities. Just relishing the weather and relaxing under the sun.

Delighted in the peaceful quiet that surrounded her, Persephone's tranquility was abruptly interrupted by distant laughter. There she saw in the far off meadow, a young man chasing after a young woman. Persephone immediately got up and went toward them to get a closer look. She hid in the bushes to sit and observe, for mortals had always captured her interest. At first glance, she thought that the young man and woman were brother and sister playing, trying to sneak away from their parents just like she had. It wasn't, for then their playfulness turned into romantic gestures. The man was caressing the woman's face and kissing her lips.

Persephone knew she shouldn't be watching the couple, but she couldn't turn her eyes away from them. She never witnessed romantic love up close before. Like a child, Persephone watched with wonder and pure curiosity. Her mother had always said that men yearn for a woman's attention only for a short while. From what Persephone saw, Demeter's adage didn't apply to this particular couple. The man gently laid the woman down on the grass and began to kiss her more passionately. They caressed one another, giving into temptation, whispering 'I love you' into the other's ears.

An aching loneliness instantly crept into Persephone's heart. Emptiness and longing, along with a seed of hope, came over her. This is all she ever wanted, romantic love, with a glorious man who would love and cherish her. Someone to have interesting conversations with, a man who understood and showed her love with each kiss and embrace. This scene also reminded Persephone of her dreams—the mysterious figure who gave her feelings of love. She began to wonder if he would ever appear.

Besides freedom and her father's attention, Persephone always felt like something else was missing from her life. Now she knew what it was, but getting it would be an entirely different escapade. Speaking of fathers, the woman promptly broke the couple's romantic atmosphere because her father was calling for her. As she ran back home, her lover watched from a distance. A look of happiness appeared on his face as he went back toward the field to work.

"Persephone!" Demeter called out. Startled and wide-eyed, Persephone rushed out of the bushes and ran to her mother. She knew that she was going to be in trouble. Her mother already gives her a hard time about being alone as it is. As Persephone got closer, Demeter had a stern look on her face with her arms crossed. Demeter may have looked contemptuous, but she was actually relieved. "Persephone, how many times do I have to tell you not to go out there alone?"

Guilt showed on her face, but Persephone tried to calm her mother down apologetically, "Oh Mother, I was collecting flowers for my headband to wear during the initiation this evening." She showed her mother the flower band. "Besides, with no one in sight, how can there be any danger around?"

"There's always danger around. It may hide in darkness, but it's always there. You must be more alert," Demeter scolded her daughter as she scanned the area with

39

her eyes. Persephone wanted to roll hers, but held back her reaction.

"Really? Where?" Persephone smiled warmly at her mother for overreacting. Demeter looked around once more, especially by the wooded area where anything could hide. Then she looked at her beautiful, smiling daughter.

"Okay, there's no present danger at the moment, but Persephone you have to be more observant of your surroundings. Above all, near the woods. You have no idea what can be lurking in there."

"Mother, I'm fine. It's a beautiful day, and I'm overly excited about seeing Olympus for the first time."

Demeter muttered a bit sarcastically, "Another place of danger." Demeter had been dreading Persephone's initiation for years.

"Honestly, Mother, who is powerful enough to attack Olympus?"

There was one person Demeter had in mind. Someone who could and would attack Mount Olympus, if given the chance, but she refused to tell Persephone about that dark part of her life. "Some beings try, but that isn't the kind of danger I'm talking about."

Persephone realized that her mother was concerned about one of the gods. "Is this about . . . Hera?"

Demeter sighed. Her daughter was starting to figure things out, but Hera wasn't really the issue. The Queen of the Gods may have an infamous reputation for how she handles her husband's affairs and their children, but Hera was not a threat to Persephone. Despite Zeus' advances, and unlike the mortals or nymphs that Zeus often pursues, Demeter was Hera's sister. "No my love, even though Hera is a concern for most, she's not the one I'm worried about."

"Then who?"

"Just the gods in general . . . especially your father."

"Mother, Father may be distant from us, but he'll never harm me."

"I know he won't, my dear. He might, however, rush you to find a suitor." Persephone felt excited. Of course, Demeter noticed this slight change in her daughter, so she took a deep breath and hoped that Persephone would choose a more sacred path. "I was hoping that you'd be a virgin goddess. I'm more than willing to convince your father . . ."

Persephone's eyes widened with horror at the thought of everlasting virginity, or not even having an intimate relationship with a man. "No, Mother! Please, no! I want to get married. I want someone to love."

Demeter sighed as she faced the reality of her daughter's desires. "Honey, you have no idea what you're asking. Men just take all they want and then leave, or they expect you to do everything!"

"Mother, I'm pretty sure you just haven't met the right man, " Persephone reasoned while she touched her unique rose necklace. Out of all the presents Persephone had received when she was born, that necklace was her favorite. She had always worn it, never wanting to take it off. Demeter revulsed every time her daughter played with that thing.

However, Demeter gave her daughter a soft smile, seeing her innocence and kindness. She looked at the flower band that Persephone had made herself. "Go get yourself ready my dear; your dress is on the bed."

Persephone was barley inside the house when her mother added, "By the way, I'm punishing you after the initiation is over."

"What for?!" Persephone exclaimed.

"Because you snuck out of the house this morning!"

"Mother, you do realize that I'm going to be initiated as a goddess because I'm grown up now, right?"

"My dear, your body may be more womanly, but you still act childish."

With a frustrated huff, Persephone went into her room and started getting dressed for the initiation. She eyed the dress her mother had laid out for her. It was a light pink chiffon toga, adorned with clusters of flowers and rose petals. In this dress, she will indeed look like the goddess of spring. Then a depressing thought came to her. *The goddess of spring? Is that my only power and reason for existence–to make flowers grow?* After all, the gods and goddesses of Olympus had more realistically essential powers, that people prayed for their assistance every day.

What power did she have? Making pretty flowers for the spring.

Persephone shrugged the thought off, as she looked in the mirror and saw her reflection. She paused, hoping that when she's initiated, things would change. No longer will she just be Demeter's daughter, no longer will she just be seen as a child, or given the right to be treated like one. "Tonight . . .," Persephone said to herself, ". . . things are going to change."

High in a sky of clouds, right above Mount Olympus, a dimension between earth and the entire universe exists. Olympus is one of the most beautifully magnificent palaces designated for gods and goddesses. It shines through all realms and dimensions. The kingdom is intricately formed like the temples used to worship the gods on Earth, except most of its walls are made out of crystals and quartz. The Aurora Borealis shines through, casting rainbow and iridescent shimmers of light.

Demeter and Persephone arrived at the palace by Pegasus and carriage, which landed in front of the castle entrance. Persephone looked around wide-eyed at its beauty and size. As they entered the throne room of the gods and goddesses, Demeter was beside her. Olympus usually had a quiet presence, especially inside the palace, but not tonight. They entered a crowded room filled with gods and goddesses. The Olympians were joined by others that had ventured from all corners of the earth. There were the Norse gods, the Celtic gods, the Hindu gods, and even the Egyptian gods. By taking in this lively sight before her, Persephone realized that the Olympians were not the only gods to exist. She saw one god that was completely blue from head to toe, while another god carried around a heavy hammer. Persephone looked at her mother with curiosity, "There are gods from other places?"

"Yes, there are many of us from different regions."

"Why?"

"Simply put, different mortals have different belief structures, even though our structures are similar."

"So . . . were we created because the mortals imagined us into existence?"

Demeter smiled, "Persephone, the gods came first, but the mortals gave us a more defined identity. Although, more often than not, our identities are skewed from what mortals choose to believe about us. So, sometimes we take a form that better aligns with what they wish to see, or what we let them see." Persephone stood a bit confused, yet fascinated by Demeter's explanation. It didn't matter, however, because she was quickly gaining attention from some of the gods who desperately wanted to meet her. Meeting this soon-to-be goddess had become everyone's priority. Persephone soaked up all the attention that the male gods were giving her. Being desired felt like a treat for Persephone, and she was enjoying every minute of it. She continued to smile and blush from every compliment that came her way.

With a smile on his face, Zeus saw his daughter from a distance. He was pleased that many gods and goddesses from different worlds came for his daughter's initiation. Especially how eager they all were to meet her, but the King of the Gods was still a little anxious. He did not see Hades, nor had he heard whether or not Hades would be attending tonight's festivities. Zeus saw Demeter walking toward him. "I'm glad you can finally peel yourself away from our daughter for once," Zeus humored.

"At least I can still see her from a distance. Besides, how can she be harmed with all of these goddesses around?"

"And gods," Zeus countered with a thick voice.

"Now, those I need to protect her from," Demeter sarcastically countered back.

"Demeter, she's not a child anymore. She's getting initiated tonight and that's a step toward adulthood, my darling."

"I'm not your darling," she said contemptuously.

Zeus ignored her comment. "Now is the time for her to start courting suitors who would want her hand in marriage."

This caught Demeter's attention. "Actually, Zeus, I wanted to talk with you about making our daughter a virgin goddess."

"Do you seriously want that for her? Have you talked to her about it?"

"Yes, I have. Persephone doesn't know what she wants, Zeus. Besides, Athena and Artemis are happy with their chaste decisions."

"Demeter–" Zeus said in frustration. "First of all, Athena didn't take a vow of virginity. She just decided not to marry. Besides, like you said, it was their decision. If you make this choice for her, you're going to destroy any love she has left for you and for herself. From where I stand, Persephone's eyes are sparkling from all the attention she's getting."

Demeter paused for a moment, seeing that her daughter was enthralled in conversation with other male gods. Frustration flashed across Demeter's face. For once, this was something out of her control. The decision whether to be chaste or not was Persephone's choice, and hers alone. Seeing this, Demeter hoped that her daughter would choose to be a virgin goddess, even though she had doubts. Especially from that conversation she had had earlier with her daughter. She looked defeatedly at Zeus and gave him a courteous nod. Demeter then looked around the entire room and saw every god and goddess, with the exception of one. "Where's Hades?" she asked Zeus.

Zeus let out a deep breath. "I'm afraid I have no idea."

"Did he tell you he was coming?"

"In his own words, Hermes told me that Hades was going to think about it. Even though he knows full well that we can't start the ceremony without him."

"That's *so* like him. Not wanting to attend celebrations or ceremonies to make other people happy. He's as depressing as the kingdom he rules."

Then, another voice interrupted them, "What would you know about depression?" Hera asked, coming out from behind Zeus' throne.

Demeter gracefully answered, "Hello Hera. I know enough."

"Then you should know sister, that when you're depressed, it's torturous to see other people be happy. When you're depressed, you become more isolated and start hating the world, as well as yourself. Trust me when I say I understand the feeling," Hera confessed in disgust, as she peered at her husband. Zeus looked guilty because he knew that Hera was alluding to his many 'adventures' with other women. Zeus focused his attention back to his young daughter, who was now talking to Athena. They were having a profound discussion.

Persephone was still trying to understand the ways of the gods. "So mortals believe that we live on the very top of Mount Olympus?" Athena nodded. "That is ridiculous! I mean, how do you expect gods to live on the tip of a mountain?"

"Well, they are half correct. We live right above Mount Olympus. That is why this palace is called Olympus. However, mortals cannot see us."

"What if they climbed Mount Olympus to the top?"

"They still won't see us. We are cloaked within another dimension, even though we are still part of the earth's plane. We can see them, but they can't see us."

"Mortals see me all the time," Persephone mumbled.

"That is because you let them. We choose who gets to see us. Most of the time, it is the believers who need to see us and seek comfort from us in their time of need."

"What if we continued to show ourselves and let mortals know that we do exist? Wouldn't they likely believe in us even more?"

"Maybe, but even if we did just that, the ones that deny our existence will still be skeptical. They will find anything to misconstrue. People only see what they want to see. Those who want to deny that otherworldly beings exist, will never believe in or see us. Those who do believe, will see us only because they have open hearts and minds. It takes a countless amount of faith, strength, and courage to believe in something that is not blatantly apparent in everyday life."

Persephone felt that what Athena was talking about just then was beyond mortal belief. "The same can be said for nearly anything else, can't it? " Persephone questioned.

Athena gave her smile as she nodded.

"Another reason why mortals see me all the time is because Mother hasn't taught me how to be invisible." Persephone sighed, for there was so much her mother hadn't taught her. Regardless, she was welcomed by many gods as she circled the ballroom.

As she kept walking with Athena, Persephone kept hearing whispers pass among other gods. She constantly heard them talk about the King of the Underworld. Persephone even heard a god say how cold and ruthless he is. "Who's the King of the Underworld?"

"Hades," Athena answered. "We are all waiting for him to make an appearance, then your ceremony can begin. Ignore the whispers and rumors, Persephone."

"Why? With everyone saying the same thing about him, shouldn't it be true?"

"My sister, everyone follows the hype and mystery that surrounds Hades, but they don't know the real him."

Persephone frowned as she subconsciously began touching her necklace, " What about you?"

"I know him well enough." Athena shrugged humbly. "Hermes, however, knows him well. He helps the souls of mortals enter the Underworld. So, he sees Hades more frequently."

It was obvious that everyone was waiting for Hades, as more gods continued to gossip about him. Athena was getting agitated because these gods were following stupid mortal fears tied to one god. "Persephone, heed my advice. Don't judge someone based on rumors and gossip. When you meet Hades, get to know him first."

Persephone nodded. "I was planning to do that already."

Athena nodded in response. "I'm going to separate myself from you now. Other gods are staring, and I've been preventing them from interfering. I'm sure you could use their company as well," Athena said cheekily. Persephone giggled. She truly loved Athena for her observation and wisdom.

Once Athena made her exit, some of the gods began flirting with Persephone, including Apollo, a handsome god with sun-kissed skin. He was truly a god that every woman and man wanted to love.

"So, you're the guest of honor," Apollo said, giving her his dashingly bright smile. Persephone quickly nodded her head while she blushed at his compliment. "So beautiful and delicate, the Goddess of Spring. How fitting for one's power, to bloom like a flower because of my sun."

Persephone felt like he was complimenting her, as well as himself. She kindly smiled at him since she didn't want to tarnish her budding reputation, alongside her respected family who she barely knew. Still, she responded, "How do you know that you're responsible for my power? For all you know, my power comes from within me, just like any other god."

Apollo kindly smiled at her, with mischief twinkling in his eye, "You are so innocent that it's very refreshing around here. As you know my dear Persephone, spring cannot survive or even begin without the sun. Without my sun, your precious flowers will wilt. So if you think about it, you and your flowers can't survive without me."

Persephone looked at him with uncertainty. "Any special reason why you're mentioning this to me now?"

"I'm saying that we are a good match," Apollo said confidently.

Persephone raised her eyebrows with questionable doubt. "Match?"

Apollo clarified, "As husband and wife. My power helps your power grow and together, with our magic, we can make the planet so beautiful. It would look like the Elysian Fields."

"You planned this out already," she said nervously, feeling as if she needed to run away. Persephone always wanted a lover, but for a man to already ask for her hand without knowing her first, Apollo had caught her off guard.

"I'm pretty sure our father will approve."

Persephone looked at her father who was talking to Demeter, which reminded her to step back from Apollo. For once, she was glad her mother was overprotective. "You will still need approval from my mother," Persephone said sweetly and smiled playfully.

Apollo looked at Demeter in the distance. He shrugged, as if accepting an easy task. "That will be no problem, sweet Persephone." He grabbed the back of her hand and kissed it. "When the time is right, I'll ask your mother for permission to marry you."

Persephone inched closer to Apollo and her face nearly touched his. Just when he thought she was going to kiss him, she turned her head. Her lips went to his left ear and she whispered: "You'll still need to court me first." Apollo looked at her confused, since he assumed that he had already won her over. As she gave him a smirk, he suddenly realized what a challenge it was going to be to win her heart.

"That's fine—I love a challenge."

Persephone nodded. "Then good luck to you sir on your conquest."

Apollo smirked, ready to embark on his mission. He never had to chase a woman before, except Daphne, the one woman that still made his heart cry. Persephone left Apollo and rejoined the rest of the party.

Everyone around here had a glorious aura around them. They all were beautiful and glowing. To Persephone, everyone looked like a supreme being. Then something caught Persephone's eye. She saw a god sitting on one of the thrones, watching and observing the party. He seemed indifferent about the festivities and did not bother speaking to the other gods. In fact, hardly anyone realized that he was there. Unlike many of the gods present, he had a dark energy that exuded mystery and power. He was gorgeous with his well-defined pale face, looking like he never saw the sun. His shoulder-length dark brown hair almost matched the color of a raven. He wore thick black armor, along with a cloak and a gold helmet encrusted with jewels, which resembled some significance. Persephone walked closer to him, trying not to lose sight of him as she pushed her way through the crowd. As she neared this dark god, the more beautiful he seemed to her. As if Persephone was in a trance, he enticed her, like a moth drawn to flame. All the while, there was something familiar about this god that she couldn't quite place.

Persephone was only a few feet away when the dark god finally turned his head in her direction. Seeing his piercing blue eyes took her breath away instantly–they were crystal sky blue and filled with loneliness. Little did Persephone know, the dark god sitting before her was Hades, god of the Underworld. They kept staring at each other, as if they were the only two people in the room. Persephone kept walking until she finally made it to his throne, as she held her breath and her heart pounded.

Hades looked at the young woman, feeling breathless. Such natural beauty and innocence bedazzled him. She had golden blond hair that was sprinkled with strawberry red highlights. It almost looked like a fire set ablaze. Her eyes were a bright hazel green that matched the earth. She had a face that looked childish and womanly, all at once. Hades knew that she was a woman, for he noticed the sexy curves of her mature body that hid under her dress. He's seen many goddesses, nymphs, fairies, sirens, mortals, and princesses. None of them could compare to this enchanting young goddess, whoever she was.

As she approached Hades, looking directly at him, he appeared slightly confused, but he also had an expression of amazement on his face. Hades instantly ignored his thoughts in that moment, so that he could greet this beautiful goddess. "Hello my lady. Why, aren't you a lovely flower."

Persephone blushed and did a little curtsy. "Thank you, my Lord."

"What have I done to deserve your attention?" he asked, trying to remain calm so that he wouldn't scare her away with his bold flirtation.

"You've piqued my curiosity," she answered back, shyly flirtatious.

Hades smirked. "Now, young one, you know what they say about curiosity."

"That curiosity killed the cat?" Hades nodded at her answer. Persephone sweetly smiled, "Then I guess death would be an adventure that the cat would view with curiosity."

Hades just stared at her, silently laughing on the inside. Nobody had made him smile. *Does this young lady know who she's talking to?* he thought. Then, he noticed the rose necklace glistening around her neck. He had made that for a particular goddess when she was just a baby. Hades was stunned to realize that the breathtaking goddess standing before him was indeed Persephone! She was wearing his necklace! After all this time, she still loved his piece of jewelry.

"Please forgive me, but I've never seen a god like you before." Hades moved his attention from the necklace to her arching an eyebrow, curious to know what she meant. "I mean, it's not like I've seen many gods myself, but out of all the people here . . . you're different."

Hades' smile returned as his eyes lit up with mischief. "Different how?"

"Everyone here has a glowing aura radiating from themselves, but yours has a dark and mysterious quality." Hades nodded. The darkness she had picked up on was his own representation of death. "Are you from another godly region?" Persephone asked and then she remembered that he's sitting on an Olympus throne. "Then again, you must belong here if you're sitting upon one of those thrones."

Hades didn't want her to know who he was just yet, afraid that his title would scare her away. "Not quite. I do belong to another part of the world, yes, but I do come here. . . rarely. I only come here on special occasions, or when I'm truly needed."

Intrigued, Persephone asked "So what kind of god are you?"

Before Hades could answer, Athena rushed to her attention. "Persephone, our father wants to see you." Athena

grabbed Persephone's hand and led her toward their father's throne on the other side of the ballroom.

As Athena tugged at her arm, Persephone looked at Hades in disappointment. "I've got to go." She continued to stare at him as Athena dragged Persephone by her wrist. With much interest, Hades continued to stare at Persephone as she slipped into the crowd.

While still being dragged across the ballroom, Persephone quickly glanced at Hades before looking at Athena. "Who was that?"

"Who was what?" Athena asked, as she looked in the direction that Persephone had turned toward.

"The god I was talking to," Persephone stated, still watching Hades on his throne. His eyes fixated on her the entire time.

Athena looked at the throne and then back at Persephone, confused. "There is no one there, Persephone."

"He's sitting right on *that* throne," she pointed.

"Persephone. . . listen to me. That throne is empty." Confusion spread across Persephone's face, especially as she looked back to the throne, seeing that it was now bare. He was gone. Athena ignored the girl's silliness and brought her to Zeus' throne. She was reunited with her mother and warmly embraced her father's hug.

Hades watched this interaction from a distance. After all, his reason for being here was to help initiate Persephone as a goddess. He suddenly felt a sense of honor and would gladly initiate her, alongside his brothers.

Zeus stopped embracing his daughter who he rarely sees, apart from looking after her from above. "My beautiful daughter, you have grown up so much. I can't wait for you to take your place on Olympus."

Persephone's eyes widened, "Will I get my very own throne here?"

Demeter immediately stepped in, "No sweetie, you'll be sharing a throne with me. Besides, most of our time will be spent on earth. You will help me with the vegetation, crops, and flowers." Persephone felt discouraged, but kept smiling. Her negative thoughts instantly resurfaced to emphasize the idea that planting flowers was her only power.

"But that doesn't limit you from coming to Olympus," Zeus confirmed, "This is your home now too." Persephone gave her father a warm smile and hugged him again.

"So when will the ceremony start?"

Feeling a little agitated, Zeus flashed a tight smile. "As soon as your uncle gets here."

"My uncle?"

"Yes, Hades. He should have been here by now."

"Hades . . . as in the King of the Underworld?" Persephone looked at her mother for confirmation. She nodded in agreement. Persephone shivered anxiously as she waited to see the god everyone fears. She's heard many mortals share their stories and fears about Hades. They are afraid to speak his name, for they believe that sudden death will strike down upon them if they do.

The whole room gasped as an apparition suddenly formed in the center of the ballroom. Through the smoke, a godly form began to appear. With his helmet off, there stood Hades holding a pitchfork, which measured over six feet lengthwise, in his other hand. He looked superior. Many of the gods and goddesses backed away fearfully from his presence. From the whispered rumors she had overheard, Persephone knew the gods and goddesses had also heard many mortals conspire about Hades and the Underworld. Even his own family had begun to believe the stories too. Only a few gods and goddesses knew the real Hades.

As her heart dropped to her stomach, Persephone stared in amazement at the god whom she had spoken with only moments ago. Then she glanced at her father. "Is that Hades?"

Relieved, Zeus smiled. His brother had shown up after all. Looking at his daughter, Zeus said, "That is him! Finally, your ceremony can begin." Zeus left his throne to greet his brother.

Persephone was stunned that he was the same man she talked to earlier. No one noticed Hades until now; even Athena hadn't seen him. Now the gods and goddess were trying to stay out of his way. But Persephone saw him and had also spoken to him. It didn't make any sense. Above all else, what bothered her even more was that she felt attracted to him. Persephone was going to be the goddess of spring. *How can I be attracted to someone who represents darkness and death?* She thought, *Was this a trick from The Fates?* She stared at his powerful, yet graceful movements that were capable of making others tremble. Loud whispers rolled through the ballroom as the other gods began to talk about Hades again.

"Brother!" Zeus exclaimed with his arms open, ready to embrace his older brother. Hades respectively hugged Zeus for the sake of not wanting to start an argument. "I'm glad you could make it! It's good to see you. It's been a very long time since you came up here."

"Well, brother, my work is never complete. After all, death happens every day," Hades said dryly.

"So does life. You must learn to take more breaks. Isn't that why you have those three judges to begin with?" Zeus asked.

"I don't exactly trust their judgment."

Zeus scoffed, "You don't trust anybody."

"With good reason," he said darkly, but Zeus ignored Hades' comment. "Speaking of which, I need to talk to Ares."

Zeus frowned, confused and frustrated, "Why? What is my son doing now?" Zeus said, placing distasteful emphasis on the word 'son.' Ares had always been a troublemaker since his birth. He's the God of War for a reason. Compared to everyone else, Hades hardly complained about Ares, but now he wanted to speak with him at once. Zeus realized it must be about something serious because Hades never wastes anyone's time otherwise.

"He's starting trouble again. Apparently, peaceful harmony among mortals is too much for him," Hades said with agitation.

"Are you certain Ares is doing this?"

"I've known from good authority."

"Are you talking about me?" Ares asked, as if ready to start a fight. He had heard them talking from within earshot. Ares had absolutely no problem with confrontation.

Zeus almost rolled his eyes, knowing that Ares would likely create an unnecessary ruckus. "Yes," Zeus admitted, "Can you explain to me what your uncle is talking about?"

"I'm surprised he found out. I haven't done enough damage yet for the Underworld to be so impacted with new residents. No more than usual." Ares smirked. "So Hermes has snitched on me, hasn't he?"

Hades confirmed this with stern sincerity. "Of course it was Hermes, so don't go blaming the messenger for being a messenger. I thought we were going to have a quiet year, nephew."

"Quiet leads to boredom, and boredom leads to insanity. I don't know about you, Uncle, but the year just got started and I'm already bored. I need to play and create some action on earth."

"Ares, can't you comprehend that the more you play, the more work I have to do?" Hades insisted.

With a careless shrug of his shoulders, Ares replied, "What an unfortunate price to pay for my entertainment!" He snickered. "Happy judging, Hades!"

Trying to suppress his frustration and fury, Hades closed his eyes. His power began to radiate around his body. Hades couldn't resist from not having the final say before Ares disappeared back into the crowd of other gods. "You know mortals are not toys to be played with! Why can't you be responsible for once?!" Sensing that a physical fight would shortly emanate, Zeus groaned. Persephone watched with wide eyes as things continued to unfold. She stayed by her mother's side.

Ares replied in an uproar, "I am responsible! Who do you think mortals pray to whenever a war battle breaks out?"

"A war battle that YOU started! That's the only way mortals pray to you!"

"Not always uncle," Ares said with a smile. "Mortals can create battles on their own without my help. That's how terrible humankind is now. Sometimes it's me or Athena who has to finish mortal conflicts."

"Don't remind me of how awful humankind can be. I see it every day in their memories when I judge souls."

"Yet you give most of them a second chance and allow their souls to be reincarnated. Why?"

"Because, my troubled nephew, they are not as evolved as us. Although, I've come across a few gods who are now steeped to their level." Hades abruptly ended the conversation and stared down at Ares, trying to hint at someone in particular.

Wanting to initiate a fight, Ares, who had no intention of holding back his anger, was ready to throw a power-ball of energy directly at Hades. Witnessing this, Zeus stopped Ares before he even threw the first punch. "ARES!" Zeus shouted and Ares froze. "NOT HERE! NOT

NOW!" Now that Hades had won the argument, Ares stomped away from his uncle to rejoin the party, fuming. Everyone just stared around the room as the feud between the god of war and the god of death ended.

Hades closed his eyes once again to calm himself down. Zeus decided to distract his elder brother, "Come now! It's time for you to meet our guest of honor!" Hades followed Zeus toward his throne. There stood Persephone, the beauty he had talked to just moments ago. Hades' pent-up agitation dissipated just by looking at her. "Persephone, may I introduce you to your uncle, and one of the three major kings of the earth, Hades King of the Underworld." Hades looked at her with a hidden smile that only Persephone could see. His icy blue eyes shone with warmth as he gazed at her.

Persephone's heart fluttered as she kindly smiled back. "It's a pleasure to meet you, my lord, finally," she said. She was happy to officially know his name.

Hades gave her a secret cautionary smile, as he took her hand and kissed her knuckles. Persephone felt as if every fiber of her being were on fire and her stomach fluttered in response to such intimate contact. Demeter was right behind Persephone, watching Hades' every move alongside everyone else. "It'll be a privilege to initiate you, my little flower," Hades said with slight seduction. Persephone blushed as Demeter scowled. She was astounded, not only because her older brother was actually here, but Demeter swore that he was also flirting with her daughter.

"As you can see Persephone," Zeus said while slapping Hades on the shoulder. "Your Uncle is not the monster that everyone proclaims him to be."

Persephone smiled warmly, "My dear father, I never once even thought of him as a monster just because he rules over the dead."

Hades showed a smile that he had fought to keep hidden. "I hope my little fight with Ares didn't scare you, little flower. His ego needs to be tampered with on occasion."

She shook her head, "No." To be honest, Persephone admired Hades' authority so much that it aroused her. She never realized that something could be so beautiful, yet so deadly.

"Well! Since we are all finally here, let's begin!" Zeus exclaimed in a booming voice for all gods to hear. Hades and Poseidon followed behind Zeus to his throne. All the gods and goddesses gathered around the head throne, watching the three major kings of the earth huddle together. A golden chalice, with sacred writings inscribed on the cup's edge, sat upon an altar. Hades held up a special vial and poured its contents into the chalice. Zeus looked at his daughter with pride, "Come here, my child."

Persephone approached the altar, facing her father and her two uncles. All of them were full of pride for this new goddess. The chalice was filled with ambrosia, the immortal drink of the gods.

Zeus began the ceremonial speech: "My dear friends across the universe. This lovely young goddess has come into her own, as she becomes one of us! May her powers reach their potential and help all beings find their greatest good." Zeus handed the chalice to Hades. One by one, all three kings of the earth put some of their own power into the ambrosia and blessed it.

Hades was first, for he was the eldest. Before he blessed the chalice, Hades glanced at Persephone momentarily. For a brief second, he felt honored to bestow part of himself upon her. "Bless this woman with my power for she is now immortal. May she reign this world with intention and power." With his hand, he poured a little bit of his energy into the chalice. Then he handed it over to Poseidon.

Poseidon blessed the cup the same way. "Bless this woman with my power for she is now divine. May she reign this world with beauty and grace." Like Hades, with his hand, he poured a little bit of his energy into the chalice. Then he handed it over to Zeus.

Like Hades and Poseidon, Zeus also executed the blessing in a similar way. "Bless this woman with my power for she is now a goddess. May she reign this world with heart and glory." Zeus placed part of his own power into the chalice to finish the blessing. Then he gave the chalice to Persephone. "Drink this, my daughter, and you'll become one of us."

Persephone gently took the chalice from her father. She was excited, but also nervous because she didn't know what to expect after her initiation. She took a deep breath before drinking the ambrosia that was mixed with the energy of the three kings. As she sipped from the chalice, the taste was absolutely divine—it was like a mixture of honey and sunshine. Persephone drank every last drop from the cup. She began to transform into a goddess as a golden glow enveloped her body. She shone so bright that, for a moment, Persephone looked like the sun. Thus, her initiation was finally over and she was now the goddess of spring and Flowers!

All of the gods and goddesses in the ballroom cheered. As Persephone's new energy subsided, Hades stared at her in amazement. She was beautiful before, but now she looked divine; he was enthralled by Persephone. To him, she was even more alluring than Aphrodite.

Zeus then made a loud announcement, "Gods and goddesses of all regions! Meet Persephone, the goddess of spring and flowers!" Zeus looked at her with both love and pride. "Congratulations, my darling girl."

Persephone couldn't be more thrilled. From this exact moment on, she is part of the Olympus Gods and Goddesses! Everyone came up to congratulate her and

Athena gave her a big sisterly hug. "I'm so happy for you! You're one of us now!"

Persephone gushed, "I know, I hope I have as interesting a story or personality like every god here."

"Persephone, as you know I'm the Goddess of Wisdom. Let me give you some advice—the more you live each day, the more your life weaves together a story of its own. Many people, including us, can see the memories from the past and sometimes a vision of the future. They can't see the present because they're living in it."

"So you're saying . . . ?"

"Live for today. Let fate run its course. The more you live, the more of a story life becomes."

"Thank you. Although, I'm not sure I completely understand your advice."

Athena gave Persephone another hug. "You'll find out someday," Athena said and she went to join the rest of the party. Persephone observed the whole ballroom—everyone was dancing, eating, and drinking wine. She looked at her mother who, thankfully, was talking to Hestia the goddess of hearth. Looking at Demeter, Persephone's heart sank upon realizing that she and her mother would have to return back to earth soon.

Needing a moment to herself, she went to the balcony where she could see the night sky and stars. She admired the godly constellations above and took a deep breath, hoping all of her concerns would dissipate from her mind.

Hades watched from a distance as Persephone took in the night sky. He began to approach her, "Persephone," he said gently.

She looked up to see Hades, and her heart fluttered as she smiled brightly at him. "So you're the ruler of the Underworld."

Pleased, Hades smiled at Persephone and his heart swelled with happiness. He was relieved that someone finally looked at him with admiration instead of fear. "I am indeed."

"Well, you weren't lying when you said that you belong here, yet you're from somewhere else."

"I would never lie to you. I did not want you to know who I was, not at that moment, " Hades said sincerely.

She nodded. "What, did you think that I would fear you?"

Hades subtly nodded at her assumption. Persephone looked at his kind, beautiful blue eyes again and smiled. Curiosity got the better of her. "So, King of the Underworld, where's the queen of your domain? My father and Poseidon have their queens. Yet, I don't see yours."

"I do not have one," Hades said somberly. He stared at her, wondering why she would pry about that.

Persephone's heart fluttered to know that Hades is still a bachelor. She couldn't help but smile to herself—she might actually have a chance with Hades. Regardless, she felt sympathetic because he's been alone for so many years.

"I'm sorry, it must be lonesome in the Underworld with no one to care for you."

Hades noticed Persephone's subtle smile as he responded, "It is. Though my servants care for me, it's not the same when someone loves you because they want to."

"So how come you don't have a queen?" Persephone asked anxiously.

Hades smirked, "Now my little flower, why are you so curious about my marital status?" Persephone blushed hard, but Hades was merciful. "Has curiosity got the better of you again?" In almost a cowardly fashion, Persephone nodded. "All of your inquiries would have made you a dead cat by now."

"Don't answer if you don't want to. It's really not my concern."

Hades decided to change the conversation; he wasn't ready to give her an answer. "What are you doing out here anyway? Shouldn't you be enjoying the celebration? After all, it's in your honor."

"I'm afraid my mother would return me to Earth without hesitation, once Father asks me the ultimate question."

Hades already knew the question that she would be asked. "Whether or not you want to be a virgin goddess?"

"Yes, that's the question, so I'm stalling for as long as I can."

Hades held his breath, hoping she wouldn't decide to be a virgin forever. "It is a big decision not to be taken lightly." Hades frowned for a moment as he dared to ask, "Is that what you want? To be a virgin goddess?"

Persephone almost snorted with laughter, "No! My gracious lord, no!" Hades let out his breath, relieved. There was a good chance for him to be with her. "I want a husband who is kind, handsome, who understands me, and holds me at night. " Hades can imagine nights with her just like that and more. Persephone peeked at him as she blushed, as if trying to hint at him. "One day I will have children with him. I want him to love me unconditionally, and see me as the woman I am, not a child nor a worthless goddess."

Ice ran through Hades veins in response to Persephone's last statement. "My little flower, what makes you think that you are worthless?"

Persephone sighed because the doubts that have plagued her for the longest while suddenly resurfaced, "I'm the Goddess of Spring and Flowers. Who would pray to that? I'm not going to be asked for very much because my powers are meaningless."

Hades understood her feelings, but he didn't want them to fester more. "I'm the ruler of death, ruler of the Underworld, and the god of riches. I'm one of the most powerful gods. There are many reasons why mortals should pray to me. Yet, I don't get a single prayer, nor do I have a temple to worship, because everyone is afraid of me. They're even afraid to say my name." Feeling instant guilt for her self-pity, Persephone sensed sorrow for Hades. She couldn't believe that a major god like Hades doesn't receive a single prayer. Hades then looked at her with a hidden smile. "Don't pity me Persephone, my world is fine just the way it is."

Hades continued to answer the question that had been plaguing Persephone's mind. "You know, flowers have great importance not only for the mortals, but for the earth too."

Smiling, Persephone wondered how the god of the Underworld knew so much about flowers. "How so? I have not had much training, other than to make flowers grow."

"Well for the earth, they attract the pollinators."

"Pollinators?" she asked, frowning.

Hades nodded, realizing that Demeter hasn't taught her daughter very much. "Bees, wasps, and butterflies– flowers attract them. These pollinators go from one flower to another, and other plants as well, carrying pollen with them. That's how new plants are created, with help from you of course." Hades smiled at her as he continued. "So the earth would be in trouble without pollinators and flowers. For some flowers, they can bring food and medicine." Hades started moving closer to Persephone and lowered his voice. "Flowers are also beautiful and are good for the soul. They sometimes bring a sense of tranquility and improve the overall quality of life. Flowers also symbolize romance, seduction, and love—like the beautiful red rose." Hades magically manifested a beautiful red rose and lifted it up in front of Persephone. He used its petals to caress her face. Persephone noticed that Hades' voice sounded more seductive as he handed over her favorite flower. Smiling, she took the rose from him, smelling its enchanting scent.

"So, my darling, you are not as worthless as you think. As you bring more flowers into this world, you will also bring life, beauty, and love. Don't worry my sweet flower, mortals will pray to you because of how beautiful and kind you are. Even if it's just to make flowers grow."

It had been a long time since someone had willfully expressed so much confidence in Persephone and she smiled. Music wafted out from the ballroom just then, and both Hades and Persephone turned their heads to listen. Hades walked toward her, closing the distance between them. He offered her his hand gracefully. "My lovely flower, would you care to dance?"

Hesitant and somewhat shy, Persephone gently set the rose down on one of the pillars to accept his hand. Warmth radiated from his palms, despite the paleness of his skin. She tried to calm her pounding heart, while his other hand held her waist. He began to gently caress her backside and they started to sway. She had never danced with a man before, especially not in such close proximity.

She stared into Hades icy blue eyes, bringing pleasurable shivers down her spine as their bodies entwined. Persephone has always dreamed of a dance like this. *How can any of the rumors about Hades be true? He is more of a gentleman than any other god that she had met tonight,* she thought to herself.

"Back to your dilemma, my little flower. It appears you already know what you want, therefore you should take it." Hades hoped that his reasoning would give Persephone the courage to detach from her mother.

"I'm afraid that it will disappoint my mother. In fact, I know it will disappoint her."

"My darling, you need to spread your wings and find your own happiness. Even your mother needs to realize that." Though Persephone's heart fluttered again because Hades had called her his darling, she shrugged it off. She believed he often said that to most women anyway. "Now, the question is: Will you have the courage to fly?"

Before she could answer him, they heard footsteps approaching the balcony. They overheard Zeus and Demeter talking nearby. Hades and Persephone stopped dancing and quickly uncoupled themselves, fearing what Demeter might think. Persephone grabbed Hades' rose and tried to hide it behind the extra fabric of her dress. Zeus came to his daughter's side. "So my daughter, did you have a nice time tonight?" Demeter was right beside him. She wasn't too thrilled about her daughter having some quality time with the King of the Underworld. In fact, Demeter was a little suspicious.

Persephone smiled at Hades, then at her father. "Yes, father I did." Zeus glanced at Hades and noticed that his brother was desperately trying to hide a look of longing on his face.

"Well Persephone, like everyone else who gets initiated as a higher being, I am going to ask you an important question," Zeus said and Persephone waited for her father to continue. "Would you prefer to be a virgin goddess or would you like to marry one day?" Even though Persephone knew exactly what she wanted, the pressure from her mother was making her decision difficult. Persephone paused and over thought her answer. Demeter interjected, "Remember Persephone, if you chose to be a virgin goddess, you cannot marry."

She looked between her mother and Hades. Upon gazing at Hades, he instantly reminded her of what she yearned after. "No father, I don't want to be a virgin goddess. That life does not suit me."

Zeus smiled and nodded. "Very well, I'll tell everyone that you're open to marriage. Come, my daughter." Zeus and Persephone went back to his throne to make the announcement. Unaware that he was holding his breath, Hades exhaled and just stared at Persephone with pride. Despite her mother's wishes, Persephone made her own decision, which Demeter undoubtedly disapproved of at once. Persephone would get an earful from her mother on their way home.

Everyone gathered around for Zeus' final announcement about Persephone. With his booming voice, he called out, "All gods and goddesses! This night has been a spectacular evening, for not only is my sweet daughter now the goddess of spring and flowers, but she has made a choice for herself. She has decided not to take the virgin path! She wants to take the path of romance and marriage!"

A big cheer rolled through the crowd, especially from the men, since a beautifully young goddess was now readily available. Hades saw the look on Apollo's, Ares', and even Hermes' faces when they heard the announcement. It was clear to Hades that he has competition. He looked at his little flower again as she smiled, hearing the other gods praise her. Hades felt his heart ache repeatedly. For the first time in centuries, he wanted a wife. Specifically, he wanted one person in particular to fill that role. He wasn't alone in his desire, for The Fates had predicted his marriage a long time ago. However, some fates can be altered. Hades promised himself that Persephone would be his wife and queen.

Persephone scanned the crowd looking for Hades. As she saw him, he looked at her with yearning eyes. At that moment, he vanished in a cloud of smoky flames. The smile fell from her face, as she had hoped the dark god would step up and court her. He was sincerely different from the other gods. Something about him made her spirit soar. Even he had helped her defy her mother's wishes. At that moment, Persephone stepped into adulthood and she knew that her mother would try everything in her power to stop it.

CHAPTER 3

THE INVISIBLE SUITOR

Persephone looked in the mirror as she put on her emerald rose necklace. In gazing at her favorite piece of jewelry, she felt its warm energy. Today was her first official day as the goddess of spring and she hoped that it would be different, perhaps more magical. She even supposed that one of the mortals would pray to her. However, Persephone doubted that many people would pray for flowers to bloom. Yet, she remembered what Hades had said last night ' *Don't worry my sweet Persephone, mortals will pray to you because of how beautiful and kind you are. Even if it's just to make flowers grow.'* Persephone should be happy that she's a real goddess now, but she couldn't help feeling the nagging worthlessness that hung over her.

Her mind wandered back to Hades, and she looked at the rose he had given her last night. As she smelled the flower, she thought of his pale blue eyes and his perfectly pale chiseled face. She loved how he encouraged her and how he listened to her about what she felt. Unlike some of the other gods that she had met last night. *Who do the gods pray to when they find themselves in a difficult situation?* she thought. At that moment, she prayed to a universal energy that she and Hades would meet again.

As she heard her mother's footsteps, Persephone quickly hid her red rose behind one of her pillows, hoping that the enchanting flower would not get smushed. Demeter walked into Persephone's room, still feeling disappointed with her daughter about her fateful decision. Persephone stopped praying because she felt the tension in the air. Instead, she played with her necklace, hoping to calm her nerves. Demeter looked at the piece of jewelry in disgust, remembering who had given it to Persephone. "I don't know why you play with that thing. Ever since you were a baby, that's the only piece of jewelry you refuse to part with."

"Do I need a reason? I love it, and it calms my nerves. Besides this piece is a work of art. Whoever made it for me, really put their heart into it. Which, by the way, you never mentioned who gave this to me," she tapped her necklace.

"I forgot who it was darling, after all, it was a long time ago," Demeter lied. She saw how much time

Persephone had spent with Hades at her initiation; she didn't want to give her daughter any more reason for her to like him. "There were many gifts that every god gave you, it was easy to lose track."

Persephone gave her mother a long, hard look. "Mother, I know you're not happy about my decision."

Demeter shook her head, disappointed. "What were you thinking, Kore?"

Persephone cringed upon hearing her nickname. She hated the name Kore ever since she figured out its meaning–Kore means 'maiden.' In fact, Demeter preferred to call her that. Persephone begged her mother not to use that name, but Demeter would use it when she's upset with her daughter every so often. Zeus, on the other hand, didn't like how common Kore sounded. It didn't sound like a goddess' name at all. So, he named her Persephone, despite Demeter's protests. Persephone supposed that if she kept Kore as her name, she'd be a maiden forever. "I was thinking of having a future with someone I love."

Her mother sighed with sadness, "Kore. . . A man's love is only temporary. He'll love you and desire you in ways that every woman dreams about." Then Demeter's eyes darkened. "Then someone new will come along, and he'll toss you aside like you were never anything special to him."

Persephone shook her head in disbelief, "I'm sure not every man is like that. Just because that's what father did to you, doesn't mean that's going to happen to me!" She stood her ground. Persephone still believed that true love exists and that it can last, despite what others think, including her mother. Unfortunately, her daughter's words struck a nerve.

"At least if you had become a virgin goddess, you wouldn't get hurt!" Demeter exclaimed.

"Mother, for me to find happiness, there's always a chance that I might get hurt. Besides, how else am I going to know what The Fates have in store for me? Suitors aren't going to knock on my door, asking for my hand in marriage if I stay here!"

Demeter let out a sarcastic laugh. "You don't have to worry about suitors not coming to knock on your door." Persephone gave her mother a questionable look. "You already have one waiting for you. That's why I came in here, to let you know that someone is outside wanting to see you. He already asked my permission to come speak with you."

"Who?" Persephone asked excitedly, hoping it was Hades.

"Apollo."

Persephone faked a wide smile. "Great! I'll go and see him now since he's been out there for a while." She wasn't too thrilled to have met him last night, but she was going to give Apollo another chance. After all, many people craved his attention, right?

"I told him he can only have ten minutes with you."

"Alone?"

"No, you two will be walking together in the fields. So that I can watch over you both from afar."

Persephone knew there was a catch and shook her head. Her mother didn't want her anywhere near a man, alone. She walked through the front door and Demeter followed. There stood Apollo with all of his charms on display. He wore a perfectly white smile and a loose white tunic, showing off his abdomen. Apollo was holding a bundle of wildflowers, which he held out to Persephone. Demeter did not like this one bit. She scowled, and it showed clearly on her face. "Apollo, remember that you have only ten minutes."

Apollo nodded as he gave Persephone the flowers. "They're an apology gift for how rude I was last night."

Persephone actually gave him a genuine smile, "You were not rude. Snobbish maybe, but not rude."

Apollo smiled, a little embarrassed, as they walked toward the fields that stretched out to the woods. He could sense Demeter watching them like a hawk. What he didn't realize was that she wasn't the only one chaperoning their courtship.

In the woods, Hades watched Persephone interact with Apollo. With his helmet on, Hades was invisible to everyone, except maybe the one person who he was watching at this very moment. He wasn't sure how

Persephone saw him with his helmet on during the night of her initiation. Perhaps, as part of her initiation, her powers were heightened before the blessings were given. Regardless, Hades didn't want to experiment with her powers today. To be on the safe side, he wore his helmet as he hid in the woods.

Apollo walked close to Persephone as he talked to her. They were in Hades' plain sight. "I might have let my ego get in the way. When I first saw you, I just thought we might pair well together. I've pictured it in my head. Then, when I talked to you, it did not come out the way I intended."

Persephone smiled and understood; maybe Apollo was a nice guy after all. "It's okay. I always give people another chance. After all, many people stumble on their words when they meet someone new. Isn't that why it's called a second chance?"

"Yes, I suppose so," Apollo said with a flirtatious smile.

"Besides, why the rush?" Persephone asked, "You were already thinking about us being married, yet we hardly know each other. Don't you want to get to know me first?"

"I do Persephone! It's just that I've always seen father take anyone he wants without being rejected. I expect the same for me."

"Zeus is our father. Of course, no one is going to reject him. Who would have the nerve?"

"That's true. What's also true, Persephone, is that no one is going to get to know you—" Apollo paused to glance cautiously at Demeter. He then whispered, "No one would really get to know you with your mother always hovering." Persephone felt discouraged, knowing that Apollo was right. How was she supposed to find the love of her life with Demeter constantly hovering over her shoulder? Even if she and Apollo courted secretly, it would only be a matter of minutes before her mother found out, or one of her nymphs would reveal Persephone's whereabouts.

Hades was thinking the same thing as he watched his beloved and Apollo. However, he too was planning out his moves, so that even Demeter couldn't catch him and Persephone. He understood what Persephone wanted and no god, not even Apollo, could give her that. Except himself. Hades knew his nephew had a completely different appetite for romance and sex. Living a satisfied life with Persephone would only last between one to five years at most, until someone else caught his eye. Apollo is just like his father, exactly as he had explained to Persephone. Unfortunately, she didn't follow that.

As their conversation continued, Ares appeared, standing like a proud peacock with a handful of flowers. Like Apollo, he was very sexy, but he was also dark and robust. His dark, wavy hair was a hot mess and his darkly powerful eyes felt dangerous. His anger made Persephone nervous. Any progress that Apollo was making with Persephone came to a halt when Ares rudely interrupted them. And for that, Apollo was evidently frustrated. Ares walked up to the couple and handed the flowers to Persephone. "For you, lovely goddess," he said smoothly.

Apollo looked at Ares in disbelief as Persephone accepted the flowers. "Can't you see I'm here with the lovely Persephone?"

Ares studied them for a moment, "Yes. I see you've set out to conquer another beautiful goddess." Ares smirked, knowing that he had just exposed one of Apollo's many flaws.

"Like you're better than me? I'm not the one stealing another god's wife!" Apollo fired back. Everyone in Olympus knew about Ares' many affairs with the goddess of love, Aphrodite, who is married to poor Hephaestus. Aphrodite is the only one who gives Ares much-devoted attention. "Even if you do conquer Persephone, you'll run straight to Aphrodite when she calls for you!"

Hades shook his head in disbelief while he watched his two nephews fight over Persephone. They really were unaware of what she truly wanted. As the situation unfolded, he saw Persephone's wide-eyed expression while she tried to suppress her laughter. However, their snarky comments held some truth to them, making Persephone rethink Apollo's nature.

Then Hades saw Demeter come toward the trio like a protective lioness. "Alright, you two!" Everyone stared at Demeter. Persephone sighed, relieved that her mother had come to rescue her. With a stern look, Demeter directed her attention toward Apollo and Ares. "Apollo, your 10 minutes are up." Apollo nodded and gave Persephone a quick smile before he dematerialized to Olympus.

Within the next instant, Demeter looked at Ares in disgust. Ares gave her a devilish grin to show that he was still determined. "Ares, what makes you think you have a chance with my daughter?"

"I think my looks and personality already answer that question," Ares said, a bit cocky. Persephone rolled her eyes in response. A god's ego never failed to amaze her.

Demeter looked down at him, "Ares, you don't have a chance with Persephone because of the way you are."

Ares' eyes darkened. He glanced at Persephone for a second before looking back at Demeter. "Yet, a god who takes pleasure in everyone's company is the better suitor?" Ares asked, emphasizing 'pleasure' with utter distaste. "You should know better Demeter; a god like that never stays around for long."

"Like you will?" Demeter challenged.

Ares just smirked as he backed away from this squabble. There was no winning an argument with an overprotective mother, especially when she made valid points. He looked at Persephone again. "You don't want to be a maiden forever do you?" Persephone shook her head no. "Young goddess, if you ever want to have a great time with me, I'll gladly serve your desire. So that you know, there's no such thing as a monogamous god. . . remember that." he said as he dematerialized back to Olympus.

"The god of war wants a relationship with my daughter!" Demeter laughed at the situation, even though the idea made her skin crawl. "That'll happen when Tartarus freezes over!" she shouted to the sky. "Come on Persephone, let's go inside before another suitor comes knocking," she said with disgust. Persephone smiled as her mother mentioned Tartarus because she instantly thought of Hades.

As Persephone walked back to their house, she sensed someone watching her from the woods. She scanned the area with curious eyes. Hades stayed perfectly still and hidden among the trees, making sure his beloved couldn't see him. The feeling dissipated, as Persephone continued to walk toward the house. Instead, she thought of Ares' warning: *'There's no such thing as a monogamous god.'* She felt that sense of hopelessness again. Her dream of having a husband would never come true if Ares was right. *Are gods not monogamous? Then again, look at her father; he's far from faithful when it comes to marriage,* she thought. It also didn't help that Apollo and Ares do not stay with their partners for very long.

Hades watched Persephone walk into her house as the sun slowly set. Through her window, he could tell that she was getting ready for bed. At that moment he got an idea. It was so simple, yet brilliant. Hades knew how he could court Persephone without anyone noticing–not Zeus, not Apollo, not Ares, and certainly not Demeter! Hades smiled. He knew that this idea would work.

Despite having loved the morning and seeing flowers in bloom, Persephone also favored the night. For everything was quiet, and the only sound audible enough to hear was the crickets playing their music. Now she can have some quiet time to herself and let her mind wander. She kept stroking her favorite emerald rose necklace while someone's pale blue eyes continued to haunt her. Apollo may have his charms, and Ares may be full of strength and courage, but none of their qualities could ever match what she saw in Hades.

Thinking about Hades taunted her every thought. He was all she could think about. *What would it be like?* She wondered, *To be the King of the Underworld's lover?* She remembered the touch of his perfectly pale skin that had never seen the sun. To be touched by the ruler of the dead, whose voice is deep and as smooth as silk. At the initiation, she was so drawn to him. His presence was so familiar, even though she had never met him until that night. His distinct uniqueness from the other gods made him more attractive in Persephone's eyes. She appreciated how he was willing to listen to everything she had to say, and how he offered his input. *Then how come he didn't show any interest in being my potential suitor?* she asked herself. *Maybe he is not interested in me.* As her thoughts became more intrusive, Persephone grew depressed.

Persephone got into bed and blew out the candle by her nightstand, hoping sleep would calm the doubtful thoughts in her mind. She silently prayed to the cosmos, wishing that the right person would come along, filled with the desire she craved. As her eyes drifted away toward sleep, she heard a familiar voice calling her. *"Persephone,"* it whispered. Her eyes opened as she heard her name again, *"Persephone."* It was the same voice she heard in her dreams, except she was awake and in her room. She looked around, confused as her heartbeat pounded loudly. Again, "Persephone," and the voice became more evident.

"Who are you?" she gently called out.

"My darling flower, have you forgotten me already?"

Persephone's heart was pounding her chest once she recognized the voice. "Hades?"

The candle at her bedside table, along with the others in her room, lit up on their own. Suddenly Hades stood there in his black robes, without his armor. The candlelight gave off a romantic glow that highlighted Hades' handsome features. Persephone smiled at him as she got out of bed.

"Nice trick with the candles. I wish I knew how to do that," she acknowledged.

"Not a trick. It is magic, my flower. Fire is one of my elements, so it's easy to manipulate and manifest. Maybe someday you will have that power," Hades replied as he stared into his lover's face. "The firelight makes your face radiant. It suits you."

Persephone blushed at his compliment, "I was hoping you would come by."

He gently smiled although, like Persephone, his heart was racing. He remained calm, trying not to rush wanting to kiss her. After all these years of being in the Underworld, no woman had seeped into his blood so quickly. "Now why would the lovely Persephone want to see the Lord of Death? Especially when she has the company of two youthful gods who want her hand in marriage?"

"You were watching me this afternoon," Persephone said flabbergasted, it was more of a statement than a question. Hades nodded with a mischievous smile. "I knew there was someone else there, I felt your presence."

Hades smirked, "Yes, I was watching you. And seeing my nephews make fools of themselves, while your mother is in denial that you are a grown woman who wants to find love."

"Apollo did try to court me with his charms and Ares tried to show off his masculinity."

Hades chuckled, "Did it work?" he asked, already knowing the answer.

"I think you know the answer to that question, but no. In fact, it was almost embarrassing."

Hades walked into Persephone's space as his eyes bored into hers. "Why not? Everyone wishes to have Apollo as a partner and Ares . .well . . . I understand why you don't want Ares." Persephone laughed. "But still, they are youthful gods who have the power make any goddess tremble."

"Maybe I prefer older gods," Persephone said flirtatiously.

"Really?" Hades gave her a genuine smile.

"Especially the handsome, intelligent ones" She whispered, again flirtatiously.

Hades held her chin gently with one of his hands, so that their faces inched closer together. Persephone's heart sped up as she looked at Hades' beautiful face. Here among the sexuality, power, and love that shone on his face, also appeared his haunting loneliness. She smelled his masculine scent that was too good beyond words to describe. It aroused her senses in such a way, which she had never felt before until now. "Do you think I'm handsome? My darling Persephone?" Hades asked, his voice heavy with seduction. As an involuntary response, the sound of his husky voice caressed her ears and sent chills throughout her body.

"Ever since I first saw you at my initiation." She closed her eyes and felt Hades' hands caress her face, while his energy caressed her spirit. Then Hades pressed his forehead against hers.

"Are you going to kiss me?" Persephone asked with her eyes still closed, and suddenly she felt Hades' breath on her mouth.

"Do you want me to?" he sounded aroused, but was still in control of himself.

"Yes." She barely said the word before she succumbed to Hades' touch upon her face.

"Do you want me to court you, my love?"

Persephone smiled as excitement coursed through her. "More than anything."

Hades felt his heart soar. As much as he wanted to kiss and ravish her, he couldn't tonight with a clear conscience. "My beloved Persephone, I would gladly court you as a suitor to try and win your love. However, I will not kiss you tonight." Persephone looked at him, confused. "I refuse to let our first kiss unfold in a dream-like state," Hades confessed.

"A dream-like state?"

"Yes my love, you are asleep. You are dreaming."

"But—" she started to say.

"Don't worry, I 'll see you at sunset. Meet me at the edge of the woods, near the lake."

With that, Persephone instantly woke up and saw through the window that dawn was just breaking. She could see Apollo's sun shining over the new day. She looked around her room for any sign of Hades. She saw nothing. No candles were lit, not a trace of footsteps on the carpet, nothing. Tears came to her eyes then, and she felt as if it were nothing more than a dream, that her romantic rendezvous was only wishful thinking. Frustration and anger washed over Persephone. She wanted that dream to be nothing more than real. Seeing Hades, and having them both confess their feelings for one another. She hoped that this encounter was real. It felt and smelled real. *Shouldn't it be real?* she asked herself. Her heart started to hurt until she saw something by her bedside candle.

There stood a green crystal ring, along with a note. Persephone picked up the letter and began to read the beautiful handwriting:

My Dearest Persephone,

Here's a little something to mark the beginning of our courtship. I thought this would pair nicely with the rose necklace I made you, when you were a baby. Like I said in the dream, meet me at the edge of the woods, near the lake. Come sunset.

Your Beloved Suitor,

Hades

"It wasn't a dream," Persephone thought out loud, peering down at Hades' letter and ring with wide eyes. "It wasn't a dream!" she wiped her tears as excitement washed to her. She kissed the note and picked up the beautiful ring, which shone multiple colors in the sunlight . Inside the ring band, *'Eternal Love Awaits Us'* was engraved. She put the ring on and it slid on her finger perfectly. It looked perfect, as if it were meant to be there.

Then she remembered something Hades had written in his note. *He had made the necklace.* The necklace she always wore, her beloved had made it for her when she was only a baby. Another tear ran down her cheek, a sign of happiness. She had finally solved the mystery that had been plaguing her for so long. She was now entering a romantic relationship with the man whom she wanted to be with for eternity. Persephone believed that fate was real as she caressed her necklace; happiness and joy filled her heart. "I'll see you tonight," she said to an empty room, hoping that he could hear her.

CHAPTER 4

THE EYE OF FATE

Hades watched Persephone through his scrying mirror. She was admiring the ring that he had left for her. He smiled with pleasure, knowing that she loved both the ring and necklace that he had made for her. He was briefly concerned that she would believe it all to be a dream. That's why he left the gift behind to show that he was there. To prove that her dream was real.

He went about his usual business like he did every day. Only this time, it was intolerable. Anticipation swarmed through his body as the time moved at an unbearable pace, as if torturing him on purpose. Hades finally had something to look forward to, come sunset tonight. Excitement coursed through his body whenever Persephone came to mind. For once, he felt like the universe was smiling down upon him, and that his life would finally change for the better.

Then a familiar voice interrupted his thoughts. "So how was the initiation?" Hades turned his head to see Hecate, the Goddess of Witchcraft and Magic. They were old friends and she lived in the Underworld from time to time, but nothing ever happened between them. At most, she was Hades' best friend and counselor.

"I think you know very well how it went," Hades said emotionless.

"I do, but I want to hear what you have to say." Hades did not say anything or hint at his feelings while he stared at Hecate.

Hades shook his head, "You are too curious for your own good." Which, of course, reminded Hades of Persephone again. "Just like her," he muttered under his breath.

"You, my old friend, are so in love. You're trying so hard to hide it. There is no reason why you should hide your feelings, Hades."

"I'm not hiding anything!" Hades said defensively. "There is nothing to hide. I'm just waiting for the right time to let everyone else know."

"So, what is she like?"

"Words can't properly describe what Persephone is like. She is exquisite, loving, and very young."

"I agree, she has much to learn, Hades. More than you know, but you need to have patience with her."

"I don't need your advice Hecate!" Hades snapped, but he instantly regretted it.

Hecate snickered to herself, knowing better not to push Hades too far. After all, Hades was not used to such intense romance. She knew best to just leave him alone. "Then I wish you good fortune in pursuing your soul mate, Hades. Since you do not want my advice, I suggest you go see The Fates and sort out your thoughts."

After judging the last soul of the hour, Hades felt obliged to follow Hecate's advice. He needed to see his three old friends who helped him out when he felt troubled. The three women weaved together life, fate, and destiny. Sometimes, they even intertwined the fates of gods. No one could control them, not Hades, not even Zeus himself. The Fates usually hid themselves away from the gods, for they were always protected in the Underworld, but Hades was their occasional visitor.

The Fates had a special place in the Underworld. On earth, there was a certain tree whose roots grew long enough to reach down into Hades' realm. The Fates always did their work underneath this tree, known as the Tree of Life.

Hades made his way over to the tree's enchanted roots, where the three fates were working. The Fates were blind, but they all shared an eye which allowed them to see the future.

Atropos, the Fate capable of ending life, felt Hades' presence before he encroached upon their sacred space. "My lord Hades, we knew you'd come visit us today," she cackled a bit cryptically.

Hades smirked, "Is there anything that doesn't get past you?"

"No," the three of them said simultaneously. "You can't hide from us. You can't sneak around us. You can't lie to us. For we see all and we know all."

"Then you must know why I'm here," Hades said confidently.

"Of course. Persephone!" Clotho the spinner answered. "goddess of spring."

"She is my queen, is she not?" Hades asked, even though he already knew the answer. Yet, Hades still had his doubts.

"We have already told you that centuries ago," they all said at once. "She is your equal, your match, but you didn't believe us. Be cautious with her, Hades! She, too, brings death as well as life whenever she's with you."

Hades frowned at their response. "How so? She is the Goddess of Spring. How can she possibly summon death? Unless she is Queen of the Underworld, of course, then she'll bring death."

"You're wrong. A mortal catastrophe will happen long before Persephone becomes your queen.

"How will it come to pass?" Hades asked, frowning. Mortal death meant nothing to him because it was just part of the life cycle. Knowing Persephone, however, he didn't want her to feel the burden of ruining mortal life.

"We cannot say, The Fates replied.

Arching his eyebrow, Hades inquired, "Cannot? Or will not?"

"Will not!" they shouted.

"What if I don't pursue her and leave her be? Free will is involved too, is it not?"

"Free will does exist. However, it cannot conquer the strength of fate. Free will only influences the pace of destiny, making it speed up or slow down. No matter how many different paths you take, you will reach the same result. We have seen it happen. You can't resist the call of her, Hades. You were already in love with the girl since she was born. You cannot ignore or deny this connection, the bond that you two share. A bond which was already started."

Hades looked at The Fates, confused. "What do you mean? Are you talking about our meeting at her initiation?"

"Before that Hades!" all of them yelled in unison.

"Stop filling my head with riddles and just be straight with me!"

"We have said enough!"

Hades huffed, hoping to get one last piece of information. "Will these deaths be prevented in any way?"

"No."

"Well, whether it's Persephone or myself who is responsible for these deaths, I'll try my best to prevent them."

"It is out of your control Hades! No matter how you try to go around it!" The Fates shouted.

"I'm the King of the Underworld! I still have some control over death, even when I hear it from you ladies!"

"Do not be stubborn!" Atropos said with concern. "Hades, you know better than this. When it comes to death, every soul agrees upon being born that they will die eventually. This is something that can't be avoided. Now go meet your future bride, for she is waiting for you. We have already said far too much!"

Hades admitted defeat. Contrary to his beliefs, he respected The Fates and, therefore, felt obligated to follow their wishes. He let them get back to weaving fates, as he departed.

He thought about Persephone and what The Fates had said. Hades contemplated if he had actually started a bond with her earlier. *Was it before her initiation? How?* Hades frowned as he pondered over his memories, but nothing was amiss. He reminded himself to be patient and to not rush getting to know her. Just because he'd known her since she was born, doesn't mean that he could automatically have her when the opportunity presented itself.

With a racing heart, Persephone nervously paced around her room as the sun began to set. She kept looking in the mirror to check that the flowers in her hair had not moved. She wanted to look beautiful for Hades.

She was ready to sneak out of her window when her name was called . . . "Persephone!" Hearing her mother's voice had not only brought her to a screeching halt, but it also made her fear that she would be late for her rendezvous with Hades. She quickly hid her bag and the new ring, which her beloved had given Persephone during their dream encounter. Persephone then picked up a book, pretending to read just as her mother came into the room. Smiling, Demeter was happy to see her daughter reading. She was completely unaware of Persephone's real intentions. "Persephone, sorry to interrupt you darling, but

I need to go to Athens. I have been receiving a lot of prayers from there about needing some assistance with their crops. I hate to leave you alone..."

Persephone shook her head almost too enthusiastically. "Mother, don't worry! The people need you. It's understandable. I'll be fine on my own. Now go and grant the mortals their prayers". Persephone said with a genuine smile. She was finally going to have some freedom, without sneaking around so much to see Hades.

"Oh my dear, you don't think I'd leave you completely alone, do you?" Persephone kept smiling, but her heart plummeted. "I'll have some of the nymphs look after you while I'm away."

"Great." Persephone mustered a fake smile. Now she would have to deal with more obstacles before going on her date with Hades. "You don't need to do this, Mother. I'm a goddess after all, which makes me more powerful than a nymph. I'm pretty sure that leaving me alone for a couple hours will be fine."

"You may be a goddess, but you are not yet strong enough to be on your own."

"Honestly Mother, what could happen? Nothing here can harm me. We live on one of the most peaceful fields of this earth, and nothing bad has happened since we left Olympus."

"Persephone, I do not want to have this quarrel again. I have told you before that unexpected things can happen at any given moment. Who knows, a satyr might come and try to have his way with you." Persephone's face instantly showed disgust, as she tried to imagine having sex with a man who is half-goat. "Exactly," Demeter said in response to her daughter's perplexed expression.

Outside, Persephone heard her nymph friends shout her name in excitement. "Oh good, they are here," Demeter said as she opened the door to let them in. "Now my baby, I'll be back as soon as I can." Demeter then transported herself to Athens.

The nymphs started to laugh, but quickly tried to hide it. "Your mother still calls you 'baby'?" one of them asked.

Persephone felt like grinding her teeth and hiding her face. "Yes, she also calls me 'Kore' or 'child'." Suddenly out of frustration, she started to rant. "My friends, do I look like a child to you? Do I look incapable of taking care of myself?"

While shaking their heads in disagreement, the nymphs all said "no." Persephone wondered if her friends would give her the freedom she craved. "Listen, will you do me a service?" The nymphs gathered closer to hear what she wanted from them. "Will you allow me to go out on my own for an hour? Just one hour alone in the fields."

"Why? What are you up to?" one of them asked, smirking. It was unusual for Persephone to ask permission to venture off on her own.

"Nothing!" she said almost defensively. "It's just that Mother doesn't trust me to be by myself, so I figured you all could pardon me for just tonight.

"What if your mother comes back before you do?"

"All I am asking for is one hour. When it comes to helping mortals, I know it takes her a while to complete her tasks. I will be back before she even knows that I'm gone."

The nymphs looked at each other hesitantly. If anything were to happen to Persephone, they feared Demeter's wrath above all else. On the contrary, the nymphs also feared losing Persephone's friendship if they don't let her go. Cadence, Persephone's closest nymph friend, chose to speak for all of them.

"Okay, Persephone, we will give you the chance to be free for one hour. However, if your mother comes back before you do— ."

"I promise that no harm will come to any of you if that's the case. Thank you so much!" Persephone quickly gathered her bag before she went out the door.

One of the nymphs looked at Cadence as if she had grown a second head. "Have you lost all sense? Demeter will send us to Tartarus if she comes back and finds that her daughter is gone."

"Which is why I'm the smart one. I'll follow Persephone to see why she's so desperate to be free."

"Have you considered that maybe she just needs time to herself?" one of the nymphs asked.

Cadence responded, "I've known Persephone for years. She has snuck out for a couple minutes of 'alone time' before, even when we were around, and came sneaking back in. Now she is asking for a full hour. What she's asking for is more than just alone time. Something is transpiring and I want to see it." Cadence started walking in Persephone's direction.

"She will know you're spying on her!"

"No, she won't, unless I make it so." Cadence continued to follow her friend, hoping to find out Persephone's secret.

The hot day was finally cooling down, just as the sun was setting. Hades was already waiting in the shadows of the trees near the lake. Like Persephone, he had been anxious all day, but was now looking forward to this moment. *What if she doesn't come? What if she changed her mind?* Doubts bombarded Hades' mind. For centuries he had been used to isolation and completing his duties. Now, after meeting Persephone, he felt like he could no longer live a life of solitude. To him, Persephone was his sun and she signified the life that he craved.

Then he saw something move in the distance. Hades saw a figure wearing white. That's when he realized that his beloved was walking briskly toward him. For the first time today, Hades felt like he could breathe again and that his life was worth living.

With the sun almost set, darkness crept across the land, especially among the woods. Persephone practically couldn't see in front of her. Her heart was beating loudly, not in fear, but out of joy because she could feel Hades' presence.

With one wave of his hand, Hades lit a tiny fire on the ground and the flames roared like a campfire. It hardly illuminated their little spot in the woods, but it gave just enough light for Persephone and Hades to see only each other.

Right when Hades lit the campfire, Persephone ran into his arms and he held her tight. "I missed you," she proclaimed while looking up at him. Though it was hard to see in the darkness, the firelight highlighted Hades' handsome facial features.

"I missed you too, even though we just saw each other last night." He smiled at the memory of their previous encounter.

"Thank you for the ring and the note. For a minute or two, I thought it was just a dream. The idea of it not being real made me sad."

Hades nodded, "I understand. To dream of something you desire, and believing with every fiber of your being that it is real, when it's actually just another dream." Persephone smiled softly at Hades for understanding. "That is called faith, but even the most faithful person can have lingering doubts. That is partly why I gave you that ring."

"What is the other reason?"

"I wanted to spoil you with all of my riches. Where I come from, I have plenty of riches."

Persephone's curiosity about the Underworld grew, even though everyone seems to fear that realm. "What is it like? This world that keeps you from me?"

Shaking his head, Hades replied softly, "It is not my kingdom that keeps us apart. Rather, it is my godly duties that keep me there."

"I can't imagine a life of eternity in a place filled with sadness and death. Doesn't it drive you insane?"

Hades began to caress her hands. Persephone felt the exotic heat radiating from her palms as he touched her. "No my love, the Underworld isn't like that all the time—with the exception of Tartarus. My world has so many different dimensions that it would take dreamers several lifetimes to imagine. There is so much beauty that my world has to offer. Including its mysteries that only I know about. It is ten times bigger than Olympus and can fill any desire that you wish."

"You make your home sound like a dream." Persephone's eyes sparkled, while Hades continued to tell her about the Underworld's unknown characteristics.

"It is. One day you'll see this dream for yourself. Trust me, darling, if the Underworld was like how the mortals describe it, my spirit inside would have died centuries ago. People forget that I'm the oldest of the Olympians, so my kind of power is earned through age and experience." His hands traveled up to caress her face and lips. The heat from his touch ignited her entire body from the neck down, trickling over her spine and making her heart pound. It felt like a raging fire had finally awakened her sensual side.

"I have something for you," Hades smiled as he grabbed a bag from behind one of the trees.

"Another present? Hades I can't—" she stopped mid sentence, as he handed Persephone a smooth black velvet cloak with purple lining. Precious stones and crystals overlaid its purple edges. "It's beautiful!" Her eyes brightened as Hades wrapped the cloak around her shoulders.

"This should help camouflage you in the darkness when we meet again. Your white dress and robes have made you more visible."

"I truly love it! Thank you! I love every gift you've given me. This cloak looks like something a queen would wear."

"You are a queen, the queen of my heart," Hades said with a genuine smile. He had almost revealed that he already saw her as his queen, but Hades didn't want her to feel pressured or fear of his boldness. "So my beautiful flower, have you received any new powers or sensations since your initiation?"

Persephone frowned. "No, I feel like nothing has changed. I just had a glamorous ceremony in my honor as a goddess, and yet I don't feel like one."

"Does your mother help bring out your strengths?"

"Only to grow flowers and plants on her behalf."

Hades shook his head in disbelief. "Alright, my love." Persephone smiled at his term of endearment. "Grow a flower for me." She looked at him with curiosity and grew the flower as he requested. Using her powers, a beautiful red rose popped out of the ground. Hades smiled at her, "Thinking about love, are you?" he teased. Persephone giggled as he plucked the rose from the dirt.

With his love's rose in hand, Hades added another request. "Now, my darling, levitate the rose using your mind." Persephone cluelessly looked at Hades, not really sure of how to make a flower float in mid-air. "Just imagine it in the air. Remember, thought and emotion give magic reality. A reality structured by rules is an illusion."

Staring at the rose in concentration, Persephone believed that the more she stared, the more likely it would float. Of course, it still rested in Hades' palm. He almost chuckled. "Darling, relax and imagine it floating before you. Just staring at it won't make it float." Persephone tried focusing her mind's eye and relaxed. Just then, the rose steadily hovered in the air and Persephone could not believe what she had just accomplished.

Hades smiled at his love's determination and power. "Now my darling, while it's in mid-air, pluck each petal one by one." The task took much energy to execute, but Persephone didn't falter. After some time had passed, not only was she able to rip each petal from the flower, but they were also floating in mid-air.

Seeing that Persephone was exhausted from using her energy, Hades took over. "Okay my love, you did the work, so now I'll create something from your magic." He took the petals that were floating in the air and arranged them into two single-file lines. Hades found a thin vine on the ground and raised it up into the air with the petals. By sewing the vine and petals together, He had created a rose headband. Hades added a bit of his Underworld touch by turning the band metallic with his fire power. Once the entire headband transformed into a gold crown with petals, it floated back down into Hades' hands.

Persephone stared at the crown, amazed by what their combined powers had created. "It's beautiful."

"It's yours, my love," He said as he placed the customized crown upon her head.

Smiling at his loving words, Persephone's heart melted like butter against the sun. "You have given me so much, but I have nothing to give to you in return."

"A kiss from you. I have longed for your kiss."

Persephone blushed at his request. "You could have kissed me last night, but you chose not to." As Hades' face came close to hers, their breathing became heavy.

"I chose not to for good reason. I wanted our first kiss to happen for real, instead of happening in your dreams. This way, the sensation of your lips on mine can linger for a little longer." Hades drew in closer, as Persephone awaited the kiss of her dreams. At first his lips gently pressed against hers, but then became more forceful. His hands held her tight. She couldn't think anymore. Her mouth opened slightly as a sigh escaped from her lips, and she felt his tongue slide in. Persephone had never felt her heart beat so fast, nor had she ever felt this feverish before. Acting upon instinct, she grabbed a hold of his neck to pull him closer. With a strong hunger, Hades continued to kiss her and both of them moaned in delight. They both felt out of breath, but neither wanted to end this blissful moment. Hades reluctantly broke away, breathing hard, and rested his forehead on Persephone's. They stared at one other, as if trying to stay connected through their mind's eye.

Persephone then started to laugh "That was amazing!"

Hades smirked at her excitement. "I hope all of our kisses are like that." He lightly kissed her cheek and neck. Goosebumps appeared on her skin and made her shiver with pleasure.

"Darling, each kiss is unique and special. However, I do hope that each one becomes a little bit more. . . sensual than the last," Hades whispered in her ear. "You have to go now, otherwise your mother will come looking for you if she sees that you're gone."

Persephone frowned and began to pout. "I don't want to leave." Hades' heart leapt in response to her confession.

"You must, my love. But hopefully I will see you soon."

"How will you contact me?"

"Same as I did last night. I will come to you in your dreams." Persephone wanted to mention the recurring dream that she's had since she was a little girl, but there was no time for it. She knew to save that conversation for another time. "You and I must go our separate ways." She nodded, disappointed.

"Goodnight Hades."

Hades gave Persephone their last passionate kiss of the evening. "Goodnight, my love."

With her face glowing, Persephone rushed out of the woods and headed back to her mother's cottage. Her new goddess powers sensed that someone was watching her, making Persephone stop in her tracks. The snap of fallen tree branches signaled nearby footfalls. Persephone called out, "Who's there?". . . No response. "I know someone is there! I can hear your footsteps and feel your presence! Show yourself!"

The footsteps approached Persephone and grew much louder. Persephone stood her ground as Cadence showed herself, looking slightly bitter. "Well, it looks like I can't spy on you anymore. It never occurred to me that your powers would grow." Persephone frowned at her comment. "Do you know what also hadn't occurred to me?", Cadence asked, "How could the goddess of life and spring be in love with the god of the Underworld?"

Persephone stood her ground once more, "If you truly were spying on me, then you would know the answer to your question. Did you really see Hades? He is treating me with love and respect?"

"The King of the Underworld doesn't love," Cadence spat.

"Says who? The mortals? The very same people who fear him only because they are afraid of death itself?"

"Persephone! Hades' only purpose is to cause pain, death, and eternal misery! Why him? Some of the more lively and most handsome gods want your love. You are wasting your love on a God that rules over death."

"Everyone needs love, Cadence, regardless who they are or what they do. Out of all the gods I've met, Hades' love puts them to shame."

Cadence shook her head in disapproval. Wait until your mother and the others hear about this!" she started to walk away.

"I thought you were my friend!" Wide-eyed with fear, Persephone didn't know what to do. She didn't want someone's big mouth to abolish any chance she had with Hades. Feeling emotionally scattered, Persephone wanted the earth to grab hold of Cadence and keep her still. Instinctively, Persephone utilized her powers to wrap weeds and vines around Candace's feet. Thick green lines covered her body from the waist down.

"Persephone what did you do?!" Candace shouted as she tried to wiggle free unsuccessfully. "See, he has already made you different! The Persephone I know would never do this nor would she be capable of doing something like this! All of this was done under his discretion!"

Persephone solemnly walked over to Cadence to observe her handiwork. She gazed at the tangle of vines and weeds in awe, feeling the magnitude of her newly discovered strength. "Yes Cadence, this is me living up to my potential capabilities as a goddess. Hades taught me that and it is a wonderful gift to have. I will not let anyone destroy my chance with Hades. Not my mother, you, or anyone else. You will never tell my mother or anyone else about what you saw tonight. Swear by the River Styx that you'll never speak to a single soul about it."

Cadence couldn't believe what her friend was making her do. Swearing on the River Styx creates an unbreakable oath. If the oath is shattered in any way, the one responsible for breaking it will face death instantly. "Surely you're not thinking this through. Do you know how serious that oath is Persephone?"

"Yes, I do. That is why I'm forcing you to swear by it. So that no one is going to find out about Hades and I. I'm sorry, but you must do this."

"I will never swear."

"Swear it!" Persephone demanded. Cadence shook her head no. Then Cadence suddenly felt the vines move upwards. "You do understand that I can make the vines grow and tighten around your body even more, keeping you still, right?" Cadence shook her head no because she couldn't understand why her friend was doing this. "The way you feel right now, being constricted, is exactly how I feel living with my mother. Staying in one spot, suffocating and shrinking the woman that I am destined to become."

The vines crawled up to Cadence's mouth and wrapped around her head. If she didn't swear to Persephone soon, she would die from suffocation. Giving in to Persephone's demand, in an attempt to save her own life, Cadence agreed to swear on the oath.

Persephone allowed the top vines to drop down past Cadence's neck so that she could talk. "Swear it Cadence. Swear it and I'll let you go."

Tears came to Cadence's eyes, "I swear on the River Styx, not to tell a soul about your secret relationship with lord Hades."

Persephone's eyes began to water as sadness accompanied her smile. Feeling instant regret for what she had done to Cadence, Persephone valued her secret relationship with Hades more than the nymph's friendship. She used her new powers to kill the thick vines and let Cadence go free. Persephone rushed to help her friend remove the rest of the dying plants. "Don't!" Cadence shouted and began coughing. She tried to steady her breath.

Hurt, but still assertive, Persephone gently spoke. "I'm sorry my friend, but you gave me no choice. I still want to be your friend, Cadence, but you must understand that I'm learning my place alongside the Olympians. That includes being by Hades' side. Hopefully, as his future wife. I can't let anyone take that away from me, just because they don't like the fact that I'm not a little girl anymore." Cadence finally understood what Persephone meant. She was no longer the little girl that Demeter wanted the nymphs to look after. She was learning to be a woman, a goddess, and Cadence was just a nymph. For Persephone to be one of the great Olympians, she had to make hard decisions, even if that meant hurting the people she loved.

Persephone arrived home, luckily before her mother returned. She still felt guilty for what she had done to

Cadence. Tears rolled down her face as she thought about her actions—she had done something that she never thought she would do. In the end, though, she felt like it had to be done. She couldn't believe the power that had manifested while she was in distress. All because Hades had awakened something inside of her, something she didn't know she had.

At the thought of Hades, she perused the new gifts that he had given her. She opened her closet and took out a golden chest that Athena had given her when she was a baby. She never had any real use for it. Until now. Not only did the chest have an excellent lock to keep the treasures safe, but it also made its contents invisible, which was unusual. When the objects were removed from the chest, they became visible again.

Persephone gathered up all of Hades' gifts and put them in the chest, including the cloak he had given her. To conceal it from her mother, she hid it underneath the floorboards near her bed. Now satisfied that her presents were safe, Persephone's mother had just come home and was calling out to her daughter.

"Hello, darling! Did you have a nice night?"

Persephone's genuine smile reached her eyes, "Yes, Mother, I did. How were the people you helped?"

"They were great. Since they gave me many offerings as a thank you, all of them shall receive a plethora of blessings." Persephone nodded back absent-mindedly, but

Demeter noticed that something was different about her daughter. "Are you okay?"

Persephone shook herself out of her trance. " Yes, I'm fine, just tired. I'll be going to sleep now."

Demeter didn't pry this time, but she noticed the dreamy look in Persephone's eyes. Demeter supposed that maybe Apollo or Ares had shown up unannounced without her knowledge. If so, she ought to keep an even closer eye on Persephone.

A couple months have passed since Hades and Persephone first started to court. They are both happier than ever before. If the Underworld allowed, Hades would often visit Persephone when he could, but sometimes weeks would pass before he saw her again. It is now just after sunset and, like many of their visits prior, Persephone is waiting for Hades near the edge of the woods, by the lake. Along with giving his beloved endless romance and gifts, Hades has been teaching Persephone how to properly use her powers. This reminds her to ask Hades about something that's been on her mind for years.

"Hades, did we know each other before actually meeting in-person at my initiation?"

Hades frowned, confused by her question. "What do you mean?"

"Well since my initiation, we have mostly communicated to one another through my dreams. Have you done this before with me?"

"Before your initiation?" Hades almost looked surprised.

"Yes. Before we met, I would always dream of a faceless man. He would call my name out in the dark, as if he was trying to reach me. I did not fear this man at all. I actually felt attracted to him. I've been wondering if that was you"

Pausing to consider his answer, Hades reflected on his memories. He remembered what The Fates had said about creating a bond with her. "Yes, I think it was me, but I wasn't sure if you would remember. Sometimes we instantly forget our dreams the moment we wake up."

Persephone gasped at his answer . "You think? What were you trying to do with me? And how come our communication works better now than it did before?" she questioned out of curiosity, rather than anger or fear.

"I wasn't trying to do anything mischievous. I found out about you, so I wanted to see if we could meet prior to your initiation. As for better communication? Well, there are two reasons for that: One, you are an official goddess with many powers. Two, we now know each other, and you have seen me before, so I am ingrained within your memory."

"Is that why your face was fuzzed out before? Because I didn't recognize you in my dreams"

"I'm no dream expert, despite my ability to appear in them, but when you aren't meant to see a person in your dreams, they will be blurred out."

"Can everyone communicate with each other through dreams?" she asked in disbelief. "Both gods and mortals?"

"With gods, yes. We have instant capability. It's the safest way to communicate with mortals sometimes. Usually, it's the only way, because many mortals will go crazy after seeing a divine presence. If it's in a dream, then mortals can handle the encounter better in the moment. Or they can ignore it, thinking it's just a dream. They often ignore us if we tell them something they don't want to hear."

"What about mortals? Can they communicate with each other through dreams?"

"It is very rare, but possible. It only happens when there is a unique bond between two mortals, like with twins or soul mates. When it comes to powers and magic, mortals have plenty of potential to practice. Unfortunately, most of them don't believe in magic, so that part of the imagination stays dormant."

Persephone moved closer in Hades' arms. "So I did see you in my dreams, and you even called my name. Did you ever see me clearly?"

"No. You were just as blurred out. If I had seen you clearly, I would have recognized you the moment we had locked eyes at your initiation."

Persephone nodded. "I guess the timing wasn't right for either of us. But if you had seen me earlier, I would have only been a child, and I doubt that you were attracted to me then.

Hades nodded at her answer. "Attraction is possible."

"It doesn't matter though, does it?" She rested her head on his shoulder.

"My love, you must understand something about the universe—regardless of how abnormal something may seem, so long as you do what needs to be done and you meet the right people, it doesn't matter at all. Fate will find its way"

Hades looked at her with love in his eyes, hoping that his wisdom would help shape her into an extraordinary goddess. However, Persephone had other plans.

Then, she kissed Hades with such passion and confidence that he could sense her eagerness to please him. As they kissed, the straps of her dress fell gently around her elbows. Hades held his breath as he took in this lovely sight. She blushed, but her confidence returned once Hades began touching her like a priceless jewel. He kissed her more passionately as Persephone removed his cloak. Whether unplanned or not, she was seducing Hades.

"Darling, we need to stop before we go any further," Hades suggested. He kissed her bare shoulder once more before setting her straps back in place.

Persephone thought that she had done something wrong and frowned. Tears threatened to escape from behind her eyes. "Don't you want me anymore?"

Hades looked at her seriously. "Of course I want you, more than anything. You have no idea how difficult it was for me to stop."

"Then, why stop?" she asked as one tear slid down her cheek.

Hades kissed her tear away. "Because, my darling flower, you're not ready."

"I am ready! I love you Hades, and I'm ready!" she blurted out without even thinking.

Hades' heart beat fast like a drum. At last, he had finally heard someone say those three words.

Persephone quickly realized what she just said and repeated herself again, "I love you. You may be the god of death and the Underworld, but you make me feel alive."

"And I love you, my precious flower. I know you are ready for the act of lovemaking. But let me ask you this, if we do consummate our relationship: will you be able to face your mother and pretend like nothing happened between us?" Persephone wasn't even thinking about her mother anymore. "Darling, let me tell you something about mothers. They can sense when something is off, especially with their children."

Out of frustration, Persephone finally asked, "When will we officially be together? I want to see you without sneaking around. Will we go on this way forever?"

"No darling, it won't be like this forever." Hades gave Persephone a comforting hug to let her know that he was just as frustrated about their current situation as she was. "Not forever. I promise you."

CHAPTER 5

BROTHERLY TALK

Out of all the things Hades disliked, he had come to Olympus to do the one thing that he despised the most. . . ask for his brother's permission. He entered the throne room to see his brother being entertained by several nymphs. Nevertheless, Zeus was waiting for Hades. Asking Zeus' permission was the only way Hades could go about marrying Persephone, so he swallowed his pride and stepped forward. If Zeus accepted, this humiliating plea would be worth the trouble.

As Hades approached his brother, Zeus dismissed the nymphs and greeted Hades with a small smile. Sensing Hades' hesitation, Zeus decided to initiate their conversation. "You know brother, your visits are becoming more habitual around here. I consistently see you more now than I ever did in the past."

Hades tried to maintain eye contact while he continued the conversation, "I am here to make a request and I need you to listen."

Zeus raised his eyebrows, "Sounds serious."

"It is serious."

"Is it Ares again? Is he still stirring up trouble?"

"No."

"Is it Cronus?"

"No. He is still chained up in Tartarus," Hades assured his brother. The thought of Cronus escaping was every god's worst nightmare. Keeping Cronus secure was one of Hades' top priorities. Hades affirmed, "Before you ask, no, it has nothing to do with the Underworld." Seeing that everything was still in order, Zeus relaxed a bit. He suspected that Hades had come to address another important matter altogether, otherwise he would not have visited Olympus.

"Brother, I have put aside my pride . . . to not only ask you, but plead with you, about marrying a certain goddess."

Zeus looked at him, flabbergasted, "I never thought I would see the day—my brother finally found himself a wife!" he said with excitement. No one thought that the god of death would find anybody. "So, who's the lucky goddess? Who will become Queen of the Underworld?"

Zeus noticed that his brother was trying very hard to keep a blank face. Before Hades answered, Zeus could have sworn that he saw Hades' smile, and it had reached his eyes. That's when Zeus realized that this was more than just two gods getting married. Hades was in love. His eyes sparkled with love as he said her name, "Persephone."

Smiling broadly, Zeus knew exactly what this was. "This started on the night of her initiation, am I right?" Hades nodded silently. "However, this began long before the initiation," Zeus avowed.

Zeus' words caught Hades off guard. "What do you mean?"

"Brother, The Fates live with you in your world. Don't think I don't know that." Hades showed no guilt for keeping that a secret. "Therefore, you knew that Persephone was going to be your wife since the day she was born." Hades stayed silent and held his head high. "Do not try to lie to me, brother. You gave her that rose necklace when she was born. It was created to the best of your ability. That piece of jewelry was—is a masterpiece. You knew she was going to be your wife!" Hades' silence told Zeus that he was right. "The Fates told you about her, didn't they?" Hades silently nodded.

"Does she know?"

Hades shook his head, "There are many things Persephone doesn't know, thanks to her mother," he muttered under his breath.

"Yes. Demeter can be protective," Zeus tried to say courteously.

"More like being overprotective. How could Demeter not teach her daughter the basics of goddess? Or not allow her be the woman that she is? Persephone. . . has the grace, the beauty, and the power of a goddess. That power she has is waiting to be released. What Demeter is doing is a crime. I will do everything I can to make sure that Persephone fully uses her powers to their potential. I will love her for the woman that she is."

"You still didn't answer my question," Zeus pressured. Hades just stared at him with no emotion. "No, Persephone doesn't know. I don't want her to think that I'm marrying her just because fate and destiny make it so. I would still choose to be with her, even if we weren't destined for each other."

Zeus shook his head and smiled. Hades has definitely fallen hard for his daughter. "You have my consent." Hades couldn't believe his ears. "What?"

"You heard me, brother. I give you my consent to have Persephone, my daughter, as your wife. Besides, you know how wrong it would be to interfere with The Fates." For the first time, Hades let himself smile in front of Zeus. As much he hated to admit, since he probably owes Zeus a favor now, this visit was worth it. "Ironically, you will be the one to marry her, yet you were the one who arrived late to her initiation."

"I was not late."

Zeus frowned in confusion, "What are you talking about? You were an hour late."

"To be truthful, I was an hour early."

"I didn't see. . . Oh! You were wearing your invisibility helmet," Hades nodded, "Why?"

"I was still debating whether or not I should join the festivities," Hades said.

"You mean you were debating whether to meet Persephone or not."

"I was debating if I should meet the person who is supposedly destined for me. Imagine waiting for the one who's meant for you, and then finally meeting her in the flesh. I thought I was dreaming every time I saw her. "

"You were scared," Zeus declared.

"SCARED?!" Hades looked ready to ridicule, "I'M THE KING OF THE UNDERWORLD!" he shouted. "NOTHING SCARES ME!"

Zeus knew he had hit a nerve, but he still needed to say what was on his mind. "Yes my brother, nothing scares you except one thing–you were afraid of being rejected." Just then, Hades began to calm down as he listened to his youngest brother. "You were alone for most of your life. You took on responsibilities that weren't meant to be yours."

Hades then spoke somberly, "Zeus, you know that The Underworld was meant to be mine."

Zeus paused, as he tried alluding something without bringing up the painful past. "I meant the responsibilities before that." Hades nodded; he understood. "Despite what The Fates told you about Persephone being your destined wife and queen, everyone has free will. You both could be married, without her loving you." Hades closed his eyes as he tried not to take Zeus' words too personally. Unfortunately, Zeus was right about Hades' fearing Persephone's rejection, and it resonated with Hades' to no avail.

"Must have driven you mad, thinking like that."

"At times it did, hearing part of your conscience agree that it's going to happen, while the other part barates you for being foolish. After a long while, I had doubted that it was ever going to happen. It made me . . ." Hades couldn't finish his sentence.

"Depressed? Bitter? Angry?"

"All three, yes. Everyone here has someone to love. Seeing couples cherish that love or, in some cases, the lust that they have for each other. I see it even when I'm judging souls, and I go through their memories." Hades recalled many sorrowful nights when he felt like the whole world hated him, including the universal energies.

"Well, that explains your infamous moods. Or why you don't join our parties like you should." Wanting to defend himself, but deciding to stay in his brother's good graces instead, Hades held his tongue. "And now?" Zeus asked.

"Timing is everything, and we all have a predetermined fate, including us gods," Hades said and turned his back toward his brother. Trying to hide the smile on his face, Hades had to admit that he's never been happier. Feeling obligated to make a confession, Hades told Zeus, "Persephone can see me when I'm wearing the helmet."

Zeus looked at his brother in shock and went closer to him. "How's that possible? Even I cannot see you with that helmet on, nor any of the other gods!"

"Perhaps she has the gift of seeing the unseen. She was probably born with it."

"If that's true, if she really can see the dead on earth, then I'm not going to say a word of this to the other gods. Even if The Fates hadn't told you who your wife was going to be, Persephone is meant to be Queen of the Underworld. After all, seeing the unseen is one of your powers!"

"I don't know if she can see the dead," Hades shook his head. "I just know that she can see me while I wear one of my greatest weapons. I mean, she can see things that are meant to be hidden from mortal eyes. Sometimes immortal eyes."

"You know what that means, right?" Zeus quietly asked.

"That she is a powerful goddess," Hades said in awe.

"Everyone sees her as this child, but she isn't. She is much more than what any of us had expected.

129

"Now, does she know about your invisibility helmet?"

"No. Persephone knows I have a helmet, but she thinks it is just part of my armor."

"Eventually you'll have to tell Persephone about her gift."

"I will when the moment arrives."

"Don't procrastinate," Zeus said sternly.

"Brother, this is not something I can just drop on her lap and see what she does with it. I'll tell her when she's close to using her powers again."

"If you and Persephone are together, then we do have a problem, Hades."

Hades' eyes darkened. "I thought you gave me your consent."

"You do have my consent and my blessing. Demeter on the other hand . . . will not let go of Persephone so easily."

"I'm not going to ask that woman's permission. No matter what I say, you know she won't even consider me. She already intercepted Persephone from Apollo and Ares."

Zeus listened to Hades, while he thought of a way to convince Demeter. "How does Persephone feel about you? Are you even exchanging conversation with her?"

"We've been meeting secretly. Mostly through dreams, but Persephone will also sneak away from her mother to meet me in the woods. She loves spending time with me.

"Does she love you?"

"I believe she does. She said that she loves me. Every time we are together, we are at peace, completely content with each other's company. No matter how horrible or beautiful eternity may be, as long as we have each other, we can conquer anything.

"Well, I am confident that you love my daughter."

"I do brother, very much. I promise to take care of her in every way a husband should."

"Then you'll need to do something drastic." Hades just looked at Zeus, confused. "Knowing Demeter, she will not let her only daughter go. No matter how old she is, or the fact that Persephone wants to find love."

"So, what do you think I should do?" Hades asked and held his breath.

"Bring her to your realm, no conversations or questions asked. When you find her alone in the fields somewhere, just take her."

Hades' eyes grew wide at his brother's suggestion. "I don't know if Persephone is ready for the Underworld yet. She does find me appealing, but I don't know about her stance on the world of death . . . I don't know if she's ready for that yet."

"If she truly loves you, then she'll adjust. Besides, there is no way around this. Not with Demeter wanting to lock up her daughter for eternity in her home."

"I'll tell Persephone about our plan."

"Don't!" Zeus ordered.

"Why? She needs to know so that she can prepare!"

"It is better if she were uninformed. That way, she will not feel guilty about leaving her mother. Or realize that many people fear her soon-to-be home."

Hades closed his eyes in frustration, "She will hate me for doing this."

"Tell me, is she hesitant about the Underworld itself?"

"I think she's like many mortals, as well as immortals, when it comes to the Underworld. She thinks about the legends of Tartarus and the pain that resides there. However, I have mentioned to her about the other places inside of my realm that don't involve pain. I told her that these painless places are beautiful."

Zeus patted Hades' shoulder sympathetically, "All the more reason not to mention anything else to Persephone. Now, when you decide to bring her there is up to you."

Hades nodded. "Thank you brother for your consent."

"May you both find happiness." Zeus smiled genuinely as Hades began to walk back toward the Underworld. Before he left, Zeus had one last thing to say, "Poetic, isn't it?"

Hades looked back at him, "Pardon?"

"It's poetic how the Lord of Death is in love with the goddess of life and spring."

On a more serious note, Hades concluded, "All the more reason why we are perfect for each other. We balance each other out. I'm the dark and she's the light. Goodbye, brother."

As Hades teleported back to the Underworld, he contemplated when to bring Persephone to his realm. In mortal words, this would be considered kidnapping. Hades thought about this over and over again. Any possible tactic he came up with led back to facing Demeter, which meant he'd lose any chance of having Persephone. Taking Persephone was the only definite way he could have her, without causing chaos.

However, age and wisdom beckoned Hades. He knew Zeus was wrong for not wanting to tell Persephone about the plan. He had a gut feeling that it was best to let her know. On the other hand, if she did know . . . he had a feeling that Demeter would find out about it. Then she would use everything in her power to keep Persephone inside her house. Locked away in her house would be more like it. "My love, please forgive me for what I'm about to do," Hades whispered to himself. He closed his eyes, ashamed for knowing that this was not the right way to bring Persephone into the Underworld. Contemplating his options, Hades couldn't think of another way. Tomorrow night, he would take his future bride to her new home—a place where she has destined to belong since birth.

CHAPTER 6

THE INFAMOUS EVENT

Keep running, just keep running! Persephone
thought, as she ran toward their usual meeting place in the
woods. She couldn't believe it. In trying to keep her
daughter a virgin goddess, Demeter had gone a step too
far. Since Persephone could barely suppress her happiness,
Demeter found a few clues about some man meeting her
daughter in secret. Despite Persephone's wishes, Demeter
believed that no man was good enough for her daughter.
She was about to make Persephone take the virgin vows
and swear the oath on the River Styx. However, Demeter
wasn't the only thing that kept Persephone away from any
man. Still, Persephone had her own suspicions about why
her mother always kept a watchful eye on her. Fresh in her

memory, her suspicion kept repeating itself as she spoke out loud:

"Mother, you don't think I can do this. Don't you think I'm going to be a great goddess? You honestly don't think I can be one of the Olympians, do you?."

Demeter looked angrily at Persephone. "Why are you saying such things? I love you! You are my daughter! Of course you are going to be a great goddess!"

"Really? When, Mother? When will you teach me how to use my power? When will I have my throne on Olympus? My temple? When will mortals start praying to me?!" At this point, Persephone's voice kept getting higher and higher, as her anger matched her mother's.

"Persephone! You are the goddess of life and spring! Eventually people will start worshiping you, but right now they don't recognize that what you have is important. They'll always come to me first, asking for their prayers to be answered about certain matters on earth. "If they pray to you—"

"If? If they pray?" Persephone looked at her mother in disbelief and with sadness. Saying the word 'IF' confirmed that her mother didn't believe in her, or her power. Demeter had more faith in the mortals who barely believe in gods, compared to her own daughter and her achievements. Persephone felt sick to her stomach and wanted to cry. Her mother stubbornly hoped that her daughter would be a little girl forever.

At that moment, Persephone wanted to leave with Hades. There was nothing left for her here. While Hades wanted to open new worlds for Persephone and give her knowledge to grow, her mother kept everything shut. Hades believed in her and what she could achieve with her power. Her mother didn't. For this reason, Persephone could no longer stay with Demeter. If she did, Persephone was afraid that her spirit would die.

Demeter suddenly broke Persephone's self-pitying mindset by saying, "I've talked to Artemis. We're going to Olympus tomorrow so that I can make you take vows as a virgin goddess."

Persephone stared at her coldly. "I told father that I wanted marriage; that I wanted to be loved. Besides, I hardly doubt that Artemis would help you, since she is Apollo's twin sister, and Apollo has been trying to court me."

"She is willing to help me because she knows how her brother would act. She has always been involved with a woman's right to be a virgin and be independent."

"Mother, you can't force me to take virgin vows even if you try. The vow will be voided because I don't mean it.

"Which is why we are making you swear on the River Styx."

Persephone felt ice rush through her veins. She knew that there was no going back after making a vow on the

River Styx. You can still take this path, Kore. Trust me, darling, it is for the best."

Persephone couldn't believe her ears. Was her mother now forcing her to take the virgin way? She didn't know how to respond. She wanted to cry, she wanted to scream in anger. Instead, with nothing but a blank face, Persephone said in a stern whisper, "Stop calling me Kore!"

After that Persephone ran out of the house, not bothering to look back. Demeter called out to her. The nymphs, including Cadence, saw their friend dart past them. Persephone had never ran so fast before, and soon Demeter's calls fell upon deaf ears. For once, Demeter didn't follow her daughter. She understood that Persephone needed some time to think things over. Demeter knew that her daughter would return once Persephone had calmed down. Cadence, on the other hand, already suspected where Persephone was headed.

As Persephone kept running, the clouds began to cover the sun, signaling that a storm was about to begin. The wind was already picking up. Nearby, a farmer who was busy gathering his sheep saw the young goddess running through the fields. He stood there and watched out of interest.

As she approached their spot in the woods, Persephone's mind screamed out for Hades—'*HADES!*. . . *HADES!*' her conscience echoed.

Then the earth began to shake and Persephone feared that she was suddenly caught in the midst of an earthquake. The ground beneath her started to shift and split evenly apart. The farmer clung to the nearest tree, trying to uphold his posture, while all the sheep scurried about. Still, he kept a close eye on Persephone.

Instantaneously, a chariot with four horses and a hooded figure rushed out of the darkness below her. Terrified by the horses' appearance, Persephone screamed. Their eyes emitted a red glow and black flesh hung from their skeletal carcasses. Frozen in terror by such a ghastly sight, Persephone failed to notice that the darkly-hooded figure was Hades. He reached out to grab her and then placed Persephone in his chariot. Once she was completely inside the chariot, with the crack of his whip, Hades ordered the horses to head back down. Persephone shrieked as they dove into the ground and the earth closed above her.

Having caught only a distant glimpse of Persephone's disappearance, Cadence quickly ran from the scene to ensure that no one could identify her as a witness. Meanwhile, the farmer, who was still in shock, cautiously searched the area for any evidence whatsoever. Unfortunately, there wasn't any to suggest that what he had just seen was real. The earth looked normal, as if there hadn't been a huge crack in the ground only moments ago. Except for seeing Hades, the King of the Underworld, enter and kidnap the lovely Persephone, the farmer wasn't sure about what else he had seen. He swiftly knelt to the ground, whispering a rushed prayer: "Almighty Zeus! I just saw death with my own eyes! Please protect me from Hades' wrath! All my gods!!!" Tears streamed down his face. After watching such a terrifying sight unfold, all the rumors about Hades seem more accurate.

Down, down, and down deeper they went. As they neared the epicenter of the Underworld, Hades' chariot sped up rapidly. Persephone continued to scream all the way.

"Persephone!" Hades called out. Just then, she recognized his voice and Persephone realized that she was in Hades' chariot.

"Hades?!"

Persephone gripped Hades tightly as they rode further into the Underworld. It registered with Hades that his love was actually afraid of the bumpy ride—her legs weren't quite steady enough to handle the realm's downward pressure. Afraid that she might fall from the chariot, Hades gripped her tightly. Thinking that she would fall out as well, Persephone continued to scream. "Persephone! Please, my love, calm down! You are safe!," Hades reassured.

She kept screaming until his words had finally resonated. Once the chariot began to fly slightly upward, Persephone caught a glimpse of the Underworld in all of its darkness and splendor. The temperature dropped and suddenly a cold dampness hit her skin. Her wailing ceased once Hades slowed his dead horses to a halt, near the corner of his castle. Even though they had made a complete stop, Persephone's eyes remained shut while she tried to control her breathing.

Hades tried to calm her, "My flower, are you alright?"

Still unable to speak, Persephone shook her head 'no' as her eyes welled with tears. Both her body and mind were processing what had just happened. Hades tried urging her to move slowly toward his home. A couple of Hades' servants came about then, "My lord, is there anything we can get you?"

"Bring some food and wine that come from the earth. Only from the earth, is that clear?"

"Yes, my Lord."

"Also, prepare a room for her. You know which one."

"Yes, my lord," they said concurrently and quickly ran off to fulfill his orders.

Hades brought Persephone to the hearth of his palace and offered her a chair to sit in. "Please forgive me for asking, but how do you feel?"

Persephone looked at Hades like she wanted to kill him. "I feel like I don't exist. The pressure in the air when we went down. . ."

"I know. The ride was . . . intense. It's something that takes some adjustment."

Persephone realized something, now that she was somewhat calm and collected. "How did you fetch me so fast? Was I that loud and clear for you to appear like magic?"

Hades shut his eyes, feeling ashamed and guilty. He needed to explain why he was there. "Not exactly, though I did hear you. I was planning on taking you down here . . . ," Hades shut his eyes once more,. ". . . by force. So that we can be together without interference from your mother." Persephone looked at him, surprised. "I didn't want to have you like this, Persephone. It was the only solution I could find."

"Kidnapping me? That's your solution for how you could bring us together?" Persephone paced furiously. The adrenaline rush from both Hades' grasp, and their trek through the Underworld's barrier, continued to surge through her body. She was still in shock from the chariot's ride and couldn't stop shaking. "I can't believe you did that to me!" she screamed at Hades with tears forming in her eyes. "You were fortunate that I even called you!"

Hades sat on his throne and watched his beloved, filled with guilt. "I did what I had to do. I just didn't see any other option, my love. Every time I found a way for us to officially be together, I saw your mother trying to take you farther away. In all honesty, my love, could you have thought of a better solution? Besides, my plan came out surprisingly well!"

Anger aside, Persephone listened to Hades while contemplating a way for them to be together, without alerting her mother. The more she thought about it, the more she realized that Hades was right. Demeter was far too smart to not notice anything different about Persephone or her behavior. "Am I so obvious? For my mother to know what's going on if we had planned this better?"

"Like I've said before my love, mothers seem to know everything that's going on in their children's lives. Especially a mother like yours. I'm sorry that I had to take you away like this, but I don't regret it. Now we can start a new life together, here in my world, without your mother interfering. I promised that we would be together; now I have kept my word."

"Have you ever thought about having a real conversation with my mother? So that you can ask for my hand and explain how you will take care of me. . . including whatever else you need to say to her."

Hades gave Persephone a skeptical look, "Have you seen how your mother treats Ares and Apollo?" Persephone nodded, she knew exactly what he meant. "If your mother were more accepting of your desire to have romantic love in your life, I would have tried talking to her. Again, my love, I'm sorry. Do you forgive me for kidnapping you?"

"You technically didn't kidnap me, because I have always wanted to come here with you. You just took action without my permission or knowledge."

"Again, my love, I'm sorry, whether you think it's kidnapping or not." He kissed her forehead as he wrapped his arms around her. Persephone felt calm, since this was something that they both had been thinking about for quite a while. "Nevertheless, why were you calling me?"

"I mentally screamed for you," Persephone admitted, as she closed her eyes. "I wasn't expecting you to appear like that. Much less hear me."

Hades nodded. "Well, the way you went about it was almost like a prayer, so I heard you." Hades suddenly felt a horrible churn in his stomach. "This was the first time that you desperately needed to see me. What happened, my flower? Why did you cry for me?"

As Persephone explained her mother's intentions to Hades, he instantly felt deep anger toward his sister. How can Demeter force her child to take an everlasting vow for something that her daughter strongly opposes? Once Persephone finished her little tale, Hades felt like his timing was perfect, and that it had saved her from taking such a vow.

"I can see that you're happy now, being with me, so I wouldn't be surprised if it showed on your face by accident. It's probably what drove your mother to make this maddening decision." Persephone nodded because she assumed the same thing. "Well my love, you must be tired after enduring our little ordeal. I'll show you to your room, while my servants get you some food from the earth."

Persephone felt a sting of disappointment in knowing that she would have her own room. "Aren't I going to be in . . ." Fearing that she might be wrong, she hesitated to finish her thought.

Hades gave her a comforting smile. "My flower, I would love for you to sleep with me. But for now, while you settle into your new surroundings and become familiar with the Underworld, you'll have your own room. This way, you can have your own space. When you are fully ready, then you will come to my bed, innocent and willingly."

Persephone blushed for asking, but at least it wasn't true that he didn't want her. Persephone looked around Hades' throne room. It was dark, but warm light from both the fireplace and accompanying torches made it feel beautiful and relaxing. She noticed the dining table was filled with different kinds of food. The pomegranates in particular had caught her eye and were sitting in a bowl next to Hades' throne. The glowing reflection from the fire hearth intensified their red exterior, making them look appetizing. Tempted to eat the pomegranates, she went to the bowl and picked one up, "PERSEPHONE! DON'T EAT THAT!"

Caught by surprise, she dropped the fruit and it rolled onto the floor, in Hades' direction. He picked it up as he went to her. "It is all right my love, you didn't eat it. Without caution, anything you eat that comes from the Underworld, will force you to stay here for eternity. These beautiful pomegranates are homegrown. They are the only fruit grown here in the Underworld."

"I'm sorry," Persephone breathed out, "I did not know."

"Everything is all right. Nothing happened. Just don't eat this. I'll show you to your room and my servants will provide you with food from the earth." Persephone followed Hades, but glanced at the delicious fruit, which had nearly cursed her, for a final time that night.

As Hades opened the door to her bedroom, the servants rushed in all at once. They turned down her bed and set a tray of fresh food on her nightstand. Although gods and goddesses can't die from starvation, they still get hungry from time to time. As much as Persephone wanted to explore, even in her own room, she was too emotionally drained from the day's events.

"Tomorrow I'll show you my world. For now, I need you to rest," Hades said gently. He could tell that his love was ready to go to sleep. Persephone looked at her food. "I assure you my love, all the food I give you is from above. I wouldn't allow you to be trapped here."

Persephone smiled, as sleep began to take over. She grabbed a piece of fruit to eat as her eyes drifted off.

Hours went by and the sun had already set. Demeter was worried about her daughter. She should have been home by now. Demeter impatiently went to the fields, calling for her daughter. "KORE! KORE!," Demeter cried out, "PERSEPHONE!" Demeter looked around and saw not a soul in sight. She realized then that her precious daughter was nowhere nearby. Nor could Demeter feel her daughter's presence. Tears sprang to her eyes with worry— Persephone was missing.

CHAPTER 7

THE UNDERWORLD

Waking up proved to be difficult for Persephone. To no avail, she tried waking herself up from the comforts of her own bed. With one eye open, she saw how dark the room still was, even though burning embers from inside the fireplace illuminated her space. Lost in thought about what had happened yesterday, Persephone realized that she wasn't even at home anymore.

Becoming more awake now, Persephone opened her eyes and peered around her room. If a single word could describe her surroundings, it would be: luxurious. The space was large and dazzling. The bed sheets she had slept upon were made of pure silk and looked like red wine. Arching above her, the iron bed frame was entwined with jewels that cast off a rainbow reflection from the glowing firelight. She remembered pleading with Hades to visit the Underworld long ago, and now he had finally brought her to his kingdom. Persephone also thought about the fight she had had with her mother. Thinking that it was still nighttime, Persephone slowly drifted back to sleep when she heard a knock at the door.

"You may enter!," she called out, unsure of who was behind the door.

A woman in her mid-forties came in with a breakfast tray. "Oh good, my lady you are awake." She placed the tray on Persephone's lap. "My king wants to see you in an hour. So please eat up, and I'll help you get dressed."

Persephone observed the servant. She seemed alive, but Persephone had a gut feeling that she wasn't, at least not entirely. "I'm sorry, who are you and . . . what are you?"

"I apologize, my lady, I didn't introduce myself. My name is Zoe, and I'm a shade. I'm one of the handmaidens assigned to you by lord Hades himself."

Persephone blinked twice. "You are dead?"

"Well, my human body is, yes. As you can see, my soul is still alive and kicking." Zoe frowned at her own pun. "Well as alive as can possibly be."

Persephone got up from her bed and touched Zoe's shoulder. It was solid, like those of any living mortal. Persephone was dumbfounded. "You feel alive, yet I can see that you don't belong to the mortal world anymore."

"My lady, you do recall that you are in the Underworld, right?"

Suddenly, an image of Hades grabbing her and standing in his chariot flashed through her mind. Persephone felt a rush of uneasiness as she remembered plunging down toward the Underworld.

"Yes. When I first woke up, it took me a while to gather my whereabouts. Still, I thought spirits couldn't be seen or felt."

"Well yes, from my understanding, most mortals on earth can't see or feel us. When we are in the Underworld, which is technically another world altogether, our souls are more transparent. Think of it as a transformation. We spirits are living in a different form of ourselves. That is why you can see us."

"Like a butterfly?" Persephone guessed.

"That's a beautiful way to put it, and I would say yes."

Persephone nodded and glanced at her food. It looked appetizing, but she hesitated, "I can't eat this. If I do . . ."

"Don't worry, my lady, the king insisted that the food must come from earth. No food on that tray will trap you here." Now, Persephone knew about the most important rule for when visiting a different realm: eat the food that is grown there, and you'll stay in that realm forever.

"So every time I get hungry, Hades has to retrieve food from the earth?"

"His people stockpile food in major quantities, so that they don't have to make a trip for each individual meal. But yes, every meal you have is from the earth."

"He sure goes to great lengths just to keep me happy, doesn't he?"

"Pardon my boldness, my lady, but I've never seen him this happy before. Not since you came into his life. Now eat up, and get dressed because he wants to see you."

Through very quick bites, Persephone finished her breakfast at once. She noticed that a beautiful long-sleeved, deep emerald green silk dress was placed on the edge of her bed. Out of curiosity, Persephone went into her new closet and opened its doors to a plethora of beautifully luxurious dresses and jewelry. "This can't be all for me, is it?"

"Indeed it is. All for you," Zoe responded. She realized that while Persephone is a goddess in her own right, she wasn't accustomed to being treated like one.

Persephone touched the luxurious fabric of her new clothes. She felt the softness of silks and other different types of linens, which was very pleasing to her skin. "This amazing man is going to spoil me."

"Lord Hades wants to make sure that you only receive the best. He is the God of Riches as well—another positive quality that many mortals forget. Now let's get this lovely

dress on you. I'm sure my king doesn't want to wait a
moment longer.

As Zoe helped Persephone into her gown, and
tightened the corset strings, Persephone realized
something. "Zoe, how come you are not in any of the other
Underworld placements? Why are you a handmaiden?"

Zoe bowed down her head as she finished tying the
laces. "Lord Hades was gracious to me, since my soul was
destined for Tartarus. Luckily for me, Hades understood
why I did what I did with my life."

Persephone frowned. "What did you do?"

"I was a murderess."

Persephone didn't know what to think. She knew she
shouldn't judge Zoe based only on the crime itself,
especially when Persephone didn't know the whole story.
She felt like she shouldn't ask questions, since it wasn't any
of her business. However, because this murderess is now
her handmaiden, out of curiosity, she had to know.
Besides, why on earth would Hades grant Zoe less
punishment for her misdeeds, compared to other mortals
who have murdered?

"Why did you murder someone?" Persephone quietly
asked, almost shamefully.

"Don't be embarrassed by your questions, my lady.
You have every right to know. I was protecting myself from
a man who made unwanted advances. Not only was he
touching me inappropriately, but he. . ." Zoe couldn't finish

the sentence and she didn't need to, because Persephone understood precisely what she meant.

"You don't need to say anything more. I can only imagine what happened next. You killed the man out of self-defense. I wouldn't call that murder, Zoe."

"It would have been self-defense if I hadn't tortured him first. I castrated this man and let him bleed out, while I mutilated the rest of his body." Persephone eyes widened more at the gruesome details. "That is why Hades took pity on me. Honestly, I think he took pity on me because of what he endured from his father, even though that's a different story."

After listening to Zoe, it occurred to Persephone that she didn't know much about her family history. Of course, her mother never mentioned anything family related. She did her best to avoid the subject. Now, Persephone began to wonder more about her lover and his past, along with everyone else's.

"They're all tied, now go check yourself in the mirror." Persephone went to the full-length mirror and inspected herself. For once, she didn't look like the Persephone that her mother knew, nor did she look like a child. Instead, Persephone saw a woman staring back at her and she felt like royalty. She looked ravishing in her emerald green dress, which glided across the floor. Her loose curls adorned a flower headpiece. She looked like a harmonious vision of life and death. A smile came to

Persephone's lips—she finally felt like the woman she was destined to be all along.

"My lady, I think we should be off. Hades awaits you and I don't want him to get mad."

Persephone glanced once more at her reflection before turning toward the door to leave. Since arriving here in his world, she had yet to see her lover through her newfound womanly eyes.

The Underworld felt like a maze—a dark labyrinth that holds many secrets. Persephone was overwhelmed and slightly nervous. She feared getting lost in the darkness. She stayed close to Zoe, who was holding a candelabra to help light their way. Despite the lit fire torches in the hallways and tunnels, darkness still consumed most spaces.

Persephone hoped that she would eventually have this place memorized. "How do you know which path leads to where? How do you remember where everything is?"

"Instinct, I suppose."

Not liking Zoe's response, Persephone questioned her further, "What do you mean instinct? Don't you know this place at all? How do you know you're going in the right direction?

"My lady, only lord Hades knows every detail of the Underworld. He allows me to go only where I'm needed. Instinct tells me where to go and then I follow that feeling. So far it hasn't failed me, and I've been doing this for almost twenty years I believe."

"You're not sure?"

"Time doesn't matter to us anymore, especially here. Time only matters to Lord Hades when a mortal must meet their end."

As they continued to press on, Persephone observed her surroundings. At the tunnel's end, they reached a balcony and Persephone saw the Underworld in its entirety. It was beautiful and mysterious, just like Hades described. Several rivers formed paths alongside the castle walls, producing mazes in different areas. Large crystals that hung from the ceiling also outlined the pathways.

Persephone's head suddenly whipped around when she heard a terrifying sound in the distance. It sounded like mortals were screaming and a monster was muttering incoherently. But Persephone didn't see anything, which made the moment more horrifying. "What was that?," she asked, as chills raced down her spine.

"A place everyone fantasizes about when they think of lord Hades. That is Tartarus."

"Do you hear that noise frequently?"

"Actually, no. You usually don't hear anything between realms. My guess is that . . ."

"What?" Persephone asked worriedly. She noticed Zoe's look of concern.

"Nothing. I'm sure it's nothing. Come along, I need to take you to Charon. He'll bring you the rest of the way to lord Hades."

Zoe led Persephone to a dock just outside of the cave-like tunnels. Charon stood there, waiting. "So there's my master's newest interest."

"Watch your tongue! Lady Persephone is the Goddess of Spring, have some respect," Zoe snapped.

"I am respectful. I meant to say that the lovely Persephone is now the owner of his heart." Persephone smiled at the sentiment.

"Uh-huh, like I'm going to believe that. My lady, this is Charon, lord Hades' ferryman. He'll take you wherever you need or want to go."

"Aren't I supposed to bring her to Hades?"

"You are! I'm just explaining that you will be there when she needs you, right?"

"Of course, I am a humble servant of Hades!" Charon said dramatically and bowed. Persephone laughed at this. "See! Someone understands my humor. Welcome aboard milady." As Persephone stepped inside Charon's ferry, Zoe kept an eye on her to make sure that Charon doesn't do anything stupid. Charon began to talk like the grim reaper again, "I welcome you to the city of woe. Abandon all hope, ye who enter here!" Persephone raised her eyebrows skeptically, but didn't bother to say anything.

"CHARON!" Zoe yelled.

"WHAT? Oh come on, this phrase will catch on! I promise you that!"

"We don't want it to catch on! If it does, then every mortal will be terrified of passing through the Underworld's entrance!" Zoe huffed.

"They are afraid of death to begin with! Doesn't change anything." As Charon started to row away from the dock, Persephone heard Zoe mumbling about Hades having mercy on her soul for putting up with Charon's antics.

Charon just ignored Zoe's ramblings and rowed on. "So where are we going?," Persephone asked as she looked out at the river.

"We are heading to Hades' judgment panel."

Persephone continued to take in the mysterious realm that lay before her, while Charon rowed. The Underworld was genuinely breathtaking. *How could mortals fear this place?* Persephone thought. Then she looked down at the river, which was very dark and misty. "Is this the River Styx?" she asked with a confused frown on her face.

"Indeed it is, my lady," Charon answered. He watched her carefully, hoping that she wouldn't put her hand in the river. Persephone began to see something move in the water and reached out to touch it. "LADY PERSEPHONE!," Charon yelled. Persephone froze and turned to look at the boatman. "DON'T TOUCH THE WATER!"

"Why?" she asked, fearfully curious. Persephone looked down again and saw thousands of souls floating in the water. The river itself was very dark, almost black. Persephone couldn't tell if the river's darkness was from the Underworld itself or from something else entirely.

"It is not what you think," Charon said aloud, shaking Persephone out of her surprised state. "They are not real shades."

"What do you mean they are not real?"

"That's the negativity of humankind."

"What?" Persephone was beyond confused.

"Well, you see my lady, before entering this realm every soul has to be cleansed. Water is a cleanser of the earth. It helps purify and shed the human ego, washing away the negativity accumulated from their human experiences. That is why the River Styx is seen as the river of hatred, and River Acheron is the river of pain. Hatred and pain have been trapped in these waters ever since the first souls were cleansed. Once someone has bathed in these waters, they can't touch it again. If someone does touch the water, they will feel extreme excruciating pain from every single soul that has ever passed through here."

Persephone kept her distance from the water at once. "Is that why the water is black?"

"Yes, my lady. That's why I carry the souls across the water."

"But, if these waters are meant to cleanse, why are some souls still going to Tartarus?"

"The waters can only cleanse so much. It rids the souls of their human ego, but not their committed crimes. You'd be surprised at how much burden mortals can carry, with just their mind alone."

She nodded. "Is it true that souls must give you a coin to board your boat?"

"Yes, it's true."

"What do you use the money for? Seems like you don't need it."

"Every once in a while, I use it for sport. The money goes toward the games I play with Hermes. However, Hades had a reason for setting up the coin system."

"Which is?"

"To pass on into the next world, one must give up a connection to the material things that they've collected during their human existence. Materialism has no necessary place here. Once I have their danakes, the soul or shade—whichever name you prefer—can mentally prepare to shed their old life and leave the burdens of their past behind."

"That makes sense. So, if only some of the coins are for your own use, what happens to the rest of them?"

"You are aware that lord Hades is the god of wealth as well as the Underworld, right?"

"Yes. Hades has proved that by spoiling me with an abundance of gifts."

"Well, lord Hades spreads the wealth around to those who need or deserve it. Have you ever seen a mortal pick up a coin from off the ground, out of nowhere?" Persephone nodded, a bit surprised. It wasn't too long ago since she had picked up a coin herself. "Or have you ever seen a monetary charity mysteriously save the day?" Persephone nodded yes again. "That, milady, is how Hades gives a bit of charity."

"I actually thought it was my father who did those things."

"Some of it probably was, but most of it came from the God of Riches himself."

Now Persephone knew about one of the Underworld's many secrets. Some financial miracles are rooted here.

"I honestly thought that only death remains here," Persephone whispered, mostly to herself, but Charon heard it too.

"My dear goddess, the Underworld is so much more. Unfortunately, I only know the way of the rivers and its common entrances. Such information allows me to bring the souls to their destination. What I know about the Underworld is only a small portion. Regardless, I know that the Underworld holds secrets and magic that no one can fathom. Of course, it's Hades' job to protect them."

"Does Hades ever stop working? Even just for one day?"

Charon shook his head no, "He has his moments, but to take a break and not work at all? I cannot remember a time when he did."

Persephone frowned. "So while everyone at Olympus is having fun, Hades is always working? Then it's no wonder why he barely comes to Olympus. Did you know mortals believe that Hades is a prisoner here? That my father banished him from Olympus?"

Charon chuckled "Mortals can be so amusing. Especially when their stories materialize from their fear and talk. Mortal stories are often so far from the truth, that it's ridiculous. However, it is true that Hades is a prisoner to his work. Hermes gets annoyed when I try to scare the shades as they board my boat. In my eyes, they deserve to be a little scared. Since most of them believe all that rubbish about Hades, or any of the gods for that matter."

"How could you do that to the mortals? They have their preconceptions about the gods because they are scared!"

"Pardon my bluntness, my lady, but people fear the gods because they assume that we think the same way they do. They fail to realize that we are not human, that the gods are not like them. The gods see the whole picture, when all mortals see is a puzzle piece."

Persephone remained silent for the rest of the boat ride, mulling over what Charon had said.

Having just finished judging souls for the day, Hades sat once again on his throne. He waited impatiently for his beloved to join him. He could tell that Charon was rowing Persephone to him, as he saw her in the distance and Cerberus barked loudly at her presence. Just as he was getting up to greet Persephone, Zoe manifested herself in front of the panel. She wanted to meet Hades in private.

Seeing Zoe appear, Hades frowned, but quickly shrugged it off once he saw her concerned expression. "What is it, Zoe? You hardly come to me for anything, so this must be important."

"Yes, sir." Zoe inched closer to him, aware that she must speak quickly, since Persephone was close by. "My lord, it's Tartarus." Her words grabbed Hades' attention. "My lord, I think the walls of the realm are weakening."

Hades looked slightly concerned, "Is there any evidence to suggest that it is?"

"When I was picking up Lady Persephone, we both heard agonizing screams coming from Tartarus' direction."

"Where were you two?"

"Outside the west wing of your castle, sir."

The screams of Tartarus reaching that far, and for people to actually hear it, was very unusual. Hades was concerned, but he did his best not to show it. "Thank you, Zoe, I will look into it." Zoe bowed before transporting herself back to the handmaiden's quarters. Hades closed his eyes, thinking that it couldn't be that serious. After all, Tartarus has never faltered before. The reality that both his most dependable servant and his beloved had heard the distant screams. That's what haunted him most about the situation. This has to be inspected immediately.

As Charon docked his boat by the judgement panel, Hades focused his attention back toward Persephone. When she spotted her beloved sitting on his throne, Persephone smiled and practically ran to him. Hades smiled, "You are the only one who has ever willingly set foot near the panel to see me, smiling."

"Are you going to judge me, lord Hades?" Hades looked seductively at Persephone, aware that she was wearing one of the luxurious dresses he had given her. By the way she was dressed, Persephone almost looked like the Queen of the Underworld.

"Darling, your judgment would've only lasted half a second because your beauty and kindness belong in the Elysian Fields. More so in the Isles of the Blessed, but I selfishly want to lock you away in my castle for all eternity."

"What for?" Persephone flirted, "So that I can be a slave for your pleasure?" She grew closer to him and touched his chest.

Hades smirked with a hint of lust in his eyes. "Don't tempt me."

Persephone decided to be bold, "What if I wanted to tempt you?" she whispered in his ear. Her hot breath sent chills down his spine.

"Now, my darling, you are playing with fire. Should I send you to Tartarus for being a naughty girl?"

"If you plan on sending me to the fire, then let it be the fire of your heart, my love." Hades shuddered in response to Persephone's alluring attempt. He tried not letting it affect him, besides he had a tour to give.

"Come, let me show you my kingdom." Hades held Persephone's hand as they walked the realm's pathways. "Did Charon advise you about the rivers?"

"Yes, he did. I am grateful for it, because I almost touched the waters."

Hades looked at her, horrified. "Darling, don't you ever—"

"Touch the water from the rivers, I know. Charon warned me of the consequences." Hades sighed with relief. "I'm amazed by how the rivers cleanse souls, while containing negative energies that are used to inflict pain."

"There's nothing to cleanse the rivers from the negative energies they absorb." Persephone was still curious about it, but she dropped the topic and continued walking with Hades.

As Hades led the way through the Underworld, giving his love a grand tour, Persephone stayed by his side. Most areas were pitch black, and without the fiery torches, they wouldn't have seen anything. Persephone didn't know what to make of it all. One minute the Underworld was enchanting, and the next minute it felt horrifying. The only thing that comforted Persephone was being next to Hades. Despite having mixed emotions, curiosity always got the better part of herself.

"Stay close to me, my love. The Underworld is a sight to see, but you need to be cautious." Hades remained calm, but could see fear in Persephone's eyes. So far, he's only shown her the judgment panel, but they've also been walking through dark cave tunnels. Of course, when surrounded by complete darkness, one's senses usually kick in and sharpen everything else. Persephone heard water drops fall from cave ceilings as they hit the ground. Then, she heard frequent screams every couple minutes. The screaming grew louder as Persephone and Hades walked on. She gasped at the growing sight of skulls and bones that lined the dimly-lit walls.

"Are you all right?" Hades asked, hoping that this tour had not changed her perception of him.

"I'm fine. Your world is very confusing to me that's all—it's mixed with good and evil things. I just don't know how to feel about it."

Hades nodded. "How do you feel now?"

"I feel a little terrified. Your castle is so dark and with the water dripping, it's like I'm walking toward my doom."

Hades nodded. "Don't let everything get to you. The shades are meant to venture down this path, that's why it's so scary."

"Well, it doesn't help that your wall decor is full of skull and bone sculptures."

Hades snickered at Persephone, "My darling. . ." She looked at him, already knowing that she wasn't going to like what he had to say. "What makes you think these bones are just artistic expressions?"

Persephone held back her surprised scream, as she inspected the piles of corpses and skulls. "Why are you showing me this?"

"I'm showing you everything I can think of. Not only to better your understanding of the Underworld, but also to show you the places I don't want you visiting."

"Why are you showing me this first?"

"I should explain what I'm doing. I'm showing you the darkest and most terrifying places first, because these are the places everyone thinks of when they hear my name.

When it comes to the Underworld, they expect to see these kinds of things."

"Well, they aren't wrong, are they?"

All of a sudden, she heard more torturous screams and Persephone screamed herself. She ducked down to cover her ears. Listening to people suffer was very overwhelming. Hades rushed over to her instantly. "Persephone!" Hades tried to comfort her, as tears rolled down her cheeks. She empathized with the shades, feeling their pain.

Persephone sobbed until the noises eventually began to fade. "What was that?" she asked. Hades used his thumbs to dry her tears.

"One of many reasons why we needed to come here." Hades took a deep, regretful breath. "We are going to Tartarus."

Persephone shook at the thought of going to such a terrifying place that all mortals feared. At the same time, she was curious to see what Tartarus looked like. "Why are we going there?"

"You are not going in, but I am. Before you came to me this morning, Zoe told me that you both heard the screams of Tartarus. Normally, those screams don't reach the west wing, so I need to go in and check for myself. It will only take a few minutes."

"I'll come with you! I want to see what it's like."

Instant horror swept across Hades' face, "This place is not for you! Please, darling stay away from this area."

Persephone looked at him with worry, but Hades smiled at her concern. "No need to worry my dear, I'm the King of the Underworld, remember? Nothing here can harm me because I am the master of these realms. I've been doing this for centuries." However, Persephone was still not convinced. Hades gave her the candelabra as they breached the door to Tartarus—it was more than horrifying to stand so close to this realm of everlasting torment. "Stay here, and I'll be back within minutes, I promise."

Persephone stood back while Hades opened the entrance and quickly went in, shutting the door behind him. As Persephone waited, she couldn't help but wander and look at the tunnels, which showed nothing but darkness. Again, sounds of dripping water sent a shiver down her spine. Every couple minutes, she still heard screams coming from Tartarus, they were loud and clear. It made her eyes well up with tears.

More time passed as she waited for Hades' return. Persephone reminded herself that Hades had done this for centuries alone. Therefore, he's an expert of the Underworld and knows how to take care of things. Suddenly, three women who looked ready for battle appeared, and passed by Persephone to enter Tartarus. "Excuse us, my lady, we need to enter. So stand back," they said.

Persephone stepped aside, surprised, and let the determined women go inside. She was confused about who these women were. Like Hades, they quickly went in and shut the door without hesitation. "Who on earth would go into that place willingly?"

After several moments passed, Persephone realized that the screams had practically stopped. It was quiet, too quiet. Then, the door opened and Hades came out. Persephone felt relief wash over her. She rushed up to Hades and hugged him. Giving her a smug look, Hades said, "I told you darling, I've been doing this for centuries."

"So what was the problem? The screams seemed to have stopped."

"Trust me, darling, they are still screaming. You just can't hear them anymore." Persephone doubtfully raised her eyebrows. "Well, I'm glad you can't hear them. That means the walls are now restored. They were weakening beforehand," Hades said while deep in thought.

Persephone silently wondered how one of the most dangerous places here could possibly have been broken. "What started it? Has it happened before?"

Hades' face was blank. "I don't know. In the time that I have ruled here, Tartarus' walls have never faltered until now. I will keep an eye on it." Something else plagued Persephone's mind about the situation, but she firmly believed that Hades knew what he was doing, so she pushed the thought aside.

"While you were inside, there were three women that entered Tartarus willingly. Who were they?"

Hades smiled. "Those my love, weren't women. They were dressed as women so as not to scare you. In actuality, they are furies. They look after and punish the shades in Tartarus. Trust me, without those disguises, you'd have been terrified. They look like monsters with large, bat-like wings. Very ferocious fighters that can tear mortal bodies apart with ease. They are the soldiers of the Underworld."

"Do they listen to you?"

"Of course. Like I said, I am the master of this realm. So, my love, now that this little dilemma is taken care of, let's start the tour again." They continued to walk through a maze of dark tunnels.

Coming from the direction of Tartarus, she heard a voice whisper, *"Persephone."* She stopped instantly and looked back at the door.

Hades quickly turned around when he noticed that Persephone wasn't behind him. He saw his love staring at the door of Tartarus. "Persephone?"

"Did you hear that?"

"Hear what?" Hades listened for a sound, but only heard water drops hitting the floor.

"I thought I heard . . . never mind. My mind must be imagining things." Hades accepted her answer because it's possible to hear things that aren't actually there, or to hear things from a distance. "Are you the only person who knows where everything is?"

"Yes, actually. Even those closest to me know only most of the realm, but not all of it like I do."

Overwhelmed by the vast size of Hades' place, Persephone tried to count how many pathways she would need to memorize. "How do you know where everything is?"

"When I inherited this realm, all of the secrets, information, and its energies just came to my head, as if it were always there. This world and I are tied together."

"So you were not taught?" Soon, they entered a beautiful room full of crystals and dozens of mirrors. Persephone looked around, amazed. She never saw a place so beautiful and elegant.

"No. Everything just came to me. It came on like a sudden headache, as a consequence of obtaining so much information." He smiled as Persephone looked around the room with admiration.

"This is so beautiful," Persephone whispered as she touched one of the crystals, feeling its energetic power. "What's with all the mirrors?"

"They look like mirrors, but they are not. They are doors to other realms and dimensions. The crystals keep the excess energy at bay."

"You mean these lead to other places with other gods?" Persephone thought of the other gods who had attended her initiation.

"That is one example," Hades nodded, "but these also lead to places on different planets and at different times. Each mirrored door goes to a different place or a different time."

Persephone looked in wonder, "You can go anywhere! Have you ever used them?"

"Yes, to see other gods and to see future consequences that are based on human choices."

"What about your choices?" Persephone alluded to their relationship.

"I choose not to look. Sometimes, my love, it's best not to know everything. That can easily be a mistake in itself, and then we forget to live in the moment and instead watch every move we make. Rather, it's good to trust the universal energy which makes everything turn out the way it is supposed to. Besides, if I want to know, I'll talk to The Fates about it. Then I'll consider their wise advice."

"The Fates are here, too?"

"Yes, including the roots from the Tree of Life and many other things that reside here in the Underworld. My love, my realm is more than just a place for dead mortals. It serves as a connection to everything between the unseen, the earth, and multiple dimensions.

They walked through more cave-like tunnels. "Can you teleport from one place to the next?"

"Yes, but I won't do that now because I know you aren't capable. However, walking around the Underworld can give you a whole new perspective."

They walked through the Asphodel Meadows, a place designated for ordinary souls. During their human lifespan, these shades didn't commit any significant crimes or accomplish anything extraordinary. Here, the souls live a numbing existence. There's no joy or sorrow for these shades. The Asphodel Meadows is an unemotional place.

Hades knew that Persephone was exhausted from walking around the Underworld. Though she was familiarizing herself with the place quite well, there was still much more to see. Hades anticipated Persephone's eagerness of making day trips to certain places in the Underworld. Still, Hades wanted to show Persephone one last place before ending the day's tour. This special place is located in a secret area that hardly anyone knows about, where some souls receive extra care.

"Alright my love, this will be our last stop for today."

Persephone yawned, "I suppose there is still more to see?"

"There is. In due time you will see everything, but, for now, at least I showed you some of the highlights."

Persephone looked around the area, which looked unusual. Again, there were crystals everywhere. As shades slept in beds, Hades' servants tended to them. "So, what's this area?"

Before answering Persephone, Hades went to check on one of the shades—a girl who was in her late thirties. "This is the healing room."

"The healing room? The shades are dead mortals, so what would they need healing from?" Persephone had trouble wrapping her head around the concept.

"Some souls become sick after experiencing ghastly things on earth. Sometimes, they still carry that burden through death. Even after being cleansed from the river, their pain doesn't vanish. Human viciousness can compel mortals to deal with grudges, unrequited love, depression, and suicide. In this room, the souls need to heal before I can send them to either Asphodel Meadows or The Elysian Fields."

"Why not give them Tartarus as an option?"

"My love, they've already suffered from so much pain. To me, that is enough. In cases like these, sometimes souls just wish to be nonexistent."

"Is it possible for a soul to be nonexistent?" Persephone inquired, feeling pity and compassion for these sleeping souls.

"No. Souls are composed of energy, and energy can't be created or destroyed."

Just then, something clicked in Persephone's brain. "Is that why there are so many crystals around here? Not solely because the Underworld is a cave, but to manage excess energy?"

"Crystals provide different energies that help the Underworld and its residential shades. Crystals come into play especially when a shade leaves Tartarus to come here."

Confusion fell across Persephone's face. "Wait a minute, souls who go to Tartarus don't stay there forever?"

"No. The souls might stay for a long time, but they don't stay in Tartarus forever."

"You know mortals won't be pleased if they discover that, in the afterlife, corrupted souls are only temporarily punished. Especially if a mortal was a murderer."

"Darling, let me ask you something. Do you view mortals like children?"

"Sometimes."

Hades nodded. "Humans usually don't think beyond the way we do. They are not as evolved, so they typically give into their mortal instincts. If you had a child, and your child did something bad, would you punish them for eternity?"

Persephone scoffed at such a ridiculous idea, "No, not forever. Just until he or she learns their lesson and asks for forgiveness."

"Exactly. For shades to leave Tartarus, they need to understand what they've done. Then shades need to ask for forgiveness, not only from me, but also from themselves."
Persephone understood the system that Hades had created.

THE SECRET LOVE OF HADES AND PERSEPHONE

"Let me tell you something, my love, the hardest part about leaving Tartarus is not realizing what you've done and then dealing with the consequences . . . it is forgiving yourself." Persephone absorbed Hades' words, amazed.

"Now, my love, let's go home. You have learned so much in one day, and I made you walk for miles on end." Persephone looked around the healing room before leaving, sending her magic to the mortals. She hoped that it would help their internal light shine outward.

Hades teleported them back to his castle. "Goodnight my love," Persephone said as she kissed Hades' lips. There was a gentle love to her touch, only because of how tired she felt. It also didn't help that she gave some of her magic to heal the souls. She went to her room and immediately crashed on the bed. Despite how tired she was, Persephone couldn't stop thinking about all that she learned today. As she drifted off to sleep, Persephone wondered what had made the walls of Tartarus collapse for the first time ever.

Hades should be concerned about Tartarus. Inside, a being of some kind knew that Hades was distracted by his newfound love. Gradually, this being had sucked the energy out of Tartarus, and weakened its walls. As part of its own agenda, this being was adamant about accumulating energy from Tartarus.

CHAPTER 8

CRONUS

"Persephone." Startled out of a deep sleep, Persephone heard someone call her name. As her quick breathing eased, she glanced around the bedroom. She remembered where she was—a guest room in Hades' Underworld castle. No being or shade appeared to be around, Persephone was alone. Perhaps she was still dreaming? Maybe Hades had called Persephone's name in her dreams, like he had done before. Or suppose she heard a sound coming from another place in the Underworld? She waited a few minutes, listening for her name to be called again.

Nothing. Just absolute quiet. Persephone lay her head on the pillow, wanting more sleep. Then she heard the voice again, a distant whisper, *"Persephone."* So she got out of bed and put on her robe. Grabbing a nearby torch, Persephone discreetly unlocked her door and peered outside.

Silence greeted her in the dark hallway. Except for her own glowing torch, the ones that lined the walls were snuffed out. Looking down the hall, in either direction, she saw nothing. When Hades is asleep, the Underworld also rests. Looking out at the infinite darkness, she heard someone whisper again, *"Persephone."* Persephone's heart beat rapidly, as the voice came from her right.

With all the courage she could muster, Persephone walked down the hallway to her right, following the ghostly whisper. It called out her name every few minutes. With each frightening step she took, her heart pounded harder. Persephone soon realized that this pathway led to Tartarus. The whispering grew louder as she crept closer to the door.

At the end of the hallway stood the door that Hades had refused to let Persephone enter. It was the entrance into Tartarus. She remembered what Hades had said earlier: *"This place is not for you! Please darling, stay away from this area."* In that moment, Hades sounded like Demeter. Feeling rebellious, Persephone opened the door to see the most fearful place in the Underworld.

At first, she thought the quiet darkness would continue. Instead, scorching heat and bright light poured out of the doorway. As she entered Tartarus, Persephone adjusted to the light by squinting her eyes. The intense heat radiated off her skin. Then she heard the cries and screams of agonized souls.

Now Persephone understood why Hades had told her to avoid this place. It was painful to be here. Some souls were being boiled in lava, while others struggled to push heavy boulders uphill. If they let go of the boulder, the shades would have to start over. Some shades were being tortured, and others worked on never-ending tasks that were impossible to complete.

As she took in such dreadful sights, tears came to Persephone's eyes. *How could Hades do this? How can he sleep while these souls suffer?* she wondered. Persephone wept, not just for these imprisoned shades, but because she missed her mother and felt betrayed by Hades. Overwhelmed with grief and sorrow, Persephone immediately turned to open the door, wanting to leave. As she turned the knob, Persephone found that it was locked from the outside.

Persephone's eyes widened at the thought of being trapped here in Tartarus. "No. . . No. . . NOOOO!!! I have got to get out of here! HADES!!!" she called out, and pounded on the door, hoping he'd hear her. "HADES! HEEELLLP! HADES!!" she screamed. Persephone began to cry uncontrollably, thinking that she'd never escape. She blamed herself for not listening to Hades. But maybe he could hear her. *Was this punishment for not following his orders?*, she thought. Persephone continued to cry as she pounded on the door again.

Thinking her efforts were useless, she eventually gave up, but Persephone could feel eyes watching her. She turned around to see every shade looking at her. A woman who had been whipped to death slowly approached Persephone. The Goddess trembled with fear. The shade snarled at Persephone, "What makes you think the King of the Underworld is going to save you from Tartarus? If you're here, you belong here! He sent all of us to this place!"

Persephone ran away screaming, as more tears filled her eyes. She believed the tortured shades would come after her and, indeed, they were. As they chased Persephone, some of the shades sent negative thoughts her way, *"I don't like you! Nobody likes you! You are nothing but a weak goddess! You don't even have real powers! Who would ever want to love you? Why do you think Hades has yet to take you as a woman? You are nothing but a little girl who no man will love! A mortal will ever pray to you!"*

"STOP!," Persephone screamed out as she kept running, "PLEASE STOP!" More tears came gushing out as their terrible thoughts shrouded Persephone in negativity.

The shades knew exactly what was going on inside her head. The power of negative thoughts can bring any mortal to the brink of suicide. Since Persephone is a goddess, it would take much more than the shades' negative thoughts for something to happen.

While she replayed their negative thoughts in her head, Persephone noticed another path leading into a cave. She ran toward it, hoping to find a way out. Inside the cave, it was cold and damp. Persephone was a little relieved from the scorching heat outside, but she was still shaken up from everything. Sitting down on a rock to calm herself, she couldn't stop crying. Through her tears, Persephone desperately looked for a way out of Tartarus.

But she was losing hope. Persephone wanted Hades to rescue her. She wanted to be safe inside his arms. Then, suddenly, she felt like she wasn't alone. She heard breathing. . . deep breathing . . . and growling. Her heart started to pound again. "Persephone," a voice growled.

Looking up, Persephone saw a giant man with his arms trapped in the cave walls. Although he looked like a man, she could tell that he was something else, something more primal. More significant than a Giant or even a Cyclops. Being imprisoned inside this cave, the man's arms seemed to merge with the rocks and stones. There's no way for him to escape. He opened his glowing blue eyes and smiled wickedly, "Come here, child."

Standing firmly on her feet, Persephone stared at this man. "Were you the one calling me to come here?" she asked accusingly.

"It doesn't take much for someone from the same bloodline to hear me."

"Bloodline? Who are you?" Persephone sensed that she was dealing with a powerful entity. Someone from her bloodline? She may be naive, but she wasn't stupid. Although her current circumstance might suggest otherwise. Persephone may not know this strange entity, but she knew that he was dangerous. She sensed an ancient kind of power radiating off him.

"I'm surprised you haven't heard about me. I'm certain every Olympus god and goddess would have warned you about who I am. Especially the one you're with now." He showed a sinister smile.

Persephone shrugged, pretending that she wasn't afraid. "Hades hasn't warned me about anyone. He only told me to avoid this place." Persephone felt guilt and worry set in."I wish I'd listen to him. Now, whoever you are, I need to find a way out of here."

"I can tell you of an escape route."

"How can you? Looks like you've been trapped here for a very long time." Persephone pointed out the overgrown weeds and his rusted chains. Persephone wondered how weeds could grow in a place like this, with no surrounding sunlight or soil. She was confused.

He looked into Persephone's eyes, "I was the first being that Hades imprisoned. Him! Him and his brothers!" he growled in anger, as he tried to move. With great effort . . . only a small vibration bounced off the walls while he slightly wobbled. Already tired, he huffed, "His brothers and . . . one sister." Persephone held her breath. "The one who cares for trees, plants, and harvest."

"My mother?" Persephone questioned in disbelief. "Now I know you're a liar. My mother has never set foot in here, let alone the Underworld!" She shouted, "WHO ARE YOU?"

Before she heard him answer, Persephone recognized a nearby voice that called her name. Happy and relieved to hear that voice once more, Persephone exclaimed, "HADES! I'M HERE!"

Hades ran toward the sound of Persephone's voice echoing from the cave. Once he went inside, he ran to her, wrapping his arms tightly around her body. For a brief moment, Hades let out a sigh of relief. Hades let go of their embrace so that he could hold Persephone's face in his hands. "What are you doing here? I told you not to come to this place!"

As Persephone pointed to the gigantic man, Hades' eyes followed her finger. "He called me, Hades. He woke me up tonight. I swear, I didn't know he was in Tartarus!"

The giant man growled, "It's been a long time, Hades, since you came to check up on me. Since I've had no visitors, I thought it'd be lovely if Persephone came to see me. Good thing too, since she doesn't even know who I am!"

Hades looked directly at the giant and spoke with threatening authority, "CRONUS, YOU STAY AWAY FROM HER! DON'T EVEN SPEAK TO HER AND DON'T CALL HER NAME!"

Cronus laughed with contempt, "What will you do?! I'm already in Tartarus! What more can you do to me, Hades! Tell me, MY SON! WHAT MORE CAN YOU DO TO ME!"

Hades didn't answer. Instead, using all of his power and pent-up anger, he hit Cronus with a blast of energy. For once, Persephone saw the King of the Underworld's powerful capabilities help knock down the giant with a single blow. The last thing that the King of Death needed to be was pissed off. She noticed that Hades' powerful strength matched her father's.

Then, Hades quickly grabbed Persephone and teleported them back to his room. Persephone held her breath the entire time. Looking at Hades with anger on his face and concern in his eyes, Persephone's eyes began to water. She had disobeyed Hades and what she had done was wrong. Persephone feared that Hades himself might punish her, so she gave him space. Hades paced around the room, trying to get his temper under control. Persephone's eyes followed Hades wherever he went and, with controlled anger in his voice, he asked, "What were you thinking Persephone?!"

Tears ran down her face, "Someone was calling my name, I . . .I . . had to answer."

Now feeling frustrated, Hades said, "Persephone my love, the Underworld is a wonderful and mystical place. However, the one place I told you never to visit is Tartarus. Any shade or being that's in Tartarus will try tricking you to go in, so that they can get out."

"How could you send all those people there?" Persephone began to cry again. "What I saw and what I felt from the souls in there—no wonder people believe you're a monster!"

"PERSEPHONE" Hades snarled. "Everyone you saw in Tartarus is there because of their actions. Actions that went beyond the Fates' control. Wherever these souls land, is based on their actions. I take everything into account before I make my final decision! In my eyes, everyone here is equal. "

"I thought you said mortals are like children to you. That they don't know any better"

Hades' anger began to crawl downward. "Yes, my love. I also said that being here is only temporary for them. No punishment can last forever, it doesn't suit the crime. Before healing themselves and moving forward, souls must realize what they've done. Some souls just require more time than others."

184

"But there were so many in there."

"Darling, that is only a small portion of humanity." Persephone was still shaken by her experience. Hades remembered to check on her then. "Are you hurt?"

Persephone shook her head no. "Not physically, no. Oh Hades, they attacked me mentally. Every pain and doubt I've ever had resurfaced in my mind, about me and you. . . "

"Don't listen, darling. It's how they satisfy themselves, by tormenting others. It is nothing but lies."

"That's the issue, Hades. They weren't lies. They were my fears brought to the surface."

Hades then went to Persephone, caressing her head with his hands. "Still, my love, don't listen. Even if it sounds true. They just want you to join their misery, by feeding off of your torment. Doubts, fears, anger, sadness, and pain. Their way of revenge is getting to you mentally."

"Does that happen to you when you go inside?"

"Yes, but I've learned to mentally block it out."

Hades no longer felt angry, while he gazed at his love with concern. "If you hear more calls from that place, ignore it. Understand?"

"Even it's you? What if you get trapped in there and you call me?"

Hades smiled at Persephone's worried concern for him. "Darling, I am King of the Underworld. I have all the power here. Everything and everyone listens to me, including the Underworld itself. We're both connected, so the Underworld cannot harm me. It's a part of me, so when I visit Tartarus to check on things, nothing harms me. Not even the scorching heat from the flames can cause damage."

Persephone looked at him in awe. Nothing could harm him here. Just then, Persephone remembered something the giant had said. "That giant . . . that man that was speaking to me . . . he called you his son. Is he your father?"

She looked at Hades for several moments. Hades seemed to age suddenly as he sifted through his own memories. "That man who you've just met, his name is Cronus, and he's my father. He's also the father of both your parents."

"He's my grandfather?" Persephone asked, wide-eyed, and Hades nodded.

"Has your mother told you a story about the Beginning of Creation?" Persephone shook her head no. Hades had a feeling that Demeter sheltered Persephone from almost everything. "Of course not. How about you come to bed with me and I'll tell you a bedtime story." Persephone hesitated at the thought of sharing a bed with him. She wasn't ready yet, and was still shocked about being kidnapped. Hades knew what she was thinking, "Don't worry my little flower, this is about comfort and the importance of history. I promise I'll be a gentleman. . . for tonight. "Hades said a little seductively, not wanting to scare her away. Persephone blushed in response.

Hades climbed into bed with his robe on, so that Persephone wouldn't worry about being intimate with him. Persephone joined him and settled in, ready to hear Hades' story.

"How come your mother never told you about how everything was established?" Hades wondered what purpose Demeter had in keeping that information hidden from her daughter.

Pausing to think it over, Persephone didn't understand why she had never heard this story before. "Maybe it never came up?"

"Haven't you ever been curious about how the world began?"

"I've been curious about many things. Sometimes Mother answers my questions, or she'll avoid it by trying to distract me with something else.

"Well then, I shall tell you how everything started and how us gods came into fruition." Persephone got comfortable laying right next to Hades. He began to recall the story from memory.

"Long ago, there was nothing but darkness. Nothing existed but Chaos. There was no light, no order, not even the earth had been created. One day, Chaos bore three children— Nyx the goddess of night, Erebus the god of underground darkness, and then there was Gaia. Gaia is known as Mother Earth." Intrigued, Persephone started to imagine the people from Hades' story.

"Gaia was the first step toward creation. She gave birth to Uranus the sky and Pontus the sea, without a man to help her conceive. Uranus' rain cast lovingly down on Gaia, which created all sorts of life. From trees and flowers, to animals and beasts. Soon after, Gaia and Uranus had children together. There was Cyclops, the one-eyed giant. Then Hecatoncheires, the monster with a hundred arms and fifty heads. There were more children, but the most favored and most beautiful of them all were the titans."

"Thinking that the titans were so captivatingly beautiful, Uranus didn't understand why his other children looked different. He despised his other children because of it and, in turn, they disobeyed him. So Uranus imprisoned the rest of his children in Tartarus. Gaia was beyond furious, so she told the titans to kill their father and to rescue their brothers. Only one titan dared to do so, a titan named Cronus." Persephone paid close attention to the story, now that her mysterious grandfather was involved.

"Gaia gave Cronus a sickle to avenge in her honor. Cronus crept up on Uranus while he slept, and castrated his genitals." Persephone made a painful expression, and seeing her, Hades had tried to stifle a laugh. "His castration thus permanently separated earth and sky. Though he succeeded in overthrowing his father, Cronus was cruel and didn't free the Cyclops or Hecatoncheires. Instead, he became the new Lord of the Universe and ruled in vain."

Hades grew somber as the story took a turn. "Later on, Cronus married his sister Rhea. They had six children, three boys, and three girls. Unfortunately, Gaia scolded Cronus for his cruelty, and warned him about being overthrown by one of his children." Hades drew in a deep breath before telling Persephone the most horrifying act that any parent could commit upon their child. "So each time Rhea gave birth to a baby, Cronus would swallow it whole. To prevent from being overthrown."

Persephone gasped and her hands covered her mouth. "How could he do that? To his own children?" Then she looked at Hades with sorrow and pity. "Cronus is your father, but you weren't swallowed whole, right?"

"Persephone, I'm the oldest. I was the first to be swallowed."

Tears formed in Persephone's eyes. She couldn't believe what Hades had endured. "After you were born, how long was it until you were swallowed? Do you even know?"

"Immediately after. . . approximately. "Hades said and dried her tears with his thumbs.

"You never saw the light of day?"

"No, I haven't. I went from one darkness to another. Born from darkness and now living in it. Since I'm the firstborn, I've stayed in this darkness much longer than the rest of my siblings."

"How did you stay alive after being swallowed?" she asked Hades. She couldn't imagine a parent being so cruel.

"I'm a god, love. I cannot die, so I lived inside my father like a baby. Every time he ate, it became my food too."

"But there was no one to teach, love, or comfort you."

"Not entirely true. During my short time alone, I heard a woman's voice, but it wasn't my mother's. I never saw her, but she would sing to me, giving me comfort, when I felt alone or unloved. Later on, she revealed her identity—the Goddess Nyx."

"The goddess of the night, the one you mentioned earlier?" Persephone asked, her eyebrows raised.

Hades nodded. "Turns out that Nyx can appear anywhere, as long as darkness emerges in corners. She would mysteriously materialize when I needed someone to love or care for me. I learned to talk from hearing her speak."

"That's still a horrible way to grow up. I can't imagine living like you did as a child. It makes the way I was raised seem easy, despite the disagreements I've had with my mother. She really does love me," Persephone admitted with almost a sliver of guilt.

Hades looked at her with certainty. "Persephone, I may not agree with how she raised you, but your mother does love you. I never once said she didn't."

"Did she. .?" Persephone closed her eyes, too scared to ask about her own mother's birth. "Was she swallowed too?" Hades looked at her sad eyes and nodded. "OH MY . . ." Tears came down Persephone's face. She couldn't fathom the pain her mother had faced. "I had no idea she went through that! Why did she hide this from me?"

"My love, this happened centuries ago. There was no need to bring up something as painful as this. It wasn't just her and I—it was also Poseidon, Hestia, and Hera too."

Persephone realized something just then, "You took care of everyone, didn't you? You raised everyone."

"I did." Hades nodded. "I had to grow up quickly in order to make sure that my brother and sisters were cared for. That way, it wasn't as harsh for them as it was for me."

"What about my father?"

"He's the reason we escaped. He wasn't swallowed because our mother had enough of our father's cruelty. She was tired of him swallowing her babies. Instead of giving Cronus another baby to swallow, she tricked him. She had swaddled a stone with a blanket. Then our mother ran off and let the nymphs raise Zeus. When he got older, Zeus married a titan's daughter, Metis, who is the goddess of prudence. She had the gift of wisdom. With our mother still angry at Cronus, he needed to be deposed. With Metis' help, both her and Mother gave Cronus a drink, promising him that he would be undefeatable."

Persephone smiled at her grandmother's cleverness, "I presume that their drink had the opposite effect."

"Not only was it the opposite, but Cronus retched up all of us. We were grown and unharmed, just like Zeus. That's when the battle of Gods versus titans began. We freed the Cyclops and the Hecatoncheires. As a token of their gratitude for releasing them, the Cyclops built our primary weapons. It took ten years of war, but we won, and all of the titans, except for a select few, were sent to Tartarus. The Hecatoncheires kept guard outside.

"Once the war ended, Zeus, Poseidon, and I discussed who would take over certain parts of the Earth. . ."

"I heard that the three of you drew straws to determine who would rule which place," Persephone interrupted, "at least that's what I heard from mortals and nymphs."

Hades arched an eyebrow, confused. "Drew straws?"

"You know, where you take straws and hide the lengths of them until you all choose one. Then, whoever gets the tallest one gets whatever he wants, while the shortest one—"

"I know the game of drawing straws, Persephone," Hades interrupted her, almost laughing. That was one of the most ridiculous things he's ever heard. "My flower, when it comes to ruling a certain area, it's because one is suited to do so; we were fated for it. Not because of a game of straws."

"But you're the oldest aren't you?" Persephone asked and Hades nodded. "The oldest usually gets the crown and becomes King," she asserted.

"I am King, Persephone." He frowned, now more confused.

"I meant King of the Gods. That should have been yours."

"I thought that too, at first. Zeus wanted the crown; it was obvious that he wanted power. I believed that it should belong to me because, not only am I the oldest, but I also took care of my siblings. I thought that I was the most responsible god. Then again, Zeus saved us all from Cronus. I failed to rescue anyone, despite my parental responsibilities to look after my siblings. So I let him have the crown, hoping that he would use his power accordingly. Poseidon agreed, granting Zeus to be King of the Gods. Poseidon felt like he was destined for the seas anyway. He loved the water, especially since it was dark enough for him to live comfortably, because he too was swallowed by Cronus and lived in darkness. He just wasn't trapped for as long as I was."

"So you took the Underworld? Without complaints or any bitterness?" Persephone felt like this was entirely different from what the mortals believed about Hades and the Underworld. Then again, they were wrong about him to begin with.

"No complaints and no bitterness," Hades replied. "I've been in darkness for so long that when it comes to light, despite my longing for it, it is still foreign to me. When I entered the Underworld for the first time, it felt like the place belonged to me. I know what needs to be taken care of and what's required to prevent chaos. From my perspective, I think that your father and I have equal power."

Confused, but fascinated, Persephone looked at Hades, wondering how he was more powerful than the King of the Gods. "How so?"

Hades smiled, "Well, obviously you've seen my kingdom."

"Yes. It is amazing and beautiful, which is completely unexpected."

"My kingdom, as you know, is ten times larger than Olympus. Zeus may be the King of the Gods who creates mortal souls, but, in the end, all souls belong to me when they die. It doesn't matter if they are good or bad, there is a home for everyone. Even all earthly riches, like diamonds and semi-precious stones, are shared between Mother Earth and the Underworld. I can easily access The Fates, along with every kind of dimension and realm that exists in the universe."

"The Underworld is more than a place destined for the dead. Rather, it's a gateway connection to all things in the universe, as I have seen with the mirror doors," Persephone realized.

"Indeed." Hades nodded in agreement. It also provides the one thing that Zeus and the other gods need, giving me the ultimate power. And it's a great bargaining tool. I'll show it to you tomorrow, my darling."

Persephone yawned. Her body and eyelids began to feel heavy. "Go to sleep, my darling. You've had a tiresome night," Hades lovingly whispered, as he pulled his silky bed sheets over their bodies. Seeing that she was going to stay in his bed for the night, Persephone gave Hades a look of uncertainty. "Don't worry, my love. We're just sleeping here tonight; nothing else will happen. I also want to make sure Cronus doesn't call you again. Acting on instinct, Hades kissed Persephone on her head and when he did, Persephone shut her eyes. As she let sleep claim her, Persephone's lips parted into a smile.

Hades moved in closer, wrapping his arms protectively around Persephone, as he let sleep come to him. For the first time, Hades went to bed filled with happiness in his heart. Hades was finally sharing his bed with his beloved. It's only a matter of time before Persephone is his entirely. He looked forward to spending eternity with her.

CHAPTER 9

THE ELYSIAN FIELDS

Demeter was losing her mind. She hadn't seen Persephone for nearly a week. Prompted to ask everyone she encountered about her daughter's possible whereabouts, with each passing day, Demeter shed more tears. She felt in her gut that someone had Persephone. Demeter would not give up until she found her. Unfortunately, since Demeter was preoccupied with Persephone's disappearance, she had abandoned her duties as a goddess. The earth looked more like autumn than the beginning of summer. It confused both the mortals and the animals.

The next morning, while Persephone was waiting for Hades, she left the palace. Her curiosity led her to try and find Cerberus, the three-headed dog. Persephone had seen dogs before, but never three-headed ones, and this dog was huge. He was almost her exact height.

Persephone tiptoed closer to the dog. Cerberus instantly sniffed something sweet in the air, and seeing Persephone come into view, barked in alert. From his bedroom, Hades heard the barking and looked out his window. He saw Persephone inching toward the ferocious dog and almost panicked, because no one but Hades could be near Cerberus. The dog could be vehemently cruel when necessary.

Dressing quickly, Hades teleported himself to where Cerberus was standing. He couldn't believe that the three-headed dog was frantically licking Persephone's face in delight. She laughed hysterically while Cerberus wagged his tail, giving his mistress nothing but love.

Hades shook his head and laughed, "Unbelievable. Count on you, my love, to tame a monster with kindness."

"Monster? He's not a monster, he's just a different kind of dog." Hades smiled at his love's indifference. "Well, he is your pet, is he not?" Persephone asked.

"He may be my pet, but my pet has a job to do. Besides, I have a surprise for you."

Persephone kissed Cerberus on each head before leaving with Hades. Cerberus whimpered before Hades ordered the dog to stand guard once more.

Hades held Persephone's hand as he led her through one of the Underworld's tunnels. So far, it looked like everything else in the Underworld—it was dark and cave-like, only aglow by small torches that hung on the walls. As they neared their destination, Persephone giggled. Covering her eyes with his hands, Hades guided his love toward an extraordinary place. He wanted to surprise her. He wanted to show her one of the few real beauties in the Underworld. She had already endured the horror of this realm, so now Hades wanted Persephone to experience the hidden pleasures that his world also contains.

With her eyes covered, Persephone relied on her other senses to figure out where they were. Nearby birds chirped and children laughed playfully, she could even feel. . . sunlight? Warmth from the sun touched her skin, as if it were possible. What Persephone felt confused her, since the Underworld didn't have any sunlight. Wherever they were, Persephone knew that it was a special and happy place.

"Hades! Please let me see!" she begged while giggling. She knew that he was having fun with her. Then he finally led Persephone to stand at a certain spot.

Hades smiled warmly at her, kissing her cheek gently. "Are you sure, darling?" he whispered in her ear. Hades' warm breath sent shivers down Persephone's spine. While he still covered her eyelids, Persephone smiled as she placed her hands over Hades'. "Okay, my love, open your eyes." Hades said as he drew his hands away.

Persephone's hazel-green eyes opened to find what she thought wasn't possible; she saw paradise. The lands flourished with green hills, flowers, crystal blue lakes, and rivers. There was everlasting food to eat, too. The bright sun shone down upon everything. While most of the children played and ran around, many of the adults were just enjoying the day. Among them, couples expressed romantic gestures to their partners. Persephone stood incredulously, still in awe that this place not only held such beauty, but also everlasting happiness for its people.

"Do you like it?" Hades asked her.

"Oh, Hades! This place is so beautiful! I love it! Where are we?"

"The one place that everyone forgets I rule over. This dimension is the Elysian Fields. The Elysian Fields is a paradise for worthy and virtuous souls."

A tear slipped from Persephone's eye when she spotted a mother and child happily together. Once the two souls saw Hades, they felt Persephone's presence and instantly bowed. Waving his hand continuously, Hades motioned for the two souls to keep bowing. A little girl carrying a basket full of flowers went toward Persephone, wanting to give her a flower. Persephone smiled at the child, "Oh, thank you! I love flowers."

The little girl gave both Hades and Persephone a wide smile. Hades returned a friendly smile as he accepted her gift. "Your flowers are beautiful today, Agatha."

Agatha curtsied, "Thank you, my lord." Then she looked at Persephone, "Will you be growing new flowers here, my queen?"

Persephone didn't know how to respond. Feeling flustered, Persephone's heart fluttered slightly at Agatha's assumption. She was not Queen of the Underworld yet. Persephone's mouth opened, but she couldn't get a word out. Luckily, Hades stepped forward and flashed a proud smile. "I'm sure my beloved will create new and glorious flowers for our world, Agatha. She's not a queen yet, but maybe someday she will be." He glanced at Persephone with a loving smile, reserving his expression only for her. Her heart sped up when Hades surmised that one day she might become queen. His queen.

"Okay, well, I need to get back to my mama. Bye bye." Agatha skipped happily across the fields to join her mother.

"She's such a sweetheart," Persephone commented as she watched Agatha and her mother embrace each other.

"Yes, she is. She even speaks to me without fear, but children are usually easy to talk to, since their minds aren't clouded with fear or judgment."

"Does she always give you a flower every time she sees you?"

"Yes, she does. She thinks I'm in dire need of more beauty in my life." Hades stared at Persephone with love in his eyes. "I truly think that will happen now. Especially since the most beautiful goddess to ever exist is now my lover."

Persephone blushed, "You know, she called me your queen."

"Yes," Hades caressed the side of Persephone's face, "like I said to her, maybe one day you will be." She looked around the Elysian Fields and smiled.

"This place makes me forget that I'm even in the Underworld or that the mortals are dead," Persephone observed. "How did Agatha and her mother die?"

"They died from influenza, but not many mortals know about the sickness. First Agatha caught it and then, of course, her mother tended to Agatha. Then her mother caught it. The medicine wasn't strong enough . . . Agatha died first. With her daughter gone, Agatha's mother felt like there was no reason to get better, so she let the virus run its course."

Persephone looked a little sad after hearing about how they died. Looking at Agatha and her mother again, Persephone saw that they both looked so happy, as if the virus had never touched them at all.

"I wish every mortal could see this," Persephone said. She looked at Hades, "Can you imagine if everyone saw what this world was like? If they did, no one would be afraid to die. They would be more willing to come see you. They might even pray to you. I feel more . . ." Persephone didn't finish her thought because she couldn't find the right words.

"At peace? At home?" asked Hades.

"Exactly!" she said and closed her eyes. Persephone stood quietly as she absorbed the realm's positive energy, along with the sunshine. "One thing I don't understand—how is there sun in this world? Is it real?"

"Of course it's real. Elysian Fields may be part of the Underworld, Persephone, but it's another world altogether. Another realm. That's what most mortals don't understand about death. Remember how I showed you the mirrored doors in my kingdom? They are the doorways to many different realms." She nodded yes. "There are many realms to visit and they are all connected," Hades said, as he picked a flower from its bush. "It's almost like having multiple rooms in one house. The Universe is the house. All dimensions are the rooms."

Persephone understood. "Including the other gods and goddesses that aren't part of our realm? Like the Norse or Hindu gods?" Hades smiled because she was right. "If that's true, then why do mortals fight over who's right and who's wrong? That's incredibly selfish."

"It is." He nodded and placed the flower in Persephone's hair. "Human ego is the simplest answer." She frowned at him, confused. "Most people want to believe that they're right, so they fail to acknowledge other beliefs. Most do not because they don't want to find fault within their own belief system. What they don't realize, Persephone, is that all beliefs exist in some form."

"Then why don't the gods reveal more of themselves to mortals? Perhaps then mortals would have more faith in the gods and their fighting would cease!" Persephone once had this conversation with Athena, but maybe Hades could offer a different perspective.

Hades shook his head sadly, "My darling, it's a lovely thought, but the truth is. . . mortals only see what they want to see, even if the truth is right in front of them. Anything that lies beyond Earth's realm is harder for many to believe in. If I stood in front of a living man and told him that I was King of the Underworld, he would probably think that I had lost my mind. Or that he lost his. As more time passes, people lose faith in the mysterious worlds that exist beyond Earth, only to rely on what's in front of them. They fail to realize that as they become more skeptical, their ties to a more universal connection is lost. Those ties—whether it's to us, other deities, or even universal energies—are severed. At that point, mortals begin to feel isolated, only believing in themselves. No faith, no magic, no universal love . . . that, to me, my love, is how Tartarus exists on Earth. Living a lonesome and painful mortal life with no hope or faith."

Persephone stayed silent and continued to stare at the realm's beauty in front of her. She absorbed Hades' comment about mortals and their lack of faith. Hades came closer to her, realizing that she had much to digest. "I'm sorry darling," he kissed the top of her head, "I didn't mean to project the mortals' depressing viewpoints onto you. I know it's not what you want to hear, how human minds work."

"Stop apologizing Hades. I need to know this. I've always wondered why we don't show more of ourselves to mortals. Now I understand that they must be ready to see us. For that to happen, they need to awaken their mind and spirit."

Hades nodded. "For those who believe, they will see beyond. For those who don't, everything will surpass them. It takes a different kind of sight to see other beings and magic." Hades caressed one of Persephone's hands, as he led her in another direction. "Come, my love, there's a section of this paradise that I want to show you."

As they walked through several fields filled with flowers and animals, Persephone loved this place more and more. There, in the center of the meadow, stood a house that looked like a Greek temple. Its columns were covered with overgrown vines and flowers. Persephone gasped at its apparent beauty. Hades looked at her beautiful smile, "do you like it, my flower?"

"Of course, I love it! Why do you ask?"

"It's yours. This, and the many acres of land surrounding it, is yours. We are standing in a special area of the Elysian Fields. This is the Isle of the Blessed. This is where the highest of good souls are found. Here, you can do whatever you wish."

"What does it take to be the highest of good souls?"

"Well, one must be reincarnated at least three times. During those times, one must maintain a good soul. They can have more lifetimes of course, but the minimum is three. The only difference between here and the Elysian Fields is more bliss and freedom, I should say."

"Freedom?" Persephone frowned, confused.

"If a shade wants to see their loved ones on earth, with my permission, they are allowed to do so. But, after a certain amount of time passes, they must return to this place."

"Interesting." Persephone didn't know what to make of it.

"If you ever want to get away—if you need space or just want to spend time with nature, you can come here."

"Get away? From what?"

"Your mother. . . or me."

"Why would I need to get away from you?" Persephone genuinely asked Hades. She looked at him as if what he had said was the most ridiculous thing in the world.

"We are a couple now, Persephone. Couples, even the happiest ones, have fights. Though my palace is vast enough for us to have space from one another when necessary, in case you need a different environment, you can come here. Being in such a peaceful setting, surrounded by nature, will surely put your mind at ease. Think about it, do you believe that you're still in the Underworld right now? Enveloped by all this beauty, do you still think you're in the presence of death?"

"No, my love, I don't. In fact, I feel free. For the first time. . ." then she drew closer to her beloved. Now, her face was only an inch away from his, ". . . I feel like I could fly."

Hades smiled as he led her into the house. Not only did he want to show Persephone the interior, but he also wanted to show her something that's most valuable to all gods and goddesses. In the fenced-in backyard, where no soul could pass through, a waterfall pours into a crystalized lake. Many beautiful flowers that Persephone had never seen before floated on the water.

She gasped, awed by the serene scene in front of her. Hades then picked a flower from the lake. "This. I've wanted to show you this since we first began courting." As he handed Persephone the enchanting flower, it perfectly balanced itself inside her cupped hands. "This is an extraordinary flower called the Lotus."

"It's stunning, but what is so unique about it?"

Hades' smile quickly turned into a smirk. "The Lotus is one of many resources that allows me to have more power than Zeus. A Lotus flower contains nectar that us gods drink to maintain our immortality and youth. We call it ambrosia. This flower not only gives us immortal life, but it can also heal and purify a soul. It has the ability to bless a person to be a god or goddess, granting them full power. Does that fragrance smell familiar to you?"

Persephone realized something just then, "Is this what I drank at my initiation?" Hades nodded. "So that's why the initiation couldn't start without you."

"This special Lotus flower only grows here in the Underworld. Of course, you may see regular Lotus flowers in other earthly areas, but these in particular only grow here, with a little bit of root from the World Tree." Hades plucked another one of the lotus flowers and placed it in Persephone's hands.

"So we can't survive without it?" she asked, while caressing it gently.

"We can and we can't. It is our top dependency. However, we only use it once every hundred years." Hades grabbed the flower from Persephone's hands. "Don't let this go to waste. These flowers are too precious. . . just like you."

Persephone smiled as she watched Hades grab a mortar. Using a pestle, Hades crushed the Lotus flower inside the bowl. As it continued to disintegrate, the essence of the flower revealed itself. Then, Hades mixed the pieces of Lotus petals with some water and honey, which he poured into a small perfume bottle. Persephone smiled at what she had just witnessed. Hades had made ambrosia.

Hades then handed her the bottle of ambrosia. "Many gods and goddesses would give anything to have this, but this one is yours."

"Hades, I don't need it. I just drank this at my initiation, remember?"

"Keep this with you anyway. You might need it for something else. Hopefully, you won't need to use it for another hundred years." With her gentle touch, Persephone took the bottle and gave Hades a quick kiss on the lips.

Smiling, Persephone looked around her safe haven. She was now Hades' complete desire and he looked at her, completely enthralled. Ever since Persephone's initiation, when he locked eyes with her, she was the only thing he worshipped. Not just with his mind alone, but also with his entire being. He couldn't peel his eyes away from her sexy body. How could Demeter still not see Persephone as a woman? Pushing aside all thoughts of Demeter, Hades couldn't restrain himself any longer.

Persephone could feel Hades stare as he inched toward her, like a lion encircling his prey. She felt her pulse quicken as the tension in the air thickened between them. Persephone's hair was up, and she felt a chill run down her spine as Hades' fingers trailed down her neck to her shoulder blade. He gently kissed the back of her neck while both his hands wandered around Persephone's torso, holding her tightly to him. She felt something hard press against the lower part of her back. Hades wanted to make his intentions about where this was going known.

Persephone' slight moan signaled for Hades to continue. She may be a maiden, but Persephone had been yearning to experience this feeling for the longest while. She had been starving for a man's love like Hades'. She molded herself to fit Hades' embrace, which left her neck exposed. Hades then placed sultry kisses on her pulsing veins that throbbed with excitement. Persephone felt like she was going to have a mortal's fever. She felt a fire below her belly that was indescribable. Persephone only knew that she wanted Hades more now than ever before. "My love, please. I want this. I want you," she panted.

Hades gripped onto everything he had within himself to not take Persephone from where she was standing. They were alone, so there was no one to disturb them, but he felt obliged to do this correctly and in his bed. If he was going to give Persephone her first night of passion as a woman, it would be done in his bed. "My darling, my love, I would be most honored to make love to you tonight. However, let's continue this someplace where we will be undisturbed. Someplace where we can have all the time in the world."

Persephone only nodded. It seemed like she could no longer speak. Being aroused overwhelmed her. Hades then teleported them both back to his private chambers. His room felt warm and was lit up from the glowing fireplace. Not wanting to break their passionate spell, Hades kept kissing Persephone. As Hades laid her upon his luxurious bed, he covered half of her with his body. Despite the heat radiating off Hades' body and from the fireplace, chills continued to course through Persephone's body. She felt consumed by her senses. She was aroused, excited, passionate, and nervous.

Hades sensed this, since his emotions were also heightened. Despite his own aroused state, he wanted to be cautious with her.

Looking into her emerald eyes, which held a hint of insecurity, Hades asked, "Darling, my flower, what are you afraid of?"

Swallowing her fear, Persephone gazed into his crystal blue eyes and saw his love for her. "I'm not afraid. I'm not afraid of you, Hades. I never was."

"That is wonderful to hear, but that is not what I meant." Hades caressed her face with a comforting touch, while his lips grazed her cheeks and teased her lips a bit. When Hades' hands glided over her bosom, his ghostly touch made Persephone's back rise into his hands. "I want to get rid of whatever is holding you back."

Persephone hesitated a moment before speaking, "What if I'm not what you're expecting, and then you think it's all a mistake? What if there's something about my body that you'll find repulsive? What if I'm horrible at it?" Hades wanted to laugh; he thought her worries were a little silly. However, he saw fear growing in Persephone's eyes as she voiced her concerns. He knew better than to laugh. Instead, Hades needed to comfort her lightheartedly, which he thought he could never do with anyone else except her.

"It is impossible for me to think that anything about you is repulsive. I was mesmerized by you when our eyes first met." Hades captured her lips again, as he cupped her precious breasts once more. Persephone whimpered in response. She loved the taste of his mouth and his warm hands made her tremble with desire. Hades whispered in her ear, "You are my love, my destiny. You were meant to be my wife the moment you were born. Even if this wasn't true, I'd still desire you."

Persephone couldn't wait anymore. She reached up to touch Hades' lips, kissing him with a fierce passion. Hades moaned, as his pent-up desires started to intensify. His restless hands moved possessively up and down her back, sliding across her spine. Persephone felt herself falling slowly into a dizzying abyss of sensuality and rousing passion.

To excite her even more, Hades removed his cloak and began to undress himself. Watching intently, Persephone's hands helped him strip down. From beneath his black clothing appeared a well-defined, pale torso.

Upon seeing this, Persephone's breath quickened and her body felt warm. She began to touch Hades. His muscles were as hard as any man's, but silky to her touch. The sensuality of the act sent electrifying nerves down to her center. Then, Persephone felt blemished skin on his back and shoulders. Persephone knew that these scattered blemishes were old scars. There were so many of them. "Where did these come from?" she asked as her fingers traced his ancient wounds. "From our battle against Cronus and the Titans."

"Shouldn't they be healed by now?"

Hades gently kissed the hand that was touching his scarred skin, pecking her fingertips. "They were too deep. It took an abundance of magic and energy to seal them shut. Sometimes, even gods can't escape permanent injury."

Persephone lifted herself up enough to kiss the scars on his shoulder. "My brave Hades. Thank you for showing me this."

While distracted, Persephone felt her dress coming undone and falling away. Acting on instinct, Persephone hid her exposed body with both hands. Hades felt himself harden as he gazed upon her beautiful form. "You are beautiful, my love, don't shy away from me."

If Hades can show me his battle scars, then I can show my bare self to him, Persephone thought. Slowly, she dropped her hands away and Hades brushed his palms against her breasts. Each of his searing kisses heightened the rapture between them. At last, Hades lifted his mouth away from hers, breathing harsh and rapidly. Persephone thought her body would surely burn like Tartarus' fire, as tender desire pulsated through her veins. Her fingers touched Hades' face, tracing his cheeks with her fingertips, until she reached his smooth lips. Then, Hades' tongue was inside Persephone and intense emotion sweetly unfolded. It bloomed vibrantly wild, with a fierceness that made her tremble.

His hands shifted, moving from her midriff to waist, then down to Persephone's lower thighs. With conscious effort, she forced her leg muscles to relax. Using her legs to clutch him to her body, Persephone buried her face against Hades' neck. The feeling of need within them grew stronger, and Hades began trailing kisses down Persephone's body once more. Shifting herself so that she was now flat on her back, Hades continued to kiss Persephone's neck and breasts, as he moved toward the inevitable.

Wanting to ask for her consent before continuing, Hades hesitated, but Persephone pressed him onward. Persephone gasped as she felt Hades gently tease the sensitive flesh between her legs. She moaned even louder. Waves of pleasure surged throughout her body, as Persephone began to sweat from the growing heat between them. She almost forgot which way was up, as the sensation surged through her mind. Hades felt this way too, and he used this powerful urge to guide him further. Persephone had never felt anything like this before, a pleasurable explosion. Soon, her moans subsided as Hades moved upwards to meet her face. She smiled as her eyes met his, signaling for him to execute what was about to happen next.

"Persephone my love. . .you're so beautiful," Hades whispered. Fully aware that he'd repeated this phrase to her several times before, Hades knew that repetition would boost Persephone's confidence. "Do not be afraid to explore—touch me any way you want. All of my flesh is yours, and I do mean all of it."

Wanting to be pleasured as well, Hades hoped Persephone would touch him without hesitation. She was already used to touching his face and muscular upper body. Of course, she was also curious about his lower region, which would soon make her a maiden no more. Hades hissed with pleasure as Persephone began stroking him. As his moans vibrated off the walls, Persephone grew more confident. She was secretly thrilled to see her love fully immersed in the pleasure that she could provide. Hades knew he wasn't going to last much longer if they kept going.

"My flower, you need to stop." He lifted Persephone upward and began kissing her in a passionate craze. He touched her again to build more arousal.

"Please, no more torture. . . please!" Persephone begged.

Hades laughed a little, "I'm the King of the Underworld darling, there has to be some torture involved." Persephone smiled back at him. She wondered if he was nervous too.

Persephone felt his entire weight as she remained underneath his warm, dominant body. Hades' knee parted her thighs, as he moved into position over her. Persephone closed her eyes and wrapped her arms tightly around the man she loved, knowing that he might hurt her, even if just for a moment.

A shudder shook Hades, as she surrendered in his arms. He slid easily into her incredible warmth, uncertain about how much pain he might cause her, but desperate to eliminate any discomfort. Their time together helped ease her passage. He felt Persephone's silken warmth tightly sheathing him, and expanding to encase him. With twisted knots of desire, Hades' heart beat painfully as he eased himself into Persephone, until he finally encountered her fragile barrier.

He withdrew by a couple inches, shifted forward again, and then withdrew once more. Poised to breach her barrier, he was desperate to bury himself within her, hating to cause her pain. Wrapping his arms tightly around her, wishing to absorb her discomfort, he spoke against her lips in a hoarse voice, "Persephone, darling, don't be afraid.

Just look into my eyes." Persephone tried to keep her attention on Hades' face. When he drove himself into her, Hades heard Persephone gasp painfully, as her arms tightened around him like a boa constrictor.

Hades waited for her pain to subside before moving inside her, gently sliding upward and withdrawing, entering deeper each time. At first, Persephone whimpered with discomfort. Slowly, her whimpers turned into pleasurable cries. Withdrawing further, his body now fully aroused and desperate, Hades fought for some control. Delicately, he circled his hips against Persephone's. His passion tripled by her soft moans of delight, as her hands glided to his hips, clasping Hades closer to her body. Suddenly, using deep, rhythmic thrusts, he plunged into Persephone and felt her body move with his. He could not believe the pleasure she was giving him and the way her body felt, clasped tightly around him.

Together, they both shared warm, blissful sensations, while their bodies began to move in an ancient rhythm. Starting slowly at first, then gradually increasing the tempo of their lovemaking, they continued to lose themselves in a world of pleasure. Their sweat mixed together as they continued to kiss and move as one.

Their tongues danced inside each other's mouths, as they continued to touch and grind together. Skin clashed with skin as Hades continued to thrust deeper into her warm interior. Persephone tightened her hold on his body with her legs, as she felt the sudden rush of mind-numbing pleasure start to surge through her body again. She wrapped her hand around Hades' neck, moaning loudly, as Persephone felt her body tense from her second orgasm. Her inner muscles tensed around Hades while she climaxed. Overwhelming pleasure sent Hades over the edge as he exploded within her, emptying himself inside of her warmth.

Hades gently withdrew himself from between her thighs, and laid down beside her. Persephone captured her breath as Hades caressed her face. He whispered, "How do you feel?"

Persephone gave him a glowing smile, "Relieved."

Hades looked at her, confused. "Not exactly the word I was expecting."

"I also feel thrilled, loved, and free. I said relieved at first because I thought I was going to stay a maiden forever. If I did, then my mother would've truly prevented me from ever being loved by a man. Now, I don't feel that burden anymore. For that, I thank you."

Hades gave her a loving smile. "Did I hurt you when I—? If I did, I'm sorry."

"Only a little, I had to . . . adjust," Persephone said, giggling. Hades smirked with pride because she was referring to his size. She relaxed against his chest and listened to his quick, but steady heartbeat. "I look back on all of the worries I had before we made love. Now, I think they are ridiculous," Persephone started giggling to herself.

Hades' soft laughter joined hers. "My love," Hades said, as his hand caressed her face. "Most virgins have those doubts and concerns before making love for the first time. It is perfectly normal. If you think that you're not good at lovemaking, then I have failed as a partner. For not letting you know what I like, while I try to figure out what you like."

"Still, I thought that I wouldn't live up to your expectations. Especially with how you see my body. Whether or not you think it's beautiful."

"Let me tell you something about beauty. Something that even Aphrodite doesn't know. Are you listening?"

Persephone nodded. Hades made sure she was paying attention. "Beauty is in the eye of the beholder. Beauty is different for everyone. Some people are turned on by something unique, or something that is not part of society's standards. What I'm saying, darling, is that what you think is a flaw, might actually be beautiful to someone else." A tear rolled down Persephone's cheek, after listening to Hades genuine words. "My flower, what don't you like about your body?"

"My eyes, for one." Hades didn't expect this answer. "They are just a plain greenish-gray. I wish I had blue eyes like yours."

"Darling, I love your green eyes. They remind me of the earth and sometimes, when the light is just right, . . . emeralds." Hades replied. "Do you know what part of my body I'm most insecure about?"

Persephone looked at him, thinking he was only joking. "How can you be insecure? You are one the major gods!"

"I am, though. I don't like my pale skin. Compared to the other gods, who are tan and have a glow about them, my skin makes me look like I'm dead or sick."

"But my love, I find your skin to be beautiful," Persephone said and touched Hades' face. "You remind me of the statues that mortals make for our temples. To me, Hades, you have perfect skin. You are the most gorgeous god that I have ever seen."

Hades smiled, he had hoped that Persephone would say that. "You have just proved my point, darling. What I think is ugly about myself, you find beautiful and desirable." He held her chin and lifted her face up, so that Persephone could look him in the eye. "Darling, I'm the eldest of the Olympians, so I've been around for a very long time. In all my time, you are the most beautiful and enchanting woman I ever laid eyes on."

Persephone's eyes welled up with tears, as she reveled in Hades' devotion, and she started kissing his chest. Not out of lust, but out of love and gratitude. "With that being said, my love, I'm not finished with you yet," Hades said with a smirk. They continued to make love into the night. Kissing, touching, and moaning in absolute bliss. The concept of time seemed to vanish as their bodies moved together in unison. Soft caresses solidified their unity now and forever.

With her mind afloat on a sea of mindless pleasure, Persephone's body began to relax, even though she was still entangled in Hades' embrace. Persephone felt Hades move onto his side, bringing her with him, as she slowly drifted back to consciousness. Beneath her cheek, she felt Hades' fast-paced, rhythmic heartbeat. She tried holding back her tears. They both fought to catch their breath, while listening to each other's pounding heartbeats. It was like a gentle beacon of love. Their naked, sweaty bodies remained entwined as they absorbed the warm, beautiful feeling of being together in such perfect bliss.

Exhausted, Persephone managed to raise herself up, meeting Hades' face once again. They both smiled warmly at one another. The happiness they felt now could never be measured. Persephone looked at Hades one more time before sleep claimed her. "I love you."

Hades sighed, now content, and moved closer to hold his love in his arms. "I love you, too. Through all eternity, in every dimension of the universe." Persephone smiled. Her heart swelled at hearing Hades' final words before drifting into a blissful sleep.

CHAPTER 10

THE HALL OF JEWELS

When she woke up, Persephone began to stretch in Hades' luxurious bed. Different parts of her body were pleasantly sore. She didn't mind it though. After all, being sore was a reminder of making love to Hades last night. Disappointed that he wasn't in bed with her, Persephone shrugged it off. She figured that he was already working. Reminiscing about last night brought a smile to her face. Persephone felt exhilarated that, at long last, she finally felt like a woman. As she inhaled Hades' scent from his pillows and sheets, Persephone was thrilled.

Someone knocked on the door just then. Persephone instantly knew it was Zoe. "You may come in, Zoe."

Zoe bowed as she entered. She tried to hide her smile—Zoe knew precisely why Persephone was in Lord Hades' room, naked. "My, my, my lady. Did you have a satisfying night?"

Persephone blushed, "It was more than pleasant."

"More than pleasant?" Zoe smirked in response.

Persephone wanted to shout to the entire world about how happy she really was. "Alright. It was pure ecstasy! He was incredible last night. I hope we get to do it all again tonight!" Moving with utter excitement, her body felt sore again, but she tried to hide her pained expression.

"My lady, how about a nice hot bath to relax the muscles?"

"That would be lovely. Thank you, Zoe."

"After your bath, you must get dressed. Lord Hades wants you to meet him in the Hall of Jewels."

Persephone looked confused. "Where?"

"The Hall of Jewels. Don't worry my lady, I'll show you there myself."

"What is the Hall of Jewels?"

"I'll let that be a surprise for you, as per Lord Hades' orders."

Persephone soaked herself in a hot bath. The water instantly relaxed her sore muscles. Despite feeling relaxed, her mind was racing—thinking about her night with Hades, wondering about the Hall of Jewels, and thinking of how worried her mother must be about her daughter's disappearance. Part of Persephone felt relieved that she was free from her mother, but she also felt guilty too.

Demeter searched the common grounds where Persephone might have been. She had no more tears to shed after constantly crying about Persephone's vanishing. Demeter had aged rapidly, looking more haggard by the day. Instead of looking like a goddess, she looked more like a crazed old maid. Demeter tried using every single power she had to find Persephone.

Then, she noticed a babbling farmer who was pacing around nearby. None of his words made any sense. For a moment, Demeter thought he was just mentally unstable. Then she heard his babbling more coherently, "Almighty Zeus! I just saw death with my own eyes. The girl brings death. The girl brings death. The girl brings death." He kept on repeating the phrase, 'The girl brings death,' which caught Demeter's attention.

Knowing that she didn't look like her usual self, Demeter slowly approached the frightened man. "I need to speak to you. Did you see a young woman come here?"

Still frightened, the man calmly responded, "The girl brings death." Looking at Demeter, the farmer failed to realize that a goddess was standing before him.

Demeter kindly touched his arm. "What do you mean the girl brings death?"

"I saw death," he confessed and began to tremble. "G-irl was here. G-irl was grab-bed by death." To Demeter, the way he carried himself made it seem like he had indeed lost his mind. Ready to walk away, Demeter then heard him say something else that intrigued her,"L-ord of th-e Under-world grab-bed g-irl."

"What did you just say?" Demeter walked closer to the farmer.

The man eyed Demeter closely and he suddenly recognized her."Hel-lo my godd-ess. godd-ess De-meter?"

Tears formed in Demeter's eyes because he was starting to come around, back to reality. "Yes, I'm goddess Demeter. Have you seen my daughter? Goddess Persephone?"

"Was that the g-irl?" his stutter began to subside. "Blonde hair with a reddish tone to it? Did she have flow-ers in her hair and an em-er-ald rose neck-lace?"

"YES! That's her! That my Persephone! Do you know what happened to her?" The farmer nodded. "Trip-tole-mu-s, knows what happened to y-our daughter."

"Triptolemus is your name?" Demeter asked. Again, he nodded. "Well Triptolemus, tell me everything you witnessed here."

With a torch in her hand, Zoe led Persephone down another path in the Underworld. Persephone's belly was filled with excitement, as she wondered what the Hall of Jewels contained.

They kept walking until Persephone saw sparks of light reflecting off Zoe's torch. Persephone looked closer, as glimmers shone on the cave walls and tunnels—beautiful stones were growing here in the cave tunnels. The stones actually grew in size, starting from miniscule to enormous, as Persephone and Zoe pressed on. Shimmering quartz, amethyst, diamonds, and emeralds created a beautiful kaleidoscope of colors. It took Persephone's breath away. "This has to be the Hall of Jewels."

"Indeed, you are right my love," Hades said as he appeared, more handsome than ever before. Persephone felt underdressed. "Zoe, you may leave now."

Zoe bowed as she made her way back to the servants' quarters. Hades went to Persephone, embracing her with a passionate kiss, wanting to relive their previous night together. She didn't want to let go, for her body ached to remember every touch from last night. Her eyes looked around the crystal room, "This is another gorgeous place, Hades. Now I see why you are called the god of riches."

Hades nodded. "All precious stones and crystals are made under the earth's surface, which is, of course, my domain. Some of the most beautiful jewelry ever made has come from these very stones."

"Another precious part of the Underworld," Persephone stated.

Another voice interfered just then, "It truly is, goddess Persephone. So, the whispers of the Underworld are true!" Hades and Persephone both turned to see goddess Hecate.

Seeing that his old friend had come to meet the woman who stole his heart at first glance, Hades smiled. "What whispers?"

"The whispers have been saying that you have finally taken a consort. You have been waiting a long time for this day Hades, I'm glad it has finally come about."

"I am sorry. . . who are you?" Persephone didn't recognize this goddess at all.

"Goddess Hecate. I'm an old friend of Hades."

"The Goddess of Witchcraft?" Persephone felt uneasy, not because of what Hecate represented, but because Persephone wondered if the two friends were ever lovers.

Hecate already knew what Persephone was thinking. "Don't worry young goddess, Hades and I were never lovers. I'm just a friend who gives him advice, nothing more."

Persephone relaxed. Hecate had put her jealous mind at ease. "May I congratulate you both! You make a perfect match, yet you both are polar opposites. Anyway, there is a storm coming, a deadly one. Take care of each other." At that moment, Hecate vanished.

"Where did she go?" Persephone looked around, hoping to find any trace of Hecate. "What did she mean 'there's a storm coming?'"

"Hecate can be a little dramatic. She doesn't like to stay in one place for too long. Besides, she needed to leave, so that I can do this." Hades lowered himself down on one knee and grabbed Persephone's hand. Persephone almost stopped breathing, as her heart continued to race. "My love, like the Hall of Jewels, you are one of a kind. You sparkle with so much love. Like a crystal, you have many faces that I adore. Like the Elysian Fields, you bring joy and sunshine to my life. Persephone, you give my soul peace, which is something I've never had before. I'm willing to share my eternal life with you. "Will you marry me Persephone? Be my wife and queen?"

Persephone looked at Hades with all the love in her eyes and the biggest smile on her face. "Yes, of course, I'll marry you! How could I not marry my heart?"

Both Hades and Persephone embraced each other with pure love and happiness. Both of their destinies had been fulfilled, as they looked forward to having a future together.

However, Hecate's words haunted Hades' mind. *A deadly storm is coming.'* It's similar to what the Fates had warned him about as well. The only thing he could do now is protect Persephone from whatever danger comes their way. No matter the what it takes.

CHAPTER 11

DEMETER'S WRATH

Athena walked around the throne room in a trance-like state, letting her mind explore the possibilities of Persephone's whereabouts. Knowing her half-sister, and relying on her own wisdom, Athena had a certain feeling that Persephone was safe. Unfortunately Demeter was making everyone miserable, both gods and mortals alike, as she continued to search for her daughter. She had been crying and probing everywhere, in desperation. Searching every possible place where her beloved daughter might be, including the common areas that Persephone used to visit.

She talked to any person who would listen. Very quickly, Demeter's search was getting old. Not only were the gods tired of her frantic behavior and constant crying, but Demeter was starting to accuse people at random.

Recently, Demeter actually came to Athena for help. Since Demeter is merely a mother looking for her child, Athena didn't blame her for being mentally unhinged. Though, Demeter keeps forgetting that Persephone is no longer a child. How does anyone know for sure, including Athena herself, that Persephone was actually kidnapped to begin with?

Approaching her throne, which was second on the right of Zeus', Athena sat down slowly and with elegance. When she sat down, she thought something would happen. Like a missing piece of the puzzle that would reveal itself to her. She didn't know why, but Athena believed that the answer she was looking for had to be right here in the throne room.

Athena repeated to herself, "No one saw anything, yet it's impossible for Persephone to go off on her own without being noticed." Athena continued to walk around the throne room, she felt an answer coming to her gradually, but she was still missing a couple pieces to the puzzle.

Her mind went back to her memory of Persephone's initiation. It really was a lovely night. Everyone almost behaved themselves. Athena remembered the conversation that she had had with Persephone. Athena stopped pacing just then, as she recalled an odd moment from that night.

"Who was that?" Persephone asked.

*"Who was what?" Athena asked, as she looked in the
direction that Persephone had turned toward.*

"The god I was talking to."

*Athena looked at the throne and then back at
Persephone, confused. "There is no one there,
Persephone."*

Athena's eyes widened at this new revelation.
Retracing her steps, Athena tried to recall which spot
Persephone kept looking at, while talking about this god
she saw, as Athena dragged Persephone to see her father.

"Okay, it was right here," Athena said, placing herself
in the same spot they had been standing on the night of
Persephone's initiation. Athena now looked in the same
direction that Persephone had pointed out.

"He's sitting right on that throne," she pointed.

"Persephone. . . listen to me. That throne is empty."

Athena walked toward the throne, giving it a good
look. "Who sat here?" she asked herself out loud, trying to
remember who it might have been. Athena looked around
the throne room. Frowning, she realized that no one had
sat there in a really long time.

Replaying the memory in her head, Athena knew the
answer was there.

"There's no one there, Persephone."

"He's sitting right on that throne," she pointed.

"Persephone. . . Listen to me. That throne is empty."

She could have sworn on her immortal life that there was no one on the throne. There were only two ways for no one to see a person, "Either he was invisible, or he is dead," Athena said aloud. She gasped when she figured it out. "Hades. He has a throne here, but doesn't use it. He must have been wearing his invisibility helmet that night." Athena was excited—not only had she figured out who Persephone had talked to, but Athena guessed that they were probably together right now. "Except. . . how did Persephone see him? If Hades was there, but no one saw him until he had made his public entrance, then how did Persephone see him? It didn't make any sense. No one could see Hades when he wore his helmet, not even Zeus."

"Can't see who?" another voice asked, and Athena turned around to see Demeter walk into the throne room. Demeter looked like she knew where Persephone was.

"Demeter I think I know where Persephone is!"

"Really?" she said in a nice tone of voice that could make anyone tremble. "So do I. I really need to talk to Zeus. Before I see him, where do you think Persephone is?"

Athena hesitated. "I believe she is with Hades."

"Yes, it is Hades. I just found out as well. A mortal farmer told me what he saw. Hades kidnapped and raped my poor Persephone!"

Athena didn't want any false accusations against one of the major gods, "I don't think he did—"

Demeter shouted, "ZEUS!!! COME OUT AT ONCE!!!"

Zeus immediately manifested at Demeter's command. "You, woman, are lucky I love you. I could easily strike a lightning bolt in your direction!"

"No threat is going to frighten me. Your brother Hades has her! He has Persephone!"

Zeus just stared at Demeter, trying not to give any indication that he allowed Hades to take Persephone. "Are you sure?" he asked calmly.

"More than sure! I have two people who witnessed the whole event!" With Demeter shouting at the top of her lungs, many of the Olympians gathered in the throne room to see what the commotion was about. "A mortal man named Triptolemus saw Hades grab Persephone from the ground, snatch her, and raped her!"

Zeus couldn't believe what he was hearing. "You actually believe the words of a mortal? Demeter, you know how some human minds get if they see an immortal being."

"It's not just him." Demeter suddenly manifested the nymph, Cadence. "She also witnessed the crime." The poor nymph was shaking, knowing that she was in trouble. Cadence was in tears because she felt death approaching upon herself. "Did you know where my daughter was the whole time we were searching for her?"

"No, my lady, I only suspected where your daughter was," Cadence replied shamefully.

"Suspected? You are her closest friend. You should know almost everything about her, just as much as I do.

Even her secrets. Not only that, but you saw what happened."

"Persephone barely has any secrets to keep because she doesn't have any privacy. Still, I know one precious secret of hers, that she tried to hide from everyone. As to what I saw, it was only a glimpse."

"Well, out with it then!" Demeter demanded.

"I can't tell, my lady. Persephone made me swear on the River Styx to not tell anyone her secret."

"Well, it looks like you are going to break your oath, Cadence," Demeter countered coldly, "You are going to tell me her secret."

"My lady, you know it will cost me—"

"Your life? You should give up your life as a consequence for not protecting my daughter in the way that I wanted you to!"

Zeus sighed as he got up from his throne and walked toward the nymph. Zeus knew the nymph was doomed either way. She tells, she dies. If she doesn't say anything, then everyone will expect Zeus to punish her in some way. All the gods of Olympus were now watching to see what would happen next. "Tell me exactly what happened," Zeus urged.

Tears rolled down Cadence's face. "You know I'll die if I speak a word of this my Lord."

"I will abolish the oath," Zeus promised. "I can break it because you were forced to comply. Hence, it is not a real oath."

After Zeus used power to break her oath, Cadence's words flowed out like water. "Persephone is with Hades. They have been seeing each other for quite a while now. I don't know if it was free will, if she was put under some spell, or if she was forced, but I did see Hades grab Persephone."

Cadence silently nodded. At the thought of her daughter secretly seeing someone without her consent, Demeter looked pale. The fact that they are courting, out of all the gods there is, she chose him. Demeter couldn't accept that.

Apollo grunted, "This has to be a mistake. Why would someone who is so innocent and beautiful be courting Hades?"

"The answer is simple," Demeter replied angrily, as tears welled up in her eyes. "Like Cadence said, Hades is controlling her somehow. He took Persephone and now she's trapped in the Underworld." Athena looked at her father, wanting to say something.

Zeus received Athena's message—he needed to reveal his own secret. "Demeter it is not that simple. Hades came to me asking my permission for Persephone's hand in marriage. I agreed." Demeter truly felt utter rage coming over her. "Before you say anything, no, I didn't know

Hades had taken her until now. The matter being that he loves her; I have never seen him so in love like this before. So, I figured it was time for Hades to be happy."

"FOR HADES TO BE HAPPY? WHAT ABOUT MY HAPPINESS? MY DAUGHTER DOES NOT BELONG IN THE UNDERWORLD! SHE DOES NOT BELONG TO HIM! YOU WILL GET HER BACK! DO YOU UNDERSTAND, ZEUS!"

"REMEMBER WHO YOU ARE SPEAKING TO!" Zeus hollered back.

"Oh, I remember! Zeus, King of the Gods! Who is also a god himself. Who takes what he wants and, when he is finished, discards of the very thing he took! A god who doesn't really care about his children! Why? Because he has too many of them to count! I have only one daughter! One! And you gave her to the lowest being in our pantheon!," Demeter spat out in total anger. Her energy was now unbridled.

As Demeter spewed her rant, every god in Olympus rushed to the throne room, to take in such a sight. While looking at everyone present, Demeter decided to make Zeus a promising threat. She was determined to follow through with it, too. "You will bring my daughter back. If you don't, I will stop caring for the earth. The earth will be as frozen as my heart. The mortals will starve, and you will not be able to answer their prayers!" With that, Demeter teleported back to her cottage.

Everyone in the room stared at each other, not knowing what to do or say. Zeus closed his eyes, knowing that he now had a dangerous situation on his hands. No matter how he looked at the conflict, he felt like this was already an unattempted loss. No one was going to win anything from this.

Amongst the crowd, a voice mumbled, "Um." Everyone turned toward Apollo because he looked ready to speak. "You don't think she really means that? Do you?"

Athena nodded. "This is about her daughter, of course she means it. We have to prepare for the worst."

"We don't need to prepare for the worst. Just give Demeter her daughter back," Hera stated, "It is that simple."

Zeus shook his head with worry. "Hera, trust me when I say. . . it is not that simple. It's not that simple at all."

Demeter returned to her cottage in tears. Hades had kidnapped her daughter and no one, not even Zeus, wanted to help rescue Persephone. She felt betrayed by Zeus once again.

She went and opened the door to Persephone's room. The thing that haunted her the most is what Cadence had said. That her daughter had been seeing Hades for quite some time. Demeter looked around, hoping to find anything that might belong to Hades.

There was nothing. Nothing in the jewelry box, or Persephone's closet, under her bed, nor her dresser. Demeter was beginning to think that either Persephone had taken everything with her when she left, or that Hades had never given her any gifts. Demeter was just about to leave the room, when she stepped on a peculiar floorboard. It sounded empty, so she tapped it with her foot. "It's hollow."

Kneeling to the floor, Demeter found a crack in the wood that she held onto as she lifted up the board. When she removed it, Demeter saw a golden chest underneath. Demeter took the chest from its secret compartment and stared at it, afraid of what its contents might be. Demeter prayed to the universe that there was nothing of importance inside the chest, even though she knew better. Persephone obviously took great pains to keep this a secret.

Using her powers, Demeter destroyed the lock and opened the chest slowly. To her surprise, there was nothing there. It was empty. Frustrated and confused, she flung the treasure chest across the floor. The chest bounced, making its secret contents spill out. The invisible charm that Persephone had placed on the chest was no longer effective. Demeter's eyes widened as she looked at Persephone's secret stockpile of gifts. Dazzling jewels and various silk fabrics, including a cloak and dress, were scattered about. There were also pouches that contained several pieces of jewelry. Everything in this chest screamed of Hades' essence and power. Demeter concluded that this must have been going on for quite a while.

Demeter started to boil again with anger. Her decision was final. With her daughter still gone, she refused to take care of the planet's harvest. Demeter went outside, letting her hands touch the ground to retrieve her powers from the earth. It would now wither away on its own. To make things worse for everyone, she also let the weather turn so cold that snow started to fall. "You will be frozen, like my heart. Only pain and suffering will come without mercy."

In the distance, farmers who gathered crops were surprised to feel a strong gust of cold air, as snow began to fall. Winter had come without mercy or warning. For the mortals though, they were unprepared, and their current stocks were bare for the upcoming winter. This seasonal change had arrived during their harvest, so the unexpected coldness would likely kill most of their newly planted crops.

Before they knew it, mortals were already running out of food. Soon, famine took place as mortals committed criminal sprees. People tried to find any available food.

When their survival instincts take over, mortals act more like monsters instead of people.

Most people perform horrific deeds in order to survive, while few visit the temples of the gods, praying with all their heart. At first, people prayed to Demeter, since this was her area of expertise. They figured that if they prayed and brought more gifts to her temple, then this unmerciful winter would be destroyed. Unfortunately for the mortals, Demeter kept her word and refused to give up her wrath. Soon their prayers fell onto deaf ears, because the goddess they prayed to only cared about one thing. She wanted her daughter back, no matter the cost.

Meanwhile at Olympus, Zeus heard every mortal prayer and discovered that most of them were asking for food. He then knew that Demeter had caused their suffering. She kept her word as promised, which forced everyone to endure the consequences.

Zeus heard their prayers, their cries, and their curses. He also heard mortal screams of sadness when someone had passed away from starvation. Brought to tears, Zeus needed to resolve this situation rather abruptly, or else the human race would become extinct.

CHAPTER 12

OVERLOAD

A call woke Hades from his peaceful slumber. He glanced at Persephone, who was still asleep beside him, with a beautiful smile on her face. Other than her breathing, she did not make a sound. At first, he thought he had dreamed the call until he heard it again. He heard not a voice, but a vibration of energy calling to him. He knew this call all too well. It was the Underworld itself reaching out to him. Ever since he had inherited the Underworld, not only did he know of its secrets, but Hades could also feel its own emotions and needs. Like the Underworld was a living being itself. When it calls for Hades, it usually means that new souls have arrived without his knowledge. However, he felt like there was something wrong about this particular group of shades.

He looked down at his beloved who was still sleeping, apparently exhausted from their exquisite lovemaking. Hades hated to leave Persephone and have her wake up alone, but he was being summoned by a potent force. As Hades put on the last of his armor, Persephone began to stir. She began to realize that she was now alone in the bed. Hades moved closer to his bed, leaning down to kiss Persephone on the forehead as she went back to sleep. Quietly sneaking out of their bedchamber, Hades instantly teleported himself to the judgment panel.

No word could describe what Hades saw when he arrived at the panel. Hundreds, if not thousands, of souls needed to be judged and placed somewhere at once. This circumstance usually happens when there is a war going on. To Hades' knowledge, there wasn't any outbreak of war at the moment. *What caused all this death?* he asked himself.

He noticed that Charon was anxious, because he was still pushing his boat filled with souls and was nowhere near done delivering them all. "My lord! What's going on? Did Ares stir up a surprise war that no one knew about?"

"If that is the reason, then I'm going to have more than just a few words with my nephew!" Hades growled. His emotions were running high; he was going to need some help. Hades needed all of his judges and servants to help maintain order in the judging process. Every soul must be calm before they could be judged. The souls were crying and were wondering what had happened to them. There were so many of them, that the souls couldn't be cleansed from the river in a timely manner. Most of them were more than terrified. Despite seeing many beautiful charms within the Underworld, the shades still feared the worst. Especially since some of these places contained human remains.

Trying to keep his emotions in check from watching such an unpleasant sight unfold, Hades took a deep breath. It would likely take long hours, and possibly days, before everyone faced their judgement.

"Oh, my—" Hades heard Persephone behind him. She had woken up wondering where Hades had gone. Persephone did not expect to see this at all. If she was going to see Hades judge, she thought that at least three or five souls would be present. Taking in this ghastly sight, Persephone gasped, "Look at all of them! What happened?"

"Persephone, darling you don't want to see this. Go back to the bedchamber!"

"What happened to them, Hades? Have you ever seen so much death? I see nothing but sorrow and pain."

"I know, my love. I will be judging them, so I'll soon find out what created this massive overload. Now go back to the bedchamber."

"No, I need to stay." Determined, Persephone wanted to know for herself what had created this monstrosity.

Hades looked at her stubbornly, "Persephone, please listen to me and go back to bed. I'll be judging every person, and they'll go where they need to be, despite what brought them all here in the first place." *I don't want you to hate me,* he thought.

"I know that."

"You will not like some of the things I must do."

"I know, and I understand that it is part of your job. Let me see this." She pleaded, not only with her tone of voice, but also with her eyes. "You cannot protect me forever, Hades" Persephone gently whispered to her lover, letting him know that she was going to be okay.

Having reached an understanding, Hades toughened up. At that moment, he realized that if Persephone were to be Queen of the Underworld, she was going to see these things eventually. In fact, she might even judge mortals herself. His own behavior quickly reminded Hades of Demeter. He wanted to protect his beloved, shielding her from any unfavorable situations. He stopped himself, though. Hades wanted to be proud of Persephone and make her feel secure. He didn't want to give into the temptation of treating her like a delicate flower, hiding her from the world.

"Okay, my love. I'll get you your own throne next to mine, and you will observe what I do."

Using his power, Hades manifested a throne as magnificent as his own. It was the same size, but it had

more jewels than his, so that it looked more feminine.
Persephone smiled at what Hades had created for her. She
slowly sat upon her new throne, feeling like Queen of the
Underworld, despite the fact that she didn't have such a
title yet. Hades sat right next to her, and as they looked at
each other, they shared a silent comfort. They both knew
that everything would be okay, or at least they hoped it
would be. "This is going to be a very long day," Hades
muttered under his breath, as Persephone held his hand
with their fingers intertwined. Off to the side, Hades saw
his three judges sitting down, while the servant shades kept
the souls in line. Cerberus was on full alert, making sure
that no soul escaped.

Hades let go of Persephone's hand just then, as he
put on his game face. He sat emotionless, like he always
does during judgment. Persephone held her breath as the
first soul of the day came toward the judging panel.

This soul was a middle-aged man who felt like he was
not supposed to be here. He believed that he still had more
years ahead of himself. Hades looked at his scroll. As a
mortal, he had been a decent man. He was a farmer whose
luck had run out on him, twice, thus creating trouble for
his family. Looking at Hades without fear, this man was
surprised—much like everyone else who comes to the
judgement panel—that Hades was not the mean old man
everyone claimed him to be. "My lord Hades, may I
speak?"

"You may," Hades responded and Persephone's interest piqued.

"My lord, is it possible for me to return to my old life? I still have a family to raise and they need someone to provide for them."

"I'm sorry," Hades looked at him with little sorrow, "There is no going back. It is nothing personal and you didn't do anything wrong. Rather, it's the rules of nature and a law that must be obeyed."

"Please!" the man begged, "I have to provide my family! All of my crops were ruined and I died! How will my family survive? They probably used the last of our money to give me a proper burial, or else I would not be here!"

Persephone felt the man's distress and understood the situation at hand. She touched Hades' shoulder and asked: "Is there any way this man can go back for just a little while?"

"Persephone," Hades started very calmly, "all souls beg for something—whether it's to go back, have mercy, pity, or a lesser punishment if they can get it. This, unfortunately, is part of the judgment process my darling. As their judge, I'll listen to whatever they need to say. Can their words change my persuasions? Possibly. Can I grant everyone's wish? No, or else everyone will think that they can do whatever they want, if I give in to every request. Going back is something I will not grant upon any soul.

Not only does it break the laws of nature, but it can have devastating consequences for most mortals who will witness it."

"Should it not?" Persephone asked, raising her eyebrows. "You mean it's possible, but it is not a good thing?"

Hades gently placed his hand on Persephone's lips. "We will talk about this later." Hades turned his attention back to the man. "I'm sorry, but there's no going back. I understand your death was. . . unexpected." Hades looked at the scroll with confusion on his face. "You died from starvation?"

"Yes sir, I. . . When it comes to food, my children come first. I sacrificed myself so that they could eat."

Persephone felt tears threatening to roll down her face, as Hades made his decision. Speaking in an authoritative voice, "You will go to the Elysian Fields. As for your family, since you can't go back, I'll make sure that they'll have some money to live a stable life."

"Thank you, sir." The man let out a sigh of relief as another shade guided him to the Elysian Fields.

Hades saw that Persephone was still wiping away tears from her eyes. "Are you alright, my love?" Hades was slightly concerned that this might chase her away.

"I'm fi-ne," she sobbed. Persephone tried to stop crying. "How can you do this every day? That was just one soul, and I'm already a mess."

"Love, this is your first judging session. It is a hard thing to do, but you'll get used to it."

"Does it get easier?"

"To be honest, no." Hades had a look of sadness in his eyes, "It's more like you develop a tougher skin and just soldier through it."

"I guess that's why you wear thick black armor."

"Remember this Persephone: sometimes mortals end up where they do because of their actions. They put themselves in these situations, but I always check to see what their previous circumstances and experiences were like, including their regrets. I always take everything into account. This is something your father would never understand about mortals."

Before another soul came forward to be judged, Hades looked at Persephone. "To answer your question my love, about a shade returning to earth, do you remember what I said about having some freedom for those who are in the Isle of the Blessed?"

Persephone nodded, showing Hades that she had paid attention to what he said, "If a shade wants to visit their loved ones on Earth, with my permission, they are allowed to do so. But, after a certain amount of time, they have to return back to this realm. This is a privilege for the shades, I know, so they must follow the rules when it comes to living mortals. Though not all shades follow those rules, so it sometimes causes damage, whether intentional or not. To give a soul that privilege, I need to know the soul personally."

"The man just wanted to see his family, Hades." Persephone insisted.

"He will, in due time. Right now, he needs to understand and adjust to the reality that he is dead. He'll be able to watch over them when he knows what to do as a spirit."

Just then, a little girl approached the panel. She looked like she was only ten years old or so. This girl had died from starvation too, which was apparent just by looking at her skeletal frame. Again, Persephone's heart softened at the sight of this dead child. As Hades read through her life scroll, Persephone immediately called out, "Elysian Fields!"

Hades looked at his love in stunned disbelief, because she had decided to pass judgment without his consent. The child gave Persephone a relieved smile, while Hades tried to put everything on pause. "Hold on, dear girl, we are not yet finished," Hades told the child. Still sitting on their thrones, Hades shifted himself so that he could whisper into Persephone's ear, "Persephone! What are you doing? I haven't even seen her life in its entirety yet, and you already passed the child onto her final destination without me!"

"Hades, I saw it clear as day. This child is innocent, and she starved to death."

Hades looked down at the scroll. "It says she's been stealing."

"Probably food, just by looking at her. Besides, my love, I can see her life in flashes."

That grabbed Hades' attention even more, "What do you mean?"

"I don't need to read the scroll to see her past life. I look at her, and I see it. My love, she was only stealing food because she was hungry. It was her last resort. As a goddess who's lived on Earth, I know that sometimes people must make difficult choices to survive. They do this when they think that there is no other choice. She didn't mean to hurt anyone. She only took what she needed."

Hades looked at his beloved Persephone in awe. He knew right then and there that she was truly meant to be Queen of the Underworld. "Well then, my love, proceed."

Persephone smiled at Hades and looked at the girl again. "As I said earlier, before I was rudely interrupted. . ." she quickly gave Hades her signature smirk. Hades wanted to burst out in laughter because Persephone appeared to have taken on this authoritative role a bit too well. "You may now go to the Elysian Fields. May you find happiness there, free from all of your sufferings."

The little girl smiled once again before leaving with another shade to help guide her toward eternal happiness. The girl went up to Persephone and hugged her, "Thank you!" Persephone smiled, feeling a sense of purpose wash over her. Even though the girl was dead, Persephone had given another mortal some peace and happiness. Hades couldn't believe what he was seeing, not once had a mortal ever come up to hug a judge. Not only that, but the girl also went to Hades and gave him a hug as well. Hades couldn't fathom what was happening. In a very calm and steady manner, he wrapped his arms around the girl to reciprocate the hug. For once, a mortal didn't look at him in fear, but rather, she seemed thankful. "Please, god Hades, this is my prayer: I hope that my mommy and daddy can come to the Elysian Fields too."

A tear escaped from one of Hades' eyes. His first prayer ever; no one had dared to pray to him before. When faced with judgement, mortals have always pleaded with Hades. They never bothered to pray for someone else who is still on Earth.

"Well, little one, I'll take your prayer into consideration when your parents come see me." Then, the little girl stepped off the judgment panel and went with a shade toward the Elysian Fields.

Hades gave himself a minute to absorb that moment. Persephone looked at him, smiling, "Your first prayer."

He smiled, feeling content. "All because of you. You've already made this place so much better, my love. With your warmth and kindness."

"Hades, I felt a sense of meaning and worth after judging that girl. I did my job and, at the same time, I loved it. I didn't realize how rewarding this job could be."

Nodding in agreement, Hades smiled because Persephone was finally starting to see how death can be a beautiful thing. "The work that I do can be very rewarding at times. What you just did, those are the good moments. They give me purpose and add meaning to my life."

Hades and Persephone continued to judge soul after soul. Some souls ventured to the Elysian Fields, while most went to the Asphodel Meadows. Others were reincarnated and very few went to Tartarus. However, both Hades and Persephone found a pattern to the death toll of so many mortals. Feeling knots in her stomach, Persephone said, "Hades I think I know why there were so many deaths."

"I think I know, too. It all has to do with food scarcity."

"Including the cold temperature," Persephone said and closed her eyes, feeling ashamed. "I think this is my mother's doing."

Hades didn't want Persephone to believe this, but even he had his own suspicions. "Yes, I believe so. I'll have to visit Earth to see if our suspicions are correct."

Just then a soul came up to the judging panel. This man gave Persephone a strong sense of animosity. The man had a cruel smirk on his face. Hades could already tell that this was not a kind soul—even he did not like the man's energy. Hades also didn't like the way this soul was staring at Persephone, looking like a starved dog. As Hades read over the scroll, he saw all the crimes that this soul had committed, with the most recent one being pathetic and inexcusable. This soul had stolen food from families and then sold it for a higher price.

With a trace of anger in his voice, Hades talked down to the man, "Anything you want to say on your behalf!"

"Why?" The man smirked again, almost proud of himself. "What does my scroll say about me?"

"It tells me every crime that you've committed. Robbery, cheating, murder, and even rape."

"Well, my Lord! Aren't you proud of my handiwork?"

Hades looked at him with anger and disbelief, "What is this nonsense?"

"Aren't you going against your brother? To take over Olympus and let evil rule over the world? I thought I'd be your best soldier when the time is right."

"You executed all these crimes . . . for me?" Hades said in disgust.

The man nodded. He was waiting for the most-feared god among the Olympians to praise his work.

Persephone's eyes went back and forth between this corrupted shade and her beloved. "Hades, what is he talking about?"

Hades stood up from his throne to face this man in a threatening stance. "I do not intend to attack Olympus, not now nor in the future. I did not ask you to carry out these crimes! Not by you or anyone else for that matter! Where in your mind do you believe that I wanted these crimes to happen?"

"You're the King of the Underworld! Everyone knows that you are the most-feared and the most horrible god of all! Including your own family!"

"Just because I rule over the dead and one of the most mysterious realms of the world, doesn't mean that I want humankind to suffer and die! Do you know how much work that is for me?"

"YOU CAN'T FOOL ME! I know you are the darkest god of all! Look at how much death has occurred! Very few mortals heard a rumor that you kidnapped the goddess Persephone! And there she is!" He pointed directly at the young goddess who had been quiet throughout the entire conversation. "Only someone with a dark heart can take someone so beautiful and keep her prisoner!" The other shades behind him whispered and pointed as they heard the conversation unfold.

Persephone wasn't going to stand for any of that. "I think it's me you should be afraid of! I am not a prisoner! I am the future Queen of the Underworld! For all of your crimes, I'm sending you to Tartarus!"

Two shade servants grabbed the soul by each of his arms. He started shrieking to Persephone, "YOU ARE THE REASON WE ARE DEAD! YOUR MOTHER MADE US

STARVE TO DEATH! SHE ABANDONED THE EARTH BECAUSE YOU WERE GONE! YOU ARE THE REASON ALL OF US ARE HERE! THE WORLD IS IN TROUBLE BECAUSE OF YOU!"

Hades went to Persephone and held her, not caring who saw. "I will go to Earth after we finish here. I will find out exactly what happened. Please ignore that shade's words, my love. Don't let them bother you."

"But, what if he's right?" Persephone looked at Hades with worry and sadness. He then kissed her, providing Persephone with his comfort and love. The last thing they heard from the shade were his torturous screams as he entered Tartarus.

Hades suddenly remembered what The Fates had said about Persephone. *"She is your equal, your match. . . be cautious with her, Hades! She, too, brings death as well as life whenever she's with you."* Hades closed his eyes at the memory. What the Fates had predicted was correct.

CHAPTER 13

THE POMEGRANATE

With the overload of souls in the Underworld, Hades needed to know what was happening on Earth. The corrupted shade's harsh words about the death toll being Persephone's fault ate away at him. After enduring days of judgment with his love, most of the souls had found their new fate. He decided to let his judges finish the rest, while he visited Earth.

Hades went to his carriage, ready to put on his invisible helmet. He then felt a gentle hand on his arm. "Can I go with you?" Persephone asked.

Hades smiled sadly, "My love, if that filthy shade is right, I don't want you to be upset."

"I know you are trying to protect me, but. . ."

"I am protecting you too much, like your mother." Hades understood that he was really beginning to cross the line between being Persephone's parental figure and partner.

He stared into her eyes and, not saying another word, nodded for her to mount his chariot. She smiled softly as Hades wrapped his arm around her and motioned for the chariot to move. Feeling a rush of air blow past, Persephone held on tightly to both Hades and the chariot, while they exited the Underworld through a separate entrance in the earth.

Icy-cold air hit Persephone as the chariot made its way toward the top of the earth. She was already shivering, totally unprepared for the immediate climate change. Hades instantly took off his cloak and wrapped it around her body. Luckily, because he was wearing his thick black armor, Hades was immune to the cold weather. "I wasn't thinking," Persephone said as she looked at him apologetically.

"We will only be here for a couple of minutes," Hades claimed. He looked at their surroundings with both determination and horror on his face. Persephone followed suit when she saw how white and frozen the earth had become so quickly.

"Hades, it looks like winter has been here for months. I was only gone for a couple of weeks."

"Your mother wants to punish everyone, just because. . ."

". . . Because I wanted to have love and freedom," Persephone said, finishing his sentence as she shed a tear for her mother's wrath. "It is my fault. The earth is like this because of me."

While looking at Persephone, Hades snarled, "Don't you dare think that any of this is your fault. Your mother is the one to blame." He pointed at the scene that stretched out before them. "She caused this!"

"But I'm the reason! If I never left. . .," Persephone couldn't finish her sentence because she knew the real truth.

"If you never left, you would have been miserable and would be forced to live as a virgin goddess for eternity." Hades finished her final thought, as Persephone closed her eyes in defeat. More tears raced down her face. He held her in a loving embrace. "No matter what you would've decided my love, your mother still would have caused misery upon Earth."

"The mortals paid a heavy price for our love," Persephone admitted, woefully. Hades nodded in silence. "Can we go home now? I've seen enough."

Hades' heart swelled, knowing that Persephone now considered the Underworld her home, with him included. "Yes, my love, let's go home," Hades said and then directed her back onto the chariot.

"What are we going to do about my mother?"

"I honestly don't know. We have to think of something fast, though, because I can't stand to have endless days of judgement or for mortal extinction to continue."

"Hades, I don't want to go back to her," Persephone said. Hades looked at the fear in her eyes. "I love you and . . . . . ."

Grabbing her face with his hands, Hades made sure that she was looking in his eyes. "Listen to me . . . You. Are. Not. Going. Back. If you go back, then your mother wins, and you'll go back to being imprisoned again. As for me. . ." Hades paused to say the unthinkable. "Living once more in solitude would be unbearable. I'd rather not exist than live an eternity without you."

"I pray that's not possible, but the same goes for me as well." Persephone sighed as they started moving back toward the Underworld.

"THIS IS A DISASTER!" Zeus roared as he threw a wine goblet across his bedroom. As a result of Zeus' apparent anger, lightning bolts flashed across the sky. He had no idea what to do with the whole Hades, Persephone, and Demeter situation.

Hera came walking into the room just then, with a charge in her step. She didn't understand what the issue seemed to be for Zeus. "What is a disaster? Is this about Hades and Persephone? My dear husband, I don't know what the problem is. Simply return little Persephone to Demeter, and she'll stop this madness. Once that is done, then everything will return to its rightful order."

"It's not that simple," Zeus grunted.

"Zeus! It has been a few weeks since Persephone disappeared. I'm sure that, when Hermes retrieves her as per your orders, Hades will be tired of her by then. I'm sure that he will have had his fill of everything that he lusted after."

Zeus began to laugh miserably. "You, my dear wife, have mistaken him for me. Hades isn't like me or Poseidon, nor Ares or Apollo, or most gods, for that matter. Once he finds an interest in a woman, he becomes serious about her. When it comes to matters of the heart, my brother takes it very seriously. Hades will not let Persephone go without a fight."

"I still don't see the conflict. You are King of the Gods! You can force him to hand over Persephone."

"Hera, no matter what decision I make, I'll lose something important."

Feelings of concern hit Hera like a splash of water. "How? So far, the only concern I see is that if Demeter continues to neglect caring for the earth, she will further hinder mortal livability. We would cease to exist in the eyes of mortals."

Looking at Hera with defeated eyes, Zeus needed to confess about how powerful his elder brother can be, "We need the Underworld's support."

"Why?"

"You know about the ambrosia we drink every hundred years or so?"

"Yes, and?"

"Guess where the flower used for ambrosia comes from."

"The Underworld? But that's not possible. Nothing grows in the Underworld."

"Not true. The Underworld not only has the ambrosia Lotus flower, but it also has connections to The Fates, other dimensions, and the Tree of Life." Hera froze in anger as she absorbed what her husband was saying.

"You mean to tell me that, despite having Olympus and you being King of the Gods, Hades has the real power?!"

"Why do you think Hades had no complaints about inheriting the Underworld? Why do you think he hardly ever comes here? There is a real, ancient power that he guards and protects. A power that most gods and mortals alike don't even know about." Hera began pacing angrily because her ego as Queen of the Gods was not as big as she thought it was. "By the way, we still have a powerful reign, my queen. I can still create life, while taking charge of the earth and its people, accordingly."

"Yet, in the end, my king, everything dies and it will all go to Hades," Hera declared. Zeus' head hung low, "Everyone thought he got the short end of the stick, including me!" Hera shook her head, "What a cosmic joke! You better have a serious talk with your brother. Until then, send Hermes to fetch Persephone and bring her to Demeter. That will put an end to Demeter's madness. Hopefully, we'll find a solution to all of this problematic drama!"

Zeus suddenly felt a headache coming on. He hoped to find a solution soon. For once, the King of the Gods didn't know how to get out of this situation. Zeus felt like the only people bound to lose in this circumstance was himself and Persephone. Telepathically, Zeus called for Hermes and Athena.

Hermes was always the first to come when needed. He's very fast. After all, that's why he is the messenger of the gods. "Father, you summoned me?" Zeus turned around to look at Hermes and saw his daughter coming toward them as well.

Zeus nodded, "Go to the Underworld and bring Persephone here, now."

"But what about—"

"Tell Hades it's urgent. If he insists on coming with her, then let him. If he intends on keeping her there, I'll go and grab her myself!" Zeus commanded firmly. On the inside, he felt anxious. Hermes instantly bowed and flew out of Olympus before anyone could blink.

Athena stepped forward. "Father, you called me."

Zeus nodded. "I have. I need your advice and wisdom right now. In this current circumstance, I'm caught in a spider's web with my daughter. I feel that, no matter what I do. . . I lose everything that matters. Regardless of what decision I make, the whole thing will come crumbling down. I must explain to you about the kind of power that Hades has."

"You don't need to explain. I have already guessed why, each time someone gets initiated, we always need Hades here. He has the ambrosia."

Zeus frowned. "How did you kn—"

"The initiations are the only events that you truly force Hades to attend with us, without question. For other occasions, you're not as adamant with him about showing up. Sometimes, you let him miss out altogether. As for this situation, father, we must talk to Persephone. Only she knows what truly happened and how she feels about it. Right now, we don't have a better option. So, let's be patient while we wait for Persephone to arrive."

"It doesn't matter what Persephone feels. Her mother still wants her back."

"Well, Demeter needs to realize that her daughter is not a little girl anymore. She should have accepted that fact the moment Persephone was initiated. And when her daughter started to take an interest in men."

"I don't think Demeter is capable of seeing reason or logic, right now. There's no way for her to change her mind anytime soon," Zeus asserted.

"We will see what she thinks once her daughter is back in her arms," Athena said with reassurance. They both waited patiently for Hermes to return with the goddess who had caused so much trouble among the mortals and gods.

Wanting to forget the images in her head, Persephone was trying to relax on the edge of a cave-like pool near the corner of Hades' castle. She placed her feet in the water and let its coolness soothe her. As Persephone stared out at the water in a trance-like state, all she continued to see was the frozen earth and all of the souls that Hades had judged. What a mess her mother had created. There were a plethora of souls that still needed to be judged, but the majority of them had been tended to. Both Hades and Persephone needed a merited break from judging.

Suddenly a big splash startled Persephone. She was so lost in thought, that she hadn't heard Hades dive into the water, and now he was swimming toward her. She blushed as she saw that Hades was naked in the water. Persephone could even see his pale skin glowing against the dark blue water. As he rose from the water, Persephone followed every droplet that traveled down his perfectly toned, pale body, which seemed to glow in the reflection of the torch lights.

"Now that I know you are truly the ruler of Tartarus, you sure know how to torture people," Persephone said while her eyes sparkled mischievously.

Hades grinned, "How so?"

"Well look at what you are doing now!"

"What exactly am I doing, Persephone?" Hades pretended to act innocently.

"Showing off such pure perfection of the male body, which I'd like to think, all things considered, now belongs to me."

With his eyes fixed upon Persephone, Hades waded closer to her as he tried to stare her down seductively. Now he was her predator and she was his prey. As Hades grabbed a hold of her foot that was submerged in the water, Persephone realized what he was about to do. "No, Hades," she pleaded, but Hades just smirked as he ran his hand up to her shin. "Don't even think about—" Persephone screamed with delight as Hades flashed a smile and dragged her into the pool.

Persephone emerged from the water, taking a deep breath, "Why did you do that?"

Hades just smiled as he began peeling her drenched dress away from her body. One of Persephone's hands touched his chest. "To let you know that this god, whose body you want to claim, is already yours."

Gazing at his lover's body, Hades made her blush again. "I'll never get used to your body. I doubt that I'll ever get used to you looking at me like this," Persephone admitted.

"Trust me, love, eventually this will all become second nature to you. I hope you won't grow tired of it later on."

She looked at him skeptically, "I highly doubt it. My blood blazes when I see you." Just then, Hades grabbed her and gently pulled Persephone underwater, with him in tow. While underwater together, he brought his lips to hers and they shared a very passionate kiss. Persephone was thrilled, and even more so, when Hades hooked his body to hers. Within a minute, they both come up for air and Hades pinned her against the pool's wall.

Persephone felt his power and domination reigning over her body, which excited her more. Still in the water, Hades quickly enveloped her with a greedy thrust. She screamed out in pleasure, as his thrusts became more urgent and violently strong. Captivated by their desires for each other, the lovers didn't notice that Zoe had entered the space. She averted her eyes as they both moaned through their climaxes. Hades grabbed Persephone's lips with his once more, as their bodies relaxed from the height of their lovemaking.

"My Lord and lady?" Zoe said, interrupting their moment.

Hades, for once, wanted to hurt anyone who intruded upon their time together. Hades gave Zoe a deadly glare. "What is it, Zoe?"

"Hermes is here to see you."

Hades and Persephone looked at each other with concern in their eyes. Their fears were now becoming a reality because they knew why Hermes had come to the Underworld.

"Thank you, Zoe," Hades said somberly as he stepped out of the pool, not caring who saw his body, and put on his robe. Persephone watched with worry as he offered her his hand to help her out the pool. "Come my darling, let's face our fears while standing our ground." Persephone nodded as she stepped out of the pool. Hades covered her in a robe and wrapped his arms around her, not wanting to let Persephone go. She could feel his determination, and Hades could feel her nervousness. "Don't worry, my love. I won't let your mother or your father break up our relationship." Persephone closed her eyes and sighed as she laid her head on Hades' shoulder. She prayed that he was right.

Hermes was in the center of the throne room. This was the first time that Hades had kept him waiting, which was very out of character for the King of the Underworld.

When it came to Hermes' uncle, he was all about business and getting things done in a timely manner. Especially with everything he must do for the Underworld.

Then Hermes saw Hades enter swiftly, almost as if he were ready to attack, if that's what the situation called for. Hermes realized that he needed to deliver this news with caution. "Hello, Hades."

"Sorry to keep you waiting. I've been . . . preoccupied." He said with a smile that surprised Hermes.

"So I've heard. It must be true then—you have Persephone and you married her."

"Not yet, but it's in the stars, and we are both looking forward to our special day." Hermes was shocked to see that his uncle was happy for the first time ever. For once, Hermes hated to deliver a message that would undoubtedly bring miserable consequences, especially for Hades.

"Then you know the reason why I'm here."

Hades' smile suddenly disappeared. "Let me guess, Demeter is having a fit about her missing daughter and she wants Persephone back. So now, she has complained to Zeus and has made a mess on Earth, which has distressed the mortals."

"You knew what was going on?"

"Of course I did, Hermes! Who do you think judged so many souls that either died from starvation or from hypothermia?! Only Demeter is responsible for all of this.

She has no idea of the damage she caused because of her little fit!"

"Little? Hades you took Demeter's only daughter who she loves more than anything. How do you think she was going to react?"

"And I love her more than anything. Persephone is going to be my wife, and she loves me just the same."

Hermes looked at him and smiled, "I'm so glad that you found happiness Hades, but the truth is, I'm delivering a message from Zeus. Persephone needs to return to her mother." While Hermes was talking to Hades, he had no idea the Persephone was also in the room, listening to their entire conversation. She was hiding behind one of the pillars.

Hades stared at Hermes, "You already know what my answer is."

"This is a direct order from the King of the Gods, Hades. I'm not asking for permission." Persephone felt her heart start to panic. Once she returned to her mother, Persephone knew that she would never see Hades again. They're not married yet, so her mother could still take her away.

"Tell your king that I can make threats too!" Hades replied, "The gods of Olympus can't live without support from the Underworld." Hermes looked confused. "Don't worry, Zeus knows what I'm talking about. You are the messenger of the gods, so that will be my message to him."

"You do understand that if you keep Persephone, Demeter will continue to neglect caring for the earth. Then, you will have to judge more souls until there are none left. What will you tell Persephone about all the deaths that have happened because of her disappearance?"

Persephone felt guilt eating away at her. She couldn't stand to listen any longer, so she finally revealed herself to Hermes. Seeing that Persephone had been there the entire time, Hermes' eyes grew wide. Hades looked in her direction. "Tell my mother that I'm happy where I am. I miss her, but I have no interest in returning."

Hermes approached her. "Persephone, this is an order from your father. You have to leave the Underworld."

Persephone shook her head as a tear escaped her eye. "Hermes, you know what will happen if I return to her."

"Not necessarily. Your father just needs to sort this out so that your mother will calm down."

"In the end, she will win with her crazy antics. Father will give in to her because he'll feel guilty for not choosing her as his queen. You know this, Hermes. I'm sure you also know about what she did when Apollo and Ares tried to court me."

"I know, Persephone, but you forget that I'm just a messenger. I have no power in this. This is an order from Zeus as King of the Gods, not as your father, and you need to go."

Persephone began to walk away, letting some of her tears flow, unseen from Hermes and Hades. She knew what would happen once she stepped foot outside of the Underworld. Going back to Olympus would be like saying goodbye to Hades forever. Hades went to Persephone then, embracing her with his strong arms and kissed her forehead. As he was hugging her, Persephone looked over his shoulder and saw a small table by Hades' throne. There was a bowl full of pomegranates sitting on top of the table.

"Don't you have somewhere you need to be?" Hades snapped at Hermes.

Hermes frowned, "I'm sorry, my lord, but I can't leave until Persephone is with me so that I can deliver her to Zeus. That's part of my orders."

Persephone stepped out of Hades' embrace, and walked toward the bowl of pomegranates. She felt that it held an answer for her. Hades continued to threaten Hermes, trying to keep his beloved in the Underworld. "Tell Zeus that if I have to create war on Olympus to keep my betrothed, then I will! I won't lose her without a fight!"

Picking up a pomegranate, Persephone knew the possible consequences of eating anything that came from the Underworld. She also knew that the outcome might work in her favor this time. One bite was all she needed. She turned around and looked at Hermes and her love. "I won't go down without a fight either!" Persephone said adamantly, which garnered both Hades' and Hermes' attention.

Hades looked at her with wide eyes when he saw the pomegranate in her hand. "PERSEPHONE, NO!" Hades ran over to the throne, wanting to stop her.

Persephone quickly took a bite from the pomegranate and swallowed it. After consuming six seeds all at once, her throat burned instantly. Then she started shaking; her body felt like it was on fire. "Hades, what is happening to me?"

Hades closed his eyes in sorrow, "Your body is being tied to the Underworld . . . permanently. Oh, Persephone! Why did you do that?"

"You know why," Persephone said in a weak voice.

"Now you have cursed yourself, my love, and you have to stay here for all eternity. You are never to see the earth, Olympus, or your mother ever again."

Persephone nodded, "I accept that if it means staying here with you."

For Hades, this was the first time someone sacrificed something on his behalf. Persephone chose him above all others. As the sight of Persephone's faithful act of love, silent tears welled up in Hades' eyes. Hermes didn't know what to make of it, other than knowing that Zeus would not be pleased because now there was yet another conflict added to the family drama.

"Well, Hermes," Hades said gently this time. "You'll have to return to Olympus empty-handed. Tell my brother that his daughter can no longer leave the Underworld voluntarily because of the ancient law about eating food from the Underworld. Therefore, she'll stay here forever."

Hermes was still processing what had just happened, but what Hades said was true. Persephone could no longer leave the Underworld. He'll have to tell Zeus. Hermes nodded as he flew off to Olympus, knowing that there would be a lightning storm tonight.

CHAPTER 14

ZEUS' DECISION

Once Zeus heard about Persephone staying in the Underworld forever, he knew that things were now more complicated. However, using his power as King of the Gods, he overthrew ancient law so that Persephone could come to Olympus. Then, everyone could discuss the conflict at hand.

"I still can't believe you ate the pomegranate," Hades said, almost whispering as they made their way toward the throne room of Olympus. They held hands as he and his love walked heavily together, both anxious about what would happen next.

Persephone looked at Hades with determination, "It was the only way for us to be together, and my mother will have no other choice but to accept this. What she's doing to the earth and its mortals is very selfish."

"Even if it means being in the Underworld for all eternity?"

Persephone stopped in her tracks, including Hades too, as she looked at him with love and longing in her eyes. "Yes. I've wanted to be with you ever since I first saw you at my initiation. You're all I want, Hades. You make me happy and, because of you, I am strong. You allow me to be myself without judgment." She reached one of her hands up to caress his face. "I love you, Hades. Even though I find it ironic that the only thing that makes me feel alive is the Lord of Death and the Underworld."

The King of the Underworld felt a tear wanting to escape his eye. His heart was bursting with happiness because he finally felt with confidence that Persephone was now genuinely his mate and queen. He bent his head down to capture her lips as they poured their love into a kiss. Hades held on to her as their kiss became desperate. Then they heard this:

"PERSEPHONE!"

Breaking their kiss, Hades and Persephone both looked in the direction of the voice. Demeter was swiftly walking toward them. She gave her daughter a quick, tight hug while giving Hades a repulsed look over Persephone's shoulder. As she broke their embrace, Demeter smiled with relief and tears in her eyes. Regardless, Persephone tried to keep herself at a distance. Though she did miss her mother very much. "How are you, my girl?"

"I'm all right, Mother."

"How can you be all right? Not only did Hades kidnap you, but he also kept you down there in that miserable Underworld. The Fates know what he was doing with you there." Hades felt like his head was ready to explode. "Everything will return normal once we talk to your father."

"KIDNAPPED! You would say that, wouldn't you, Demeter! Is that what you told everyone? That I kidnapped and raped your precious Persephone, without caring about the consequences?" Hades' voice grew lower and lower in disgust. "What else have you told them, dear sister? To your nymphs and mortal followers that worship you? That I'm a monster. . .a god that brings death everywhere he goes?"

"THAT'S WHAT YOU ARE!" Demeter screeched out.

"ENOUGH!" Zeus shouted across the room. Persephone was speechless about what to do in this situation. The two people she loved the most were fighting over her. She hoped her father would find a solution. Still, she was committed to being with Hades no matter what. Persephone watched her father stomp toward them with anger and authority. He needed to be King of the Gods right now. "All of you at the throne room now! We need to discuss this civilly!

Zeus remained calm, though his power was raging, as he sat on his throne. "I'm going to treat this like an actual court. However, even though no one here is a criminal, none of you are completely innocent."

Demeter was the first to say something. "I am more than sure that your statement is inaccurate." Both Hades and Persephone looked at her, waiting to hear more. "Everyone knows that Hades kidnapped my only daughter. We all know that nymph Cadence had witnessed the event. Including the farmer Triptolemus, who also saw the whole thing! Hades kept her in the Underworld unwillingly! If she were there out of her own free will, she could have traveled back and forth when she wanted."

"Mother, if you found out that Hades was courting me, you would have locked me in my room for eternity."

"Courting?"

Persephone looked at her mother directly in the eyes. "Yes. Hades and I were secretly courting without your permission, unbeknownst to you. After the restrictions you placed on Apollo and Ares when they were trying, I had to be with Hades this way."

"How long has this been going on?" Demeter asked in disgust. " I saw your hidden stuff, Persephone. Stuff I know that belongs to Hades."

"Around the time that Apollo and Ares both tried to court me, but I was already attracted to Hades from the first moment I saw him," Persephone said as she looked at

Hades. He stood there with an invisible smile that was reserved only for her. It was time for him to speak up and, unfortunately for him, Hades might have to discuss his emotions once more in order to keep his love.

"I must confess that when I first saw Persephone, I felt at peace. I knew that this woman was going to be my wife. My love for her runs deep. Unfortunately, before we had arrived here, Persephone ate some of the pomegranate fruit." Upon hearing this, Demeter's face grew pale. "By ancient law, Persephone would then stay in the Underworld for eternity."

"NO!" Demeter felt like she was going to faint, "Persephone, what did you do? You ate food from the Underworld?"

Persephone looked guilty as she sought for a lame excuse, "I couldn't help it, Mother. I was starving."

Demeter crossed her arms and gave her daughter a stern look, "Gods and goddesses don't starve, Kore."

Knowing that her deific mother had seen right through her excuse, Persephone closed her eyes and drew in a deep breath before speaking again. "All right, I ate the fruit and swallowed it willingly. I wanted to be with Hades, and I was afraid that this would happen, so I took a drastic step to ensure that nothing would stop me."

Demeter didn't know what to believe. How could her daughter make such a hasty decision? She looked at Hades with absolute hatred. "What did you do to her? Did you brainwash her? Or put a spell on her!"

Hades now had enough. There was only so much he could take. "Don't you see your daughter as this powerful being, capable of making her own decisions? She wants to be with me! She loves me! Why is that so hard for you to grasp?"

"Because she is still a child!"

"NO, I'M NOT, MOTHER! I'm a woman who is in love! I'm a woman who is finally utilizing her powers! I'm not even a maiden anymore!"

Hades silently snickered as Demeter's pale face held a shocked expression. Once again, Demeter looked at Hades like he was some kind of disease. She spoke in a harsh whisper because Demeter could barely get her words out, "You raped her, didn't you?"

"Mother! Hades did no such thing!"

"I'll ask again!" Demeter yelled directly at Hades as he walked toward her, ready to stand his ground. "Did you . . ."

"Repeat the word rape and I'll cut off your tongue!" Hades snarled. His powers were ready to explode in full force. Persephone couldn't tell who was most angry— Demeter and her wrath or her lover ready to attack on Persephone's behalf. One thing that Persephone knew for sure, she felt pain for the both of them. Seeing them ready to kill each other, made her heart ache and her mind fill with guilt.

Zeus had had enough. He wanted this to be over and done with. "Silence! All of you!" He took a deep breath and looked at his precious daughter who was full of sadness and guilt. He got up from his throne and went toward her, wanting to give her some compassion. "Persephone, do you love your mother?"

"Of course I do. My mother, we do everything together, no matter how overprotective she is." Zeus paused, waiting for Demeter to be done with her fury. "But, if I didn't sneak around and do the things that I wanted to every now and then, how was I supposed to enjoy my life? How was I supposed to find my lover, if she's by my side all the time? I'm not a little girl anymore."

Demeter closed her eyes, feeling guilty that maybe, instead of protecting her daughter, she had harmed her unintentionally. Zeus nodded because he too felt robbed of not spending enough time with his daughter, since Demeter didn't want her near Olympus. "What about Hades? How do you feel about him?"

Standing her ground, Persephone smiled as she looked at Hades' handsome face. "I love him with my entire being. He's my best friend, my mentor, my lover, and my partner. I've learned and grown so much from him so quickly. He has brought me such happiness that I never thought could be possible. He has made me into the woman that I was destined to be." She said with such sincerity and pride, as she took Hades' hand, showing her father and mother that separating them apart was not an option. Hades gave his love a genuine smile for everyone to see, which was a very rare thing, coming from him.

Zeus knew that this was going to be tough, but he had made his decision. It was going to be a win-lose situation. "Persephone ate the pomegranate and its seeds. According to the ancient ways of all realms in the universe, anything you eat within that realm binds you to that realm forever. That includes the Underworld. We have to respect that law and Persephone has to be with Hades." Hades smiled as if he'd won, and Persephone would finally be his forever. Then Zeus looked at Demeter with compassion in his eyes. "Though no child should be away from her mother forever. However, Persephone is no longer a child, as she strongly claims, which is true, so it shouldn't matter. Unfortunately, I know what the consequences will be if she doesn't return to her mother. Humanity will suffer Demeter's wrath inevitably."

He then looked at Persephone with pity as he concluded, "Persephone, you ate six seeds from the pomegranate. I am counting one seed per month, which means you'll spend six months with your mother, and the other six months with Hades. To be fair, there will be no visitations from either side when Persephone spends her time with one of you. No conversations, no visits, and no letters." They all felt a dreadful sadness just then, especially Persephone. "Persephone, when you visit your mother, Hades will be forbidden to contact you. The same goes for Demeter when you visit Hades."

Demeter's bitterness was suddenly provoked. "You do realize that every time my Kore goes down to that dreadful place, the mortals will suffer again during those six months. I will bring ice and snow to cover the land so that few things grow."

Hades interfered. "Yes, Demeter, we know how much damage you have caused. Persephone saw the death that you produced just because you missed her. We judged those souls together, and you have killed thousands of mortals from your wrath!"

"Enough, Hades! Yes, Demeter, I knew you would do that. I accept that, which is why I charge you with teaching the mortals how to farm and store food properly. So that they won't extensively suffer your wrath." Demeter remained quiet, as tears started to flow, because she knew nothing would change Zeus' mind.

"Who gets her first?" Hades already had an idea as to where Persephone was headed.

Zeus closed his eyes, he hated to do this to Hades. "Nature needs to get back on course. In order to do that, Persephone will have to go back with her mother." A tear escaped from Hades' eye just then.

Persephone saw the sadness that crept inside of him. Not caring who saw, Persephone went to Hades, embracing and kissing him with all the passionate love she could give. Hades shed more tears. He had found his love and now he was going to lose her. "It's only six months, my love. We can handle this," Persephone whispered as she started to cry. Hades could only nod while his forehead touched hers.

Demeter was about to interrupt, when Zeus cut her off. "Not one word, Demeter. They've gone through enough."

"What did they endure? What about me? I looked all over for Persephone, worrying every single minute about what had happened to her."

"Nothing happened to her," Hades commented. "She was with me the whole time. She was safe. Maybe if you let her have some room to grow, we wouldn't be where we are now. Sneaking around to see each other, without your interference. When it came to her powers, she didn't even have half the common knowledge of a goddess in that regard."

Demeter was looking more haggard by the minute. All the chaos that had happened within the past month had made her tired. For the first time since they were both at Olympus, she looked at Hades with dull eyes and talked to him with parental authority. "Hades, when you have children, which something tells me that will happen soon, you will do everything in your power to make sure that they are safe, loved, and cared for to the best of your ability. You will worry every single minute, even over the smallest things. You'll try to watch your every step when it comes to making decisions. You will question yourself, asking whether you are doing the right thing or not. I am a mother, and I will always be Persephone's mother. Nothing in the universe is going to change that. She will always be my baby, no matter how old she gets. When you finally become a father, Hades, then you can come to me and preach about parenting." Demeter now had her say.

Hades just looked at Demeter, absorbing what she had said. She was trying to be a good parent, unlike the parents that raised them. He had a taste of parenting when they were living inside of Cronus' stomach. Parenting is more complicated than it looks. Demeter's only flaw, when it came to Persephone, is loving her too much.

"I will now go to the Underworld and pack my things," Persephone said before teleporting back to their realm.

"She knows how to teleport?" Demeter asked Hades in awe.

"Yes. Persephone's powers have grown considerably," Hades said in a respected manner. "She has learned so much."

"Because of you."

Hades nodded, as Demeter walked away to return back to her cottage on earth.

Hades and Zeus remained, staring at each other in gloomy silence.

Zeus was the first to speak. "I'm so sorry, my brother. This was the only solution I could think of to solve the problem. It is in everyone's best interest. You and Demeter can both be with her for a certain amount of time. At least you didn't lose her completely."

"Here's what I don't understand brother," Hades spatted, "You and Poseidon have so many wives, mistresses, and bedmates to keep you satisfied. All I wanted was Persephone. One woman to be with me for all eternity. Only with her, do I feel at peace and content. She even brings life to the Underworld; the souls are happy to see her. Why would the universe want me to have the only woman I love for just six months out of the year? Explain that to me brother!"

"Hades, you can always have a nymph to keep you company while Persephone is away."

Hades shook his head violently. "Brother, the one thing you'll never understand is that Persephone is the only one for me. No woman could ever capture my heart and attention like the way she did. I feel a deep sorrow for Hera, for all the pain you give her, every time you find yourself another woman."

"Again, I'm sorry Hades."

Hades couldn't hear Zeus' apologies. He once again felt like the universe had hurt him for no apparent reason.

Why the separation? Why be apart from the only woman he loved, while his brothers have so many?

He turned around and teleported back to the Underworld, where he saw Persephone slowly rifling through her stuff. With every movement she made, Persephone felt unbearable pain in her heart. Hades went to her, giving his love all the comfort that he could provide.

CHAPTER 15

SUMMERTIME SADNESS

Persephone got dressed with a heavy heart, dressing herself slowly, while Hades watched with sad eyes. Usually watching his beloved getting dressed or, most times, getting undressed would give him a sense of delicious pleasure. Tonight was the exception, because they both felt the inevitable pain of separation. Now that Persephone was almost fully dressed, the closer she was to leaving Hades. Six months with Demeter now and the other six months with Hades. That was Zeus' order for this so-called peace treaty he had made between Demeter and Hades, over the one thing they both loved the most.

Persephone was wearing a blood-red silk gown and many jewels that came from Hades. She looked like a beauty queen with her hair up—roses and thorns encircled her head like a crown. Her beautiful hazel green eyes were outlined with thick, black eyeliner, which gave her appearance a dramatic look. Persephone might be returning to her mother, but she wanted to leave here as the future Queen of the Underworld. She looked elegant and authoritative. Persephone glanced at her soon-to-be husband with both love and sorrow. "It's only six months. It really isn't that long."

"It'll feel like an eternity in Tartarus."

Persephone went to Hades, giving him a desperate and loving embrace, which he also reciprocated. He held back his tears, while she gave in to hers. Hades used all of his strength to give his love the comfort she needed to leave. "I'll come visit you in your dreams, my darling. That is the one way we can see each other, without anyone ever knowing. Maybe I'll even sneak above ground at night."

"It is not the same."

"But it's something. It's a way for us to connect, it's a way for me to say 'I love you' before you fall asleep. We did it successfully the first time after your initiation. We'll just have to do it again more carefully."

"Still, I am used to sleeping beside you in your bed." She softly smiled.

"Our bed and it will miss you. Not as much as me though," Hades gave her a sexy smirk.

As much as Persephone loved his sexual intent, she just nodded, feeling numb. She was so depressed that Persephone kept how she really felt hidden. Only a few tears escaped from her eyes. What will she do once she goes back to her mother? Grow flowers? Play with the nymphs again? Why would she want to make things pretty and playful when she felt so sad about being away from her lover? "How can I revert to my old self again when I'm with my mother? How can I go back to the way things were before I met you?"

Hades spoke tactfully blunt, "You don't. Persephone, you have grown so much in the little time that you have spent here. Now you need to show the world, and your mother, what you can do. It is she who needs adjusting to who you are now. You can't escape destiny, no matter how many different paths you take. Destiny brings you right where you're meant to be. And you were meant to be my wife and queen since birth. No matter what your mother says, you will always be mine and I'll always be yours. Don't be scared of your mother."

Persephone gave a little chuckle, "After experiencing this place. . . nothing scares me anymore," Persephone said, hoping that she was right.

"Good, because you shouldn't be. You are the future Queen of the Underworld. There is no reason for you to be afraid." Jokingly, Hades added, "Don't be surprised when mortals and nymphs start to fear you." She laughed, but doubted that it would ever happen.

The Underworld called Hades, which meant that Hermes had arrived to retrieve Persephone. The realm itself felt the couple's sadness, especially in response to Hades, since he was tied to the Underworld. Persephone grabbed her bag of many treasures. "I have to get going, my love. Do you like my outfit?"

"You look like a queen. The Queen of the Underworld to be exact." He looked at her proudly.

"Excellent! That's what I was going for. I want to show my mother that her virgin daughter no longer exists."

Hades held up his hand, waiting for Persephone to be silent. "You are still the beautiful woman I saw on the night of your initiation. You are just. . . more. As much as I don't like what your mother is doing to us, give her some credit, my love. She does what she does because she loves you." Persephone looked at Hades like he had grown two heads. "I have that urge, too—wanting to protect you from everything, even if I can't," Hades admitted.

"You're thinking about that time I went into Tartarus, aren't you?"

"It's more than just that. To me, you are more precious than any earthly riches in the caves. While your mother and I can't stand to be near each other, we both just want to love and protect you. We can't help it,

Persephone, because that's what happens when you love someone. So, darling, go a little easy on her if you can."

Persephone nodded. Hades' wisdom still continued to surprise her. Every day, he proves mortal beliefs about him wrong. They started walking to the judgment panel where Charon and his boat were waiting, along with Hermes hovering from above. The shades watched as they saw their future queen walk toward Charon's boat.

"Wait!" Hades said and he grabbed one of her hands. "Kiss me once more before you go."

"Like I wouldn't give a proper goodbye to my future husband."

"It's not a goodbye. I'll see you later, my love." He stroked her cheek as he gave her a passionately heated kiss. This is what Persephone would miss the most, his hot kisses that burned her spirit.

Hermes observed the unhappy couple, sure that for the both of them this was torture. Out of all the gods and goddesses of Olympus, these two were the most loving and loyal to one another. Yet, they have no choice but to separate. "Come Persephone, your mother is waiting for you on the other side."

"I'm sure she is," Persephone said bitterly as she boarded Charon's boat. She looked at Hades one last time while Charon began to row away. "Think of me, my love."

"Always. Whether I'm awake or asleep, you are always in my thoughts." Hades stayed put while he watched Persephone fade into the distance. Charon's boat soon approached the entrance of the Underworld.

Before Hermes left to escort Persephone out of the Underworld, he glanced at his uncle and saw the apparent sadness and anger on his face. He knew that Hades was using every ounce of control to restrain his fury. "Hades," Hermes called, but Hades remained silent. He only looked at his nephew in discontent. "I'm so sorry. What happened between you and Persephone was most unfair." There was nothing for Hades to say; he didn't want to lash out at Hermes. The best thing for Hades to do was just to nod and not say anything more. He wanted to go to his room now. Realizing that it was time for him to leave, Hermes flew away to join Persephone.

As she was leaving, Persephone tried to absorb all of the beauty and mysteriousness that the Underworld had to offer. She noticed Cerberus just then, and heard him whimpering for her not to leave. "I'm so sorry, boy. I'll see you in six months, okay? Then, when I come back, I'll give a nice belly rub!" Cerberus barked at her in agreement.

"Everyone here is going to miss you, my lady," Charon said as he kept rowing. "You have brought such happiness to this place, especially to our king."

"I'm happy to hear that, Charon."

"Yeah, well . . . I hope that, because you won't be here, Hades doesn't take it out on everyone."

"I'll talk to him if he does."

"Don't, My lady, don't! He has every right to be angry." Persephone looked guilty, because she and Hades were not the only ones to suffer from this separation. The Underworld would also be in agony.

"I'm sorry, Charon."

"Oh no my lady, this is not your fault. We will all be waiting patiently for your return. Who knows, we might actually have a party down here!" For once today, Persephone actually laughed at Charon's humor. Charon looked at Hermes, who was still hovering above them. "What do you think, Hermes? Should Hades throw a party in the Underworld once Persephone gets back?"

"I don't know. The first thing Hades will do is hide her in his bedchamber for a month." Persephone blushed in response.

"Want to make a bet?" Charon suggested, excitedly. Hermes just rolled his eyes at him.

Persephone smiled sadly because she was now near the cave's entrance, inching closer to the light, and she was feeling homesick already. She realized something then, as she felt the sunlight on her skin. The Underworld is her home. Hades is her home. That old saying about home being where the heart is . . . Hades now owns her heart, and she was already missing the Underworld and the Lord of Death.

"Kore!" Persephone heard her mother's voice as Demeter stood there, waiting to grab her daughter with open arms. As Demeter came closer to Persephone, her arms dropped to her sides. Her mouth was agape as she observed her daughter's new clothing attire. Looking at Persephone from head to toe, Demeter felt like she was looking at a complete stranger. She really was staring at the Queen of Death. "Well . . ." Demeter said with distaste, ". . . I'll give Hades credit for making you look like the Queen of Death."

Persephone shook her head a bit angrily. "No, Mother, I dressed myself. It's true that Hades provided me with beautiful gowns and jewelry, but I chose to dress like this."

"For what reason? You know that you can't grow flowers or plants by wearing that!"

"To show you, Mother. To show you that I'm more than just the goddess of spring and flowers."

Demeter raised her eyebrows and looked bitterly at her daughter, knowing Persephone would rather be with Hades, than with her own mother. "What are you, then? The Queen of the Underworld and death, I think not! Kore, you are meant to be with me, helping the earth and harvesting plants. Hades committed a crime! He kidnapped you! He stole you from me!"

"He did no such thing, Mother! I called him and I begged him to take me away from here!" Persephone shouted. She closed her eyes, feeling a little guilty about shouting at her mother. However, she sensed that Demeter was getting ready to preach. Her mother would try convincing her that Hades is an evil god, just like the mortals do. "Mother, let's just go back to the cottage. I've already had a long, emotional day. It was hard enough for me to leave Hades."

For once, Demeter didn't say a word. She was still shocked that, not only had her own daughter shouted back at her, but Persephone had also confessed that she let Hades take her willingly. It was too irrational to believe.

When they returned to the cottage, Persephone went straight to her old room. She already felt like she didn't belong here anymore. This room belonged to a little girl who had not yet found love. Hades was right about how much she had grown up since being with him. Now, looking at her room just made her feel uneasy. As if she were going backward in time, a time before Hades.

Persephone rifled through the bag that she had brought with her from the Underworld. Mostly, she brought crystals, like amethyst, and placed them on the side table. She took out the jewelry that Hades had given her, along with some of the clothes as well. Persephone tried to make her room feel more like the Underworld, so that it reflected a more mature version of herself.

Looking in her closet, she saw nothing but white linen dresses that made her appear so innocent. Persephone decided to keep two of these dresses so that she could wear them while working in the field. In an angry haste, she removed the rest of them from her closet. She wanted to burn them! *Too bad I can't go to Tartarus and burn them there,* she thought to herself.

Then, Persephone looked for her magic trunk, which contained all of Hades' gifts that he had given her while they were secretly courting . It was nowhere to be found. All of her anger was now overwhelming. "MOTHER!" she screamed in fury.

Demeter rushed into Persephone's room, worried. She thought that something had happened to her precious daughter. "What is it, darling?" Demeter looked at Persephone's face, which was full of contempt and disgust. At that moment, Demeter truly felt like she lost her daughter. "What's wrong?"

"WHERE IS MY TRUNK?!"

Demeter swallowed hard. She was no longer answering to her daughter, but to the future Queen of the Underworld. "I threw it away." She spoke gently, so as not to choke on her own words. "I'm trying to rid Hades' influence from you. I promise everything will go back to the way it was, once everything that belonged to him is gone."

"WHAT! GIVE IT BACK!"

""NO!" Demeter shouted back.

Persephone glared at her mother while she inhaled and exhaled, trying not to let the anger consume her. Hades' words rang in her ear just then, *"She does what she does because she loves you.*" In a very calm and stern manner, she replied back, "Mother, please give me back my trunk. I treasure everything that Hades has given me as a precious memory. I need you to return those items. If you don't, I will go to Father and plead with him, asking to stay with Hades forever. Then, you will never see me again."

Demeter exhaled defeatedly. She couldn't believe that this was her daughter now. What happened to her sweet and innocent Persephone? She looked at her and nodded. Demeter went to retrieve the trunk.

It took a while for Demeter to return with Persephone's trunk. At first, Persephone wondered why until she saw how dirty it was. Her trunk was covered with dirt. "You buried it?" she asked, while she held onto the trunk with her life.

Now it was Demeter's turn to be cross. "Be lucky I didn't burn it! I don't know why you love the stuff that he gives you so much. It's not like it matches your wardrobe as the goddess of—," Demeter paused as she noticed the white dresses laying on Persephone's bed. "Are you reorganizing your closet?"

Persephone looked at her bed. "You can say that. I'm getting rid of these old dresses, except for two, so that I can wear them while working in the fields."

"But darling, you'll need more!"

"No, I won't. I now have elegant gowns that make me look more mature!"

"You can't work out there wearing dark, heavy fabrics darling! You'll start to sweat within three minutes!"

"That's why I'm only keeping two old dresses, specifically for fieldwork."

Demeter closed her eyes, feeling frustrated. "My daughter. . . when you are here, you are the goddess of spring. When you are with. . . Hades . . . then you can be the Queen of the Underworld."

Persephone shook her head as tears started to flow. She felt like all she did today was weep. Persephone cried over her lover, their separation, and her mother's denial. She screamed because Persephone felt like her life was going backward. All she wanted was to be loved by a man, and she had finally found him. Now, her mother just wouldn't accept reality. "When are you going to realize that I am both?"

Demeter ignored her daughter's question. Instead, she hoped that tomorrow would be a better day. Maybe Persephone just needs sleep. "Goodnight my Kore. Tomorrow will be better, you just need to get some rest."

With that, Demeter closed the door and Persephone sat down on her bed, feeling exhausted. She touched the linen on her bed and it felt. . . wrong. Persephone had gotten used to the luxurious fabrics on Hades' bed, that her own linen felt scratchy and stiff. She rummaged through her trunk and examined all the gifts that Hades had given her. Especially the black velvet cloak. She wrapped it around herself and smelled it, hoping to find a trace of Hades' scent. His smell was there, even though it was faint. Her tears returned once again, as she laid down on the bed. She'd be sleeping alone tonight. Hoping that Hades could hear her, Persephone whispered to the empty room, "Goodnight my love. I miss you already, and I wish you here with me." With tears still spilling out, she closed her eyes and waited for sleep to come.

Looking into his scrying mirror, Hades saw his beloved crying herself to sleep. "I hear you, my love. I'm so sorry that you are in pain. I will come visit you soon. I'm always with you." Hades touched the scrying mirror with his hand as a tear escaped his eye. "Sweet dreams, my love."

Consequences meant nothing to Hades. After all, he is one of the three mighty kings of the earth. Nothing was going to stop him from contacting his soon-to-be wife. He may visit her only in dreams for now, but he wanted to contact her with something more substantial, something for her to hold onto. He started writing a letter to his beloved, knowing full well that this wasn't part of the treaty. Hades didn't care. He needed to tell Persephone how much he loved her and how much he missed her.

Hermes had just flown in, bringing a new batch of souls that were waiting to be judged. As he flew over to Hades, who was sitting on his throne and writing like a madman, Hermes suspected that he was writing to Persephone. "Um, Hades?" but Hades didn't even bother to look up. "You are not writing to who I think you're writing to, are you?"

Without looking up from his letter, Hades answered almost innocently, which was odd coming from the King of the Underworld. "I have no idea what you're talking about, Hermes."

"You know exactly what I'm talking about! That is a letter to Persephone, isn't it?"

"Why do you question something when you already know the answer?"

"It's going against the treaty! Demeter is not going to like this!"

Hades stood up and stared into Hermes eyes, "Which is why Demeter will never find out that I'm contacting Persephone in any way, especially from you." Hermes remained silent, feeling terrible about what had happened to Hades and Persephone. Once Hades finished writing his letter, he rolled up the scroll and wrapped a gold bracelet around it. On the gold chain was a flower charm engulfed by flames.

"That is daring, don't you think?" Hermes asked nervously, "Giving Persephone a piece of jewelry and a letter?"

"This separation is not going to stop me from loving or spoiling her." Hades then handed the decorated scroll over to Hermes. "Guard it with your immortal life and ensure its deliverance," Hades sounded threatening and simultaneously stern.

Hermes bowed more seriously than ever before. "Yes, my lord." Hades watched him as Hermes swiftly flew away.

In the middle of the harvest fields, Persephone disguised herself as a working mortal. She hoped that work would distract her mind from thinking about Hades and her mother. *Her mother. More like a prison guard,* she thought to herself. Regardless of how hard she tried to concentrate on something else, Hades always came to mind. Each time this happened, her heart would ache and tears threatened to flow.

Then she heard a whistle from above. Hermes appeared for only a second and dropped a scroll at her feet. As quickly as he came, he was gone without a word. Persephone's heart quickened. There was only one reason Hermes would deliver a message and fly away that fast, making sure no one saw anything. She picked up the scroll and sat down to read it. The tears that Persephone kept holding back all day finally gushed out. Of course, this letter came from the one person she had wanted to hear from the most. Nervous about Hades breaking the treaty, she hid the scroll with her hair, keeping it hidden, while she started to read its contents.

My dearest Persephone,

I know it has only been a couple of days since we saw each other last, but I already miss you, my love. My body and heart crave you every day and every night. I miss your hazel-green eyes, your smile, your voice, and your body that I love to touch. I count the days until you come home and sleep in our bed once more. I feel as if death has consumed my heart, I feel like I am now becoming the king that everyone has feared me to be, but I do my best not to be, because of you. I love you dearly, my darling future wife. Here's a token of my love for you.

Your devoted fiancé,
Hades

As Persephone read the letter, tears blurred her vision. She looked at the bracelet he had given her. She really started to cry when she examined the flower pendant surrounded by fiery flames. Knowing that the flower represented her, and that the fire represented both Hades and his raging passion for her.

"Is that a letter from your sweetheart?" Persephone gasped in surprise, unaware that someone was standing right next to her. It was a young, mortal woman who was also working in the fields. She had noticed Persephone's attentive interest in the scroll that she was holding. The mortal woman smiled because she loved listening to romantic stories about other people.

"Yes, it is. We're separated until autumn arrives and miss him terribly. When I'm not with him, my heart hurts with each day that passes."

"Oh, I understand. My betrothed is a soldier, and I heard there's a war about to break. He was summoned two months ago. I worry that I'm never going to see him again."

Persephone couldn't place her face, but this woman looked very familiar. Persephone swore that she had seen this mortal before. "There's a war coming on? I thought Ares stopped creating war amongst the mortals this year."

The woman looked at her, confused. "Why would you think that the god of war would prevent warfare from happening?"

Without thinking, Persephone gave the woman a blunt answer. "My fiancé told him not to, and my father made Ares settle it. To everyone, my father's word is the law."

At first, the woman stared at Persephone in shock, and then she bowed before her. "I'm so sorry, my lady. I didn't realize that I was talking to one of the goddesses. Please forgive me for thinking that you were one of us."

This was the first time, ever, that anyone had recognized Persephone as a goddess. Now this woman wanted her forgiveness. She was in awe of receiving praise, while simultaneously feeling awkward about it. A sense of insignificance clouded her mind. "Please, you can stop kneeling. There's nothing to forgive. In a way, I am also a part of you. I help the earth just like you do."

"You are still a goddess though, and you are supposed to be worshiped, if you don't mind me saying so." The mortal woman finally looked into Persephone's eyes.

"All I do is summon the arrival of spring and help flowers grow. Also, I assist my mother with the harvest," Persephone said humbly.

"You're Persephone! Goddess of spring and flowers. You are Demeter's daughter!"

A smile spread across Persephone's face, "You have heard of me?"

"Yes, everyone has. Well, everyone who worships the gods of Olympus." Persephone understood what she meant; there are other religions with different gods, but she decided to keep that to herself. She didn't want to overwhelm this mortal woman even more.

"Forgive me, my lady, may I ask you a personal question?" The mortal woman had her eyes on Persephone's scroll. "That letter you were reading, you said it was from your fiancé?"

"Yes," Persephone confirmed with a sad smile.

"Is it true that your fiancé is Hades, King of the Underworld?" she asked fearfully.

"Yes it is, and I miss him so."

"You miss him?" The mortal woman frowned, not wanting to say the wrong thing to a goddess. So, before she decided to say anything more, she wanted to hear the whole story. "Then, perhaps, you can educate me my lady. What's he like, our King of the Underworld?"

Persephone smiled as her mind clouded with images of Hades. "He's tall and handsome. He has the best icy-blue eyes that you've ever seen. He is so kind and understanding, and also very wise."

"That's not the Hades I was raised to know. I heard that he was cruel, that he is an old man with a grudge. That's why I'm afraid to die. I'm afraid he'll put me in Tartarus for just one mistake. I've been a good person, I promise!"

Persephone wanted to ease this woman's apparent fears. "You have absolutely nothing to fear about Hades.

He's not like that at all. You fear him because he rules over death and the Underworld, that's all."

"What about Tartarus?"

"It's there, but you have to be evil to the core for your soul to end up there. So it's rare for a soul to be sent to Tartarus. Besides, for those who do end up there, it's only temporary."

"Temporary?" Suddenly the woman's emotions changed from anxiousness to anger. "Why should the bad souls only serve a temporary punishment for the crimes they've committed here?!" The mortal woman covered her mouth with both hands, realizing that she had just yelled at a goddess. "I'm sorry, my goddess!" She bowed down again. "I didn't mean to speak out of line."

Persephone looked at the woman with compassion. "What's your name?"

"Frona, my lady."

Persephone laughed at her answer. "So, you've been given a name that means self-control? Yet, you do everything but that." Frona smiled because she knew that she had no filter for her big mouth. She always let curiosity get the best of her.

"Indeed, my lady. I'm sorry."

"Please, you can stop referring to me as 'my lady.' It's Persephone. Again, you have nothing to apologize for. To answer your question about punishment, I'll ask you this. . . do you have a child?"

Frona looked at Persephone with a sense of guilt and joy. "Not yet."

Persephone looked surprised. "You are pregnant right now, aren't you?" Then, out of instinct, Persephone did something that she had never done before. She put her hand on Frona's flat, lower stomach. Persephone utilized her powers, feeling for any sensation in Frona's belly. She instantly felt life stirring from within Frona, and the energy of her baby being created. It was conceived about two months ago, approximately. Persephone couldn't help but smile for Frona. "So, your betrothed gave you a proper goodbye before he left?" Frona laughed as she blushed. Frona looked at the young goddess because Persephone also knew about something else. "It is going to be a boy."

Frona was ecstatic. "A boy? Oh, I hope he looks exactly like his father!"

"How are you going to raise him?"

"I'll raise him in the same house that I grew up in, right over there," Frona pointed in the direction of Demeter's cottage. Persephone now realized why Frona looked familiar. Frona was the woman she had seen with that man on the day of her initiation. She didn't say anything, and instead just gave Frona a pleasant smile. Persephone was happy that their love had progressed into something more. "I plan on giving him the best possible education that I can and with his father being a soldier, it's feasible. I'll love him unconditionally and play with him too," Frona said excitedly.

Then, to help redirect their conversation, Persephone asked, "What about discipline?"

"Well, of course, there will be discipline. I'll reward my son for being good and punish him when he is being bad. That's the way most people discipline their children."

Persephone challenged Frona to consider this, "So, if your child does something bad, will you punish him forever?"

"Punish him forever?" Frona laughed like that was the most ridiculous thing she's ever heard. "Of course not. No one deserves to be punished forever. He will need love, support, and understanding after his punishment ends. How else will he learn?"

Persephone gave her a big smile, "Exactly."

Frona paused just then. She quickly realized that's why punishment is only temporary in the Underworld.

Persephone cradled Frona's face with both of her hands. "To us gods and goddesses, you mortals are our children. No punishment can last forever, whether it's for one or multiple crimes. Those who have done extreme harm, on the other hand, stay in Tartarus for a longer period of time. However, for them to leave Tartarus, they must accept what they have done and learn to forgive others, including themselves. Trust me when I say that it is probably one of the hardest lessons to learn, which is why it's so difficult to leave Tartarus."

Tears formed in Frona's eyes because she suddenly felt Persephone's strong aura. She may be a young goddess, but Frona could tell that Persephone was coming into her own. Here she was telling Frona that there was no reason to fear death or the Underworld. "Is there really a paradise there, too?"

"When you die, you must see the Elysian Fields. It is beyond beautiful than any place here on Earth. Everyone forgets that Hades is also in charge of that place, too."

"Persephone, forgive me for asking, but didn't Hades kidnap you? Didn't he force you to live with him? I also heard that he raped you, too."

Almost offended, apparent anger appeared on Persephone's face. Though she was vexed, Persephone had to find out where Frona had gotten this information. "Of course not. How can I still yearn for him if he had done those things?"

"I'm sorry, my lady, but that's what the mortals are saying about him in regard to your disappearance. A man named Triptolemus saw Hades grab you and take you down below the earth. Because of your disappearance, your mother has punished us for his actions. Now, people are more scared of Hades than ever before."

Persephone closed her eyes, wanting to scream, but she kept it all inside. In this moment, she now understood what Charon meant when it came to mortals and their storytelling. "Triptolemus has no idea what he saw. In his eyes, he witnessed the horrifying Lord of Death grab a young goddess. He has no clue about the true story behind it." Now, there was more damage caused than the gods had anticipated. In the eyes of mortals, Hades already had a feared reputation, but now her assumed 'disappearance' had turned Hades into an absolute monster. The story of their romance had become a mother's nightmare instead. Persephone had no doubt that Demeter had spread this false version of the story everywhere.

Persephone's heart grew heavy for Hades because, not only was she missing him and his presence, but now he would go down in history as a villain, regardless of him being her savior.

CHAPTER 16

SUMMER SOLSTICE

Once again, Hades was in a foul mood. Before Persephone, he was accustomed to being alone in the Underworld. Ruling over it, making judgments, and carrying out his daily routine. To ensure that everything was in place, Hades checked on all parts within his realm. But, ever since Persephone left to be with her mother for six months, he was now unbearable to be around. Since Hades' temper was more easily aroused, his people often walked on eggshells so that they wouldn't trigger his detestable mood.

Hades lived in constant torture as time dragged on, as he waited to see Persephone again. Feeling miserable and somewhat guilty about how he's treated everyone in his realm, including Charon, Hades counted the days until Persephone would be with him. With each passing day, Hades would not find any relief until she was in his arms again.

Just then, he sensed Hermes enter the Underworld. Hades didn't want to partake in any judging at all today, but Hermes was flying right to him with a scroll in his hand. Sadly reminiscing about the last time that Hermes had handed him a scroll, Hades remembered it being when Zeus had called upon him and Persephone, thus concluding his miserable state. Hades knew that he was already turning into the dark god that everyone believed him to be, in the first place. He really didn't want to be a dark god, but he just couldn't control the emptiness that he felt inside of himself. Fearing that misery would cloud his judgment, for once, Hades allowed his three judges to carry out judgements without having a final say.

After landing near Hades' throne, Hermes never saw such anger and sadness in his eyes. Hermes felt his pain and, wanting to give Hades sympathy, Hermes blurted out, "I'm sorry about what happened."

"I don't need your pity," Hades growled, "I just need everyone to leave me alone, in peace."

"For how long? Until Persephone comes back? Which, you know, she will. You just need to wait three more months Hades, and then she'll be here with you once more. You're treating this like she is dead, as if you'll never see her again. I have to admit, though, this is odd behavior. Especially because you are the ruler of the dead, after all. If Persephone was dead, you would have seen her already."

Hades growled again more angrily, "Hermes, if you have nothing important to tell me, I suggest you leave before I put you on the lowest floor of Tartarus!"

For once, Hermes looked at his uncle with fearful eyes. Having never seen Hades like this before, Hermes did not know what to expect. Hermes cautiously handed Hades the scroll. Hades sighed in response, not wanting to know what the scripture said. "Trust me, you'll want to read it. There is no sad news or orders," Hermes assured.

Hades read over the scroll with a bit of skepticism, while Hermes held his breath. "It's another invitation to Olympus. A ball?" Hades asked curiously, "What for?"

"Summer Solstice," Hermes replied with a slight smirk. "Demeter is going to showcase her plants for the event. The fun part is that her only daughter will also be there. . ." Hades looked at Hermes with wide eyes, as his heart began to quicken. Hermes continued, ". . . I heard that Demeter's daughter is a real beauty and that she's waiting for her future husband to come see her."

Hades shook his head, "We are not allowed to see one another while she's spending time with her mother."

"You're not allowed to speak to Persephone while she is with Demeter. However, there's no rule that forbids you from seeing her at a public party. Every god and goddess will be in attendance and, to make things even more fun, everyone will be wearing a mask. It's a masquerade ball, so everyone will be dressed as different beings or creatures." Hermes gave Hades a sincere smile, hoping that his uncle would take the hint.

"This is tomorrow tonight?" Hades asked and Hermes nodded.

Hades now felt guilty for how he had treated his nephew. It wasn't Hermes fault that Persephone was no longer here in the Underworld. He was, after all, just the messenger. "Hermes, I am sorry for my temper."

"Uncle, you really don't want to turn into the fearful god that everyone thinks you are, do you? For the first time ever, since I brought souls down to you, I am afraid of you. Are you going to be like this every time Persephone leaves? What would Persephone say? Do you want her feeling guilty once she finds out that you've been a monster to everyone around you, just because she isn't here?"

Closing his eyes in shame, Hades knew that Hermes was right. He was the oldest Olympian, and yet, he's been carrying on like she had died. She's not dead, though. Hades peered down at the scroll with joy in his heart. Now he can finally see Persephone outside of their dream visits. While their dream visits have kept both of them sane, it is still not enough. "Thank you, Hermes. Thank you."

"I assume you are going?" Hermes asked while trying to hide his smirk, but having no luck.

"You don't need to ask me twice this time."

"See you there Hades," Hermes said as he flew back to Olympus.

Hades smiled to himself, feeling relieved. He'll soon see his beloved Persephone without breaking the treaty that he and Demeter had established, without suffering any consequences. Now, the only thing that concerned Hades was figuring out what to wear for such a special occasion. What disguise should he adorn? Hades smirked as he thought of the perfect costume and mask. He couldn't wait for tomorrow night, when he would finally see his beloved Persephone again.

Summer Solstice had arrived, and every god and goddess came to attend the Olympus masquerade ball. Everyone was already dancing and having a good time, as the party transformed into a vibrant sea of masks and elaborate costumes. The throne room looked like an enchanted forest, with much thanks to Demeter, since she and Persephone had decorated it together. With help from Dionysus, the god of wine, party, and chaos, the room's atmosphere was vivacious and entertaining. The sound of dancing footsteps and constant laughter echoed throughout Olympus.

Looking around in anticipation, Persephone was eagerly searching for the one person she had hoped to see tonight. However, it was difficult to distinguish anyone because of their masks. Everyone was dressed as something—another being, an animal, or just someone who wore an exotic mask. So far, the only person easily identifiable was Hera, because she dressed as her favorite animal and also her signifier—a peacock.

Persephone herself was almost easily recognizable, since her lace mask only covered her eyes, highlighting their hazel-green color. Wanting to look like a fairy queen, she was dressed in a beautiful lavender-mint ombre chiffon dress. Along with her golden fairy crown, flowers decorated her hair as well, and Persephone's costume moved with her every step. The best part of her entire ensemble, though, was her iridescent wings that flapped in the wind. She was wearing the necklace that Hades had first made for her, along with an engagement ring that shone brightly from the light's reflection.

With a strong feeling of desperation, Persephone walked through the dancing crowd, searching for a certain someone. Seeing couples as they danced together made her feel so alone. Then, a voice suddenly interrupted her search. "Hello, Persephone." She looked around and saw Hephaestus, the god of metalsmith. He is also the husband to the goddess of love, Aphrodite.

"Hello, Hephaestus," Persephone said, giving him a genuine smile. She always treated him with kindness whenever they crossed paths. Out of all the gods on Olympus, Hephaestus was still in a lot of emotional pain. Despite his significant metalsmith achievements, his lower body was slightly deformed from the waist down. He could walk, but it was not a normal gait. The gods and mortals believed him to be unattractive, especially his own wife. He sees his unfaithful wife go from one lover to the next, leaving him discarded. Despite everything that she has done, Hephaestus still loves his wife.

"Looking for someone in particular?" he asked knowingly.

"I think you already know the answer to that one, sir." Persephone sighed as she searched the crowd again with wondering eyes.

"I know how it feels." Persephone looked at him as he continued to speak with sorrow in his voice, "I know how it feels to love someone who you can't be with, at least not fully. I know our situations are vastly different, but to have that heartache, because you are nowhere near your love, is unbearable."

"Why don't you get away from Aphrodite, if she hurts you so?"

"You should know the answer to that one, Persephone. You can't help who you love, no matter how much it hurts."

Gently, she defended her lover, "Hades doesn't hurt me."

"No. . . but you'll be pained every time you are separated from one another. You didn't exactly choose a common spouse, my dear. He is the Lord of Death, after all. You will be in the Underworld for half the year."

"I actually love the Underworld. It's a fascinating place . . . just like Hades. However, I do see what you mean. I feel depressed when I think about Hades because I can't be with him or touch him." A tear fell from the edge of Persephone's eye.

"Sorry, Persephone. I didn't mean to make you cry."

"No, Hephaestus, I have been crying uncontrollably quite often. All of this has been tough for me."

"I am sure it has been rough on him as well," Hephaestus said as he looked around the dance floor, seeing everyone sway in rhythm to the slow melody that played before them. "I know I'm not the most fluid dancer, but would you like to dance with me until your real dance partner arrives?" he offered Persephone his hand.

Persephone smiled softly, "I would love to."

They started to dance along with the crowd. As Hephaestus watched his every step, he also noticed that Persephone was trying to enjoy herself. Still, every minute or so, Persephone would scan the room as she continued to dance with Hephaestus.

Demeter was watching her daughter dance with the gentle Hephaestus. She knew her daughter was just being sweet to him, but she could tell that Persephone was also distracted. Her daughter had begged Demeter to attend this ball, and she knew that the only reason Persephone had wanted to go was to see Hades herself, without breaking the treaty. It's a public celebration, after all, so there were no rules to break, except for speaking to each other.

Even Zeus was watching what Demeter was observing. He approached her from behind. "Was it worth it, Demeter, to starve the world? To punish both the innocent and the guilty? For you to separate your daughter from her only love?"

Stubbornly, she stated, "It's not real love. There might be lust between them, but not love."

Zeus frowned in response to her denial. "You know why our daughter is here, don't you?"

Demeter frowned in disgust, "Of course I do! She is searching for Hades."

"A desperate search, might I add, since Persephone keeps glancing around the room while she is supposed to be dancing."

"It's just infatuation! A major crush that was blown out of proportion. He'll hurt her in the end!"

"Why? Why must you believe something like this is going to happen between Hades and Persephone?" Zeus paused, waiting for an answer that didn't come. "The reason you believe this, my fair Demeter, is because I did this to you. I promised that you would become Queen of the Gods and become my true wife. Instead, I chose Hera over you. I'm very sorry that I hurt you, my love. If I could take the pain away, I would. I will always love you, Demeter."

"I want to regret ever loving you. I wanted to hurt you in return," Demeter admitted, feeling herself trying to forgive Zeus, "But. . .I can't. Out of our love and shared experiences, we put our cruel ancestors away, including our father. Then came my beautiful Persephone. I'll never regret our union together because of her. For that, I will thank you." Demeter finally looked at Zeus, as tears welled up in her eyes. Zeus enclosed the space between him and Demeter to give her a comforting hug. After that, Demeter reverted to being the powerful and determined goddess that she had always been. However, her heart felt like it was finally starting to heal from past wounds.

Hephaestus was enjoying Persephone's company, especially once she had stopped looking for Hades. They both concentrated on their footsteps as they danced together.

Suddenly, over Hephaestus' shoulder, Persephone saw a tall man wearing a black mask. His black mask highlighted his icy-blue eyes. Persephone held her breath as her heart beat fast with excitement. She already knew who he was. The man came forward and tapped Hephaestus' shoulder, giving him a silent nod, showing that he wanted to cut in. Knowing that this mysterious man was Hades, without any hesitation, Hephaestus was stepping aside to let him dance with Persephone. Before Hephaestus moved away, though, he gave the couple a simple reminder, "Remember you two, everyone will be watching. No speaking to each other." Hades and Persephone both nodded in response.

Persephone looked at her future husband with a sad, but happy smile. He was as handsome as ever—wearing Celtic black armor that had the same shades of red and purple that matched his cloak. He was also wearing ram horns that were covered in dark roses and vines. To Persephone, he looked like a dark fairy prince, which perfectly complemented her own costume.

She reached out, touching his smooth face, wanting to remove his mask. Persephone needed to see his eyes without any interference. As she removed his disguise, he caressed her own beautiful face, while he lifted away her mask as well.

Everyone in the room stared at the gorgeous, yet torturous, couple because they had all sensed what was about to happen. News spread faster here within the spirit realms, as opposed to Earth.

Seeing Hades, Demeter was ready to interfere, but Zeus stepped in front of her. "Demeter, no treaty will be broken tonight since they are both at a public gathering. As long as they don't speak to one another, they will still be adhering to the rules." Demeter nodded in response. For once, she was going to let Persephone enjoy spending time with her future husband. After all, Persephone had been depressed ever since she came back to Earth with her mother. It was nice to see a genuine smile on her face, one that reached her eyes.

Everyone in the ballroom continued to stare at the infamous couple, while Hades led Persephone to the dance floor, as they began to dance before everyone else joined in. The rules of the treaty forbid either of them to speak to each other until Persephone could live with Hades for six months. Regardless, to each other, they could both read the other person's body language just by staring into their eyes.

As they were dancing, Hades' fingers intertwined with Persephone's, while his other hand lovingly wrapped around her waist. Their foreheads touched together, while they both shared each other's air. Were they even allowed to kiss? At this point, they didn't care. Hades moved in, letting his lips touch hers with a forbidden kiss. All of his emotions were held within that kiss, letting Persephone know just how much he loved her and had missed her. He craved her so much. Persephone gave Hades the same passionate kiss in return. Tears came to her eyes as

Persephone stared at her beloved, showing Hades how much she had missed him.

Hades used one of his hands to wipe away Persephone's tears. He then gave her a soft smile that was reserved only for her to see, which let her know that everything was going to be all right. It was almost time for them to be reunited once again. They heard the quiet whispers of gossip that echoed through the ballroom as everyone watched the couple interact. But it didn't matter and they didn't care. Hades and Persephone just continued to dance and sway to the music. as they silently communicated their love to each other.

Hours quickly passed, as morning approached, and the party reached its end. There were only a few handfuls of gods that lingered around. Persephone's head rested on Hades' chest as they swayed together. Hades concentrated on how it felt to have her in his arms, the very feeling of Persephone herself, and he breathed in her scent. Every precious moment together was not wasted tonight.

Zeus walked up to them just then, hating to disrupt their romantic moment. Demeter was ready to return to their cottage home, so Zeus didn't want any angry confrontation between the three of them. Hades looked at him, knowing that it was already time to let go. Persephone looked up at her beloved and Hades gave her a sad smile, kissing her lips for the last time until they met again. Then, he kissed the back of her hand as a way of saying goodbye to his love. Persephone felt tears threatening to fall again as Hades turned to leave.

Breathing in deeply to stop her tears, Persephone looked at her mother who was waiting for her. "I hope you enjoyed yourself," Demeter said in an almost genuine way.

Persephone held her head high as she looked at her mother, "Yes, Mother, very much so."

"I'm surprised you two didn't sneak away to talk."

"We don't need words," Persephone said in almost a whisper. "Mother, what Hades and I have is so much more than you can imagine. We don't need words to tell each other how we feel." Persephone went to gather the rest of her belongings so she and her mother could return to Earth.

Demeter gathered her new plants that she had showcased for the evening, which no one had seemed to care about when everyone's attention was focused on Hades and Persephone. They had all anticipated one of them to slip up.

"What were you expecting tonight?" Demeter looked up and saw Athena. How weird was it that she hadn't seen her all evening, and now she had appeared.

"What do you mean?" Demeter asked as Athena came closer to her.

"What were you expecting to happen between Hades and Persephone?"

"Maybe a slip up from either of them?" Demeter guessed.

Athena frowned, "What good will it do for either of them to break the treaty by saying something?"

"It would let me have more time with my daughter, of course."

"Demeter, did you not see the real love being displayed here tonight? Hades might be in love wholly, but he is not an idiot. He knew that this would be a break for him and Persephone, from being separated, but he also knew that this was a trap you had set for him as well."

"It was not a—"

"Oh, Demeter! For once, you let Persephone attend a ball with zero restrictions. You even let her wander around the ballroom without you chasing her, which you have never done before."

"Maybe it's time I gave my daughter some independence!" Have you thought about that, Athena?"

"I know you, Demeter. You wanted Hades to fail."

"What would you do if your daughter, hypothetically speaking, was engaged to the god of death?"

Athena gave Demeter an unexpected answer, "I'd say 'Congratulations, you found a great catch'."

Demeter was dumbfounded, "What?"

"I am going to tell you something that you don't want to hear, Demeter."

"Oh! I am confident that you will impart some wisdom that I don't want to hear!"

"Out of all of us gods and goddesses on Olympus, Hades is the wisest, most intelligent, and most understanding god around. His wisdom even beats mine."

Demeter started to laugh, "Okay, Athena, now you are joking."

"Do I look like a goddess who jokes around?" Athena asked seriously, which stopped Demeter from laughing.

"Hades is the oldest of us all. He carefully judges souls, each and every one of them, taking their prior circumstances and everything else into consideration. Hades makes sure that there's a balance. I don't know if you remember, but he took care of you and everyone else as you all grew inside of Cronus' stomach."

- "I remember being inside of that horrible place!" Demeter snapped.

Calmly, Athena countered, "Do you remember Hades taking care of you, when neither of your parents would?"

Guilt hit Demeter like a ton of bricks. She closed her eyes, having forgotten everything that Hades had done to protect his siblings, while they were trapped inside of Cronus. Athena could tell that Demeter really was reflecting back on that horrible time in her life.

"People tend to forget that Hades is just as equally, if not more, powerful than Zeus," Athena added.

"How so?" Demeter asked, voicing her concern.

"Zeus may create life and rule over the gods, including Hades, but, in the end, everything belongs to Hades—the souls of humans, the jewels, different dimensions, the invisible beings, and creatures that many mortals wouldn't dare dream about or believe in. It all belongs to Hades, even the Underworld. His world is more vast than Olympus or the earth itself. He has to watch over it every single day."

"What are you trying to say, Athena?"

"That Hades is a mighty god who is always misunderstood because of what he does. This amazing powerful being of a god loves your daughter with all his heart. With everything that he has endured, don't you think you should give him more credit? Shouldn't you trust him to be a loving husband for your daughter? After all, she's happiest when she is with him."

Demeter just stood there, absorbing Athena's words, while Athena left Demeter alone with her thoughts. Maybe Athena was right, perhaps Hades was the perfect god for Persephone. She had completely forgotten about Hades' admirable qualities, just like the mortals had as well. The one thing that Demeter kept thinking about was the last thing that Athena had mentioned, *"After all, she's happiest when she is with him."*

CHAPTER 17

LOST SOULS

Though depression still weighed heavily upon her heart, Persephone kept herself occupied as she helped with her mother's harvest. Wheat fields had grown long, tall, and almost golden. The earth and its food had finally been replenished from Demeter's wrath. Persephone counted the days until she would be reunited with her love. She couldn't wait to return to the Underworld, so that she could be with her future husband.

As Persephone reaped wheat from the fields, she looked up at the sound of something rustling in the tall grass, sounding like a soft whimper. She knew that someone was there because she felt its energy, and it was getting closer. Persephone followed the direction of the energy's vibration, as her heart beat fast. At that moment, Persephone reminded herself of what Hades had taught her, *I'm a goddess for Earth's sake! I'll soon become the Queen of the Underworld! I shouldn't be afraid of anything!* Persephone put her fears behind her and took charge. "Look, whoever you are, I know you're there! So, come out of the wheat grass slowly!"

Persephone braced herself as she got closer to the rustling. A small boy who appeared to be no older than five, slowly showed himself from behind the tall wheat grass. Relief washed over Persephone just then; she had been scared over someone so small. His gentle eyes began to well up with tears, as they threatened to run down his face. Persephone bent down to the little boy's level. "I'm so sorry, I didn't mean to frighten you, I thought you were. . . something else." Persephone spoke gently, "Are you okay? What can I do for you?"

Tears escaped from the boy's eyes as his voice cracked when he tried to speak, as if he couldn't say the words, "Wh-ere do the l-ost peo-ple go?"

Persephone's heart filled with sorrow as she absorbed the boy's question. "What do you mean, 'Where do the lost people go?' Are you lost?" The boy shook his head yes. "Did you lose your mother or father?"

More tears streamed down the boy's small face. "I-I was w-with my gr-ran-d-dma." Persephone used her hands to dry the boy's tears. "I w-was walking with he-her. N-ow she is go-ne. Pl-ease he-lp me."

"Shhh. It's going to be okay, I promise. I'll help you find your grandmother."

"Re-ally?"

Persephone smiled. His pronunciation may not be precise, but to her, it was adorable. *One day, Hades and I will have a child of our own*, she thought. Persephone felt a flutter in her chest and smiled at the boy, "Yes, really." She grabbed the boy's hand, determined to help him find his grandmother. As they walked through to the other side of the wheat field, Persephone saw a dirt path which led into the woods. She then understood how the boy had gotten lost. When you don't know your way around in the woods, it's easy to lose direction. After all, any path in the woods looks identical. For some reason, this particular dirt path stood out from the rest. How the boy found her, to begin with, was a feat in itself. "Is that the path that you came from?" The boy nodded. If Persephone were an ordinary mortal, it would have been impossible finding the boy's grandmother. Luckily, for the boy, she was anything but mortal.

Still holding the little boy's hand, Persephone walked in the direction where the energy source was being emitted. They walked on the dirt path that had been created over the years by many carts that had passed through this area.

They walked into the woods together and the boy grasped onto Persephone's hand for comfort. Persephone concentrated on summoning any power that she could muster, hoping to find the boy's missing grandmother. Visualizing the area in her mind, she used her energy to sense any nearby human vibrations. Within a minute, she had felt something. She sensed a mortal's energy source, but it was very weak. Persephone continued walking toward the energy source until. . . she encountered a smashed cart that was surrounded by dead bodies. Their throats had been slashed.

Persephone held her breath as she took in such an unsightly scene. Trying to remain calm, she took the boy and hid him from the ghastly site that lay ahead of her. Persephone brought him over to a few trees and bushes where he could hide easily. "I need you to stay here. I need to make sure that it's safe and see if anyone is hurt."

"No! Don't l-eave me alone!"

"Shhh! Shhh, I'm not going to leave you alone. I'm right here. I just need you to stay put while I check everything out. . . alright? To make sure that it's safe. Now, please stay here!"

The boy hid in the bushes as Persephone walked up to the horrific scene. The truth was, everything that Persephone had seen in the Underworld, and what Hades had taught her, had made her self-confidence blossom. Compared to what lay before her, she had seen worse. To a mortal, this was a tragic circumstance. To a god or goddess, this was just part of daily human life. Pieces of gold were scattered around the dead bodies and Persephone shook her head in disbelief. "All of this was caused by a robbery?" she said to herself out loud, feeling sorrow for all of humankind. They were driven by greed more and more each day.

She heard labored breathing coming from underneath the cart. Cautiously, Persephone slowly bent down to look at what lay under there. She saw an old lady who appeared to be half conscious, trying to stay alive. The goddess noticed fatal wounds on the woman's body that needed immediate medical attention. When it came to assisting mortals, Persephone remembered that her help had to be executed through influence or advice from her inner thoughts and dreams. Directly, gods and goddesses can help when it's essential—when a mortal has no control over the situation.

Knowing this old woman's fate, Persephone looked around, hoping that Thantos would come to collect her. But there was no one. Unless Thantos had arrived earlier to collect these deceased bodies already. "Please." Persephone looked back at the old woman, as she tried to keep her attention with all the strength Persephone had left. "Please help me," the old woman begged.

Persephone bent down under the cart, reaching for the elderly woman's hand. "I'm here. Can you move?"

"Barely," the woman said, choking on the word in pain. Persephone looked for what was causing the woman immense pain. A piece of wood that jutted out from her hip, down to her leg, was pinning her to the ground. Persephone closed her eyes, realizing that there was no way to save her. By the time she calls upon Apollo for help, it'll be too late. Persephone may be a goddess, but healing was not one of her powers, at least she didn't think so.

"I'm the goddess Persephone. So, maybe with my powers, I can try and heal you."

"Don't bother to try, my dear. I appreciate your offer, but I can feel my soul slipping away. Besides, there's nothing left to live for," she said tearfully.

The goddess looked around for Thanatos once more. "Are you the grandmother to a five-year-old boy?"

More tears flowed from the elderly woman's eyes. "Yes."

"Then fight to live for him! He came to me looking for help!"

"My dear goddess, what are you talking about? He's. . . he's. . . " She couldn't talk anymore as she became overwhelmed with more tears. Instead, she pointed toward the opposite direction of where the cart currently laid.

Persephone followed the grandmother's pointed finger, and as she walked toward the spot, she gasped at what she saw. There he was, the same boy who had come to her, crying for help, lying dead on the ground. *How can*

333

this be? she asked herself before saying it out loud. "How can this be!"

She dashed to the spot where she had hid the boy. He was still there, with his eyes watering with worry. "Did you fi-nd my grandma?" Persephone, at that moment, calmed down enough to realize that he was only a shade looking for help. Without Thanatos' arrival or Hermes assistance, the boy is now a lost soul. He was lost indeed.

How can I see him? Is it because of my connection to the Underworld, and to Hades, that created this power? Persephone thought.

"Yes, honey, I found your grandma. . . but you must wait a couple of minutes." Persephone knew that the grandmother's death wouldn't take long. She just knew that The Fates were ready to end the woman's life cord with just the snip of scissors. "Sweetie, what happened to you and your grandmother?" Persephone asked, trying to distract him. But she already knew what had happened.

"Bad people hurt us. They wanted money, so I kept screaming for help. Then it got dark."

Persephone closed her eyes just then. This precious child was killed because he was trying to get help. She'll never understand humanity and their dark side of nature. Taking something that isn't theirs, to begin with, and hurting several innocent people along the way. Where were the gods when this happened? Where was her father? How come he did not do anything? "You are a very brave boy.

The gods smile upon your bravery," she said with determination. "I should know, because I'm one of them."

The boy stared at her in wonder, because he had asked a goddess for help. His grandma had always told him to love and respect the gods. 'Do that,' she had advised, 'and when you need help, they'll be there. He knew all about them because of his grandmother's stories. "Which one are you?" he asked curiously.

"I'm Persephone."

"The goddess of sp-ring?"

She smiled, "That's right. I'm also Hades' future wife now. I see that you know your gods!"

"So that's why you can see him!" Persephone heard the grandmother's voice and turned around to meet her soul. She quickly looked down and saw her lifeless body still under the cart. Persephone felt sorrow because she had now seen a real death. "Don't feel bad for me, my goddess."

"Grandma!" the boy leaped into her arms. "Are you okay?"

The grandmother smiled, relieved. "I am now."

"Grandma? Are we dead?"

"Yes, sweetheart, we are," she said tearfully.

"We have to go to Hades!" the boy said, proudly sharing his knowledge.

"Yes, my love. We do."

She looked at Persephone, hoping that this goddess would give her further explanation. "You being betrothed to Hades probably gave you a gift of seeing the dead, my lady. So, what happens now?"

Persephone shook herself out of her own stupor. "Thanatos was supposed to pick you both up and bring you to Hermes."

"Then to the Underworld?" the grandmother asked, knowing full well what the answer was.

"Yes. I don't understand why I still don't see Thanatos anywhere. I don't want you two wandering around."

"My goddess, you have forgotten the rules. Thanatos doesn't pick up every shade unless there's to be a burial, along with a coin for Charon. There's no one we know that can bury my grandson or me. Nor do we have a coin to pay Charon." The grandmother took an unnecessary breath full of sadness. "We have no choice, but to wander. We are lost souls."

Inner rage was growing inside of Persephone because this situation was not fair. "What about the boy's parents? Can they bury you both?"

"They are already dead, my lady."

"Grandma," The boy interrupted, "When will we go see Hades?"

"Soon, sweetheart." She tried to comfort the boy, fearing that they might be ghosts for a long while.

Persephone had to solve this problem. She's going to be Queen of the Underworld soon, anyway. She has some

power now, doesn't she? She can order her people of the
Underworld to do whatever she wants, right? However, for
her to do that, there will be consequences to face. She'd
have to break the treaty set between her mother and
Hades. "I'll bring you to the Underworld myself."

The grandmother smiled softly. "My goddess, it
would be an honor."

"Are we going now?" the child asked impatiently, just
like a typical little boy would.

Persephone gladly took the boy's hand. "Yes, we're
going right now. Now, come and follow me."

Unfortunately, since they were new souls and
Persephone was still learning how to properly use her
powers, they had to walk to the entrance of the
Underworld. Over an hour had passed before Persephone
found the entryway. She looked at the grandmother and
the boy. Persephone quickly grabbed the grandmother's
hand, "Follow my every step. It can get very dark, and only
I can open the veil."

The grandmother and the boy walked as close to
Persephone as possible. Using her fingers, the young
goddess lit a torch that hung on the wall. The boy looked at
her in amazement.

Persephone guided them further down from the
entrance to Charon's dock. Both the grandmother and the
boy looked around in awe. They didn't expect the
Underworld to hold such beauty,as they heard water drops

fall to the floor. "I never expected this place to be beautiful," the elderly woman said with sincerity.

Smiling, Persephone replied, "Everyone is surprised when they first arrive here. Mortals created such scary stories about Hades over centuries, that they began to believe in them to be true. All because they are scared of the unknown, so they think the worst.

The grandmother nodded as she gripped her grandson's hand. They had finally reached the dock where Charon's boat waited. There stood Charon with a shocked expression on his face. "What are you doing here, my lady? It can't be time for you to see Hades, already."

"No, Charon. As much as I miss my love and can't wait to see him, I'm here doing my duty as future Queen of the Underworld."

Charon looked behind her and saw the two shades. "Them?"

"Yes."

"I'm sorry, my lady, but they can't come onto my boat without a coin. They'll have to wander the earth until they do, or wait until a hundred years have passed."

"They were murdered on a forest road. There was no preparation for their deaths, or a planned burial. So, I'm permitting them to enter the Underworld without their coins."

"Again my lady, I'm sorry, but I can't allow them on board. It's the law."

Persephone looked at Charon straight in the eye, determined to get her way. One way or another. She spoke to him in a very stern voice, "Are you questioning your future queen, Charon? Must I go to Hades and tell him that you've disobeyed my order?" Charon fearfully shook his head no. He loved his king, but he knew how brutal he could be, especially when it came to Persephone. "Then, Charon, let me and these shades come aboard your boat. Take us to the judging panel."

Charon bowed his head, stepping aside to let his future queen and the shades board his boat. As he started rowing, Persephone held her breath while she looked at her other home. She had missed Hades wholeheartedly, but she also missed seeing the beauty and the mystery of the Underworld. It felt as if this place was welcoming her back with open arms. She couldn't wait to see Hades again.

"You missed us, my lady," Charon said, as more of an observation, than a question.

Persephone looked at Charon and smiled, "Of course, I missed all of you. How could I not?"

"This world misses you. The entire place became more depressing than usual, since your absence."

"How is Hades? Is he well?"

"My lady, he has been depressed since you left. He finally felt a little relief because of the Summer Solstice ball. It has been better since then because of it. Still, Hades misses you so," Charon said genuinely, as he kept rowing to the judging panel. Persephone knew that feeling all too well. The ball brought temporary relief from their long separation, but her heart still ached for her lover.

Now, Persephone's heart was pounding excitedly as the boat drew closer to Hades. Then she heard three loud dog barks. Persephone smiled because Cerberus was barking wildly, because he saw that his future queen was coming home now. The grandmother and the boy huddled together, out of fear and confusion, as they watched Persephone eagerly wanting to reach out and hug that dangerous creature. "Hi, Cerberus! How are you, boy?" Persephone shouted across the river as Cerberus continued to bark loudly. His tail wagged with happiness.

Hades could hear Cerberus' constant barking, and grew curious because he had never heard him bark so loud before. He rushed over to see why the dog was barking so much. As he went to the dock near the judging panel, he stopped in his tracks. There he saw the most beautiful thing he had ever seen since the Summer Solstice ball— Persephone on Charon's boat, which was sailing toward him.

Happiness encircled his heart, but at the same time, he was also concerned. It was not the right time for her to be here with him. Persephone smiled when she saw Hades, feeling very giddy as the boat drew closer. She reached her arms out to him, as Charon docked the boat. Persephone squealed as Hades grabbed her, embracing her with the tightest and warmest hug that she had ever received. She inhaled the earthy scent of his neck as she felt him kiss her cheek. A tear escaped from one of her eyes; she couldn't hold back any emotion.

"I missed you, my love," Hades said before kissing her sweet lips. Persephone reciprocated his passionate kiss, showing Hades how much she had missed her lover.

As the grandmother stood behind Persephone, she knew that this sweet moment was something that most people would never see from the King of the Underworld. She remained quiet, letting them cherish their time together. The boy, however, had other plans. "Ewww!" he cried out, as he observed Hades and Persephone's tender embrace.

Hades stopped and looked at the boy with an arched eyebrow. Then, he looked at the grandmother who was right behind his beloved. "Persephone? Why are there two shades with you?"

Persephone looked at Hades and said in all seriousness, "They're the reason why I am here."

Hades smirked momentarily. "I thought you had come here to see me. I thought that you just couldn't stay away from me and my charming looks that you love so much."

Persephone smiled and giggled at his flirtatious efforts. The burden she had felt since their separation no longer weighed on her heart. "Hades, I do miss you and I'm ecstatic to see you, but I think you know better than that. I've come here for an important reason and I'm breaking the treaty with my mother to see this through. Persephone turned back toward the grandmother and the little boy, motioning for them to come closer. She looked at her love with pleading eyes, "Hades, I know that for shades to enter the Underworld, they must give a danake to Charon, but this little boy had cried for help." Persephone held her hand out to the boy. He grabbed onto her and inched closer to the Lord of Death without any fear. "He and his grandmother were murdered in the woods. There's no one left in their family who can give these two a proper funeral. Thanatos didn't show up, so I took this into my own hands and brought them here."

Acting more like the King of the Underworld now, Hades stared at the boy and then looked at the grandmother. "You are fortunate to have had your future queen escort you both here."

The grandmother spoke, "We know that, my lord. I beg you to let us through, despite having no form of payment. If not both of us . . . at least take my grandson. He needs to rest and if I have to wait for a hundred years. . ." Tears started flowing from her eyes. The woman was crying not only for the possibility of being left behind, but also for everything else that she had endured today. "If I have to wait, I will. Just please take . . ." Hades held up his hand, which forced her to stop talking.

No one was aware that, during the entire time that she was talking, Hades was already judging her soul. After sifting through her mind and reviewing her memories, Hades saw a kind-hearted soul who had loved her children and her grandchild more than life itself. Despite having endured several major tragedies that had surrounded her kids, this elderly woman still had a warm heart and had always prayed to the gods for comfort.

"While you were talking, I was judging your soul," Hades said. "Persephone escorted you to my realm and as her future husband, I will allow you and your grandson to enter my realm. Now, let me escort you both to your new home. Please, follow me."

Hades kept to the left of the judging panel and made a quick turn. Persephone was unsure if he would let them reside in the Asphodel Meadows or the Elysian Fields. As they walked on, she knew the answer. Persephone's heart was full of happiness, not only because of Hades' kindness, but also because she knew the destined fates of these shades. Where they were headed would be splendid.

As they entered the Elysian Fields, the grandmother and her grandson felt a sense of peace and contentment. Out of everything in the Underworld, this was Persephone's favorite place. Indeed, it is a place full of pure happiness and peace.

Then, they heard a voice utter, "MOMMA! PAPA!" the little boy yelled out as his parents came into view. He

ran to them at light speed. Meanwhile, the grandmother
suddenly felt guilty as she went to see her children.

"I'm sorry. I'm so sorry," The grandmother said as
she began to cry, "I didn't protect him well enough."

The boy's parents looked at her sympathetically and
with forgiveness. "It was not your fault. How were you
supposed to know what would happen? After all, the gods
didn't grant you the gift of foreseeing the unknown," The
boy's mother said, as she gave her own mother a giant hug.
The grandmother was overwhelmed with tears because she
was finally reunited with her family again, including her
husband, who had also joined them.

Watching them brought joyous tears to Persephone's
eyes, as she felt Hades wrap his arms around her.
Together, they both observed this sweet family gathering
and felt a sense of tranquility. "See, my love," Hades said,
"There is joy in death. Being reunited with your loved ones
is one of the perks of being dead."

Persephone laughed. "The perks of being dead?"

"Well, it is true. As you can see, a little boy is now
reunited, not only with his grandmother, but also with his
parents." Then Hades whispered in her ear, "All because of
you, my love. Look how much eternal happiness you have
brought to these people." Hades looked around the Elysian
Fields and saw all of the happy and carefree souls. "This is
why I love what I do."

"I can see why," Persephone nodded in response, "It really is an incredible feeling—leading the souls to their final resting place. I feel like I'm providing an important service."

"That is what many gods don't understand about why I prefer not to leave this place. There is so much beauty here, as well as on Earth. As a god, I love what I do."

"Tell that to the mortals. They still think that you're some kind of monster."

Hades frowned. "Do you think I am a monster?"

"No! Of course not!"

"Then that's all that matters, my love. Your opinion is the only one that matters to me."

Persephone continued to watch the reunited family. "Where was my father when this happened?"

Hades looked at her, frowning, "What do you mean?"

"Why didn't he hear the old woman's prayers as they were being attacked? Didn't Father hear her?"

"I'm sure he did," Hades replied unsarcastically.

"Then how come he allowed for this to happen?" Persephone turned to look at Hades with sadness in her eyes.

Hades took a deep breath, hoping that Persephone would understand the ways of life, including those of the gods. "My love, sometimes people die because they are destined to die. In other words, their time is up, even if their lives end violently. Zeus and The Fates have control over that."

"So, you are saying that the grandmother and her grandson were destined to die today?" Persephone asked skeptically.

"Yes."

"No! No! I refuse to believe that! The boy was only five years old! How can you say that the boy's time was up?"

"Because he did what he was supposed to do—he was there for his grandmother until she died. Now, some souls return to Earth, helping out other souls that they have been assigned to assist. Once their time is up, then it's time to go home, which is here. There was no reason for that boy to stay any longer. His family is here, and there was no set destiny for him, other than being the light of his grandmother's life. Would you want the boy to live alone on Earth for the rest of his life?"

"Why would a soul go through all that trouble of being born, just to live a short life?" Persephone asked, as more tears threatened to fall.

"Usually, it's to keep a promise that they once made in a previous life, which has yet to be fulfilled. It could also be a way to give back to someone who didn't have a chance to give because of their untimely death. Sometimes a soul could be there for just a few days, to give a lesson or the love that a soul needs."

"There is no such thing as an untimely death, is there?"

"No, there is not. Even murder and deadly accidents are planned ahead before they actually happen."

"So what? Does this mean that it's okay to murder because The Fates make it just?"

"No, it's not okay. Yes, fate and destiny do manifest. However, there is free will. Can you change the future? Yes, it is possible, but The Fates have the upper hand.

"What if something shouldn't continue, even if it's a good thing, like relationships or a leader's rational plans?"

"Then we gods have a meeting and discuss changing it. If something isn't right or needs to be taken care of, then we can talk to The Fates and Zeus about changing it."

Persephone looked at her beloved as an unexpected thought came to mind. "What about our relationship? Is that destined too?"

Hades swallowed hard. He knew that he would have to answer this question at some point. "It is."

"Then how do I know that you love me?"

"My love, you have it backwards. Knowing your destiny only confirms what you are meant to do and what you want to do. It doesn't mean that everyone is a puppet, following the puppet master. How you arrive at your destiny and how you feel about it, is up to you. Yes, we are destined to be together, but we still need to make certain steps for our relationship to exist. Yes, we are meant for each other. That doesn't change how much I love you, no matter if I'd known our destiny or not."

"I still don't fully understand this."

Hades nodded in agreement. "I know, and it's all right. We'll discuss this another time. As much as I hate to bring this up, my love, you must return to your mother before she brings upon another wrath to Earth. Then I won't see you for another six months!"

But before their conversation ended, Persephone remembered something. "Hades, how come I saw the shades on Earth? Was it because I ate the pomegranate or is it because of my betrothal to you?"

"That is something you must talk about with The Fates. Personally, I don't know because you had this ability before we met."

Shaking her head, confused, Persephone thought hard about when that might've happened before having met Hades. "That can't be. It wasn't until after I met you that I could do such a thing."

"On the night of your initiation, while all of the gods and goddesses were enjoying your company, no one saw me . . . except you. No one, not even you, was supposed to see me. When you saw me, I was wearing my invisibility helmet."

"I was wondering why no one saw or spoke to you." Persephone thought about when they had first met. It felt so long ago now. "Even Athena thought I'd grown a second head when I pointed to you, wondering who you were. But you were invisible to everyone else?"

Hades nodded. "I was surprised when this beautiful goddess not only spotted me, but began talking to me with curious eyes. It turns out, my love, that you can see the invisible. To see beings that are meant to be hidden from both mortal and god eyes." He smiled as Persephone gave him a passionate kiss before boarding Charon's boat.

Persephone knew that her time with Demeter would soon come to a close. Even so, it hurt her to walk away from Hades again. At least this time she felt a sense of purpose as Queen of the Underworld, after delivering the two shades to where they belong.

CHAPTER 18

TIME OF THE SEASON

The early morning was creeping upon the earth as Persephone tried to tiptoe back into the house, praying that she wouldn't wake her mother. After having spent time with Hades and breaking the treaty, she dreaded facing the consequences. Persephone then heard a concerned voice.

"Where were you?" Demeter demanded angrily. She had waited up for Persephone all night long. She sat in her chair with her arms crossed and a stern look on her face.

After releasing a breath she didn't realize that she had been holding in, Persephone answered her mother in goddess-like manner. "I had something to take care of. A couple of mortals needed my assistance, so I answered their prayers."

Demeter didn't expect that kind of answer from Persephone. "You actually received a prayer?" Demeter asked with genuine surprise, but Persephone couldn't help but sense her mother's doubt.

"You sound so surprised. Did you not think that I was going to be worshiped at all?"

"No, I didn't think that at all. I knew the mortals would need you in some way, eventually. But why did they need you for such a long time yesterday? No mortal would pray out of desperation for flowers to grow at night." Persephone knew what her mother was getting at, she could tell just by the way Demeter looked. She looked at her daughter suspiciously.

"I'm not lying, Mother, if that's what you're thinking. Mortals needed my help yesterday and for most of the night, too!" Persephone knew she had to tell her mother the truth. "I was helping a lost child find his grandmother."

Confusion struck Demeter just then, "Why would you help them, Persephone? I mean, that's kind of you, but that's not your area of expertise my dear. I think that kind of responsibility belongs to Hermes."

"At first, I thought it would be a simple task. I just needed to find the grandmother and leave the child with her. Except, by the time I found the grandmother,. . . The child that I was helping . . . I found his body. The grandmother was dying too."

Everything suddenly became clear to Demeter, "The boy came to you, asking for help, as a shade?"

"Yes." Persephone held her breath again, afraid of her mother's reaction.

"How could you see him? You are not Queen of the Underworld, yet."

"According to Hades, I was born with this ability. It's not just the shades mother, I can also see things that are meant to be hidden. At my initiation, I saw Hades while he was wearing his invisibility helmet. I was the only one who saw Hades while Father was looking for him. Even when I was talking to him, with Athena standing right next to me, she couldn't see Hades and he was right in front of her."

"After all these years, not once did you show any sign of seeing hidden things when you were younger."

"Mother, I didn't know that what I saw was invisible to everyone else. I just assumed that whatever I saw was meant to be there in the first place."

She didn't know what to do or say. For the first time, Persephone couldn't read what was going through Demeter's mind. In fact, her mother just looked numb. "You went to the Underworld, didn't you?"

Gently nodding, Persephone replied, "I had to. I had no choice. I couldn't just leave the shades there."

"If I recall the death protocol correctly, Thanatos was supposed to bring about death and lead the shades to the Underworld entrance. Then, Hermes is obligated to guide them the rest of the way."

"That is the correct protocol. The problem was, no one came to guide the shades because they were murdered, since they weren't going to have a proper burial or burning. They didn't have danakes either. As the future Queen of the Underworld, it was my duty to bring them to Hades. Otherwise, their souls would have been lost, wandering around like ghosts."

"Do you realize that you broke the treaty Hades and I had created?"

Persephone felt infuriated, as she gave her mother a confident response, "Yes, I know that I broke the treaty. In fact, Hades was worried that he wouldn't see me for a long while because of this." Persephone raised her voice. "But I did what I had to, Mother! I'm the future Queen of the Underworld! Mortal souls are my responsibility, no matter what season it is. If one calls for my help, I will answer! It is my job. If you think that helping a soul is breaking your treaty, then go to Olympus and talk to Father about it."

Demeter didn't even budge. She didn't even blink. In fact, Persephone saw something she had never seen on her mother's face before. . . Defeat. Shame. Guilt. These emotions showed Demeter's true age within her eyes. Feeling more than a thousand years older, the goddess of agriculture and harvest moved slowly out the door of their home. "I need to talk to someone. You have been up all night, why don't you get some rest, Persephone."

As Demeter closed the door behind her, Persephone stared at the entrance, dumbfounded. She was tired, but more than anything, she was also anxious. She had no idea what her mother was going to do. Who was she going to see? Her father? One of her friends that owes her a favor? Demeter didn't even tell her to stay inside, nor did she call for a nymph to come watch Persephone. Fear kept gnawing at Persephone, because her mother honestly wasn't acting like herself at all. The one thing Persephone felt obligated to do was pray to the universal energy, hoping that everything would be all right.

While Charon rowed his boat, he felt someone's presence at the entrance of the Underworld. As he whistled while he rowed, Cerberus stood at the edge of the river, barking like a mad bloodhound. "What's got your heads in a twist?" Charon asked, but Cerberus continued to bark. Charon grew concerned because he didn't see Hermes, nor a any souls, in the near distance

With Cerberus barking, Charon was on alert. By using his own personal power, he gave a gentle wave of his hand and every torch that burned near him grew brighter. He made sure that not only did the torches on his boat burn brighter, but that every torch in the Underworld did as well. Hades had granted Charon the power to control light, in case anything happened.

There, by the Underworld's entrance, stood Demeter. Upon looking at her, Charon's mouth had a bitter taste. Charon spoke to Demeter as he docked the boat. "Now I know why Cerberus went nuts. He really is a good guard dog, especially when a threat to the King's happiness is present."

Demeter was stunned by Charon's disrespect, "How dare you. As your goddess, you need to treat me with some respect!"

"You are not my goddess. You are not my queen either. You might be the mother of my future queen, but you have no authority or respect here otherwise."

Ignoring Charon's comment, Demeter demanded, "Speaking of your King, I need to speak with him."

"Why? Why should I bring you to him? So you can cause continued suffering and misery? To remind him that Persephone is with you? I think not."

"I am concerned about Persephone, that is why I am here." Demeter for once had to swallow her pride. " I . . . I need Hades' advice when it comes to my daughter." It may have only been one sentence, but for Demeter, it was a mouthful. Charon just stared at her with his eyebrows raised, speechless. He didn't know what to think. Part of him wanted to laugh in her face for needing Hades' help, but he also felt sorry for her. He knew that what she was doing wasn't easy for anyone, let alone a goddess who believed that she had done everything right.

"Please, Charon, bring me to Hades." Demeter then put ten danakes into Charon's hand. Business got the better of him. "Come aboard, my lady."

"Thank you," Demeter said as she stepped onto Charon's boat. As Charon rowed them toward their destination, Demeter took in the current state of the Underworld. The last time she had come down here was before Hades had inherited the place, giving it life and order. Back then, it was merely just a cave filled with darkness. Now, she saw it the way Persephone had described, seeing the real beauty and majesty that this realm contained. As they neared the judging panel, Demeter felt nervous. She had no idea how to resolve this issue between her and Hades.

As Charon docked the boat, Demeter noticed Hades was already standing there with his arms crossed. He looked disgusted. "What are you doing here?" Hades growled.

Demeter knew she had to be careful; she took Charon's words to heart. She decided to take a very calm and civil approach. "I came here to talk to you . . . about . . . Persephone."

Hades suddenly looked concerned, "Is she all right?"

"Physically, she is fine. Right now, she is resting at my house."

"Well, I don't know about you, Demeter, but if I had only six months to spend with her—which will happen when my time comes around—I'd spend every minute with her. If I recall correctly, that is what you use to do before her initiation. Now you are wasting your time with me, when you should be with her."

While Hades was talking, every nearby shade had crept up behind him, trying to eavesdrop. They wanted to find out what was going on between Hades and their future queen. Demeter noticed this and really began to feel uncomfortable because a plethora of shades had now joined in on her conversation with Hades. Demeter was trying to keep calm as she felt their eyes staring at her. "Can we talk privately somewhere else?"

Hades smirked while his eyes scanned the room full of shades. "In my palace. Go on, I'll be there in a minute."

Demeter walked hastily to Hades castle, nearly running. Hades almost chuckled at the sight. It has been a long time since he saw Demeter look afraid. He walked toward Charon who stood by the dock. "You actually brought her here?" he asked seriously.

"I warned her that she had no authority or respect by being here, my lord. I even told her how unhappy I was to see her, but she insisted on seeing you."

Hades looked at him with slight doubt. "She paid you, didn't she?"

Charon closed his eyes shamefully, "Ten danakes."

Hades crossed his arms again. "I know about the game you and Hermes play, betting on the deaths of new shades that come here." Charon didn't say anything and just stared at Hades. "Should I ban shades from coming into the Underworld without a fee from the ferryman?" Charon looked at him with horror. "After all, everyone who comes to the Underworld is supposed to be free, right?"

"My Lord, I'm sorry that I brought Demeter here, but what else was I supposed to do? Just keep her there?"

"Yes. Eventually Demeter would've just turned back anyway. She can't be away from her daughter for too long. Speaking of which, I have to go see her."

"Are you going to punish me?" Charon asked suspiciously.

Hades gave the ferryman a dark smirk. "We will see. It depends on what Demeter wants." Hades went toward the direction of his palace, leaving Charon to wonder what his master would do. Whether he would receive punishment or not.

Hades braced himself, knowing that Demeter wanted to talk about Persephone's visit from last night. There stood Demeter, next to his living room fireplace. She just stared into the hearth, like she was enchanted by the flames. "Demeter?" Hades spoke gently, wanting not to startle her.

Demeter looked at Hades with sadness in her eyes. "I can see why Persephone was so in awe of this place. She mentioned wonderful things about the Underworld. Though I haven't seen all of it, based on what I've seen so far. . ." Demeter didn't finish her sentence because she was overwhelmed with tears. "You spoil her with riches and jewels, I take it?"

"Of course. Persephone is going to be my wife and queen, she deserves to be treated like royalty. She is everything to me."

"And to me, as well! I can't compete with you Hades."

"As much as I like to hear that, we are not supposed to be competing against each other. You will always be Persephone's mother, Demeter, nothing in the universe can change that. And I'll be her husband. Though, they are very different roles. Is that what you are afraid of? That I'm replacing you as a parental figure?" Demeter just stared at him silently. "I'm not going to be another parent to her."

"But you did that with me, and you are my brother!" A tear escaped from one of her eyes.

"I had to. Despite being in Cronus' stomach, I wasn't going to let my siblings live in despair. I did it out of love, so that everyone involved wouldn't be bitter about the experience like I was. Why do you think I'm the most responsible? The serious god who hardly enjoys any festivities? We may be gods Demeter, but being swallowed by our father did do something drastic to us both, whether we realize it or not. Are you going to keep Persephone under lock and key because of what we had to endure together? After what Zeus did to you?"

Demeter closed her eyes, "Zeus didn't do anything wrong."

"No?" Hades asked, his tone sounded disagreeable. "He didn't make you Queen of the Gods like he promised, did he?"

"You know about that? I thought only Athena and Hestia knew about that."

"We ALL know about that, Demeter. Another reason why you continue to hold on to Persephone so tightly."

"She is the only precious thing I have, the only valuable thing that Zeus ever gave me."

"She is precious, yes, but Persephone is also a grown woman who wants a husband and a family of her own. She wants her own life as a goddess. You have no idea how powerful she really is."

"That's where you shine, Hades. You saw her spark and I didn't. I don't want Persephone to endure any of the experiences that I had. Not just with Cronus, but what had also happened with Zeus. . ."

Hades nodded, "I understand, but that is not going to happen to her, Demeter. I will love her and be faithful to her for all eternity."

"She admitted that she had come here last night, to complete an errand for a couple of mortals who had passed on." Hades just nodded, hoping that this wouldn't make things worse for everyone. "Is it true? That she can see things of the unknown?"

"Yes. Persephone was born with this gift, Demeter."

"That is when I knew for sure." Her tears were now making themselves known.

"Knew what for sure?"

"That she was meant to be yours. Seeing death and the unknown, that is your area of expertise, Hades."

"She is still the goddess of life and spring, though. That is something you need to understand. As I said earlier, Persephone is a powerful goddess. She will be in charge of life and death, noticing the unseen, and seeing the beauty that is all around her. She needs to have more freedom so that she can be powerful."

Demeter nodded. "I'm letting go of my pride by asking you this. You are closer to Persephone than I ever was. How can I make my little girl happy again when she stays with me?"

"I think we should get rid of this treaty," Hades said simply enough.

"You know if we do, she'll spend more time with you than me."

"Honestly, even if it kills me to say it, we should stick to the six-month time frame. The earth needs her to spread new life and flowers. Then, she'll spend six months here with me. Spring and summer seasons will need her. So, during the fall and winter, she will be with me. You can still spread your wrath without having serious consequences for the mortals to live with," Demeter stared at Hades sternly, "Less for me to judge."

"Then, what is the point of breaking the treaty, if you believe that the same time frame is still efficient?"

"I just want no more rules. In other words, if I need to speak or see Persephone while she is with you, I may do so. The same goes for you. Also, if Persephone is needed elsewhere for some purpose, I don't want our treaty to stop her. She will be a great goddess, but she needs that freedom to fully embrace her powers. You know Persephone would love you if you were the one to break the treaty. In her eyes, you would no longer be a villain."

"Yes, I'll do it," Demeter answered with her eyes closed, feeling defeated.

Hades, for once, gave his sister a genuine smile for coming to her senses. "Don't feel so defeated, Demeter. You are actually saving your relationship with Persephone. I may be the God of the Underworld and Death, but I don't want to be the reason that destroys a precious relationship between mother and daughter."

Demeter nodded as she made peace with Hades. Charon rowed her back to the entrance. Hades watched as the boat faded from view, and he smiled softly to himself.

He felt the tension between Demeter and himself dissipate. He hoped that Demeter would keep her word and break the treaty, which would give Persephone her freedom. As Hades returned to the judging panel, Charon was at the dock. Hades knew why he was there and smirked. Charon looked at him worriedly, "My lord? What is my punishment?"

"I should give you one, but you are lucky, Charon. Demeter and I resolved our conflict, so there's no consequence for you." Charon let out a sigh of relief. "However, take five of those danakes that she gave you and give them to some worthy mortal in need."

Charon gladly accepted Hades' request. "Thank you, my lord."

Persephone couldn't stop pacing around the house. She had no idea where mother went or who she was speaking to. She felt her stomach churn at the thought of what her mother was doing right now. Will she be taken away from Hades forever, because of what she had done? If that is the reason, Persephone will fight with everything she had to prevent that from happening.

Hours passed before her mother finally returned home, looking slightly defeated. Persephone was ready to defend herself, anticipating what her mother would say, but she paused instead. Persephone wondered why her mother was so upset, because Demeter really looked like a centuries-old woman.

"Hello, my Kore."

Persephone rolled her eyes, "Mother, I told you not to call me that."

Demeter nodded, "Forgive me, Persephone," she rephrased, as she sat down in a chair by the table. She really looked as if she had no power left to use.

Cautious about what to say, Persephone moved closer to her mother, "Where did you go?"

Demeter couldn't look at her daughter, but she mustered up the courage to do so. She must confess, which is out of character for herself. "I went to see Hades." Persephone closed her eyes, assuming the worst. "Trust me, darling, it's not what you think. It was just him and I having a civil conversation. I needed to know about you and the unknown gift that you possess."

"You actually sat down with Hades and just talked?" Demeter nodded in response. "Did you threaten him?"

Demeter wanted to be angry at her daughter's accusation, but how could she? All she accomplished was making threats and being too stubborn to actually listen, in the first place. "There were no threats. There was some anger and a misunderstanding, but there were no threats. Although, I did not feel welcomed by the Underworld citizens, I tell you."

"Can you blame them? It truly is another kingdom down there and you hurt their king, as well as their future queen."

"I'll never be totally all right with this, Persephone. You are still my baby, no matter how old you are. Just the idea of you marrying someone who rules over death. . ."

"He's more than that, Mother," Persephone responded kindly. "He really loves me and will do anything for me. Hades won't run off like Ares or Apollo."

"I know that, which is why I was so scared about your marriage once I found out that you can see the dead all by yourself. You and Hades are supposed to be together, but I was afraid that you wouldn't be with me anymore. That, instead, you would be trapped forever in the Underworld."

"Everyone loves me there, Mother, especially Hades." Persephone paused, fearing what Demeter's next question might be. "Are you going to visit Father, so that you can punish Hades and I because of what I had to do for those shades?"

Demeter shook her head no. "I spoke with Hades and realized that I was truly hurting you when I took you away from him." Demeter started to cry. "I didn't realize that I was losing my daughter because I was being so possessive. As your mother, I wanted to separate you from someone who loves you just as much as I do."

"Is it because of what Father and Grandfather did to you? That's why you overprotect me, isn't it?"

Confusion showed on Demeter's face, "I never told you about Cronus."

Persephone nodded her head, "Hades told me."

"Why would he tell you about . . . ?"

Persephone looked sheepishly at her mother, "I accidentally went into Tartarus and got trapped there. I bumped into my grandfather who was chained to a wall."

"You met him?" Demeter felt all of her worries come creeping back.

Persephone nodded. "What's scary is that he knew who I was. He called me in the middle of the night, that's how I got trapped in Tartarus." Demeter looked horrified. "Don't worry, Hades got to me just in time."

"Then you know it's not my first time being in the Underworld. It didn't look like that when I came down there."

Persephone nodded, "I saw your handiwork on Cronus."

"Next time when you are in the Underworld, and especially around Tartarus, ignore your grandfather's call. He's very manipulative. That's how he became king to begin with. That's why he is so dangerous." Persephone genuinely smiled at her mother. "What is it, darling?" Demeter asked.

"You are actually giving me real advice for when I visit the Underworld again. You aren't hiding information from me anymore."

Demeter gave a little smile of her own. "There is no point anymore. You have seen so much, Persephone, more than most mortals and even gods, for that matter. You have a powerful gift that even your father wishes he had. Hades believes you are a powerful goddess. . . . and so do I. I don't want to interfere with your growth and happiness anymore." Tears of joy started to fall down Persephone's face.

"Speaking of which," Demeter continued, "The treaty between your future husband and I. We still believe that you should have six months with each of us." Persephone frowned for a moment. "But if you ever need to see one of us or need to be on either side for anything, even if it is just to talk, we believe you should have the freedom to do so."

"So, if I'm here with you, I can still see Hades whenever I wish?" a smile began to spread across Persephone's face.

Demeter nodded, "As long as you come back to me on that same day during those six months. The same thing applies for Hades. If you ever need to see me, you can."

"Does Father know?"

"I'll inform him tomorrow."

Persephone gave Demeter the biggest hug ever, including a kiss on the cheek. "I love you, Mother. Never forget that; just because I'm grown and about to be married."

"And I love you, my precious daughter, so much."

Persephone hesitated, but she had to ask, "Can I?"

Demeter didn't need any more of a clue about what her daughter was asking. "Yes, you may go see Hades. Just come back before it gets dark."

Persephone gave her mother another quick kiss and rushed off to the Underworld, ready to see her fiancé. Demeter sat there, as a feeling of tranquility washed over her. Not only had she let the past go, but she had also released her daughter from Demeter's overbearing grip, letting Persephone have her own path. The bitter tension between mother and daughter was gone.

"Charon!" Persephone shouted excitedly from across the Acheron River. "Charon!"

"I'm coming as fast as I can, my lady!" Charon saw Persephone with the biggest smile on her face. He docked the boat, letting her come aboard. "My lady, what an honor for you to be back so soon."

"Please take me to him."

"I'm sure he'll be thrilled to see you, and I'll gladly take you to him." Charon rowed faster than usual, trying to return his future queen back to his king, where she belonged.

Then they heard loud and excited barks coming from Cerberus. "Hello, boy!" Persephone called out. "I'll see you soon!" His barking continued, which, of course, made everyone in the Underworld stand at attention. Including Hades, whose attention was focused on Charon's boat. He never saw anything lovelier than his beloved, who carried a big smile on her face. Hades knew that her smile was meant for him.

Persephone exited the boat and ran to Hades. He instantly encircled her with his arms and captured her lips. She moaned for his fiery kiss. Persephone couldn't contain her love and kissed Hades back with much more enthusiasm, locking her arms around his neck. A low moan escaped from Hades' throat, as he passionately explored her mouth. Before they got too carried away, Persephone rested her hands on his face and looked into his eyes. Hades spoke first, "Your mother broke the treaty?"

"She broke the treaty! I can see you whenever I want!"

Hades gave her a bright smile. "I wasn't sure if she was going to do that. I mentioned that's what she should do, so that your relationship with her would not grow bitter."

"I still have to stay with her for six months, like I do with you, but at least I can still visit! No restrictions! Well, I shouldn't say that. I still have to return to her before nightfall."

Hades nodded. "Sounds fair."

"I'm so happy right now, I have no idea what to do!"

Hades grinned wickedly, "There many things we can do right now." Persephone blushed. knowing full well what he meant. "It is amazing that despite everything we have done, you still blush as if it is your first time."

"I think I'll never get over the fact that someone so powerful and so handsome can love . . ."

Hades interrupted her sentence, ". . . A powerful goddess who, very soon, will not only have the powers of life, but also death as well. Also, this amazing goddess has the power to see the invisible. She is so beautiful that any god would want her as a lover and consort." Persephone was silenced by Hades' profound words. "I'm the luckiest god in the world, not only for ruling over a powerful kingdom, but also because I have a lovely and powerful goddess who loves me in return."

Persephone smiled and leaned into his embrace. Hades remembered to give Persephone something to think about. "There's another thing you can do now, since you can freely visit your mother and I."

"Which is?"

"You can plan our wedding. I'll do some of it here, but if there's anything you want to do while you're up there, you have the freedom now to do as you wish."

Love and excitement ran through Persephone's body, like Zeus' lightning bolt. "Where shall we have it?"

Hades smiled, "Here in the Underworld, there have been enough parties at Olympus. It'll be nice to have everyone come here for a change."

Persephone agreed, "Everyone should get to know the Underworld as well."

"We can even get married in the Elysian Fields, so that you can have all of your flowers when we say our vows to one another. Then, you will be Queen of the Underworld."

Persephone smiled. She could just imagine what their wedding would be like. "I'll be the most beautiful wife." "How can I forget?" Hades gave Persephone a passionate kiss before carrying her into his palace. He wanted to make sweet love to her, as they embraced a bright future together.

CHAPTER 19

WORLD COLLUSION

Hades and Persephone slept peacefully in each other's arms. Exhausted from their lovemaking, they decided to take a nap together. They both fell into a deep sleep, despite Persephone having to return to her mother soon. Contentment and happiness filled their lives like a shield. Nothing could penetrate their love and joy for one another. At last, after so many centuries, Hades felt at peace with his life and his purpose.

Then, suddenly, Hades gasped himself awake. He felt terror spread over his entire body like one of Zeus' lightning bolts. Something was wrong, very wrong. The

Underworld itself was calling to Hades, warning him that danger lurked nearby. The threat was waiting in Tartarus.

With caution, Hades silently slipped out of Persephone's arms, as he tried not to wake her. In a flash, he was dressed in his robes and armor. As more time passed, the more Hades felt danger intensify. His gut was full of extreme fear. He quickly grabbed his pitchfork and the invisibility helmet, ready to put on the helmet, when he heard his lover's voice, "Where are you going?"

"Go back to sleep, my love. Our domain calls for me, so I must find out what it needs."

With her eyes barely open, Persephone saw the weapons that Hades held in his hands. She noticed his armor, too. She frowned with concern, "Judging souls with weapons? What's wrong, Hades?"

"Darling, it's probably just a tiny issue. Please, go back to sleep." Persephone felt sick to her stomach. She had never seen Hades worry so much about the Underworld. She watched him leave their chamber. There was no way that she could possibly go back to sleep now. She had a terrible gut feeling about this.

Hades walked slowly down the hall that led to Tartarus. Walking was safer than teleporting, since he had no idea what danger was lurking within his domain. The horrible feeling he had grew more as he inched closer. . . and closer. As he neared Tartarus, Hades slowed down as he heard the shades scream again. The walls were thinning once more. *For what reason?* Hades thought in frustration.

As he touched the walls, Hades felt a wave of energy vibrating through to the other side. The walls of Tartarus were extremely thin now, which made Hades more than just a little nervous. He utilized his own power to strengthen the realm's barrier. It vibrated out only a small amount of energy now. As Hades touched the hallway wall again, his eyes widened. He barely felt any energy at all.

Hades had no idea what was going on inside, but he knew that, for once, he was going to need his brother's help. Including help from all the other gods as well. Hades sensed that Tartarus was on the brink of collapsing in only a matter of minutes. If he opened the door to Tartarus now, it might cause even more trouble. Hades immediately teleported back to his palace and tried not to panic.

Once Hades returned to their chamber, his beloved was already dressed in armor that fit her quite well. "Did you feel the Underworld's outcry?" Hades asked Persephone, as he held his helmet under his arm.

Persephone frowned and closed her eyes again, trying to feel what he felt. Like the danger had done with Hades earlier, it startled Persephone and now made her fully alert. "It's Tartarus."

"It is. The walls are disintegrating." Hades was giving her a command as calm as he could. Though it barely hid the fear in his eyes. "I need you to go to Olympus and call every god for help."

Persephone looked at him with fearful wide eyes. "My love, you are scaring me. I have never seen you—" Her words were cut short when they both heard sudden, ferocious screams. They listened as the demons and furies made frightening noises. At last, they heard Cerberus barking wildly. The energy barrier of Tartarus lasted for only a few seconds more.

"The walls of Tartarus are now gone. Go and get your father! I'll escort you to the chariot, so that you can get out of here. Then when you exit from here, as quickly as you can, go to Olympus and tell your father what happened. Round up every god who is willing to come here and help us." Hades took a deep breath before giving Persephone his final instruction, "Also, I want you to stay at Olympus until this is over."

"Hades, I think I need to be here with you this time."

"No. I need you to stay at Olympus. It will be easier for me to fight, knowing that you are safe." They hugged each other tightly, as Persephone began to cry. How many times had fate intervened between her and Hades? Hades grabbed Persephone's hand just then, "Come on, my brave flower, I'll protect you as we walk to the chariot. You have to leave now!"

Cautiously, Hades and Persephone left their palace at once. Still, from all of the noises that surrounded the couple, they could tell that some of the beasts and deadly souls had been released. Zoe came running up to them and whispered, "My lords!"

Persephone gave Zoe a quick hug. Hades interrupted their embrace, asking for critical information, "What have you seen?"

Zoe didn't know where to begin. "My lord. . . Whoever was in Tartarus is now on a rampage in the Underworld. More importantly, my lord, some of your subjects are no longer with you."

"What do you mean?" Hades frowned out of significant concern.

"One of the main prisoners that escaped has now gained a favor."

Persephone instantly knew who this was, "Is it Cronus?" Zoe nodded.

Hades couldn't believe what he was hearing. His own father was running loose? Not only that, but now Cronus had convinced some of Hades' Underworld subjects to betray him. Hades understood that Tartarus was indeed growing weaker by the minute. This problem has been going on for quite some time. It was his own father who had been trying to escape and, at last, Cronus had finally succeeded. "Persephone, now you have to tell your father that Cronus has escaped. We've got to get you out of here!"

They ran toward the chariot, as Zoe fetched the steed horses. As Persephone hopped into the chariot, one of the furies came at her, screaming. Sensing the attack, Hades killed the furie with his pitchfork, as Persephone ducked down. Things were getting out of hand.

"You have to go!" Hades yelled.

Persephone gave him a quick, passionate kiss, full of desperation and fear. She was afraid that she might not see him again. "I will come back with father and save our world."

Looking over Hades' shoulder, Persephone's eyes widened as she saw a fire from Tartarus spreading throughout the Underworld. With a fierce speed, the dead steeds and their future queen left the Underworld and flew to Mount Olympus.

Hades made sure that his beloved exited the Underworld safely.

Goddess Hecate ran toward him just then. "Hades! Chaos will spread even more if anything from this realm escapes into the mortal world. With your permission, may I create a barrier for the entrance?!" She had to yell because the noise from Tartarus was growing louder, as more souls roamed free.

"So be it, Hecate. Just let the gods enter our realm when they show up! How many souls escaped?!"

"I am not sure, Hades. They are all over the place."

While they were talking, several furies came over and started to attack. For Hecate and Hades, the furies were nothing difficult to destroy, it just took great strength and use of their powers to get the job done. "We have to return all of these souls to Tartarus!" Hades shouted. "Put order back into the realm!"

"Hades! Listen to me! There are no more walls surrounding Tartarus! The energy level from that realm is gone! Cronus took it all!"

Coming from the direction of Tartarus, in the distance, Hades heard someone call his name. Chills ran down his spine as he recognized his father's voice.

Persephone commanded the dead steeds to go faster, because she knew that her love was in genuine danger. The last thing she heard before leaving the Underworld was Cronus' voice calling her love's name. She finally reached the entrance of Olympus and, without hesitation, she quickly ran to the throne room.

When Persephone entered the throne room, she ran up to her father. Luckily for her, all the gods, including her mother, were there in the middle of discussing an important matter: The War of Troy. All of them stared at Persephone, bewildered. They had never seen Persephone so panicked before, as she rushed into the room, not caring that she had interrupted their meeting.

Persephone collapsed by her father's feet, trying to catch her breath. "Persephone!" everyone shouted as

Demeter and Zeus rushed to her side. Everyone started to whisper, wondering what had happened.

While still trying to catch her breath, Persephone spoke up, "Cro-Cronus. . .is. . .loose!"

The whole room fell silent as fear seeped into every god's eyes. The mighty titan that had created the gods, and who also had the ability to destroy them all . . . is now free.

Zeus grew more concerned than ever before. "My daughter, is he still in the Underworld?"

Persephone nodded. "When I left to come find you, he still was, but he is no longer in Tartarus. Some of Hades' subjects are now serving Cronus and the walls of Tartarus have collapsed."

Right then and there, Zeus gave commanding orders. "Everyone, arm yourselves by gathering your powers and weapons. Hephaestus, make as many thunderbolts as you can! We are all going to the Underworld."

Ares shouted out in prideful joy, "FINALLY! THE DAY JUST GOT BETTER!"

Hera hissed at him, "ARES! THIS IS NOT THE TIME TO SHOW OFF!"

"Mother, this is my shining moment! I should take charge of this!"

Athena moved in front of his face just then, "Ares! This is the Underworld we are talking about, not some human-infested land. We can't just use some of our power and expect for it all to be over! We are dealing with so many things—demons, furies, multiple dimensions—and, more importantly, the titans! If they escape, the mortals will see us and their world come to ruin!" Then, Athena instructed everyone in the room, "We have to do this strategically and fight with caution. We are dealing with unknown territory!"

Everyone quickly realized that, for most gods in the room, this would be their first trip to the Underworld. "The only ones who have visited the Underworld are Hermes and, of course, Persephone," Apollo stated, "So we don't know how to prepare."

Demeter began to speak, "I've also been down there as well. I would say that the Underworld is an amazing place. However, given the circumstances we are facing right now, we are going to see the Underworld at its worst. Whatever mortals fear most about that place, is what we will be up against. That is what we are about to encounter."

Everyone saw Persephone stand up as she finally caught her breath, "I need to go with you!"

Zeus stepped in, knowing that his daughter would be stubborn about this. "I'm surprised that Hades is letting you go back at all."

"He isn't. He ordered for me to stay here, actually."

"For once, I agree with him," Demeter said. "You need to stay here. You have no idea what Cronus is capable of, Persephone."

"I'm the future Queen of the Underworld! That realm will soon be my kingdom, too, and I'll be cursed if I don't help Hades. No matter what challenges we face, we are supposed to endure this together. Unfortunately, Hades is so used to doing things himself, that he forgets to let people help him. This situation is the exception."

Demeter nodded. "This war is beyond dangerous. He must swallow his pride twice, once for letting you go and then once more after calling upon his brother for help. This battle is not something that Hades would usually commit to."

"Which is why we are going right now!" Zeus commanded. Looking at his daughter once more, Zeus said, "Persephone, I won't stop you from coming with us if you think that you must join the fight."

Feeling determined and embracing her power, Persephone was ready to save her future husband and his realm.

Poseidon went to Zeus's side, "If the walls of Tartarus have indeed broken, then we need all of our powers, including Hades', to restore those walls."

"That is the least of our problems. I am hoping that none of the creatures, including Cronus, have yet to reach Earth's surface. The last thing I want is for mortals to find out that we can't control our enslaved demons."

All gods of Olympus, except for the hearth goddess Hestia, gathered at the entrance of the Underworld. Hermes and Persephone led the group, since they both knew the Underworld better than the rest. For once, they were both scared about how much damage has occurred since Persephone left to get help.

All Persephone could think about was Hades, wondering if he was still all right. Zeus, Poseidon, Demeter, and Hera stared at the entrance, knowing that they would soon be facing their father once again. "More than a millennium has passed since we had trapped our father here," Zeus declared, "We can do it again."

Ares was more than ready to jump in, "With all of us here, it shouldn't be a problem. We should be done in ten minutes!"

"I wouldn't be so confident," Athena said as she stood next to her father. "He not only got loose without Hades knowing about it, but now he has allies, including other titans, in there as well. We also don't know if things have gotten worse."

"Then we will enter with caution," Zeus said with determination.

With that, Persephone frowned as a question came to her mind at that very moment. "Wait a second, why is everyone so afraid? We are gods, are we not? So we are immortal. Why, all of sudden, are we afraid? We can't die."

"That is true, unless we get hurt or killed by one of our own," Athena answered. "The titans are our ancestors, after all. They are more powerful and are also quite large."

"Yes, I know. I have seen Cronus." Persephone remembered being trapped in Tartarus with her grandfather.

Athena continued, "They can squash us like mortals if they really wanted to."

Fear now entered Persephone's mind. "So we can die from this?"

Athena nodded. "Just don't let any of the titans get close to you. Other than that, you should be fine."

"But that doesn't make any sense. If that is true, then how come Hades, and everyone else who was swallowed by Cronus, survived?"

"Cronus didn't want us dead. At the time, he just wanted us to be imprisoned so that he couldn't be overthrown. For us gods and our immortality, we can be swallowed without dying. If done properly by a titan or a god, it is their powers and their weapons that can destroy us," Demeter answered with worry in her voice. "This is why Hades didn't want you here. Persephone, are you sure that you want to join this fight?" All the gods stared at Demeter and Persephone, unsure of what they were hearing.

"You are giving me a choice?" Persephone asked, not believing that her mother would just let her do this.

"Persephone, if it were up to me, you would be locked away in your room and tied to the bed, with nymphs watching over you. But knowing you . . . You would escape and try to rescue Hades. This is your world now."

Smiling, she gave Demeter a silent nod. Her mother finally understood where she was coming from. With that, Persephone gave the final command, "Come, we have wasted enough time. Let's get the Underworld back in order."

Everyone, including Hermes, walked through the Underworld entrance. They did what any mortal would do, since no one knew what to expect. What scared them the most was how quiet the Underworld had become. They only heard dripping water falling from the ceiling, near the cave's entrance.

Aphrodite looked around and shrugged her shoulders, "Maybe Hades got Cronus back into Tartarus? I mean, it's too quiet down here, isn't it?"

Every god looked around, while Persephone searched for Charon. All she saw was the Acheron river. . . empty. No Charon, no souls being cleansed, it was just the water itself. Persephone walked closer to the water's edge, with a hand out in front of her, trying to feel for anything. Zeus looked curiously at his daughter. "What are you trying to find?"

"I know it's quiet here, maybe too quiet. So, I'm wondering if there's a barrier somewhere around here."

Persephone put out her hand again, trying to feel for some kind of force field. Within minutes, Persephone felt heated energy pushing against her hand. "I was right! There's a force field! That's why it's so quiet."

"I don't remember Hades having that kind of power," Poseidon said.

"I think Hecate created it. So, once we cross it . . . that's it," Persephone suggested.

Zeus then felt for the barrier with his hand. "We have to end this quickly. I'm very sure that Hades asked Hecate to create this energy barrier, so that no one can get out, but it's fragile. Once we get in, we can't escape until Hecate brings down the wall herself." Everyone nodded, as they all prepared for what's to come. "Let's go, then."

Once they had passed through the barrier, the gods were instantly hit with loud screams coming from the Underworld. The fire from Tartarus had spread throughout the realm as well. The shades were wreaking havoc everywhere. Horrified, Persephone had never seen her home like this before. It was chaotic and all of the monsters were unleashed. Some of the wicked shades had crossed over to the Elysian Fields, and were trying to torture the good souls.

"I have to find Hades! Persephone shouted, as she continued to walk on while ignoring the surrounding chaos. The rest of the gods wanted to stop her, but as soon as they tried, they were attacked by furies that were now under Cronus' control.

Using their weapons, the gods fought back. Since they were furies, it took very little for the gods to kill and destroy their attackers.

Meanwhile, Zeus and Poseidon rushed over to Persephone. "We can't restore order until the walls of Tartarus are standing once more. My daughter, lead us to Tartarus. I'm sure that is where your love is." Persephone nodded.

Demeter stepped in, "I'm coming too."

"Demeter, now is not the time to—" Zeus began before she cut him off.

"Don't you dare patronize me. Yes, I'm here to protect my daughter, but you forget, Zeus, that I was the one who kept our bastard father trapped inside those walls."

Zeus actually had forgotten that Demeter had much to do with imprisoning their father the first time around. "Very well. Let's go now! We don't have much time."

With the walls of Tartarus down, every horrendous thing that was previously imprisoned before—unpleasant souls, demons, and titans—was now set free. Chaos bled into various areas of the Underworld, spreading like a disease, infecting everything else.

Hades gathered up all of his people that still served him, since half of his furies were now controlled by Cronus. Furiously, Hades used every ounce of his power to strike anyone who tried to attack him or tried to escape. Cerberus ran around wildly, barking and biting at the furies and monsters who were trying to escape. Trying to protect the souls in the Elysian Fields and the Asphodel Meadows, Hecate used her powers for good.

"HADES!" Cronus roared. He had now officially escaped Tartarus, no longer chained to the walls, and no longer weak. But Cronus was not alone. Other titans that had been imprisoned were standing beside him. Like Cronus, these titans were just as huge and equally as powerful. Hades remained unseen, thanks to his invisibility helmet. While wearing his helmet, Hades had been able to sneak in and annihilate what needed to be killed. "HADES!" Cronus roared again, "Show yourself! Only cowards hide themselves!" Hades wasn't going to let his father belittle him.

Cronus immediately thought of something that would bring Hades out into the open. "You know, Hades, I see your siblings in the distance! Along with your special Persephone!"

Anger hit Hades like an electrical current. To Hades, the idea of Cronus hurting his love was the most significant crime that ever existed. Hades removed his helmet so that his father took notice of him, drawing attention away from

Persephone. Once Cronus saw Hades, he instantly attacked his son with the firepower that Cronus had obtained while imprisoned in Tartarus. Zeus and Poseidon rushed to their brother's side, ready to defend Hades by using their powers. They both stood with their weapon of choice, Zeus with his thunderbolts and Poseidon with his ocean waves, which he had created from the river of the Underworld.

Cronus instantly fell over from the big attack that his sons had created. They had caused the ground to quake. The fire from Tartarus was still spreading, and now volcano fireballs added to the fiery chaos that had erupted from inside of the realm. Hades thanked his brothers with a simple nod. He then saw Persephone with a look of relief on her face. Hades looked at his brothers, "Try to rebuild the Tartarus walls before Cronus rises again. I'll be there shortly!" He rushed over to his love's side and gave her a tight hug. He started to yell, not only because of the loud noises within the realm, but Hades could not believe that she was here against his wishes. "What are you doing here?! Are you crazy?!"

She yelled back in response, "Did you honestly think that I was going to let my beloved fiancé and my future home be destroyed, while I sat at Olympus, wondering if you were all right?!"

With their powers combined, Zeus and Poseidon rebuilt the walls of Tartarus, all while fighting the furies and other demonic beings. Cronus was starting to find his renewed strength once again. "HADES!" Cronus shouted.

Hades looked at Persephone once more before attacking Cronus again. "We will talk about this later, if we are still alive! Hades went to help his brothers rebuild the wall and keep Cronus grounded.

Demeter came to Persephone just then. "Come, there is something we can do to keep Cronus in place. It will buy the men some time to finish the walls."

"How? I don't have the full powers of the Underworld, yet. We only have powers designated for Earthly duties." Then, Persephone suddenly remembered how Cronus was chained to the walls of Tartarus. Vines were wrapped around his arms and the rocks that surrounded his huge body. It reminded her of what she had done to Cadence, when her nymph friend threatened to tell her mother about her Hades. "You have been here before. Long before I was born. You had trapped Cronus here with your vines!"

Demeter nodded in surprise. "How did you know?"

"I did the same thing to Cadence, she was about to—" Persephone didn't want to finish her sentence.

"She was about to tell me about Hades, right? That's why you made her swear on the River Styx?" Demeter asked, already knowing the answer.

"Well, my daughter, I need you to get angry again because that is exactly what we are going to do." Demeter put her hands on the ground and, by using her powers, she made vines grow from out of Underworld's dirt floor. Persephone followed suit, doing the same thing as her mother. By now, Cronus was up again and ready to attack once more. The two goddesses used all of the power that they had to grow the vines until it reached Cronus and wrapped around his feet. Coincidentally, this got his immediate attention.

"Demeter!" Cronus growled. "Do you think your vines can stop me again?!" He was trying to set himself free. With Persephone's help, the vines not only grew faster, but she also added some thorns, which made their grip even more painful. She remembered how she wanted to stop Cadence from talking. Persephone used that as inspiration to keep her beloved family safe, especially Hades. Persephone smiled with pride as she saw her powers manifest significantly. Hades had been watching this scene unfold, , as his future queen took down his father. This was more than Hades could have ever imagined. Demeter was also watching her own daughter, as Persephone became a powerful goddess in that moment.

The vines nearly encased Cronus' body, to the point where he had only one free hand left, which he used to strike again. He threw one last fireball at Demeter's side.

"MOTHER!" Persephone screamed. This got every god's attention. Now, half of Demeter's body was scorched in flames, and she was bleeding out rather rapidly. The vines no longer continued to grow as Persephone rushed to her mother's side. She wanted to stop the bleeding somehow. Tears streamed down Persephone's face.

Hades ran to Persephone's side. "Persephone! Don't stop the vines from growing, you were almost done!"

"If I don't do something for my mother, she is going to die!"

"Listen to me, Persephone! I'll keep her death at bay, but you must grow those vines until Cronus can't move! Zeus and Poseidon are almost done rebuilding the walls."

Persephone listened to Hades. With anger as her inspiration, Persephone used every ounce of her power and continued to rapidly grow the vines. Meanwhile, as he held his beloved's hand and used the life force from their shared touch, Hades made sure that Demeter was still alive. Just as Persephone had finished wrapping Cronus in vines, trapped against the new walls of Tartarus, Zeus and Poseidon had finally exhausted both of their own powers to finish building the walls.

The other gods had already defeated the rest of the titans. Luckily, compared to Cronus, the titans proved to be not much of a threat. Persephone went straight to her mother, who was now barely alive. She looked at Hades with tears in her eyes. "How can we help her?"

"The only thing that can help her is the ambrosia Lotus flower. However, with all that has happened here, it could possibly have been destroyed among all the chaos."

Persephone stopped crying because she suddenly remembered the vile that Hades had given her on the day that they had made love for the first time. Luckily, she still carried it in her pocket, in case of an emergency. Persephone smiled because she had the ambrosia with her, ready to use. Smiling, Hades knew that Demeter was going to be okay, once she drank the nectar.

"Mother, please drink this." Persephone held the vile to Demeter's lips. Knowing instantly what it was, Demeter gulped the liquid down without hesitation. Within minutes, her body had almost fully recovered. Letting herself rest, Demeter knew that the danger had passed. Relief and happiness had spread throughout Persephone's body. She looked at Hades in that moment. He appeared to look older than before, his age showed especially in his eyes. Between Cronus, the Underworld, and giving his life force to Demeter, he took quite a toll in a very short amount of time. "Oh, my love, thank you for chasing away death from both my mother and everyone on Earth."

Hades chuckled, "That is my job, Persephone."

"I didn't know that you can chase death away."

"I'm the master of death, my love. I can either bring it when needed or chase it away."

Zeus, Poseidon, and all the other gods gathered around the entrance to Tartarus. Many of them were dirty, with scratch marks from the furies and wicked souls that had attacked them. Though, it was not as serious as Demeter's wounds. Using his water power, Poseidon extinguished the remaining fire clusters that still burned in Tartarus. Then, Aphrodite used her love energy to bring all the shades back to exactly where they needed to be.

Hades and Persephone watched as the Underworld slowly regained its natural order. Hecate went to Hades, looking exhausted. "Are all the shades accounted for?" he asked her.

She shook her head no. "My lord, I apologize, but the shield I created for the entrance . . .wasn't strong enough to withstand the fight. Some shades escaped."

Hades nodded, disappointed in himself. He had a reputation for never letting a soul escape without permission. "It's to be expected. How many?"

"At least a couple hundred."

"With your magic capabilities, is there any way that we can bring them all back?"

"I can call to them, like an instinct, signaling for the souls to return, but they need to come back on their own," Hecate responded. She turned to leave so that she could gather her energy.

"So, what happens to them?" Persephone asked, as she looked at Hades.

"On Earth, they become ghosts," Hades answered. He felt his head starting to ache. "So, some mortals will just be terrified of living in their own houses."

Persephone smirked a little, "You know what that means? The mortals will pray to you, wanting to get rid of ghosts!"

Hades had to laugh at the idea, "It would be a lovely gesture, my darling, but I doubt that will happen."

"You know, it won't be as much of a pain as you think. When it's time for me to be with my mother, then I can look for the souls that escaped and bring them back down to the Underworld. Just like I did with the grandmother and her grandson."

Hades smiled, "If you can, I would very much appreciate it. Just keep in mind that these escaped souls are less than friendly. Some of them will be difficult to remove." Persephone nodded, she understood. "Speaking of which, what were you thinking? You really wanted to come down here for this?" His voice was filled with emotion. "You could have possibly been killed. Look at what happened to your mother!"

"I'm your future queen. Did you really think that I was going to leave you, and my kingdom, in ruin? I would have gone nuts if I had stayed at Olympus, wondering if and hoping that you were all right. If I didn't love you so much, I would have stayed behind!"

Without another word, Hades passionately kissed Persephone, which took her breath away. For a few moments, she gave into his passion, since she had thought that she might lose him to Cronus. "I love you too, my love." Hades proclaimed, as he gave her one more gentle kiss on the lips.

"I did help you with Cronus, did I not?" she asked.

"You did, which I'm so proud that I have a queen like you."

Persephone blushed, "I'm not a queen, yet."

Hades nodded. "Yet. But, very soon, that will be rectified."

CHAPTER 20

QUEEN OF THE UNDERWORLD

For the first time in centuries, Hades' throne room, and most of the Underworld, was filled with guests instead of souls waiting to be judged. The crowd consisted of souls from the Elysian fields, his servants, minor Underworld deities, and all of the gods and goddesses from every culture.

For the first time ever, anyone who was ever curious about Hades' domain will finally get to see the realm for what it really is, free from war or judgement to cloud its mystery. Cronus was placed in the lowest part of the Underworld, in the deepest part of Tartarus, so that no one could see or hear him unless they went down there themselves.

It's been months since Persephone's "abduction" happened and the story of her love affair with Hades has been told through both god and mortal realms alike. So, of course, those who were invited came to witness the marriage of Hades, King of the Underworld and Persephone, The goddess of spring and life.

Everyone glanced around the space, in awe of how vast and beautiful the Underworld really was. Hera was especially taken aback by what she saw around her, as she gazed upon miles and miles of the Underworld's grandeur. Then she saw the Lotus ambrosia flower that was growing near the lake, in the garden. She huffed at everything Hades had in his kingdom. "Short end of the stick, what a joke! He truly has everything here!"

"What are you complaining about now, Hera?" Athena was standing at her side.

"I'm not complaining, I'm just noticing how we've misunderstood Hades' domain. Everyone thought that he only received very little when, in reality, he and his brothers had divided the earth into thirds. No one had wanted the Underworld, nor its responsibility. Now I look around, and see that he has everything! He holds the real power!"

Athena nodded, understanding what she meant. "Have you thought about why The Fates gave him the

Underworld? Perhaps he is responsible and wise enough to rule it? He has never abused its power, and he has taken great care of it. Now, even more so, with a kind-hearted woman by his side. Zeus would never be able to run the Underworld. This place needs constant care and compassion for everything to run its course. Look at what happened with Cronus, Hades has to constantly be on guard about that titan, or else everything that we hold dear could easily be ruined."

"I still can't believe that Zeus let Hades have all of this."

"Hera, do I need to remind you that no one knew how powerful the Underworld actually is? Besides, please be content with the fact that you are Queen of the Gods."

Hera sighed, "I may be Queen of the Gods, but I envy what Persephone has. She has more than I could ever hope for myself."

Athena knew exactly what Hera was talking about. Persephone not only has the Underworld kingdom to rule over, which includes the power of life and death, but she also has the one thing that Hera wants the most—a faithful, devout husband that would love her and do anything for her. Athena looked at Hera with pity on her face as she observed Hera walking toward Zeus, who was already engaged in conversation with Hades. For the first time, a bright smile showed on Hades face for everyone to see.

Hades looked around, seeing happiness spread throughout his kingdom. Even the souls from the Elysian Fields were happy to witness this blessed event. He was delighted himself, only something else was bothering him. Zeus sensed his elder brother's uneasiness. "Are you getting cold feet?"

"No. I could never second guess marrying Persephone. In fact, I can't contain my joy that she will soon be my wife," Hades admitted somberly, as his eyes sparkled.

"So, my brother, what is the problem?"

"I was just thinking about Cronus and how he escaped."

"Hades, you have been watching over our father since the day we overthrew him, which happened many centuries ago. The first time that he had ever escaped."

"Do you know why he escaped?" Hades said as more of a statement, than a question.

"You know why he escaped. He was draining Tartarus' energy source by trying to make it his own. As a result, he had gradually weakened the walls."

"Without me noticing. I look after the Underworld like a tight ship, making sure that everything is in order. I didn't notice because—"

"Because of Persephone?" Hades nodded, as his brother finished the sentence. "Hades, you were in love and when love takes over, everything else fades into the background."

"I'm still in love, whether Persephone is with me or not. She is always on my mind, but I'm losing discipline on how to take proper care of everything."

"That is not necessarily a bad thing."

"Yes, it is. Persephone is my weakness, and Cronus knew that. I was so preoccupied with Persephone and the resolving conflict with her mother, that I lost sight of what was going on in my own kingdom."

Zeus patted Hades on the back, "Welcome to my world."

"What?"

"You don't think I lose sight of my own duties as King of the Gods because of Hera or my children?"

"Or the affairs you've had?" Hades smirked, trying to prove a point.

"I'm trying to give you some perspective about this situation, Hades. What I'm saying is that it's okay to occasionally indulge in something or someone that you love, and forget the world for a while. You slipped up one time, Hades. You need to forgive yourself for what happened with Cronus. You have to balance work and pleasure, that is all you need to do. Besides, I don't see Persephone as your weakness. Not when she gives you the strength and an extra hand to help you run things. Especially how she helped you defeat Cronus. Even I admit that I had underestimated her." Zeus gave him a friendly smile before joining the rest of the crowd.

Hades smiled as he thought of his bride, who would be coming out shortly. Everyone else was finding their seats. Hades had never seen so many guests before. He felt nervous, as he began to pace near his throne. Impatience was getting the better of him, until an old friend quietly joined him. "Congratulations on your marriage, my lord," Hecate greeted him. She would be the one to perform the ceremony. Hades nodded to her out of respect and appreciation. Hecate gave him a hug and whispered in his ear, "Don't worry, she is very excited to see you." Hecate released him as she went to prepare the altar for their ceremony.

The room hushed as a beautiful woman, who was dressed in silver and black, appeared. Rose petals decorated the top part of her corset and the bottom of her dress. Hades looked at his beautiful bride with such pride and joy. Not only was she dressed as the bride of the Underworld, but she already looked like a queen who was ready to take her place by his side. Her long veil dropped to her waist in the front, but almost touching the floor from behind. Regardless of its length, the veil could not hide her divine face. Hades ached to touch her face. He never thought that anything could be more torturous, as he waited for Persephone to walk down the aisle toward the judging panel.

Persephone never felt so light in her life. Instead of walking, she felt like she was flying toward Hades. She couldn't wait to be with him. Everyone in the room saw happiness in her eyes and a smile that showed through her veil. No one had ever seen a couple more in love. Hades only had eyes for his bride, and for the both of them, everything else had disappeared into the background. Demeter, on the other hand, had nothing but tears in her eyes, She genuinely felt like she was losing her little girl forever. Hestia held Demeter's hand, hoping to provide her with some comfort, and whispered to Demeter that her daughter would be happy. Demeter knew this to be true, especially now that her daughter could take care of herself. She had proved herself to Demeter in the way that she had dealt with Cronus.

Finally, after what seemed an eternity, Persephone came to the altar and stood in front of Hades. He offered her his hand, which reminded her of their first dance together at her initiation. In that enchanting moment, they had become a couple. She smiled, took his hand, and he led her right to the steps where Hecate stood. Beside her was a small table where both a golden chalice and a golden silk cloth lay. Hades smiled as he lifted her veil. He held her hands once more, not wanting to let her go.

Everyone remained silent as Hecate initiated the ceremony of their union.

"Marriage is a blessing between two people who have found an eternal partner. A partner that is supposed to be the other half of one's soul. It is not only a joining of two bodies, but of two souls, for the rest of their lives. To the mortals, who have short lifespans, this unity will breeze right past them. For us immortals, however, it's a decision not to be taken lightly. To us, forever truly means forever. We have here the god of death and the goddess of spring and life. Despite their age, their powers, and what each of them represents, they see each other as loving equals. They are complete polar opposites, yet complement one another perfectly, for where there's life, there is also death. You cannot have one without the other. It's a life balance that no one, not even the gods or The Fates, can control. Hades, Persephone, and their love for each other remind us of that fact. We are here today to see these gods, one of life and one of death, become forever united as husband and wife. We are blessed to see such a rare occasion."

Hecate took out a golden box that held the wedding rings. Hades had them made special for Persephone and himself. The rings were designed with the Lotus ambrosia flower, along with a diamond human skull in its center. Indeed, both rings signified the unity of Hades and Persephone. The rings looked both masculine and feminine and signified life, death, and immortality. "These rings represent the symbol of your love, as well as each other. These rings tell the world that you now belong to someone, that you are committed to someone. These rings represent that vow."

Hades took Persephone's ring first and placed it on her finger, and then she took his ring and did the same. Their right hands now adorned the rings. Some of the gods thought that this was the most human thing that they could have done. Gods don't wear wedding rings, but with Hades and Persephone's constant contact to the mortal world, they thought it would be a beautiful tradition for them to partake. Then, Hecate took the gold silk cloth and wrapped it around their wrists.

"As this golden cloth ties your hands together, it will also tie your lives together. You are now one complete soul." Hecate picked up the golden chalice and brought it over to them. "This chalice is filled with water from the River Styx, which is more powerful than anything else in this world. As we all know, no promise or vow can ever be broken when you swear on or drink from its waters. If you both drink this water, you shall be bound together for eternity. This is the moment, the final step, where you each pledge yourselves to each other. Hecate offered the chalice to Hades first, and he gladly took it. Looking at Persephone with love in his eyes, he begins:

"I, Hades, King of the Underworld, swear myself to you, Persephone. I offer you my heart, my body, and my soul for all eternity. May our love grow each day and may it bring you happiness and joy during every step we take together." Hades brought the chalice to his lips and drank from it.

Now it was Persephone's turn. She took the chalice in her hand, and looked at Hades with the same love and devotion:

"I, Persephone, Lady of Spring and Life, swear myself to you, Hades. I offer you my heart, my body, and my soul for all eternity." Persephone drank from the chalice. She felt the power of the sacred water as it coursed through her body. It was complete, Hades and Persephone are now connected more than ever, in a spiritual sense. It was like Persephone could feel Hades, and vise-versa. They both smiled at each other, in awe of their newfound connection. Hecate unwrapped the ribbon from around our hands.

"Now you are both bound by the River Styx. You are husband and wife." Looking at Hades, Hecate said, "You may now kiss your bride." Hades leaned in and captured Persephone's lips in a passionate kiss. Everyone cheered and clapped for the newly-wedded couple.

As the goddess of marriage and family, Hera blessed both Hades and Persephone. May you both be faithful to each other, and may you be blessed with children. Persephone blushed at the thought of children. Hades had already smirked at the idea, then he kissed his wife again, uttering a passionate growl that made everyone laugh.

After the kissing ends, they both climb the stairs to his throne, but now his throne doesn't stand alone. A smaller throne stands right beside his. In the shape of a flower with skulls, her throne is made from pure silver and purple velvet. Hades placed Persephone in her new throne. Zoe appeared just then, holding a golden pillow. On the pillow cushion, lies a small crown. The crown was made from silver flowers, along with the Underworld's rubies and emeralds. Hades held the crown in his hand and placed it on Persephone's head. Zeus and Demeter looked at their daughter in awe. Then, Hades turned to the crowd and declared: "Let everyone be merry! The Underworld finally has a queen!" The crowd cheered and applauded frantically.

Persephone looked out at the crowd and at her loving husband. This was precisely what dreams were made of, this was what she had wished for. Then she felt something else, another connection, besides Hades. She closed her eyes and felt a different kind of love, not for someone, but for something. That's when she realized it was the Underworld making its own connection with her. Not only was Hades in charge, but she was as well. The Underworld was sending her its love and secrets. Just like Hades, Persephone now had the power to control and know of this realm's every secret.

Confidence, purpose, and happiness overwhelmed Persephone. She became the powerful goddess that Hades, and The Fates, had predicted. She became in charge of not only new life and flowers, but also the dead. She can still see the unseen. She can control life and death at her fingertips.

Persephone sat on her throne, beside her proud husband who never felt happier. The Underworld itself has become a much more comfortable and bright place. Of course, it darkens once Persephone has to return to her mother, but it soon became a routine that everyone was used to.

Both Hades and Persephone judged souls together. Everything was going smoothly until one particular shade encountered Hades and Persephone. "So, it's true then. The King of the Underworld has indeed kidnapped Persephone! He probably rapes and enjoys her, while Demeter makes us suffer at his expense!" he shouted to the other shades behind him.

Persephone stood up immediately. As she faced this shade, Hades tried to stop her, but Persephone's determination and strength got the better of herself. She stared directly into this shade's eyes, as she spoke with such authority and grace. Persephone made sure that every soul in the Underworld heard her "What do you know about me? About us? The gods? You have these assumptions solely based on mortal stories and fear. Let me tell you something, you poor soul, when a god or a goddess asks you to do something, we make sure that you know it is us. Not just a voice in your head, or some hallucination, or your imagination. Do you see me tied to a chair? Do you see me locked in a cage, only for his pleasure, using me to his heart's content?

The soul could see that Persephone was as free as a bird. He shook his head no, almost shamefully. "No, my lady."

"Do you know why?"

"No, my lady."

"Because I wasn't kidnapped. Hades loves me. He is not the monster that you and other mortals make him out to be! Maybe if humans weren't so closed-minded when it comes to the things that they fear, then they would be surprised how much they could be open to. This is why, most of the time, you don't see us! Because you all have blinded yourselves to fear, doubt, reasoning, and lack of faith. Not only in us, but also yourselves!" Persephone looked at the shade once more before passing judgment. "Where did you hear that I was kidnapped?"

"All mortals know about your abduction," the shade responded.

Persephone nodded with sadness in her eyes, as she looked at her husband. "Asphodel Meadows."

"Don't be sad, my goddess." Hades said as he grabbed her hand.

She shook her head almost defeatedly. "Despite everything we fixed, all mortals still think that you are a monster. One who rules over the dead and has kidnapped me."

"Do you think I care about these mortal assumptions?"

Persephone looked again at her loving husband. "I think you do, at least on some days."

"On the bright side, it just makes me more mysterious."

"More fearful is more like it," Persephone mumbled. "What if this continues? That you remain forever in history as an 'evil god' among the Greek gods?"

"Then, one day, whether it's soon or in the distant future, I'll have someone write about us. It will be the true story," Hades said, planning to salvage his reputation. "Someone who knows the gods and knows how to communicate with us. It will be someone who doesn't look at us in fear."

Persephone almost laughed, "Good luck with that one, my love. That is almost impossible."

Then Hades gave Persephone a kiss of loving reassurance. "I got you, didn't I? To me, that was almost impossible. All we need now is a mortal who can see us through new eyes, who doesn't let society tell them what to believe."

"This will most likely be in the future then, Hades. When most mortals will only think of us as a myth or a fairytale," Persephone said sadly. She then felt a small shift in current religious beliefs.

"I know, but it's worth waiting for, just like I waited for you. At least now, we both have many things to do until that time comes."

Persephone trusted her husband and his words, but she still valued her own opinion, "Still, it is unthinkable."

Hades smiled at the one person who gave him more meaning than anything else. "Only The Fates would know."

The End

ABOUT THE AUTHOR

L. E. STARDUST studies all different types of religion, spiritual beliefs, supernatural beings, and experiences. She uses her passion about these subjects to show other people the connection to, and the possibilities of, other realities. These interests appear across other creative outlets that she enjoys, including: fashion, music, art, and the written word, such as this book. Her skills and interests are extensive, they often connect to one another in some way.

While L.E. STARDUST lives in California, this story was written during her time in Bismarck, North Dakota, where she worked as a sales associate at JCPenney and a bookseller at Barnes & Noble.

Made in the USA
Monee, IL
02 June 2025